Praise for *Year Zero*

D0149888

"Hilarious, provocative, and supersmart, *Year Zero* is a brilliant novel to be enjoyed in perpetuity in the known universe and in all unknown universes yet to be discovered."
—JOHN HODGMAN,
resident expert, *The Daily Show with Jon Stewart*

"[Rob] Reid's extreme imagination never wanes as he builds an entire universe solely on how alien societies would react to our music and culture. Nothing is typical or obvious. Reid uses the lens of an outsider to unleash a sarcastic— and hilarious—rant on how obsessed we are with technology and greed."
—*Associated Press*

"Holy hilarity! A new force in geek humor is upon us. You'll never think the same way again about extraterrestrials, bad music, buggy technology—or lawyers!"
—CHRIS ANDERSON, TED curator

"I loved it. Funny, smart, silly . . . three things I also happen to admire in a novel. Bottom line: recommended. Buy it and read it."
—PHIL PLAIT, *Discover* magazine

"*Year Zero* made me laugh out loud *and* taught me stuff about copyright infringement: It's clever, smart, and so original that people are probably already trying to rip it off."
—CHARLES YU,
author of *How to Live Safely in a Science Fictional Universe*

"All in all, it's a supremely fun read which will remind you how much you love science fiction comedy—and how much you hate the music industry."
—io9

"My pick for best (and funniest) sci-fi book of the year."
—CHRIS ANDERSON, editor in chief, *Wired*

"[*Year Zero* is] an often hilarious satire on much of current entertainment, including reality TV, the legal profession and fandom (interstellar and otherwise), but the book's crowning achievement is that it actually makes copyright funny."
—*Toronto Star*

"*Year Zero* is ROFLMAO funny, insightful, and sly: A sort of Hitchhiker's Guide to our own tortured commercial/litigation culture, by way of planet Zinkiwu."
—MARK JANNOT, editor in chief, *Popular Science*

"Fans of Douglas Adams will rave about this smart, funny satire. Debut novelist Reid, founder of Listen.com, has crafted a masterly plot that deftly skewers the American obsession with music, money, and power. Fast paced and original, this is highly recommended."
—*Library Journal* (starred review)

"Witty and original—I loved it. *Year Zero* is a biting satire of the record business and those who run it . . . and ultimately ran it into the ground."
—CLIFF BLESZINSKI, creator, Gears of War

"Smart and wacky."
—BOB BOILEN, NPR's *All Songs Considered*

"Reid . . . takes aim at many targets—technology, the
music industry, hipsters—and nails them all hilariously."
—*Parade*

"What if aliens heard our music—and really liked it? You
could 'what if' for the next millennium and still not come
up with as many zany scenarios as Rob Reid does in this
tale of copyright law, astrophysics, biophysics, and crazy
physics that hasn't yet been invented. So sit back, hold
your sides to ease the laughing pains, and find out
whether Earth survives."
—JILL TARTER, director, Center for SETI Research

"*Awesome* . . . Think *Hitchhikers Guide to the Galaxy,* but
with copyright law driving a major plot line. A mainstream
humorous sci-fi novel that uses the Berne Convention
as a key plot point and tosses aside casual references
to Larry Lessig and Fark? Yes. Count me in."
—Techdirt

"*Year Zero* is a brilliant satire of the American
entertainment industry, and I never stopped grinning."
—KEVIN HEARNE, author of The Iron Druid Chronicles

"Light-hearted, intelligent and just plain silly . . .
Year Zero is very clever and has wonderful fun with
themes I think you'll enjoy."
—Boing Boing

"The fun in *Year Zero* comes from the banter among the main characters, all of whom are well drawn and hilarious in their own right. While the novel satirizes the music industry, it's obvious the author feels as passionately as some of the alien characters about the power of pop music."
—Shelf Awareness

YEAR
ZERO

By Rob Reid

YEAR ZERO
AFTER ON

YEAR
ZERO

A NOVEL

ROB
REID

BALLANTINE BOOKS

NEW YORK

Year Zero is a work of fiction. All incidents and dialogue, and all characters with the exception of some well-known public figures, are products of the author's imagination and are not to be construed as real. Where real-life public figures appear, the situations, incidents, and dialogues concerning those persons are entirely fictional and are not intended to depict actual events or to change the entirely fictional nature of the work. In all other respects, any resemblance to persons living or dead is entirely coincidental.

2013 Del Rey Books Trade Paperback Edition

Copyright © 2012 by Rob Reid

All rights reserved.

Published in the United States by Del Rey Books, an imprint of The Random House Publishing Group, a division of Random House, Inc., New York.

Del Rey is a registered trademark and the Del Rey colophon is a trademark of Random House, Inc.

Originally published in hardcover in the United States by Del Rey Books, an imprint of The Random House Publishing Group, a division of Random House, Inc., in 2012.

Library of Congress Cataloging-in-Publication Data
Reid, Robert.
Year Zero : a novel / Rob Reid.
p.   cm.
ISBN: 978-0-345-53451-4
eISBN: 978-0-345-53448-4
I. Title.
PS3618.E5474Y33 2012
813'.6—dc23
2012010001

Printed in the United States of America

www.delreybooks.com

9 8 7 6

Book design by Susan Turner

FOR MORGAN

ACKNOWLEDGMENTS

I'd like to thank my wife, Morgan, for believing in *Year Zero* when it was just a wisp a of story. I never would have started writing it if it weren't for her. I also certainly wouldn't have finished it without the steady feed of encouragement, edits, advice, caffeine, patience, treats, cajoling, laughter, and love that she sustained me with. I may have been the one at the keyboard, but this was a two-person project from start to finish. So thank you, Morgan. This is our book.

Writing fiction can be a very solitary pursuit. But I was blessed in having a few people who kept me company, in a sense, by reading and commenting on multiple drafts of *Year Zero* throughout its development. It isn't an outlandishly long novel, but Scott Faber and Alan Peterson read enough versions of it to make *War and Peace* look breezy by comparison. Arch Meredith also went through multiple editions, and all three of these guys had a huge impact on the book's final form through their generous feedback.

Susanne Losch was another source of priceless input, above all her polite but firm suggestion that I consider adding a plot to the book after reading an early draft of it. Susanne then introduced me to Lynn Hightower, a twelve-time novelist who is also an instructor with UCLA's writing program. I spent several months restructuring my story with Lynn as a mentor, coach, and taskmaster, and the results were transformative. Dan Muth, Jim Gable, and John Hlinko all gave me detailed written, annotated, and verbal feedback on the first truly complete draft of the book, and each of them pushed me to hone and sharpen the story in ways that improved it significantly. Chris Alden and John Battelle helped me in similar ways with my final major rewrite.

Several more people were generous with their editorial input after reading full drafts of the book, including Avril Love, Bob Lesko, Drew Curtis, Eric Kronfeld, George Gilder, Juan Enriquez, Miles Beckett, and Ryan Vance. Others shared their expertise in areas as diverse as lobbying, the law, office politics, geek culture, and kick-ass rock 'n' roll by reading focused parts of the book, or by answering detailed questions from me. They include Dan Horowitz, Diana Woods, J. P. Shub, Julia Popowitz, Kevin Kiernan, Lawrence Lessig, Matt Keil, Scott Sigler, Stephen Bishop, Tim Chang, Tim Quirk, and Zahavah Levine. Kevin Pereira, meanwhile, had almost nothing to do with the creation of this book, but I'd like to thank him anyway. Let's just say he's owed.

Before sending *Year Zero* out to publishers, I approached four people who I admire in hopes of getting short written endorsements from them. After reading the book, all of them pushed me hard to revise and revisit it in ways that significantly improved it. Chris Anderson, Jill Tarter, John Hodgman, and Mark Jannot therefore have my deep gratitude not only for giving *Year Zero* their blessing, but also for helping it to become the book that it is. Excerpts of their comments are now on its cover, along with a few others from people that I approached after Random House/Del Rey agreed to publish it.

Speaking of Del Rey, I would like to thank my editors, Betsy Mitchell and David Pomerico, for believing in this book, and for their wise and generous counsel as I honed and polished the story under their guidance. My profound thanks also go out to my agent, Alice Martell, both for believing in *Year Zero* and for finding it an amazing home at Del Rey.

Finally, while this book doesn't have a co-author, it does have something of a co-pilot. Ashby the Dog stationed herself on a chair next to my own throughout its creation, and kept a careful eye on everything. I couldn't have written this book had my office been overrun with noisy, distracting squirrels, and with Ashby on duty, this was never a danger.

CONTENTS

YEAR ZERO

ZERO

Aliens suck at music. And it's not for a lack of trying. They've been at it for eons, but have yet to produce even a faintly decent tune. If they had, we'd have detected them ages ago. We've been scanning the skies for signs of intelligent life for generations, after all. And we've actually picked up thousands of alien anthems, slow dances, and ballads. But the music's so awful that it's always mistaken for the death rattle of a distant star. It's seriously that bad.

Or more accurately—we're that good. In fact, humanity creates the universe's best music, by far. We owe this to a freakish set of lucky breaks. For instance, the combined gravitational pulls of the various bodies in our solar system tug the fluids of our inner ears in *juuuuust* the right way to give us an exquisite sense of rhythm. Certain deeply bewitching tonal patterns are meanwhile wired right into our brain stems, because they map to the sounds that our distant ancestors' ancient prey once made. These two, and several other long-shot rarities combine to give us musical super-powers that no other civilization can match.

The irony is that in every other artistic form that matters to the rest of the cosmos, we're the dullards. In sculpture, fashion, and synchronized swimming, we rank in the bottom percentile, universe-wide. Découpage and pyrotechnics aren't even considered to be high expressive forms here, grotesquely stunting our development in those fields. And while we did manage to get off to a decent start in stained glass, we lost all interest in it just a century before LEDs and nanopigments would have taken it to radical new levels. Meanwhile, the plays, dramatic series, and films that we make are in the "so bad, it's good" category, with our crowning achievements providing ironic late-night amusement to smirking hipsters on countless planets.

All of this is according to the standards of the Refined League—an obnoxiously brilliant and peaceful confederation of alien societies that spans the universe. To join it, primitives like us first have to attain a certain middling mastery of science. Pull that off, and we'll be promoted to the Refined ranks. We'll then be handed all of the technological secrets that we haven't yet cracked for ourselves, as a sort of cosmic graduation gift. And that will free us up to spend the rest of eternity creating and consuming great art—just like every other Refined species.

The bad news is that most societies destroy themselves with nuclear, biological, or nanoweapons long before achieving Refined status. And when this happens, Refined observers do nothing to stop the annihilation. This may sound heartless. But it's actually a prudent form of self-defense—

since any society that's violent and stupid enough to self-destruct on H-bombs might easily destroy the entire universe if it survives long enough to invent something with real firepower.

Humanity first drew attention to itself back when the Pioneer 10 probe crossed a certain threshold out beyond the orbit of Jupiter. When a planet lobs something that far into space, it tends to mean that intelligence has arisen on it. And so the Refined League's equivalent of an admissions office—which was already dimly aware of the Earth's existence*—decided to check in to see if we had any artistic potential (as well as to see if we planned to keep throwing crap into space, because at some point, we might hit something). A scouting craft soon entered our solar system. It detected several broadcast signals, and routed the strongest one (WABC-TV in New York) to a distant team of anthropologists—who then found themselves watching a first-run episode of the hit sitcom *Welcome Back, Kotter* (the one in which Arnold Horshack joins a zany youth cult).

Before I get into what happened next, I should mention that music is the most cherished of the forty so-called Noble Arts that Refined beings revere and dedicate their lives to. It

---

*Our planet was previously visited by some kids on a joy ride during a time geologists call the Cryogenian period. The kids were looking for fun—but the only cool thing about the Cryogenian was that its name could be rearranged to spell things like Organic Yen, Coy Grannie, and Canine Orgy. The Earth itself was nowhere near that fun back then, being barren, rocky, and home only to some microbes. So the kids took off. But they dutifully logged our planet's coordinates with the appropriate authorities, who in turn set up the tripwire that Pioneer 10 hit eons later.

is indeed viewed as being many times Nobler than the other thirty-nine Arts combined. And remember—their music sucks.

The first alien *Kotter* watchers initially doubted that we had music at all, because everything about the show screamed that we were cultural and aesthetic dunderheads. Primitive sight gags made them groan. Sloppy editing made them chuckle. Wardrobe choices practically made them wretch.

And then, it happened.

The show ended. The credits rolled, and the theme music began. And suddenly, the brainless brutes that they'd been pitying were beaming out the greatest creative achievement that the wider universe had ever witnessed.

Welcome back, Welcome back, Welcome back. On Earth, these lyrics were a humble cue to hit the bathroom before *What's Happening!!* came on. But everywhere else, they were the core of an opus so sublime that the Refined League reset its calendars to start counting time from the moment it was first detected. And so, October 13, 1977; 8:29 p.m. EST became the dawning moment of Year Zero to the rest of the universe.

Countless Refined beings perished before the new era was even a minute old. The delight triggered by the *Kotter* song released so much endorphin-like goo in their brains that they hemorrhaged, bringing on immediate, ecstatic death. *Welcome back, Welcome back, Welcome back!* Others died from neglecting sleep, meals, or bathroom breaks as they obsessively replayed the *Kotter* theme over the ensuing weeks.

The period following the "Kotter Moment" (as it's known) passed in a haze. Everyone was so stunned that it was months before they thought to scan our TV spectrum more deeply. Once they did, more waves of rhapsodic joy swept the cosmos. *Good Times. Happy Days. Sanford and Son.* Each new theme song added to the ecstasy—and to the casualties. Soon they discovered the Top 40 stations of the AM spectrum. They listened to "Stayin' Alive" by the Bee Gees, "Seasons in the Sun" by Terry Jacks, and the immortal "Boogie Oogie Oogie" by A Taste of Honey. More rhapsodic joy. More hemorrhaging brains.

But with every deadly new discovery, the survivors got a bit hardier. *Kotter* was like an inoculation that toughened everyone up for Olivia Newton-John, who in turn prepared the cosmos for Billy Joel. So as the music got marginally less awful, the mortality rate paradoxically dropped. And by the time they started exploring the FM frequencies, most Refined beings were ready for what they found. By then it was mid-1978. The FM dial was jammed with what we now call Classic Rock, and some stations occasionally played entire albums from start to finish. The last big die-off occurred when WPLJ broadcast both sides of *Led Zeppelin IV.* And anyone who survived that had what it took to safely listen to even the most stellar rock 'n' roll.

Decades later, the exaltation inspired by our works had barely diminished. But the universe had ignored its inboxes, errands, and to-do lists for decades. And so, everyone reluctantly started returning to business. Politicians started governing again. Accountants started accounting again. Most significantly, alien anthropologists began studying other aspects of human society.

And that's when it hit them. They owed us an ungodly amount of money.

ONE

ASTLEY

Even if she'd realized that my visitors were aliens who had come to our office to initiate contact with humanity, Barbara Ann would have resented their timing. Assistants at our law firm clear out at five-thirty, regardless—and that was almost a minute ago.

"I don't have anyone scheduled," I said, when she called to grouse about the late arrival. "Who is it?"

"I don't know, Nick. They weren't announced."

"You mean they just sort of . . . turned up at your desk?" I stifled a sneeze as I said this. I'd been fighting a beast of a cold all week.

"Pretty much."

This was odd. Reception is two key-card-protected floors above us, and no one gets through unaccompanied, much less unannounced. "What do they look like?" I asked.

"Strange."

"Lady Gaga strange?" Carter, Geller & Marks has some weird-looking clients, and Gaga flirts with the outer fringe, when she's really gussied up.

"No—kind of stranger than that. In a way. I mean, they look like they're from . . . maybe a couple of cults."

From *what?* "Which ones?"

"One definitely looks Catholic," Barbara Ann said. "Like a . . . priestess? And the other one looks . . . kind of Talibanny. You know—robes and stuff?"

"And they won't say where they're from?"

"They can't. They're deaf."

I was about to ask her to maybe try miming some information out of them, but thought better of it. The day was technically over. And like most of her peers, Barbara Ann has a French postal worker's sense of divine entitlement when it comes to her hours. This results from there being just one junior assistant for every four junior lawyers, which makes them monopoly providers of answered phones, FedEx runs, and other secretarial essentials to some truly desperate customers. So as usual, I caved. "Okay, send 'em in."

The first one through the door had dark eyes and a bushy beard. He wore a white robe, a black turban, and a diver's watch the size of a small bagel. Apart from the watch, he looked like the Hollywood ideal of a fatwa-shrieking cleric—until I noticed a shock of bright red hair protruding from under his turban. This made him look faintly Irish, so I silently christened him O'Sama. His partner was dressed like a nun—although in a tight habit that betrayed the curves of a lap dancer. She had a gorgeous tan and bright blue eyes and was young enough to get carded anywhere.

O'Sama gazed at me with a sort of childlike amazement,

while the sister kept it cool. She tried to catch his eye—but he kept right on staring. So she tapped him on the shoulder, pointing at her head. At this, they both stuck their fingers under their headdresses to adjust something. "Now we can hear," the nun announced, straightening out a big, medieval-looking crucifix that hung around her neck.

This odd statement aside, I thought I knew what was happening. My birthday had passed a few days back without a call from any of my older brothers. It would be typical of them to forget—but even more typical of them to pretend to forget, and then ambush me with a wildly inappropriate birthday greeting at my stodgy New York law office. So I figured I had about two seconds before O'Sama started beatboxing and the nun began to strip. Since you never know when some partner's going to barge through your door, I almost begged them to leave. But then I remembered that I was probably getting canned soon anyway. So why not gun for YouTube glory, and capture the fun on my cellphone?

As I considered this, the nun fixed me with a solemn gaze. "Mr. Carter. We are visitors from a distant star."

That settled it. "Then I better record this for NASA." I reached across the desk for my iPhone.

"Not a chance." She extended a finger and the phone leapt from the desk and darted toward her. Then it stopped abruptly, emitted a bright green flash, and collapsed into a glittering pile of dust on the floor.

"What the . . . ?" I basically talk for a living, but this was all I could manage.

"We're camera shy." The nun retracted her finger as if sheathing a weapon. "And as I mentioned, we're also visitors from a distant star."

I nodded mutely. That iPhone trick had made a believer out of me.

"And we want you to represent us," O'Sama added. "The reputation of Carter, Geller & Marks extends to the farthest reaches of the universe."

The absurdity of this flipped me right back to thinking "prank"—albeit one featuring some awesome sleight of hand. "Then you know I'll sue your asses if I don't get my iPhone back within the next two parsecs," I growled, trying to suppress the wimpy, nasal edge that my cold had injected into my voice. I had no idea what a parsec was, but remembered the term from *Star Wars*.

"Oh, up your nose with a rubber hose," the nun hissed. As I was puzzling over this odd phrase, she pointed at the dust pile on the floor. It glowed green again, then erupted into a tornado-like form, complete with thunderbolts and lightning. This rose a few feet off the ground before reconstituting itself into my phone, which then resettled gently onto my desk. That refuted the prank theory nicely—putting me right back into the alien-believer camp.

"Thank you very kindly," I said, determined not to annoy Xena Warrior Fingers ever, ever again.

"Don't mention it. Anyway, as my colleague was saying, the reputation of Carter, Geller & Marks extends to the farthest corner of the universe, and we'd like to retain your services."

Now that I was buying the space alien bit, this hit me in a very different way. The farthest corner of the universe is a long way for fame to travel, even for assholes like us. I mean, *global* fame, sure—to the extent that law firms specializing in copyright and patents actually get famous. We're the ones who almost got a country booted from the

UN over its lax enforcement of DVD copyrights. We're even more renowned for our many jihads against the Internet.* And we're downright notorious for virtually shutting down American automobile production over a patent claim that was simply preposterous.† So yes, Earthly fame I was aware of. But I couldn't imagine why they'd be hearing about us way out on Zørkan 5, or wherever these two were from.

"So, what area of the law do you need help in?" I asked in a relaxed, almost bored tone. Feigning calm believably is a survival tactic that I perfected as the youngest of four boys (or of seven, if you count our cousins, who lived three doors down. I sure did). It made me boring to pick on—and useless as a prank victim, because I'd treat the damnedest events and circumstances as being mundane, and entirely expected. It had also helped me immensely as a lawyer (although by itself, it had not been enough to make me a successful one).

Sister Venus gave me a cagey look. "It's sort of . . . an intellectual property thing."

"Of course," I said. "Is it media? Patents? Trademark?"

"It's kind of a . . . music thing." She and O'Sama exchanged a furtive look.

---

*No, we haven't stopped the spread of pirated music or movies online, nor have we slowed it even slightly. But we do get paid pornographically vast sums for trying our very best.

†Our client didn't have a leg to stand on. But the Big Three paid a half billion dollars to get rid of us rather than cede the market to the Japs (their word, not mine) while awaiting trial. Within the firm, this is remembered as our finest hour.

"I see. Is it related to royalty payments? Piracy?"

Now O'Sama jumped into the action. And I mean that literally—he leapt to his feet, and practically screamed in my face. "Who said anything about *piracy*?"

The nun hit him with a lethal glare. "Zip it," she hissed. He plunked right back into his chair, giving her a hurt, sullen, but obedient look. *Impressive*, I thought. It was like seeing that dog whisperer guy make a pit bull back down.

"I do have an extensive background in music law," I said, clenching my nose to stop the sneeze molecules from breaking out.

Sister Venus rolled her eyes. "No duh, Mr. Carter. We've done our homework."

Well, yes, up to a point. True, they'd chosen a fine law firm from an impressive distance. But I was beginning to suspect that they had mistaken me for *the* Carter in Carter, Geller & Marks, rather than a lowly associate who happened to have the same last name as the founding partner. And did she seriously just say *no duh*?

"Also," O'Sama added breathlessly, "we simply adore 'Show Me the Meaning of Being Lonely,' and every one of your other songs."

"Ex*cuse* me?" I asked.

But I knew exactly what he was talking about. And if you're a woman born between the years 1984 and 1988, you probably do, too. Otherwise, you're hopefully only faintly aware of the Backstreet Boys—the vilest confection ever to emerge from a "boy band" factory. Like me, one of their alleged singers is named Nick Carter. He's two years my junior, so I was here first. And I got as far as age twenty-one with a wonderfully anonymous name. Then Nick and the boys unleashed an abomination called *Millennium* that sold more than forty million copies. I still get about a dozen Backstreet Boys jokes per week.

That said, something told me O'Sama wasn't joking. He just seemed too . . . earnest. "I do not have, never have had, and never will have any relationship whatsoever with the Backstreet Boys," I said, hoping to forever banish the topic from the intergalactic agenda.

"Really?" O'Sama's obvious devastation confirmed that he had been completely serious.

Sister Venus gave him a shocked look. "You didn't *honestly* think—"

And that's when we got Rickrolled. If you're not familiar with the aging prank, it's a sonic ambush that causes you to hear a snippet of Rick Astley's foppish late eighties hit, "Never Gonna Give You Up." Rickrolling had its heyday during the late Bush era. But like bell-bottoms, it stages occasional resurgences, and we were in the midst of one. I figured that the culprit was my unattainably gorgeous neighbor, Manda Shark. We'd had drinks the night before, and at some point she must have slyly changed my phone's primary ringtone. And now someone was calling, filling my office with that cheesy chorus.

Normal reactions to Rickrolls range from eye rolls to ironic sing-alongs. But my visitors started trembling, almost convulsing. And as they clung to their chairs for support, they took on an ecstatic air that was almost smutty. I instinctively grabbed my phone and muted the ringer.

"Big . . . music fans?" I ventured as they calmed down.

The nun nodded, catching her breath. "Almost any of your music can prompt that sort of reaction from us. Which is why we chose outfits with headdresses. They conceal devices that can completely silence our hearing when we're not in a sealed room, to protect us from the ambient music that fills the public spaces in your society."

O'Sama reached a finger under his turban and made a flicking gesture. *"You see, I can't hear a thing now,"* he bellowed, then flicked his finger back the other way.

"Then I better change a setting on my computer," I said, sliding over to my keyboard. "Otherwise it'll play some Michael Bolton whenever an email comes in." That was a lie. Neither of them could see my monitor, and I was actually launching the software that I use to record depositions and other interviews. If they wouldn't let me shoot the meeting on my cellphone, an audio recording would be better than nothing. "Anyway. You know my name. Do you mind if I ask for yours?"

"You can call me Carly," the nun said.

I nodded agreeably, although I'd been hoping for something a bit more exotic.

The mullah smiled gently. "And you can call me Frampton."

"Pleased to meet you both. So anyway—it sounds like you're big music fans. And you need representation. In what specific ways can Carter, Geller & Marks be helpful?"

Carly leaned toward me, almost conspiratorially. "We need a license to all of humanity's music. One that will allow . . . a rather large number of beings to play it. Privately and in public. And to copy it. And to transmit it, share it, and store it."

Decades of marveling at Hollywood aliens hadn't prepared me for this dry request. But my career at a sharp-elbowed copyright and patent law firm absolutely had. "That should be feasible," I said, managing to sound like

Carly was the third extraterrestrial to make this request today. "And exactly what music are you seeking licenses to?" I struggled not to sniffle as I said this. I failed.

"Every song that's been played on New York–area radio since 1977. Or has ever been sold or widely traded on the Internet."

"That would be . . . complicated, but quite manageable." This thigh-slapper came straight from my firm's equivalent of a cunning marketing script. The partnership owes much of its lavish income to conversations that begin a lot like this one (albeit with Earthlings). A prospective client imagines that our music-saturated society must surely have a rational and well-defined set of rules governing music licensing. They come to us because we famously know everyone in the industry. So naturally, we can get them their licenses in a trice—right?

You'd think. But music licensing is an arcane thicket of ambiguity, overlapping jurisdictions, and litigation. This is a disastrous situation for musicians, as well as for music fans and countless businesses. In fact, it suits absolutely nobody— apart from the cynical lawyers who run the music labels, the lobbying groups, the House, the Senate, and several parasitic law firms like my own. Collectively, we are wholly empowered to fix the entire mess. But that would result in a needless loss of extravagantly high-paying legal work for all. So we indignantly denounce the situation to our respective patrons, wave our fists at each other in public, and then privately chuckle slyly over drinks.

In this environment, conversations with prospective clients need to be handled delicately. You don't want them to look back later and think that you were overpromising in a no-win situation. But you certainly don't want to talk them out of attempting the impossible.

"Why would it be complicated?" Carly asked. "Is it . . . hard to get this sort of music license?"

"No, I wouldn't say *hard.*" This part of the pitch calls for offering some misleading relief. But as I started to deliver it, I recalled with a pang that the firm was about to trim some deadwood, and that I was a likely victim. They didn't hate me around here; I just wasn't viewed as being partner material, and would probably be shown the door within weeks. So why should I loyally push their greedy agenda until the bitter end? Particularly to a pair of extraterrestrials who probably lacked American currency anyway?

Carly tugged impatiently at her crucifix. "So, if it's not *hard,* what is it?"

"Utterly impossible," I said, with the reckless swagger of the noble corporate renegade that I'm not. "You can get close to a license as sweeping as that. But it'll cost you a fortune. And it'll take months at best—more likely years. And once you think you're done, there will always be lots of loose ends. Thousands at least. Ones that people can sue you over. And when they do, your defense could drag on for years—at four to nine hundred dollars per billable hour."

"But what if we want a license for places where no rational person would expect any of your music to ever sell, or even be played?" she pressed.

"Like where?"

At this, Frampton got to his feet and leaned across my desk. "The far side of the Townshend Line," he intoned, with the gravitas of a wizard invoking dungeons deep and caverns old.

Carly glared at him. "How would he know about the Townshend Line? You and I are the only beings who have ever crossed it." She turned back to me. "The damn thing's completely overrated anyway."

"Com*pletely*," Frampton agreed, retaking his seat.

"Anyway," Carly continued. "We want a license to regions that your record labels can't possibly care about. Specifically, all points one hundred forty-four light-years beyond your solar system."

Frampton stretched his arms wide. "That's over a hundred *trillion times* the distance from here to Staten Island!"

"I'm afraid the music industry actually cares immensely about even the remotest markets," I said. "In fact, almost every contract that it generates contains language like this." I picked up a document at random from my desk and gazed at it. " 'The terms of this contract shall apply past the end of time and the edge of Earth; all throughout the universe; in perpetuity; in any media, whether now known, or hereafter devised; or in any form, whether now known, or hereafter devised.' " I actually know this clause by heart, and can reel it off like a cop reciting the Miranda rights. But unless I pretend to read it from a document, people think I must be joking.

A brief, gloomy silence followed. "Well, if that's the case," Carly finally said, "it'll be a lot harder than we thought to save your melodious asses."

Save our asses? "From what?" It took every bit of self-control that I'd honed as a kid at the bottom of the testosterone pyramid to say this with professional calm.

"Self-destruction," Frampton said grimly.

"Yeah," Carly said, then mimed ironic quotation marks with chilling enthusiasm. "Self-destruction."

"Oh, *that*," I said languidly, while teetering on the brink of terror. "But why come to me about this?"

Carly's testy façade dropped, and admiration flitted briefly across her face. "Because we need to enlist the greatest copyright attorney on Earth. If not . . . the universe."

I allowed myself to savor the sound of this for a few moments. But there was no sense in pretending they had the right guy. "Then you really ought to talk to *Frank* Carter, who started the firm back in the seventies. Old guy, rich as hell. Sits in a huge corner office two floors up. Although he only comes in about once a month these days. No relation to me, I'm afraid."

Carly looked horrified. Frampton looked terrified. She pointed at me and fixed him with a murderous look. "I thought you said he ran the firm."

Frampton quaked. "I thought he *did*."

Carly paused, apparently putting two and two together. Then, "No, *you* thought he was a Backstreet Boy, and were looking for any excuse to meet him!"

"Well—not en*tire*ly."

Carly looked like she might hit him.

"Because there's the firm's name! It's *Carter*. And something, and something!" Frampton pointed at me. "Nick *Carter*!"

"You honestly thought a Backstreet Boy was moonlighting as a *lawyer*?"

"As a *music* lawyer!"

"Seriously?"

Frampton just grinned obsequiously and gave her a terrified shrug.

Carly turned her withering gaze to me. "Why doesn't anybody ever tell me *anything*?" she demanded, as if I was part of some conspiracy.

I shrugged neutrally and turned to Frampton, angling to keep the spotlight on him.

Carly kept staring me down. "Mr. Carter," she continued, after reining in her outrage somewhat. "How senior are you around here?"

"Well, it's hard to say exactly. But out of a hundred and thirty attorneys, for now I'm probably . . ." I thought for a moment. "Top hundred?"

Frampton cringed further. Carly glowered as if I'd somehow arranged all of this just to spite her. "In that case," she said, "it seems that my colleague and I have pulled you into deadly waters that are well over your head."

Whatever you might think, it's no fun when aliens talk about drowning you, even metaphorically. "But luckily there's a lifeguard out there, and his name is *Frank* Carter," I said brightly. "His old assistant has all of his contact info. So why don't we track him down and pass the baton to him?"

"Because it sounds like he's retired, and probably half senile," Carly snapped. "And besides, we don't have time. The gateway back to our planet closes in one minute. If we don't leave before then, we'll be stuck here with you for almost a day before it opens again. And I don't think you want that."

You got that right, I thought. In fact, I wanted nothing to do with these extraterrestrial freaks. Ever. "Well, then," I chirped. "We better get you into that gateway of yours pronto, huh?"

Carly shook her head. "We still have forty-nine seconds. And we need to arrange our next encounter with you, because it looks like you're all we've got. The gateway will reopen for roughly twenty minutes tomorrow morning. Since you've now met us, we won't need to come in person. Instead, we'll connect to an Earth-based dataspace. You will meet us there. And you will need these."

She held up a set of pink, wraparound safety lenses. They looked a lot like the odd specs that Bono always wears.

"They have been specially built to interface with one of your primitive computers. We will teleport this pair to you tomorrow at eleven oh-three a.m., and simultaneously email you instructions for joining us in the dataspace exactly three minutes later. Frampton and I will now exit by way of a Wrinkle. Don't be alarmed."

"By way of a what?"

"A Wrinkle," she said. And then added enigmatically, "The universe is pleated."

And that was when I finally sneezed—while making a botched effort to rein it in, which only made it sound like I was gagging on a pool ball.

"We could probably help you get over that cold," Carly said, cocking an eyebrow. And with that, the two of them knelt to the floor and bent low, as if praying toward Mecca. Then, in the course of about three seconds, they faded entirely from sight.

TWO
PIECES OF EIGHT

I used to think that English-speaking aliens who conveniently look, dress, and act human only turned up in lazy science fiction. But as Carly and Frampton dematerialized, I became grimly aware of how well they'd also fit into a psychotic hallucination. My distant uncle Louie blathers constantly about aliens. He's completely unhinged when he's off his meds—and they say that stuff runs in families. Meanwhile, no physical trace of my close encounter remained. There was no blinking ray gun carelessly left on a side table. No dropped Space Pesos made from strangely durable alloys that would confound scientists. My iPhone was also in perfect working order. And even if I turned out to be entirely sane—well then, great, it meant that an alien advance party was suddenly nosing around my planet. Worse, they were lawyering up.

Then I remembered my audio software. I couldn't have

imagined the meeting if my computer recorded it! I giddily tapped the space bar to get rid of my screensaver. Nothing happened. So I clicked and jiggled the mouse. Nothing again. Then I jabbed several times at the keyboard. Finally, I twisted my fingers to hit the defibrillating CTRL, ALT, and DEL keys—a gesture I associate so strongly with both annoyance and panic that my hand now reflexively makes it when I'm caught in traffic, stuck in a long line, flying in extreme turbulence—you name it.*

Click. Click. Click!

Several seconds of blank screen were followed by a flurry of digital Post-it notes. The top one declared that `~e5D141 .tmp has encountered a problem`. Next we had `Windows is currently in the middle of a long operation`. This was followed by `Cannot delete ysh53qch .3w4: There is not enough free disk space`, and so on. The gist of this trove of insight was that my audio software's recording (if there ever was one) had drowned in the maelstrom of the Windows OS. I was about to ritually denounce the entire Microsoft empire when the door flew open.

"Dude, got a moment?" It was the guy from the next office over, Randy Cox. Not waiting for an answer, he slid onto the chair that Frampton had just vacated. Six-two, brawny, and with a thick head of wavy brown hair, Randy's a decent guy who joined the firm two years after me. "Fido's coming to New York the day after tomorrow," he said, fixing me with a meaningful look. "I thought you might want to know. Given that you're due for the Omen, and all."

---

*You laugh, but it's usually just as helpful in those situations as it is on a Windows machine.

Our firm has so much internal jargon that we could probably foil a wiretap with it, and I know its terms as well as I know the names of the states. But I was too frazzled to muster anything more than a shell-shocked gaze.

"Fiiii-do," Randy repeated, as if teaching a new word to a thick preschooler. "Coming to town. Senator Fiiii-do. Fido."

I nodded mutely. Fido is our hazardously impolitic nickname for a man who can only be described as the music industry's pet senator—a high-ranking Republican. I think he honestly views himself as a fiercely principled advocate of The People. But he's firmly on our leash. And like any good pet, he obeys his master's voice.

"He's coming through town the day after tomorrow for some fund-raising," Randy continued. "Judy's got an hour on his calendar."

"Of course she does," I said, partially regaining my wits. Judy is one of the firm's most powerful (and dreaded) partners, and manages our relations with countless outside bigwigs. She meets privately with Fido almost monthly.

"I thought you'd find this interesting. Given that it may be your turn."

I nodded again. Each year, our firm hacks mercilessly at its cadre of long-serving associates, dropping the ones with no hope of ultimately making partner. And I was now in my seventh year—a notoriously lethal time. You know you've survived year seven if (and only if) you receive The Omen. This comes when a senior partner (like Judy) takes you around to meet privately with some of the firm's most prominent outside allies (like Fido). If you don't get The Omen by early March, you never will. And with February almost over, I was running out of time. I was also battling political headwinds that were bigger than me—and even Judy—in that our firm's patent litigators were starting to eclipse the copyright group that Judy heads. Our group was still printing money. But with patent troll clients shaking down businesses for ever-larger payouts over ever-more questionable patents, we were no longer the firm's ascendant team. This made it that much harder for copyright associates like me to survive.

I managed to give Randy a calm, skeptical look. "Do you honestly think Judy will let me through the gate?" She had been openly hostile toward me for months.

"Of course she will. She's like a lazy seventh grader. She only bothers to be mean to the people she really likes."

Randy wasn't just being nice, as this interpretation was actually consistent with Judy's odd temperament. But unlike him, I had read my performance reviews. "Nick gives good meeting," she had written recently. "But does NO original thinking." Sadly, I could see where she was coming from. I do *give good meeting*—a result of my ability to stay weirdly cool under fire, and to make people think that I know what's happening when I don't (another old survival tactic. I defused countless childhood plots by conning my brothers and cousins into thinking I was on to whatever they were planning against me, and had already alerted the grown-ups—when in truth I had no clue). The trouble is that this sets expectations high—so high that when people figure out that I'm occasionally quite clueless, they tend to overcorrect their assessment of me, and decide that I must be a full-time idiot.

"Thanks for the warning," I said, as my phone vibrated from a text message landing in its gullet. I slid it from my pocket. "I assume your info came from The Gretch?" Judy's assistant Gretchen has a harmless crush on Randy, which he parlays into a steady stream of intelligence about the mighty boss's calendar.

"Of course."

I glanced at the inbound text.

Take me to your leeeeeea-der, Earth boy!

My hands turned to ice as my thoughts returned to my alien-addled Uncle Louie. I meanwhile noticed that my phone had matched the sender's callback number to "Paulie Stardust"—which made zero sense, because that name wasn't listed anywhere in my contacts.

"I figure that if the partners are thinking of Omening you, they may give you a little trial by fire over the next couple of days," Randy continued. "And forewarned is fore-armed."

I forced my mind back to our conversation. "I know. I . . . really appreciate the heads-up." Randy was in fact doing me a huge favor. If the partners are on the fence about someone, they'll often stage an ambush at Omen time to see if the person can think creatively under acute, unexpected pressure. Last year, they gave a woman ten minutes to prepare an hour-long rebuttal to a *Wall Street Journal* editorial that denounced a growing tsunami of frivolous patent litigation for smothering the tech industry (no mean feat, as the piece was essentially correct on every point). The associate had to present her rebuttal to the full office, and did a great job.* The next day, she received The Omen, and is now very much on track for partner.

---

*She quite literally brought tears to the eyes of a senior partner who the *Journal* had denounced by name when she declared that he was, in fact, "a hero of American law" for pioneering an entirely new

"I bet if they're gonna mess with you, it'll be at the weekly meeting with Judy tomorrow morning." As Randy said this, my phone vibrated with another message from Paulie Stardust:

All your base are belong to us!

"I . . . I'll bet you're right," I answered.

Randy rose and opened the door. "So. You may want to brace yourself."

The phone vibrated one last time as he left:

Come directly to Eatiary. All will be revealed.

This was followed by an address I didn't recognize. I looked it up on my phone's map as Randy left. Eatiary, whatever it was, was on the Meatpacking District's outer fringe. Spooked to the core, but determined to get to the bottom of this, I headed to the elevators.

Soon I was down on the icy, bustling streets. New York in February is New York at its worst, unless you count those hundred-degree August weekends when everyone's off at the Hamptons but you.* The cheery buzz of the holidays is long gone, and the spring thaw is too distant to provide any solace. Add a three-inch layer of blackened slush, and it can feel like Moscow without the twelve-cent vodka. I started walking toward the Meatpacking District.

Eight blocks on, I found a cab. The crosstown traffic turned out to be so bad that walking might have been faster. But it was nice to get my stricken sinuses out of the freezing

---

scorched-earth approach to patent litigation (one that's so effective that entire sectors of the semiconductor industry are leaving the U.S. for less litigious shores).

*Which I suppose you should count. So let's call February New York at its almost-worst.

rush-hour air. As I settled into the backseat, my phone started humming from a flurry of inbound texts.

OMG, EATIARY? I'm sooooooo jealous.

That came from a girl I faintly remembered from college. Next in the queue was this from the cousin of a long-ago roommate:

You must must must have the Stuffed Marrow Rings with Aduki Bean reduction!!!

And on it went—fifteen texts from distant acquaintances, as well as an actual friend or two. After wondering if everyone I knew was in on some ingenious belated birthday prank, I figured out what was happening.

Phluttr.

Phluttr is a smartphone app that lets you trumpet your every thought and action to an enraptured world by pushing out mini press releases via Facebook, Twitter, SMS, email, and, for all I know, telegrams and carrier pigeons. Being this fascinating can be taxing, even for clinical narcissists. So Phluttr makes it easy by infiltrating your phone and automatically publishing whatever it learns. In my first twenty minutes of experimenting with the service, every classmate and co-worker that I'd ever had was told that "NICK just arrived at 200 Park Avenue!" and, "NICK just called United Airlines!" and, most embarrassing, "NICK is listening to 'Bye Bye Bye' by 'N Sync!'"*

However awful this sounds, the reality is far worse, and I soon quit the service. I'd since uninstalled its diabolical software a dozen times, but somehow it kept reappearing. This

---

*For the record, I was in a goofy mood, and listened to it strictly for its kitsch value—but good luck explaining the concept of irony to a smartphone.

time I thought I'd finally foiled it—by quite literally buying a new phone. But now, after a month's sulk, Phluttr was baaaaaack. It had apparently matched the address that I'd looked up on my phone to Eatiary (a faddish restaurant, it seemed). And once my GPS signal indicated that I was actually heading there, it had informed my breathless public.

When I got to the texted address, I found a cheap, bustling, overly lit restaurant. Outside was a gigantic mural of several figures raising a Greek flag in poses cribbed from the Iwo Jima Memorial. I faintly recognized them as the cast of an old sitcom set in a Nazi prison camp (isn't it amazing what they used to get away with?). The sign above them said Hogan's Gyros. No hint of anything called "Eatiary." Inside, the restaurant was packed with pierced kids in ball caps ironically touting mideighties metal bands. As I puzzled over this, a six-foot goddess of the night strode through the front door. Dressed for Miami weather, she was barely of the same species as Hogan's crowd, and made a beeline for an unmarked green door toward the back of the tiny dining area.

Could it be . . . ? I opened the door myself, and entered a darkened oasis of LED lighting, leggy models, and thirty-dollar appetizers. All the young dudes in the Twisted Sister caps stayed out with the short-order pita chefs—this side of the green door was for bosses, hotties, and investors. Years ago, my jaw would have dropped at the drastic shift in scenery. But these days, Manhattan is late into a romance with ironic speakeasy entrances from incongruous premises. I had entered a throbbing nightspot through a shabby taqueria's kitchen closet, a high mixology temple via a phone booth in a hot dog hut, and even a boutique hotel through a unisex bathroom in a bowling alley.

My path was blocked by a towering hipster whose ironic,

midcentury math teacher glasses were thick enough to stop bullets. "And we are joining . . . ?" he asked, with an arch mix of deference and disdain. Clearly a lowly suit like me was somebody else's plus-one in this postmodern nightscape.

"Paulie Stardust," I said, feeling like a complete ass.

He squinted at his list. "I see. The Stardust/Carter reservation. Walk this way."

He led me around an intricate series of waterways. Some rushed under Lucite beneath our feet, others along shoulder-high aqueducts hammered from distressed iron and brushed steel. The water flowed above, around, and under the diners, setting each table apart from its neighbors, and drowning every sweet nothing, deal term, and harsh ultimatum in its busy murmur. It was all just some Tiki wood and a barnacle-covered treasure chest short of god-awful tackiness. But the goth-industrial fixtures and the steampunk plumbing made for a masterful effect. Every table was full.

"No music?" I asked. You'd think the place would be pulsing with smooth Euro-beats, but there was nothing but the sound of running water.

The host shook his head. "The birds don't like it."

As if on cue, a bright red parrot landed on a nearby railing. "I'm sustainable," it chirped. Then, "Biodiesel!"

Another free bird zipped by overhead, then another—and I got it. Eatiary was a dine-in aviary (I could barely see the soaring ceiling), and home to dozens of chattering birds of paradise. Several seemed to be entertaining diners with their stock phrases. And all of them were brilliantly trained—none were swiping any food, and their bowel control was a marvel.

The host took on the air of a bored tour guide. "All of

the winged fauna at Eatiary are rescues. None were bird-napped from the wild. Many were liberated from abusive domestic situations." He gestured at a footbridge. "The timbers used in our interior were reclaimed from long-ago shipwrecks in the Great Lakes. No tree was harvested for the building's renovation." What a relief! Although the place must have had the carbon footprint of a small county. Arctic evening be damned, it was mai tai weather in here—sultry and humid, with fertile scents percolating from a tropical jungle of potted trees that ringed the dining area.

A sky-blue parakeet landed on an aqueduct as we turned a corner. "Bikes, not bombs," it urged. Moments later, we arrived at a spacious table with one other diner. And as I recognized him, I reeled from a strange mixture of ecstatic relief and moral outrage. "Paulie Stardust" was apparently Henry Pugwash—the youngest, smartest, and most obnoxious of my three smart, older, jackass cousins. No doubt he was behind everything that had happened that evening—including those awful thoughts about losing my mind. Muttering into his cellphone while skimming the news on his iPad, he nodded absently as I took my seat. "What's up, Pugwash," I murmured. No one calls him Henry (including his brothers and parents) because he just looks so . . . *Pugwashy*. All of five foot six, he's always been chunky. And he has dark, narrow-set eyes under this dome of coal black hair that always manages to contort into something like a bowl cut, regardless of how it's styled.

The host unfurled my napkin for me as I took my seat. "Tonight's special is a grass-fed, free-range Wagyu petite fillet. It's sourced from an agrarian coöperative that's run by differently abled ranch hands. Waitstaff will bring you some Hopi blue corn piki bread shortly. Meanwhile, you may wish to examine our butter list." He handed us two heavy cards that were no doubt repurposed strike posters from a hemp factory. They listed twenty separate butters, broken down by region and species of "milk-giver." "The *beurre du jour* is a clarified preparation derived from Tibetan yak milk," he added.

"I'll just have the whale burger and panda ears again," I said. I caught the host stifling a chuckle as he left, and savored the low-rent thrill of a tourist making a Buckingham guard smile.

"Dude, that's sick," my cousin snapped, setting down his phone. "The most sustainable restaurant in town, and you're making jokes about our ecological crisis."

I was tempted to ask him what was so ecological about sustaining a little patch of Singapore in wintry Manhattan— but I let it go. My cousin's a master of progressive rhetoric and loves to lure moderates (*fascists,* as he calls us) into political debates. He invariably wins these with a deft mix of data, wordplay, and self-righteous sloganeering. At heart, though, he's a true social Darwinist, and his other hobby is protecting his prodigious wealth from government attempts to tax and redistribute it. He'll never admit it (above all to himself), but Pugwash really only dallies on the Left because he's heard there're some easy chicks there.

"So, how's business?" I asked. Although I was dying to learn about Carly and Frampton, I couldn't let him know this, or he'd be sure not to mention them until dessert.

Before he could answer, a smug cockatoo landed on the back of the empty chair next to him. "Go solar!" it demanded.

An instant later, something swooped in low from the far side of the restaurant, grazing the hair of a waiter as it zeroed in on our table. It landed on the back of Pugwash's chair, then swatted the cockatoo on the beak with a muscular wing. The smaller bird tumbled backward, and fell almost to the ground before fluttering off jaggedly, like a dazed housefly. The newcomer was twice the size of all the other birds. It was mostly yellow, with a stark white face and chest, and a black targetlike pattern around its left eye. "Pieces of *EEEEEEIGHT!*" it cawed.

"Holy crap," Pugwash yelped, pulling back reflexively.

The parrot saw this and jumped right onto his shoulder. "Swab the mizzen-mast!" it commanded in a thick Scottish accent. "Scurvy me sextant! All hands to the Lido deck!" Clearly this one had been liberated from a marauding corsair, instead of an eco-boosting reëducation camp. Pugwash tried to slide away, but the parrot held on tight. So he brushed frantically at his shoulder. This irked the bird, who grudgingly hopped over to the back of the empty chair that he'd just evicted the cockatoo from. "Tree-lubber," it snorted.

"So . . . you were about to tell me how business is going," I said.

The parrot cocked an ear and struck an attentive pose.

"Business? It's awesome!" This conveyed zero information, since Pugwash would claim it from the very throes of bankruptcy. That said, business does tend to go rather awesomely for him. He graduated college three years before me, with so-so grades from a no-name school (smart as he is, he's even more lazy). He moved back into his parents' home with no discernible prospects. But just as he was starting to delight his sibling rivals by amounting to nothing, a Magoo-like stroke of random fortune swept him into a job at Google. It was 1999, and the company had about thirty employees.

Within a few quick years it had over ten thousand. This happened through absolutely no fault of Pugwash's. But his stock options became outlandishly valuable as a result, and he'll coast forevermore.

"So how'd you score this table?" he demanded, clearly as close to being impressed with me as his constitution would allow. "Eatiary's tougher to get into than the Waverly these days."

"How did . . . *I* get this table?" Even as I said this, my spirits collapsed as I realized that my cousin hadn't sent the chilling texts that had brought me here. He just saw that I was going to a hyperexclusive restaurant on Phluttr, and showed up to leach on to my reservation.

"No, I'm talking to birdbrain here." Pugwash jabbed a sarcastic finger at the chair next to him.

The rowdy yellow parrot was still perched there—far enough back that my cousin couldn't see his face. Apparently taking advantage of this privacy, the bird caught my eye, and winked conspiratorially. Entirely freaked out, I looked away, trying to write this off as a standard parrot trick, like saying hi or mimicking the ring of a telephone. I mean, all parrots can wink. Conspiratorially. In perfect sync with your conversation. Right?

"By the way, you don't have a *cold,* do you?" Pugwash instinctively cringed back in his chair—and he had good reason to be worried. Whenever any guy in our family got sick growing up, we'd all catch it within minutes. To this day, Pugwash and I can swap a cold back and forth just by passing through the same room.

"Guilty as charged," I confirmed. "You'll be a sneezing wreck by midnight." I chanced a second glance at the parrot. The little fucker gave me another wink.

"Well, being a good cousin, I got you something other than a *disease* for your birthday." Pugwash pulled an oddly shaped cigarette lighter from the pocket of his plush cashmere jacket. It was bulbous, almost spherical. "I picked it up last week, down in Pahra*khwai*." It sounded like he was gargling with marmalade when he hit that last word.

"Paraguay," I corrected. An obsessive traveler, my cousin's always zipping off on quick, pricey journeys. No place is too random for him. But *Paraguay*? He must be running out of countries to visit.

"Yes. Pahra*khwai*," he said, with an even harsher gargling sound. Pugwash can't bear to mention any Latin American location without making some pathetic gringo stab at sounding native. He thinks it makes him sound worldly and liberal—like those NPR reporters who make pretentious gagging noises whenever they utter a faintly Hispanic name.

"Well, thanks," I said, looking at my fabulous gift. "But you . . . know I don't smoke. Right?"

"Of course. But this is no ordinary lighter."

I flicked it suspiciously. Your basic flame leapt up from its nozzle.

"It's the world's first carbon negative lighter," Pugwash continued proudly. "It's shaped like a *khwa-ra-NAAA* seed. And it's made by indigenous persons."

"So it . . . takes CO_2 out of the air?"

He shook his head. "For every one you buy, a tree in the rain forest is conserved. Carbon sequestration. Much more efficient. And I'm gonna make a fortune by investing in the tribe that's making them."

I nodded politely, sliding the lighter into my jacket pocket. Pugwash left Google years ago, and these days he fights boredom by pumping his winnings into business ideas. He's had some surprising successes (e.g., Amish vs. Aliens—a maddeningly addictive Facebook game). He's had some awful flops (e.g., Forever 29—a store for older women who liked to dress like trashy youngsters, and lie about their age). And he's had one monstrous win (Phluttr, in which he was the first investor). Rather than launching businesses himself, he invests in start-ups, and trolls Union Square bars for entrepreneurs like a pederast cruising bus stations for runaways. He generally positions himself as a "tech guy." But Internet fortune aside, he has no hard technical expertise. His Google job was in "business development." From what I can tell, this is a worldwide backslapping society whose members jet off to conferences, discuss strategic partnerships among their companies, and then race home to ignore each other's emails.

Before I could ask how the Indigenous went about sequestering trees, Pugwash's phone started vibrating so violently that it almost leapt from the table. He grabbed it and gazed at the screen. His eyes went saucer-wide, then platterwide. And then he took off at a trot, without a word.

With that, the parrot hopped right onto the back of his vacant chair, regarding me at eye level. "So who invited dat guy?" he asked, the Scottish brogue suddenly replaced with Dodgers-era Brooklynese.

Practically gagging from shock, I managed a blasé tone. "Phluttr."

The parrot nodded.

I gestured at the table. "Your reservation, I assume?"

The parrot nodded again.

"So why meet here?"

"Where else can a guy like me connect up without stickin' out? Apart from a pet store." As if on cue, a forest green parakeet flew past us, nattering about urban composting.

I nodded absently as if this was just an obvious, throwaway fact. But I was furiously analyzing the parrot's every word. Hundreds of depositions had taught me that idle chitchat can be a great source of useful information—and I wanted to learn everything I could about this guy.

"Anyways," the parrot continued, glancing from side to side, "I guess this is how they roll . . . on the richest planet in the universe." His eyes narrowed as he made this bizarre statement, and he looked at me intently—and I realized that we were playing a similar game. He'd probably just said something that was mundane and obvious in his circles, to see if it confused or surprised me (a technique I often use myself). If I was a nobody, I'd respond with a silly and basic question. Whereas if I was plugged in, he probably hadn't betrayed any facts I didn't already know. It was a no-risk way to get a sense of who he was dealing with.

"I hear it's the best restaurant on this side of the Townshend Line," I said, like a fellow tourist sharing a tip. Carly and Frampton had used this term, and it seemed like it would fit here.

The parrot opened his beak to say something, then clammed up. Then he did it again. *Was I getting to him?*

"But why'd you drag me out tonight?" I continued, pressing him to talk before he could come up with something cunning.

"'Cause . . . I know all about the alien visitor you just had," he said slyly. "And I'm here to tell you: you're in danger."

Gotcha. He was fishing—and he blew it by saying visi*tor*, instead of visi*tors*. He didn't even know how many beings had visited me, much less who they actually were. But he wanted me to think he'd positively identified them as bad guys. Time to go on the offensive.

"You don't know a *goddamn thing* about my visitor," I said, leaning in toward him. "So why am I even talking to you? Tell me what you're after, or this meeting's over."

The parrot's eyes narrowed, and he glared at me. Then finally he snarled, "Aright!"

Excellent, I thought. If my iPhone has taught me anything, it's that angry birds make boo-boos.

"I'm here doin' . . . asset recovery," he continued. "For my team."

"Of course. And how much did you guys lose?"

"More than anybody else." The parrot hopped from the chair to the table and took a few steps toward me. *"Anybody."*

Dammit—he was right back on to his game. That sweeping superlative should tell me exactly who he was working with—so now I couldn't ask for that information and still come off as an alien-savvy sophisticate. But he had left me a toehold by implying that lots of other groups had also lost assets.

"Hey, everyone's down a bit these days." I shrugged, like he should just get over it already. His short temper seemed like an asset to me, and I hoped this would inflame him further.

"But who the hell else lost a *third of the assets* in the goddamn universe?" he growled.

Bravo. I shrugged again. "Just you guys, obviously."

The parrot's eyes narrowed again, as he realized he'd just given something away. Then, "Aright, Mac. Your turn to talk. What th'hell do you know about the Townshend Line?"

Absolutely nothing, I thought. Then I remembered Carly's odd little statement. "Just that it's completely overrated," I said, rolling my eyes.

The bird backed up a few steps, and almost fell off the table. "Who . . . who told *you*?" he finally managed.

I arched my eyebrows sarcastically. "A little bird."

The parrot leapt across the table toward me, and lowered his voice. "Listen, Carter. I ain't no goddamn *bird*. I'm a *rap*tor. And I'm very, very *large* for my species. Got that? But enough about me. Who are *you*? And what are *you* doing on Earth?"

I had one last serviceable phrase to parrot back from my previous alien powwow. "Just trying to keep these crazy humans from . . . self-destructing," I said, miming jokey quotation marks like Carly had.

This completely silenced him for a moment. Then he exploded. "But you can't *do* that! That—that's against the *rules!*"

At this, a mad fluttering broke out overhead. I looked up. The cockatoo that my guest had bitch-slapped several minutes back was dive-bombing him, along with two cohorts. "Go *green!*" it squawked.

The alien parrot launched himself like a cruise missile. He collided head-on with his lead attacker, knocking it out cold, and sending its limp body reeling into a beef chutney soufflé three tables away. Then, in a blur of avian jujitsu, he reversed direction, grabbing his second attacker's shoulders in his talons. With a few powerful thrusts of his wings he dragged it into an aqueduct, and left it flailing in the water. The third attacker darted off in a panic.

Kung-fu parrot rejoined me. We were getting lots of stares. "Pieces of EIGHT," he bellowed, trying to convince the room that he was just another three-phrase knuckle-head. "Set the controls for MogadiSHU!"

"I don't think it's working," I said drily, wishing I had a shaken-not-stirred martini to sip at debonairly. More and more people were looking our way, and a knot of irate para-keets was gathering overhead. This round was mine.

"Yer right," the parrot whispered, scanning the room anxiously, and focusing on a massive bouncer who was now approaching. "And here comes the heat." He seemed to spy an escape route. "I'll be back," he vowed.

"Hasta la vista," I said, as he rocketed straight at the bouncer's face. At the last second he pulled up toward the dis-tant rafters, and vanished.

"That was so weird." I looked up and saw that Pugwash was back. He was staring at his cellphone rather than the scene unfolding around us. "Check this out." He handed me the phone.

He'd been texted a picture of two ridiculously sexy blondes. One was exposing her breasts as her friend nibbled on her ear. They were standing right outside, next to the Hogan's Gyros sign. PUGGY-BEAR! the text said. We'RE eye-ing You & your Friend. Come out and say hiiiii beFore we Leave!

Pugwash was inconsolable. "I went outside, and they weren't there. I looked everywhere."

I quietly admired the parrot's technique. He wanted a few minutes alone with me, and he'd pushed Pugwash's but-tons just right.

Suddenly another commotion began in the center of the room. The alien parrot was now dive-bombing the bouncer. He pulled up a few feet short, releasing a payload of what had to be alien parrot droppings right into the poor man's

eyes. The bouncer bellowed in disgust and staggered frantically, colliding with a small reservoir, which collapsed and
unleashed a deluge onto three tables of diners. The rest of
the irrigation system shuddered, springing dozens of leaks
throughout the room. Our urban biodiversity sanctuary was
about to become a wetlands preserve.

"We should be elsewhere," I said. Pugwash, still bereft
over the vanished hotties, followed me mutely toward the
exit.

THREE
STRAY CAT STRUT

We hit a Thai place after Eatiary, and put away a few bottles of Singha. That, and the familiar drone of Pugwash deconstructing Pugwash made it feel like things were almost back to normal, and I gladly let dinner unfold at an especially unhurried pace. Although, of course, nothing was normal. God only knew what the aliens were up to. Indeed, only He knew if they were real. My cousin had at least seen the parrot—but my conversation with it could have easily been the product of a freshly deranged mind. Still, I left dinner determined to enjoy the sudden normality.

With this in mind, I shut Pugwash down when he invited himself up to crush me at Scrabble after dinner. The reason wasn't aliens, but my neighbor, Manda Shark. She's the one who teed up that intergalactic Rickroll by naughtily changing my ringtone the night before. Midway through dinner, she had sent me a text:

Hey if you get n by . . . midnight? Come buy
I'll have a fun present for you. To say thanks for
the pep talk last night it really helped!

The pep talk was over a late glass of bourbon. I suggested it after I found her pacing in the basement laundry
room, fretting about a big show tonight (opening a lengthy
bill that would climax around midnight with the Decem-
berists). Manda's something of an It Girl on the independent music scene. Her haunting, melodic songs have obtuse
lyrics, and meld folklike arrangements with swish electron-
ica. She's gifted and respected. But since indie cred doesn't
pay the bills, she also works as a paralegal at a midtown law
firm. Our faint professional overlap is a godsend, as it gives
me something completely unconnected to my puppy-dog
fascination with her to discuss when we cross paths.

We live in Murray Hill—a hill-free neighborhood whose
minute claim to fame stems from its being the site of the
Ricardo household in _I Love Lucy_ (it's a fancy way of saying
"the East Thirties"). Our apartments are in a prewar building with maybe forty units on its eight floors. It has clunking
radiators, gothic-looking water towers on the roof, and an
old-school elevator with a sliding steel gate. The chummy
doorman gave me an unsolicited Knicks update when I entered the lobby (they'd won, but there was a key injury to
fuss over). I thanked him, and took the elevator to six—the
floor that both Manda and I live on.

By then, the two of us had caught up for semi-
spontaneous dinners or drinks thirteen times since she
moved in (and yes, that's an exact count). She lived just two
doors down from me (another exact count). So if I timed it
right (and I really did my best), we'd cross paths at least
briefly maybe twice a week. In the interim, I'd develop

stockpiles of quips and pithy observations to weave into our conversations. I'd prepare little insights that could help her in her paralegal work. I'd also listen to any albums or songs that she might have mentioned in passing, so as to be informed and opinionated if they came up again. I once even read three kitschy romance novels by one Robyn Amos, because I mistakenly thought she was Manda's favorite author (who in fact turned out to be some Brit named Martin Amis).*

When I got to Manda's door, I paused before knocking. I could faintly hear some humming, and some stop-start strumming on an acoustic guitar. She was working on a new song. I stood at the door and listened, hating the thought of interrupting. Manda had told me that she holds all the parts of a new piece in her head at once—even if she's just playing a simple chord. If I knocked now, I feared that they'd scatter like the tiles of a detonating Rubik's Cube, because her songs are intricate, almost baroque. Each has multiple synthesizers and at least three guitar parts—one of which hammers out rapid arpeggios that wrap the music in ornate, almost percussive textures. Add drums, bass, and several vocal tracks, and there's a lot going on.

After about a minute of listening I started feeling like a stalker. But I still didn't want to interrupt her, so I shuffled

---

*Luckily, Manda didn't drop in during the week when the Robyn Amos canon was casually arrayed throughout my apartment in hopes of catching her eye. While I had presented myself as a Renaissance man with diverse interests, a taste for African-American bodice-rippers might have seemed odd. From its product suggestions, Amazon.com is now convinced that I'm a middle-aged black woman.

down the hall to my own apartment while pecking out a text:

I'm back! Drop by/call whenever you feel like it—I'll be up really late!

I paused at my front door and read it over. Friendly is good, but this bordered on goofy. So I surgically replaced the exclamation points with periods. The goofiness was gone. But now it seemed almost . . . chilly. Didn't it? So I reinserted the second exclamation point, leaving the first one out. *Better.* It now ended with a little crescendo of enthusiasm, but without that Ned Flanders vibe. The only problem now was grammatical fussiness. I mean, the slash was a bit much—wasn't it? I certainly didn't want Manda thinking that I was some kind of dork who obsessed over punctuating texts. So I dropped the hyphen, replaced the slash with an "or," and kept the final exclamation point. That done, I courageously hit Send and entered my apartment.

I flipped on the lights. My setup is nice enough—your basic one-bedroom that's furnished maybe a half cut above Ikea. But it's clearly the work of a heterosexual man who works long hours and has no design sense. A couch and a fifty-inch plasma screen dominate my small living room, predictably arrayed against opposite walls. The one hint of style comes from a gorgeous rosewood bookshelf that I splurged on when I first joined Carter, Geller & Marks. My plan was to gradually fill it with hardbound copies of only the very best books that I read in my new life as a New Yorker—ones that truly moved me, or made me think. They'd be first editions when possible, and some would be autographed. But I've since been lucky to find time for maybe a half dozen books per year, and most of them are crap. So my glorious shelves hold DVD sets from voguish TV shows like *The Wire, Fringe,* and *Breaking Bad* (which will probably be viewed as my generation's Great Works anyway).

Manda's shelves are way more interesting, and most of her living room walls are lined with them—mainly particleboard kits that she nails together herself. All are heavy with reading matter that she's devoured in the three scant years since she graduated NYU. There are classics, modern novels, graphic novels, dozens of issues of *Vice* magazine (a fire hazard she can't bear to toss), evolutionary biology (she was a premed for two years), evolutionary psychology, scholarly musical histories, and an entire shelf dedicated to weighty art books.

My pocket hummed briefly as Manda responded to my text:

Cool m coming byy now w my new man

My new man? The phrase punctured my heart, and brought my post-Singha rally to a crashing end.

Moments later she was knocking. I braced myself for the worst and opened the door, and . . . she was alone. And as always, she was a vision. She does some careful hair and makeup work before going onstage, and always looks incredibly put together after a show. Her hair is a satiny, full-bodied mahogany. It falls to her shoulders in big, soft curls, and marches across her forehead in short, uniform bangs, framing her bewitchingly dark eyes. Manda's also fairly tall, and is curved in the ways that artists, sculptors, and designers idealized from Sumerian times until the bulimics' recent rise. All this was wrapped up in a cute, fuzzy Radiolab sweatshirt.

"I see you haven't had time for a wardrobe change since you left the stage," I teased. Below the sweatshirt she was wearing a pair of skinny black jeans that I'm a huge fan of. Those she probably did wear onstage.

"I haven't had time for a wardrobe change since I left college."

I smiled. She did wear that Radiolab sweatshirt a lot. The jeans she didn't wear anywhere near enough.

"By the way," she continued, "it sounds like you're fighting quite a cold."

"It would kill a lesser man, but it's no match for me." I struck a mock-heroic pose. My wimpy nasal voice upped the comic effect, and Manda smiled. "So, uh," I continued, "where's the new man?"

"He's being shy all of a sudden." She bent down and leaned off to the left of my doorway, extending an arm. "C'mon little buddy—Nick doesn't bite." And with that, an exceptionally long and slender cat strode regally into view. He was coal black, with bright green eyes. The vise of tension that had clutched my shoulders since the *coming byy now w my new man* message instantly released.

"Awesome—I love cats," I said, bending down for a closer look. I actually love them about as much as I love Robyn Amos romances. But no way was I going to blow the moment by admitting that. And of course, any creature was better than the fashionably tattooed Lothario that I was expecting to see. "What's his name?" I asked as they entered, and I shut the door.

"I'm calling him Meowhaus. Say hi, little buddy."

Meowhaus dutifully let off a full, perfectly rounded *Meow*.

"He's wonderful," I said. At this, Pinocchio's nose would have impaled the little beast and burrowed clear through to China. But mine didn't betray me. "When did you get him?"

"He turned up in the dressing room tonight before the show. Maybe five-fifteen, or six? I'm not really sure."

"A fan, huh?" I asked, forcing myself to squat down and pet him.

"More like a stalker. He's followed me ever since."

"Around the dressing room?"

"Around everywhere. I hit a couple stores on the way home, and he tagged along like a little brother."

"You did *errands*? Coming home from the biggest show of your life?"

"I was hunting for your thank-you gift," she said, smiling like a deity. And with that, all thoughts of aliens and schizophrenia left me for seven seconds straight. *Sweet respite . . .*

"So the cat came into the stores with you?"

"Yeah, like he owned them. No one minded. They let dogs into most places these days. A smart cat can just slip in like a spy."

Like a spy. Respite over. The events at Eatiary had made me highly suspicious of large, charismatic animals.

"Hey, I think he likes you," Manda said as I rubbed a reluctant finger against Meowhaus's left cheek. He shut his eyes, and leaned hard into my hand. As Manda looked on, I fought off a Tourette's-like urge to make childish puns about petting her pussy. After months of meticulously gaining her trust, the thought that a single moronic phrase could dash it all was giving me a sort of verbal vertigo.

Manda joined me on the floor and gave Meowhaus a little neck massage. This prompted a low, smooth rumbling that sounded more like the purr of a top-end sports car than of a stray cat. For the first time since I met her, Manda and I were hovering cheek to cheek. And that was all it took for me to renounce decades of bigotry and realize that cats were awesome after all. *Really* awesome! And as for Meowhaus— why, I'd take a bullet for my wingman! I rubbed his cheek a bit harder. He purred a bit louder. I quietly wished he had a twin that I could adopt. Or a septuplet, or whatever the little monsters came in.

"So he doesn't have an owner?"

"Not as far as I can tell. No collar. Tomorrow I'm gonna go to a vet to see if he has an ID chip, look for flyers around where I found him, check Craigslist—that sort of thing."

"And if your new man's really single, is he a keeper?"

"Hell yes!"

"Great. And the two of you can come by for a drink and some catnip whenever you want." A brief, cuddly montage filled my mind of Manda and me watching TV with Meowhaus; of Manda and me reading on the couch with Meowhaus; of Manda and me screwing athletically with Meowhaus nowhere to be seen.

"Cool—and we can get started on that right now." I tried very hard to believe that Manda was miraculously referring to my montage's glorious finale. But she just pulled a bottle from a canvas bag that she'd brought in. "Is this the stuff you were talking about?" she asked, handing it to me.

By God, it was. When I poured her a humble glass of Maker's Mark the night before, the conversation turned to bourbon, and I mentioned that the best stuff I'd ever tasted was this twenty-three-year-old hooch named after a guy called Pappy Van Winkle. A classmate of mine at law school who's part hillbilly on his mom's side sourced some out of Kentucky once, and I hadn't tasted the stuff since graduation. Now for the umpteenth time since meeting her, I fell in love with Manda Shark. "How in the world did you find this?" I asked.

"I shouldn't admit it, but it was pretty easy. I only had to go to three places. They'll cough up the good stuff if you bat your eyelashes the right way."

I nodded. Bat them the right way, and the Librarian of Congress would cough up the Gutenberg Bible for you, I thought. "You need to try this. I'll get us a couple glasses." I headed into my kitchen, which is about the size of a jet's galley. A normal person would find it maddeningly small. But anything beyond a fridge and a cereal cupboard is wasted on me.

Just as I was grabbing the glasses, this crazy sound started coming from the living room. I dashed out and saw Meowhaus squaring off with my bedroom doorway. Crawling toward it in a low, predatory posture, he was hissing like a cracked airplane window. The bedroom was dark. The door was half open. I was starting toward the bedroom myself when the lights suddenly cut out in the rest of the apartment. Then Manda screamed. I pivoted and saw a pulsating red orb emerge from the floor in front of her.

FOUR
METALLICAM (ME)

The orb was maybe three feet wide, and it rose majestically. Heavy gray smoke poured from its surface and oozed to the floor. There it spread, until we seemed to be adrift on a roiling, fog-choked sea. The orb was translucent, and a deep, red, pulsating glow emanated from its core. It rose to chest height, then stopped.

"Smoke on the water," it boomed in the sort of voice that Zeus might use if he were auditioning to play Satan in a Russian speed metal video. The fog beneath our feet churned and convulsed.

"Fire in the sky!" Bolts of flame shot up from the fog. Searingly bright, they weirdly gave off no heat.

Manda was deeply spooked, but also bedazzled by all this Sturm und Drang. And I wasn't unimpressed. But this was my third alien encounter, and so far they had been harmless. So my main feeling was one of relief. *Manda was seeing this, too*—and I no longer had to worry about my sanity!

"What . . . are you?" she managed, gazing at the orb.

"I'm jet fuel, honey." This odd claim was followed by a blinding red flash, along with an infrasonic thud that rocked my innards but was barely audible.

This seemed to render Manda mute, so I leaned forward. "You're *what?*" I asked.

"I'm . . ." The orb paused awkwardly, clearly expecting more shock & awe, and less Q&A. Then, **"I'm TNT. I'm . . . dynamite."** At this, it unleashed a cool explosion effect, with flames in the shape of a skull.

"You're not the first to make this claim," I said, affecting an urbane calm that I hoped would fluster our visitor. I'd heard the TNT/dynamite thing before, although I couldn't quite place the source amid all the excitement. "Try being more original."

"I'm . . . a mean go-getter," the orb sputtered. That one I knew. It was a lyric from that Quiet Riot song. Not "Metal Health"—the other one. "But enough about me. I'm here to learn about you, Carter. To start with—why did an alien infiltrator just cross the universe to visit you in your office?"

At this, Manda fixed me with a look of unbridled awe, which was most welcome. No way was I going to admit that I'd been mistaken for a Backstreet Boy moonlighting as a copyright lawyer.

I was thinking up a response when the orb's form started distorting madly. First it stretched violently into a tall, narrow oval. Then it jerked into a short, wide oval. Then it smeared into an S shape, then an arch. As it shifted forms, it cycled through colors—blues, oranges, yellows, and countless others beyond the Crayola basics that I can name.

Suddenly the silhouette of a cat appeared in the orb's center. This was accompanied by an angry *screeeeeech*, which came from right behind us. I spun around, and saw that Meowhaus was battling a waist-high, Tinkertoy-looking contraption just inside the bedroom door. Actually, "mugging" may be a better word. His foe was a sleek metal skeleton made of brushed steel, with a giant purple sphere at its base. It almost looked like a Dyson vacuum cleaner—only it had spindly arms and wiry hands. It was clutching a small, glimmering object that Meowhaus was clawing for. The object fell after a brief struggle. As it hit the ground, an explosive *crack* sounded from the orb in the living room. At that, the orb jerked upward—then it shrank, until it looked like a harmless, shriveled disco ball hanging from the ceiling.

"Stupid cat!" High-pitched and nasal, the vacuum cleaner sounded like a cartoon rabbit with asthmatic lungs. He retreated deeper into the bedroom, rubbing one wiry hand with his other wiry hand. Meowhaus ignored him, utterly transfixed by the strange, alien lump on the floor. As the glowing object cycled through colors in perfect sync with the shifting colors of the shrunken orb, he batted at it repeatedly. Each time, I could see a little silhouette of a paw flash through the orb's center. So the lump was a projector of some sort. And Manda's new cat had a violent weakness for shiny things.

Seeing that Manda was taking all this in with the thunderstruck gaze of a geek on the holodeck, I turned to the vacuum cleaner and pointed theatrically at the lump. "Tell me about your little toy," I commanded, showing off a bit.

"It's a stereopticon," he answered in that wheezing squeal. "It makes projections."

"So it projected that . . . globe thing? How?"

"Self-organizing light. It bounces in a way that forms solid-looking images before the eyes of every conscious being in the room."

"I assume it also does something similar with sound?" I asked, starting to miss the orb's orotund boom. The vacuum cleaner's squawk really savaged the ears.

"Clearly."

"That aside, breaking and entering is a serious crime," I said, suddenly very harsh. This guy seemed to fluster easily, and I wanted him back on the defensive.

"But I didn't break *anything*," he wheezed. "I came in through a Wrinkle."

Wrinkle. Carly and Frampton had used that word in discussing their transit to a distant star. "Whether you slip in through a Wrinkle, or barge in with a bulldozer, it's still breaking and entering. Not to mention—" I groped for a more serious charge, but criminal law isn't my thing. "Aggravated attempted ambushing."

"But I didn't even mean to lay *eyes* on you," he whined, and started pacing—or something like that. He'd roll a few feet in one direction, do a hundred-eighty-degree pivot, then roll back. "My boss sent me here a couple hours ago, and a Wrinkle's scheduled to pull me out in ten minutes. I honestly didn't think you'd be back this quickly!"

"Oh please. That orb of yours was clearly designed to give us heart attacks."

Our visitor started pacing faster. "Was *not!* That was just a stupid animation that came with the stupid stereopticon when it was assigned to me. It's a harmless cartoon! And I wouldn't even have projected it at you if that *stupid cat* hadn't assaulted me before my Wrinkle took me away!"

I turned to Manda. "Wrinkles are . . . kind of like teleporting." Might as well start the explanations somewhere.

"Riiiight," she said softly, still struggling to process everything without going into shock.

I turned back to the vacuum cleaner. "So where did you Wrinkle over from?"

"Somewhere . . . local."

"Well, you better cough up more detail than that, or you'll be spending the night in the local jail," I bluffed gruffly. "And trust me—the inmates there will make short work of a little plastic vacuum cleaner like you."

"Goddammit, I'm *not* a stupid vacuum cleaner," he shrieked indignantly. "And I'm certainly not made of plastic. I'm made of metal. *Heavy* metal. The heaviest metal—in all of the cosmos!"

"Seriously?" That actually sounded kind of cool.

"Yes. That's why they call me . . . Özzÿ."

"Wa-wait," Manda said. After all the organic chemistry she suffered through in college, she couldn't let that one go by, however freaked out she was. "You're saying that your metal can form into . . . organic life?"

"Yes. It's a superheavy element that your scientists haven't encountered yet," Özzÿ squawked. "You'd probably call it something stupid like unseptiquadrium.* But we call it

---

*Manda later told me that physicists have been creating increasingly heavy elements in nuclear reactors and particle accelerators for years. Each new one gets a temporary Latinate designation based on its atomic number, as scientists work to come up with a permanent name for it. The heaviest element that our physicists have synthesized thus far has the temporary name "ununoctium," after its atomic number of

metallicam. Because it's the heaviest metal that can possibly exist in this universe."

Manda looked at him blankly.

"Look," I told her. "I've got a lot to explain to you. But the CliffsNotes are that these guys *really like* human music." There was a pause. Then—

"Wait," she said. "Metallicam?"

I nodded.

"As in—'Metallica'?"

"Yep."

"As in . . . *the band*?"

"I was disappointed, too," Özzÿ said, making a shrugging gesture. "I was hoping for ironmaidium. But back when we renamed it, the votes were with Lars and the boys."

"And what other . . . superheavy metals do you have?" she asked, clearly more stunned than ever.

"Well, there's vanhelium, which is tough as steel but has a negative mass that lets it float heavy objects. Defleppimite, which is used in prosthetic limbs. And of course, slayerium, which is the most energetic element in all of creation. And then, let's see, you've got your megadeathium, your ledzeppimite, then there's anvilium, sabbathide . . ." As he went through this list, Özzÿ's voice seemed to be getting higher, raspier, and softer.

118—with each "un" representing a 1, the "oct" standing for 8, and the "ium" suffix giving it that papal flair. Like all of the heaviest elements that we've created, it decayed into nothingness in fractions of a second. But it's long been thought that superheavy elements deeper into the sequence will be stable, and could have amazing, unpredictable properties. As for Özzÿ's element, the name "unseptiquadrium" implied that it had an atomic number of 174.

"What about bonjovium?" I asked. I've always had a weakness for "You Give Love a Bad Name."

"Of course, it exists. But bonjovium is *certainly not* a heavy metal by our standards," Özzÿ sniffed. "It has an atomic number of just fifty. You call it 'tin.'"

"Well, thanks for the science lesson," I said, remembering that a Wrinkle would be pulling this guy out of our hands in a few minutes. "But it's time for you to tell me what you're doing on Earth."

"What would a metallicam creature do, anywhere, but handle metallicam?" This aphorism seemed like a bumbling attempt at being cagey. But it came out in such a harsh rasp that it was hard to interpret.

"Hey, what's up with your voice?" I asked.

"My . . . atmosphere is quite . . . sssssimilar to yours," Özzÿ hissed, now sounding almost woozy. "Except there's a teeeeeny lit-tle trace of iodine in our air. And I seem to be more sssssensitive to its absence than expected. It's making me—what did the bards say? Dazed and confused . . ."

"Well, that Wrinkle of yours will have you out of here in a jiffy, so I wouldn't worry about it," I said, angling to keep him calm and milk his growing delirium for useful information. "Meanwhile, what were you saying about . . . handling metallicam? On Earth?"

"I'm sorry," Özzÿ slurred. "Must not say anything about . . . canceling our debts to humanity."

"*What* debts to humanity?" I said slowly and succinctly, hoping he wasn't about to clam up. I wondered if Google had any thoughts on how to waterboard a vacuum cleaner.

"Ssssso ssssssorry. Feels like . . . going off the rails. On the crazy train . . ."

I looked at Manda. "I think we're losing him."

The need for action yanked her out of her daze. "He needs to inhale iodine," she said, dashing into my eensy kitchen. "So let's burn up some fish, fast! Do you have any?"

That threw me. "In my *kitchen?*" In my world, fish comes from restaurants.

"Exit light, enter night," Özzÿ rasped, drifting around my living room in a vague figure-eight pattern. "Off to never-never land . . ."

Manda was already ransacking the refrigerator. "You seriously have nothing in here but *beverages.*"

"I'm sure there's some butter, too," I said defensively, trying to keep myself between Özzÿ's swaying form and my plasma TV.

"On my way to the promised land," Özzÿ gasped weakly, waving his spindly arms like a televangelist leading a pledge drive. "Na na na, highway to hell!"

Manda was now rummaging through cabinets that hadn't been opened since the day I moved in. "You literally have *one pan!*"

"Seriously?" That was precisely one more than I thought I had.

Özzÿ was now holding out a beseeching hand toward Meowhaus, like a dying sensei imparting life's secret to a loyal apprentice. "If there's a bustle in your hedgerow, don't be alarmed now," he advised in a hoarse whisper.

"Salt!" Manda was gazing in disbelief at another empty cupboard. "You *simply must* have salt. Where is it?"

"The spice drawer," I yelled, and with one small step I burst into the kitchen* and yanked open the cache of

---

*Like most of the places in my apartment, the kitchen is remarkably close to all of the other places in my apartment.

ketchup, soy sauce, and mayonnaise containers that years of takeout had deposited in my home. Several packets of Burger King salt were among them.

Manda splashed my lone pan with scalding tap water, set it on a gas burner (which amazed us both by working), and threw in the salt. "It's iodized, so it may help. Get him over here so he can breathe it."

The heavily salted water boiled quickly as I rolled Özzÿ into the kitchen. Figuring he took in air like your basic vacuum cleaner, we stood to either side of him and lifted, positioning his base over the rising steam. This involved bracing ourselves against each other, because he was remarkably hefty.* So we ended up cheek to cheek again. And once again, I felt a sudden, mad loyalty toward the creature who had brought this about.

"Come *on*, Özzÿ," I urged.

Nothing happened. The water boiled. Manda spied an additional salt packet, and added it to the brew. But Özzÿ was silent.

Just as I was losing hope, Manda held up a finger. "Did you hear that?"

"What?" I asked.

"Shhhhhhhh."

Listening intently, we barely detected a faint whisper. I pointed at a small orifice at the top of Özzÿ's handle. "It's coming from there." We lowered him to the floor and hovered our ears over it.

---

*Özzÿ wasn't kidding about metallicam being heavy. Luckily, metallicam-based life-forms aren't composed of pure metallicam (just as carbon-based critters like us aren't one hundred percent carbon), or we wouldn't have been able to lift him at all.

Moments later we heard an even fainter whisper. It began with something indecipherable, followed by "over the water."

I was about to hoist Özzÿ over the boiling pot again, but Manda stopped me. "I think he's trying to tell us we're doing something wrong." Then, "Özzÿ, can you hear me? If you can—say that again!"

There were several seconds of silence. Then, as we both held our breath, we could barely make out "I'm not a goddamn vacuum cleaner! That's my *ass* you were putting over the water!"

"Flip him over," Manda shouted.

"Right!"

We lifted Özzÿ, turned him upside down, and held him over the boiling pan. Within moments, we could feel a tiny breeze trickling into the opening at the top of his handle. And within seconds, he was sucking in air like—well, like a vacuum cleaner; inhaling every puff of iodized water vapor rising from the pan.

"Thank you," he said in his normal atrocious, high-pitched wheeze about a minute later. We flipped him over and set him down on the kitchen floor.

"You're welcome," I said as he settled onto his little rubber wheels. "And by the way, there's no need for any secrets between us. Your boss told me everything." I'd been wondering who his boss was since he first mentioned having one, and figured this lie might trick him into shedding some light on that.

"He told you about humanity . . . destroying itself?"

Manda's eyes widened with horror. I just nodded at the now-familiar theme.

"Yeah, we seem to have a knack for that," I said obtusely, hoping to provoke a reaction.

"A *knack* for it?" Özzÿ wheezed. "You mean you think you're *good* at it? Please. We hacked every firewall on your stupid little Internet looking into this last week. And trust me—you *suck* at it!" This fact seemed to personally offend him. He started pacing again. "A devastating ice age should have started in the nineties. I can show you the data! But your *stupid* CO_2 *emissions* staved it off completely," he wheezed. "Then a tropical bacterium evolved that should have wiped you all out. Some clueless grad student sequenced its DNA, and parked the data on a genomics site that we've examined. It was a *monster!* But some idiot ranchers burned down its corner of the Amazon before it could infect anyone! And you think you're *good* at destroying yourselves? Please."

Özzÿ's voice was getting higher, and more strained again. "Then back in '03, Saddam came within days of figuring out how to trigger a war between Pakistan and Israel. But then *you* had to go off and invade Iraq. And that was the end of that, wasn't it?"

"That was close," I said, feeling guilty about my decade of anti-Bush tirades.

"Close? That was nothing! Just a few months ago, an al-Qaeda cell in Chicago came within hours of getting its hands on a Russian H-bomb!" Özzÿ's voice was definitely fading fast again.

"And uh—remind me what happened with that one?" I asked. *Holy shit!*

"Some idiot gave them an Arabic copy of the new Glenn Beck book, and they weren't even five chapters into it before they all defected and joined the Tea Party movement!" The effort of shrieking this left Özzÿ gasping, and brought his pacing to a halt.

"Whoa," Manda murmured after a long, stunned pause. "There goes my entire worldview."

"The parrot told me that you felt passionately about all of this," I said. Özzÿ's appetite for our self-destruction had given me a feeling that the two of them might be working together. I was going out on a limb by mentioning the parrot, because if they weren't working together, there was no reason for Özzÿ to know that I'd met the guy. But my hunch was strong.

Özzÿ instantly confirmed it by bubbling over with incredulous joy. "Really? *Really?* What else did he say about me?"

"That you're . . . a mean go-getter." That was lame. But Özzÿ was too starstruck to notice.

"He said *that*? About me?"

"He did."

"Wow! You know—he's a Senior OmniSteward. And he selected me for this mission. Personally!"

"It's impressive that he recruited you personally," I said, now angling to drive a wedge between him and his boss before the Wrinkle took him away. "But he'll be so disappointed that you let me catch you searching my apartment."

Özzÿ started pacing again. "You're right. But how was I supposed to know when you'd get back?" His voice was getting fainter and fainter.

"You couldn't have," I said, sympathetically. "But Senior OmniStewards expect so much from their protégés. And he seems to be very hot-blooded. So I suppose he'll fire you."

"FIRE me?" Özzÿ was now pacing at an Olympian

speed. "But that's not fair! Where was I supposed to hide before the Wrinkle opened?"

I sighed. "You know . . . you're right, Özzÿ. It's not fair. And back when I was starting out, I had some pretty tough bosses myself." I pretended to carefully weigh the situation. Then, "Okay—I'll tell you what. I won't let on that I caught you here. It can be our little secret." I prayed that Özzÿ would go along with this. The parrot was clearly the brains of the operation, and I didn't want him to find out how much information I'd clawed out of his underling.

"You'll keep it a secret? Really? Oh, I'll never forget this. Truly, never! And—well, I'd say more, but I better go. The Wrinkle's open now, and I'm feeling a bit faint again, and there's iodine back at the local base."

As he said this, Manda's eyes widened with astonishment—which seemed odd, as this was far from being the most jarring thing Özzÿ had said. Then I realized that she was reacting to something that she'd just seen over my shoulder, toward the living room door. I was about to turn and look when she said, "Before you take off, Özzÿ, don't you think you should vacuum up the mess you made in here?"

I cringed. This was not going to go well.

"GODDAMMIT, I AM *NOT* A STUPID GODDAMN VACUUM CLEANER!" Özzÿ bellowed. Or tried to bellow—his voice was straining mightily with the effort.

Manda rolled her eyes. "Oh, come on. You are so. And I'll tell you what. I have a hot little Electrolux over at my place. What say we get the two of you together so you can— *make some DustBusters!*"

Özzÿ said nothing, but I thought I could see him trembling slightly. There was a long pause.

"You know," Manda said. "By . . . fucking?"

Okay, he was definitely trembling. Make that vibrating.

"Because DustBusters are like baby vacuum cleaners?"

Make that shuddering.

"And they'd be, you know—your offspring?"

Massive undulations . . .

"Hey, Hoover—are you even getting my joke?"

Oh, but he was. "VERY FUNNY!" he finally exploded.

Manda caught my eye and we both started giggling despite the crazed situation.

"HARDY-HAR-HAR. YOU'RE SO FUNNY THAT—" Özzÿ gasped.

"THAT—" he wheezed.

"THAT—"

At this he made a horrible gagging sound, hacked a few times, and then faded from sight, as he caught his Wrinkle back to the safety of his base. I instantly spun around to see what had caught Manda's eye and prompted her bizarre outburst.

It was a giant paw attached to a furry arm the size of a telephone pole.

FIVE
MOVING IN STEREOPTICON

"Meowhaus, you're a hero!" Manda said, dashing right through the paw itself as if it were a puff of steam.

I tried to avoid its spectral claws, and followed her into the living room. There I saw that Meowhaus had gone back to batting curiously at Özzÿ's stereopticon, which he'd apparently nosed out of the bedroom. The paw in the kitchen was a live feed of his batting arm, massively enlarged and projected in three dimensions. When he saw us, Meowhaus bit into the stereopticon and the projection shut off. His teeth got some kind of purchase on it, and he proudly dragged it to Manda's feet. *Gggggggggh!* he trilled, and started nuzzling her legs.

"I was hoping Özzÿ would leave this thing behind," Manda said, picking up the glimmering gadget, then setting it gingerly on my coffee table.

"I'd forgotten that he'd left it on the floor."

"So did I—until the mighty Kong started swatting around the kitchen door. It scared the hell out of me, until I saw the black cat fur. Then I did everything I could to get Özzÿ to beam up before he remembered his toy."

So that was why she started taunting him. "Brilliant," I said. "You really got him gasping for breath."

"Well, he wasn't the only one. Nick, what the *hell* is going on?"

As I started into a rundown on my first two alien encounters, we sat down at the coffee table and popped open the Pappy Van Winkle. We both urgently needed a drink or four. And the luscious stuff indeed helped us both to calm down.

"Well, I'm glad we got this thing," Manda said when I finished my story, picking up the stereopticon again. "I don't trust Özzÿ one bit. And maybe losing this will mess up his plans, whatever they are." She held the alien device up to her eye, squeezing and tweaking at it.

"Whoa, lookithat," I yelped. A giant 3D projection of Manda's squinting eye was suddenly suspended above the living room.

"*Wow*," she whispered as she saw this. She squeezed one of her fingers slightly, and the image vanished. She squeezed another finger, and the projection of Meowhaus's thwacking paw reappeared. Apparently, the stereopticon was a recorder as well as a projector. "Check it out," she said, handing it to me. "It suddenly has these . . . buttons on it. And it feels *incredible* in your hand."

I took it from her. It was almost transparent when it was shut off, like a chunk of Lucite. It also had a perfect heft to it—enough weight to feel substantial but not a gram more, so I felt like I could carry it effortlessly for hours, even days.

I tightened my grip. It fit my hand as if an ergonomic wizard had shaped it precisely to my palm. As I was admiring this, a tiny bulge under my index finger smoothed itself away into a glasslike nothingness, and I realized that it was dynamically reshaping itself to my grip. I squeezed harder. It gave slightly in some areas, and bulged out in others, establishing a flawlessly comfortable equilibrium in moments. I squeezed harder still. The glassy surface became almost rubbery, and allowed itself to squish in a downright therapeutic manner—like one of those squeezy balls that the HR people hand out at crunch time to keep you from climbing a clock tower with an M16. I squeezed a couple more times and felt tension melting away from my shoulders and back. *Awesome.*

I loosened my grip and ran my fingertips across its surface. They immediately slipped into four faint indentations. These had to be the buttons that Manda had mentioned. They seemed to have materialized because the device somehow sensed that I was looking for them. I squeezed the one under my index finger. It slid downward with an almost sensual clicking action, and the recording of Meowhaus's swatting paw reappeared. I squeezed again, and the image switched to a recording of Manda's eye. I squeezed with another finger, and it shut off entirely.

"In*cred*ible. Wanna give it another try?" I handed it back.

Manda took it and clicked a few times. Soon she had Özzÿ's giant orb emerging from the floor. **"Check it out,"** she said—but somehow her voice was muted entirely out of our hearing and replaced by the deep, menacing boom that had emanated from the orb earlier. This put us both into hysterics—with Manda's laughter rendered as a demonic **Mwahahaha!** Delighted, she used her cool new voice to bel-

low **"Silence, Earthling."** Then, **"By Grabthar's hammer—
you shall be avenged!"**

I was enjoying this and draining my glass (on the vague
logic that fine bourbon must surely fight colds) when the
parrot suddenly materialized on the coffee table. I would
have done a spit-take if the whiskey hadn't been quite so
awesome.

"So, we just had a lovely chitchat with your co-worker,"
I said in a raspy, flu-infected voice that was starting to sound
as bad as Özzÿ's.

The parrot sat motionless, staring hard at a point in the
middle distance.

"By the way, this is my neighbor, Manda Shark. Have
you met?"

He continued to stare, unblinking and motionless.

"Would you . . . care for a drink?"

At that, Meowhaus rose, stretched languidly, and leapt
over to the coffee table, where he passed through the parrot's body just as easily as Manda had passed through the
image of his paw. Manda was still holding Özzÿ's stereopticon, and I could see that it was glowing softly again. As
Meowhaus settled back in the space between us, she and I
both realized that the parrot was just a projection.

I peered at it closely. "That's definitely the guy from dinner. And it's a perfect image." Even from inches away, the
parrot looked entirely real and present.

"I can feel some buttons under my fingers again,"
Manda said, hefting the stereopticon. "They disappear if
you hold on loosely. But they're back now." She started flex-
ing her fingers in different combinations, trying to see what
other tricks the device had up its sleeve.

After a moment, the parrot came to life. "Listen,

Roomba," he said in his Brooklyn voice. "I just met with Nick Carter. And he know things. Things no human oughta know. So I figure, he's gotta be one of the nine trespassers. You know . . . from way back. Worse, he seems to know the truth about the Townshend Line. And no one but a Guardian should know that. So he might even *be* a Guardian. And if he is, we can't do nothin'. He could have spy gear down here. Full support from HQ. The works. And with all that, he'd already be on to us. In fact, I kinda think he *is* on to us.

"So me, I gotta file a report with Central. Right now. So you need to step in. And here's whatcha do. Book the first Wrinkle you can into Carter's apartment. And prebook the very next one out. Should give you an hour or two at his place. Then go through everything. His papers. His music. His goddamn socks. Figure out if he's a Guardian. If he is, we can't do *nothin'*. But if he ain't . . . it's showtime. Now that the Townshend Line is down, ain't nothin' can stop us. 'Cept a Guardian." With that, the projection vanished.

"A sort of 3D voice mail?" Manda guessed.

"Yeah—those had to be Özzÿ's marching orders from the boss."

"And did any of it make the slightest bit of sense to you?"

"No."

"It sounds like we want them to keep thinking you're a . . . Guardian," Manda said. "Or else. I didn't like it when he said 'it's showtime.'"

"I'd keep working on my Guardian impersonation, if I only knew what one was."

Manda nodded gravely. "Meanwhile, what's that Townshend Line thing that he mentioned?"

I shook my head. "Carly and Frampton mentioned it, too. But I don't know what it is."

Manda started methodically pressing different key combinations into the stereopticon. "I'll try to get the message back. Maybe it'll make more sense the second time." After a few tries, something radically different materialized a few feet above the coffee table. *"Whoa . . ."*

It was the size of a basketball and looked like a dazzlingly ornate gem. It had thousands of glowing facets, with countless colors, textures, and levels of opacity dancing between them. For a moment I thought it was spinning. But it was actually standing still, as its facets shuffled and re-sorted in ways that suggested a clockwise rotation. Then I realized that depending on how you looked at them, the shuffling facets could also suggest rotation on several other axes as well. Then for the tiniest moment, I could perceive rotation on a dozen different axes at once. It was a sensational bolt of clarity—a billion-megawatt version of the *aha!* moments that I'd get from those Magic Eye stereograms as a kid. What I was seeing was an extreme physical impossibility. And for that one instant, the glittering projection was more beautiful than anything I'd ever imagined.

Moments later, it emitted an agonizingly harsh sound. It was like hundreds of consonants crammed together over the din of a paper shredder gagging on shattered glass.

I shook my head slowly when the noise finally stopped. "That was *awful*."

"I am sorry," a flat and oddly genderless voice said. "I detect that you speak English. American, yes?"

"Bull's-eye," I said, guessing that the dreadful noise had been the sound of an alien language.

"You are now in Ersatz Concierge Mode. You may ask any question."

"Any . . . question?"

"Of course. This is Ersatz Concierge Mode."

I considered this, then went with a classic. "What's the fastest animal on Earth?"

"The cheetah," the voice answered immediately. "Why not try something harder?"

"Sure. Um . . . what's the Townshend Line?"

"The Townshend Line is the notional surface of a spherical region centered around the planet Earth," the androgynous, expressionless voice said. "It has a one-hundred-forty-four-light-year radius, and is the boundary of the most powerful force field ever created. It was built in 1978 to keep several trillion fans of The Who from storming the planet in hopes of attending one of the band's shows. The Townshend Line was designed to be impenetrable. However, nine unidentified trespassers are known to have infiltrated to Earth prior to its creation. They are still believed to be there."

Manda and I exchanged stunned looks.

"What else?" the concierge prodded. "You are starting to bore me."

"Okay," I said. "Then tell us about . . . Wrinkles." That was another word that seemed to keep coming up.

"Wrinkles enable the near-instantaneous transfer of matter or data in three-dimensional space. They become accessible in irregular, but predictable intervals between any two given locations. They remain open for periods of roughly nineteen minutes. If two locations lie nearby each other in three-dimensional space, connections open between them perhaps a dozen times per day. If they are far apart, they open less frequently."

"That explains everything," Manda said, nodding slowly.

"It does?" I asked.

"Well, not *every*thing. But it explains a lot. Carly and Frampton must have been on a long-distance Wrinkle, because if they stayed more than a few minutes, they were going to get stuck—for almost a day or something, right?"

I nodded.

"And it sounds like Özzÿ was in your apartment for maybe two hours. So he must have taken one Wrinkle in, and then a later one out. And since the Wrinkles were just a couple hours apart, he must have come from someplace 'nearby.' Whatever that means." She turned to the glittering concierge. "What constitutes 'nearby' for Wrinkles?"

"Distances less than roughly four thousand of your statute miles."

Manda and I swapped a worried look. It seemed that Özzÿ and the parrot were staying somewhere on Earth.

"Got it," Manda said, looking around for something to take notes with. "And how do Wrinkles work?"

"Your language lacks the necessary vocabulary for a technical explanation. I could attempt a more informal description. But first, I would suggest that we switch to an interface that is native to your own society."

"To a what?" I asked.

"A native user interface. They are preferable because a great deal of communication is nonverbal. I am currently using a visual and cultural layer that conveys context, emotion, and emphasis in a manner that's inscrutable to you, but plainly obvious to certain aliens, including the one who previously carried this stereopticon. For instance," the concierge paused. "How are you feeling?" As it asked me this, a beguiling pattern of ruffling facets and blinking colors unfolded on the projection's surface.

"Fine, I guess."

"See? You missed that," the projection said in that tone-less voice.

"I beg your pardon?"

"When I asked you how you were feeling, my visual cues conveyed sarcasm, condescension, an absence of genuine concern for your well-being, carnal interest in your female companion, and an utter lack of physical strength or stamina on my part. You should have belted me."

"But you're just a projection!"

"True. And I am also just a computer algorithm." The image unleashed another achingly beautiful kaleidoscopic pattern as it said this. Then, "I cannot believe that you let me get away with that."

"With what?"

"With this." The sublime light pattern repeated. "Ghastly wars involving entire galaxies could be justifiably waged over far less insulting conduct."

"I guess I'll have to take your word for that."

"Thank you," the concierge said, flashing another gorgeous pattern that was no doubt a grievous insult. "I have now scoured your Internet, and have identified several ersatz concierges that were created by your own society, and are in current and active use throughout it. I strongly suggest that you allow me to import and implement one of them."

I caught Manda's eye. She shrugged. "Sure," I said.

"Earth's most popular ersatz concierge has had hundreds of millions of users—although its usage has declined rather dramatically in recent years. Shall we try that one?"

I really, really, really should have asked why the thing was shedding users. Instead I shrugged and said, "Why not?"

The dazzling, octodimensional projection instantly transformed into a flat rendering of a paperclip with googly eyes.

"*That's* an ersatz concierge?" Manda whispered after a shocked silence. "Dear God . . ."

As she said this, the paperclip's eyes darted cunningly from side to side. Then a cartoon bubble appeared above its head reading, "It looks like you're writing a letter. Would you like help?"

It was Clippy—the despised emcee of Microsoft Office. I knew him well. Because while he had allegedly retired long ago, my firm—like so many others—had clung to the Clippy-infested Windows XP operating system for years beyond its expiration date, staving off the expense and trauma of a Windows *upgrade*. That process had finally started eighteen months back. But copyright associates are low in the priority queue—and I had been slated to get upgraded "next month" for as long as I could remember.

"Okay, go back," I said.

Clippy stared at me impassively.

"Stop it. Cut it out. Go back. Use the other interface. Use the gem thing."

As I said this, Clippy's eyes started darting again as he scribbled on a notepad with an animated pencil. Another cartoon bubble appeared. "It looks like you're making a list. Should I format it?"

I fell into an appalled silence. Then Manda gave it a shot. "We do not want to use this ersatz concierge," she enunciated clearly. "Please return us to the previous one."

Clippy gazed back with bovine incomprehension.

We went on to try every command, plea, and threat that we could think of. But we couldn't get back to the prior concierge. Luckily, the stereopticon's projector mode was still working fine ("If you download Windows Media Player, I'm throwing you under a bus," Manda warned it). But we wanted the old concierge back. We had a thousand questions, and Clippy couldn't answer any of them.

Or could he?

"Okay, so we're stuck with Clippy," Manda said, over an hour later. "But I'll bet the same knowledge base is still sitting beneath him. We just have to figure out how to access it. So let's think—is there *any* way to get useful information out of Microsoft Office?"

Now that was a stumper. "Well . . . it has a Help menu, right?"

"It does. But that's barely useful when you actually have questions about Office. You're thinking the right way. But we need to get the software to kick out information that's not just about the software itself."

"Well . . . it puts squiggly red lines under words that are spelled wrong, right?"

Manda nodded slowly. "Right. So it must have some kind of embedded dictionary. Do you have a pen and a piece of paper?"

I grabbed both from my desk, and handed them over. She positioned the paper on the coffee table right under Clippy and wrote "S-P-E-L-I-N-G." Clippy got that pervert-on-the-playground look again, and a squiggly red line appeared beneath her word. A small menu popped up next to it. It included four guesses at what Manda was trying to spell, an "Ignore" command, and a few other options.

Manda touched a finger to the correct spelling of "spelling," and the word was immediately corrected. For a moment we thought the device had actually rearranged the ink on the page. But it was just projecting the correct spelling in a way that blotted out the misspelled word. With the correct spelling now displayed, a new menu appeared. One of the options was "Look Up." Manda touched this, and a definition for "spelling" appeared.

"Cool," I said. "But I don't really see how—"

She was already scribbling something new on the page. G-A-R-D-I-A-N.

"Brilliant," I said, realizing what she was up to.

The new word got a squiggly red line. She selected the proper spelling for "Guardian," and selected the Look Up command as soon as it appeared. The first definition to come up was "Protector." The second was far more interesting:

One of 5,000 members of the highest governing body in the universe, the Guardian Council.

"Pay dirt," I whispered.

Manda gave me an amazed look. "So why would Paulie and Özzÿ think that *you're* one of those?"

I shrugged. "Maybe Carly and Frampton's visit to me made me seem . . . important to them, in some way?"

"Despite the fact that they don't know who Carly and Frampton are."

"Or maybe *because* they don't know who Carly and Frampton are. I mean, they could be nobodies. They came to me because of a dumb mistake, after all. So maybe the parrot's jumping to conclusions based on their screwup."

Manda nodded slowly. "Possibly. Then again . . ." She looked at me intently. "Maybe the parrot's right."

"What?"

"I mean, are you *sure* you're not a Guardian?"

"Of course I'm sure. I don't even know what a Guardian is!"

"Well, maybe it's like being the Dalai Lama, and you don't know it yourself until someone shows up and tells you."

I considered this. "Well, maybe. But . . . a parrot?"

"Probably not, but . . . hey, how about this? Are you totally sure you were born on Earth? I mean, you're not adopted or anything, are you?"

"No, my mom gave birth to me. In *Denver.*"

"And you've seen the birth certificate? The long-form one, I mean."

"Manda!"

Eventually we turned our attention back to Clippy, but he didn't have a lot more to tell us. We spent the next hour scribbling countless words onto the page (Humans, Earth, Carly, and so forth). Almost everything produced a simple, standard-English definition. The one word we scored on was "metallicam"—the element that Özzÿ had apparently come to Earth to "handle."

Metallicam is the universe's heaviest element. In its inorganic form, it can conduct current from the Zero Point field, making it a source of almost unlimited energy—or a weapon of immense power.

"Good God . . ." Manda said as we read this. "It's like plutonium on steroids. What are these creatures up to?"

I shook my head slowly. "Whatever it is, it . . . has something to do with our music."

Manda nodded. "With all those Who fans out there."

"Yeah, and that strange license that Carly asked me about."

"So what do we do now?" Manda said after a long pause. "Call the FBI? The air force? NASA?"

I shook my head. "We may as well go straight to Bellevue and ask to be fitted with straitjackets."

"Not if we show them the stereopticon." She held it up. "If this isn't proof that we've met aliens, then what could be?"

"It's an extraordinary machine. But it won't make anyone believe in little green men. It's much easier to think that the CIA—or Apple—can build something that cool in a secret lab."

Manda nodded slowly, unconvinced.

"And speaking of Apple—I hear they can shut down a stolen iPad remotely," I continued. "And I'm sure Özzÿ can do that with his stereopticon. So by tomorrow, we may not have anything more than a clear plastic chunk to show off."

"But you can convince anyone to believe anything— even *aliens*. I mean, I just saw you turn Özzÿ into putty. You're the best talker I know. It's like your . . . superpower."

Well, that was an awfully nice way of putting it. And maybe my knack for steering through loaded conversations was something of a white-collar superpower. I had seen others practiced in the workplace, after all.* But as anyone

---

*For instance, my old roommate could use PowerPoint to bend almost any organization to his will. But he was seduced by the dark side of his superpower, and used it to get a $25 million investment from CBS Interactive to launch a Facebook knockoff. Since he doesn't know squat about running a business beyond making great slides, this was just as disastrous as you'd expect.

who has one will tell you, the real trick with a superpower is knowing its limitations. And mine has plenty. It can help you ace a job interview, but it won't make you partner. It can get you a second date, but not a girlfriend. And when it comes to Saving the World—well, give me invisibility, telekinesis, or omniscience any day.

With that in mind, I shook my head. "I may be kind of smooth, sometimes. But I'm still just a midlevel lawyer who can't tell the Big Dipper from Ursa Major.* If I thought I'd have an ounce of credibility with him, I'd take the stereopticon straight to Carl Sagan.† But I don't know the first thing about cosmetology.‡ So if I tried to tell him that we'd swiped it from an alien, I'd probably end up drinking hemlock in a loony bin. Just like Galileo."

"You're right," Manda agreed, suddenly looking quite concerned. "You should absolutely not talk to any scientists about this."

"It's a deal."

"So now what?" she asked.

"Sleep, I'd say. Then, as for tomorrow, I should go into work first thing. If all of this really is connected to our music, then my firm's probably the best place in the world to figure out things like Carly's licensing situation."

"But isn't that practically impossible?"

"*Getting* her the license is probably completely impossible. But that may not be necessary."

---

*This was an even more embarrassing confession than I intended, because it turns out that they're kind of the same thing.

†Another doozy. Apparently he died in 1996.

‡Oops again. This is the study of makeup and perfume (unlike "cosmology," which is the study of the universe).

Manda gave me a hopeful look. "Why not?"

"Well, I've been thinking about this thing called the Berne Convention. It's over a hundred years old, and basically says that each nation that signs it will honor, and help to enforce, the copyrights of the other signatories. Every major country in the world has signed it, and most of the ankle-biters, too."

"But not many alien planets."

I nodded. "Exactly. And I can't think of any reason why the Convention would apply to actions taken in nonsignatory territories. So even if the aliens are determined to follow our laws for some deranged reason, our own legal frameworks probably don't indicate that our laws apply to them."

"So Carly's people can probably do whatever they want to without a license."

"Exactly. Which means there may not be any problems at all. Not with her, and not with Özzÿ and Paulie—although I want to do a bit of research into this to be sure."

"Then you should definitely go to the office tomorrow. Is there anyone there who could help you with this?"

I nodded again. "Potentially. I've got this weekly meeting at eight that's led by a woman named Judy Sherman. She's one of the most powerful partners in the firm, and she knows the copyright laws inside and out. In fact, she literally wrote a lot of them. She also knows everyone who matters in the music industry. Not only that, but she must have pictures of most of them with goats, or something. I mean, they'll seriously do whatever she tells them. So maybe I should try to recruit her somehow?"

Manda nodded energetically. "That sounds perfect."

"One problem though. She kind of hates me. In fact, she's probably about to fire me."

Manda thought about this. "Well, what if Özzÿ's heavy metal orb tells her not to?"

"What do you mean?"

Manda hefted the stereopticon. "I know you're skeptical. But if I can figure out how to work this thing, it could be an awfully persuasive tool. Seriously—if she sees it in action the way we did tonight, she'll believe whatever you tell her about the aliens."

I nodded slowly, only partly convinced. "You may be right. So assuming someone doesn't disable it, you can call in sick or something, and work on it some more while I'm at the office."

Manda nodded. "But as a first step, I'll try to get the old concierge back. There's a ton that we could learn from him."

"Totally agree. Also, at eleven oh-six, I'm meeting with Carly and Frampton in that 'Earth-based dataspace'— whatever that is. Assuming they actually send me the glasses that I'll need to interface with it beforehand, like they said."

Our plan now set, I walked Manda and Meowhaus down the hall and got a chaste good-night hug, then went home to toss and turn the night away.

SIX
SHERMAN'S SPAWN

The next morning I found an empty seat next to my buddy Randy Cox in the main conference room at exactly 7:59. I'd hit the snooze alarm three times, and arrived with a minute to spare at the cost of not having breakfast. My stomach was growling audibly.

"Dude," Randy said in a private murmur. "Why don't you grab one of those crêpes?" He pointed at a side table, where mounds of Manhattan's freshest fruit and finest pastries were arrayed.

I just glared, sniffled, and gave him the finger.

The only associate to arrive after me was a cocky blond loudmouth named Errol Stanton. He slid in moments before the clock hit eight, flirting with disaster. This is what passes for macho brinksmanship in our paranoid and hierarchical firm—our equivalent of playing chicken with freight trains in a cow town. Cutting it close is fine. But no one arrives late to a Judy Sherman meeting.

Apart from Judy herself, that is. She's eerily punctual whenever someone else is not. Otherwise, she's invariably late. Her casual tardiness broadcasts her dangerous eminence— much as plumage and pheromones signal deadliness or virility in nature. You laugh, but it works. I was once in her entourage when she visited the head of a major movie studio that we were wooing as a prospective client. We got to his office right on time. So she had us kill twenty minutes in the parking lot before going in, to make it clear that she was too damn important to run any way but late. I doubt this guy had waited on anyone since the eighties, so I was aghast. But within three months, his studio had become our firm's top client. Recalling this, I wondered if Judy would keep an alien delegation cooling its tentacles out in reception while she pretended to wrap up a conference call. *Of course she would*, I realized— and somehow, this would get them eating out of her hand.

My stomach growled again as Errol took his seat, and Randy caught my eye. "Dude, you should grab some of that *pain au chocolat*," he murmured. "I hear it's . . . *incroyable*."

My stomach snarled madly at the thought. So I glared, sniffled, and gave him the finger.

Thirteen of us were there for the Critical Environment Committee's weekly meeting, which Judy chairs. And no, we don't save whales, plant trees, or spread panic about global warming. Instead, we try to anticipate, or (better yet) engineer shifts in the legal environment—ones with the potential to dramatically benefit our firm.* Our main tools are

---

*Actually, make that "to dramatically benefit our *clients*," because we wake, toil, and breathe with the sole purpose of promoting our clients'

lobbyists and litigation, and we focus on copyright matters (a sister committee on the firm's patent side shapes the Environment using similar weapons & tactics).

"You know, those exact pastries go for twelve bucks a pop at the Four Seasons," Randy whispered, making one last pitch. *"They're that good."*

"Why don't you just shut up and transfer to London?" I hissed back.

He smiled at our running joke. Being named Randy Cox amounts to a de facto ban on ever living or working in the UK. "I'll transfer to Siberia if you'll just help yourself to some breakfast."

"I'd rather streak through a partners' meeting," I snapped. And I was almost serious, because *one does not eat* at a Judy Sherman meeting. Sure, there's always a mesmerizing spread in the room. But everyone knows it's a trap.

"All right, where the hell's Jack?" Judy demanded an instant after rolling in at 8:22. One of her lesser superpowers is an ability to take full roll calls in a single glance.

"Honeymoon," a younger associate reminded her.

"Dammit, that's right. But why isn't he dialing in? I mean, didn't he go to Albania? Or Taiwan, or something? It's gotta be ten at night for him. He's done with dinner, right? So he should dial in—and *bang* . . . the *bride* . . . after . . . the *call.*" This last bit was slow and overenunciated, as if it was a basic point of etiquette that we all learn as kids.

An awkward silence followed.

---

interests. Any advantage that accrues to us as a result is incidental. And you should pity the fool who implies otherwise (particularly in writing).

Then, "Jesus, I'm kidding, people. Even *I'm* not that much of a bitch." There were chuckles all around, and everyone relaxed just a notch. Judy really isn't that much of a bitch. But she's awfully close, and she knows that we know it, so she goads us with jokes that we're scared to laugh at until we're completely sure she's kidding. They say that Idi Amin had a similar sense of humor.

"By the way—nice look, General." This came from Greta, a brash, pretty third-year associate out of Duke. Today's outfit was a high-waisted gray skirt, a white blouse, and pumps made from the skin of some endangered reptile. Wardrobe flattery works well with Judy. Greta also got bonus points for using Judy's sanctioned nickname. *General* invokes her distant ancestor, William Tecumseh Sherman, whose march through Georgia prefigured her own scorched-earth assault on copyright infringers throughout the world.

Judy smiled. "Thanks, Greta. The devil wears Chanel today." Specifically, Chanel in a size 2, because Judy has a tighter body than most college girls. It's topped with a flowing black mane whose gray streaks confidently acknowledge her maturity. This inspires her unsanctioned (and much more popular) nickname—Cruella, after the villainess in *101 Dalmatians*.

"Okay, gang," Judy continued, while shooting me an unprovoked withering look. "Time to play some defense. Any trouble in paradise this week?" *Playing defense* is a euphemism for flagging developments with the potential to offend or spook our clients into taking pricey legal action against someone.

As usual, Errol Stanton had something up his sleeve. "A new TiVo-for-radio system was just reviewed on Tech-Crunch. It's particularly targeted at Sirius/XM subscribers."

In other words, some nitwit had shipped a product that would make it simpler for people to record radio broadcasts for later playback.

Judy shook her head in mock disbelief. "God, it's the gift that never stops giving. Don't these dolts ever learn?"

It was a good question. We had already sued three start-ups out of existence for launching virtually identical products. And that should have made it clear to one and all that the music companies don't *want* people recording radio broadcasts.* Not that there's a law against it. But there doesn't have to be, because legal bills can destroy a company just as thoroughly as Senate bills. We've shut down countless other operations that probably weren't breaking any laws over the years. They include companies that made products to record free Internet broadcasts, to fetch lyrics to songs playing on a computer, to back up store-bought DVDs to hard drives—the list is long. We just claim there's a slight chance that a company is hypothetically violating a subclause in some arcane copyright law, and our prey immediately starts suffocating on legal expenses.

The start-ups we go after are usually penniless. But that's fine, since the music labels and movie studios pay us by the hour to strangle them in their cribs.† For their part, our clients never expect to collect any damages. The fees

---

*The fear is that if people record radio (particularly digital radio), they'll surely record some music shows, which can easily lead to music piracy, which itself leads swiftly to meth addiction, human cannibalism, and societal collapse.

†Although of course we prefer it when our quarry is able to fight long enough to run up the bills for a while. That said, we never feel great when they go bankrupt with lots of unpaid debts. After all, defending counsel deserves to get paid, too.

they pay us are investments in a reputation for deep-pocketed ruthlessness that will keep tomorrow's investors and entrepreneurs away from their turf. It was scary to think of how hard they'd fight if there was actual money to be clawed out of one of these lawsuits. I could see them fighting to the death before compromising. Perhaps to the death of the human race.

As Errol was wrapping up his rundown of the new TiVo-for-radio company, a text came in from Manda:

Clippy more resilient than Freddy Kurger. Can't get rid of him, focusing on mastering stereopticon

Dammit. The original concierge could have told us about Özzÿ's organization, explained how our music fit in with the rest of the universe, and a lot more. Hopefully Manda would have better luck learning how to wield the stereopticon, so that we could use it to recruit Judy. I imagined Özzÿ's orb blasting out of the whiteboard, and commanding her to do my bidding. What fun!

I dragged my attention back to the meeting when Judy asked for another new business idea. If nobody volunteered one, she'd point at someone and tell them to start talking. And in light of Randy's warning that I might be due for a little trial by fire, it could well be me.

Luckily Josh Weisner raised his hand. He's a quiet, brainy guy—the sort that either washes out instantly or goes on to great things at our firm. So far, he was showing no signs of washing out. "Well, Judy," he said, in that professorial tone of his. "I think it's time that we built upon some of your own landmark legislation."

Judy gave him an intrigued look. "Which piece?" She's been the de facto author of many laws over the years, and spends at least an hour working Washington for every hour she spends on client business. The laws we care about all pass through the Judiciary Committees (both the House and the Senate have one). And no client, however lucrative, gets the kind of service and attention that Judy lavishes on those committee members and their senior staffers.

"I'm thinking of the Copyright Damages Improvement Act," Josh said. Judy basically wrote this legislation verbatim on behalf of a Judiciary Committee staffer who was conveniently distracted with wedding plans back when it was wending its way through the Senate. Passed in 1999, it famously legislates penalties of up to $150,000 for *each and every copy* of an illegally downloaded song (or film, TV show, etc.). It has enabled the industry to sue over 35,000 individual Americans for swapping music files—some into bankruptcy.

"I'm all ears, Josh," Judy said. "Tell me what you've got."

"I think it's time to expand the footprint of the piracy we address. To include luxury brands—and consumer products." Now *that* was a pin-drop moment. Our firm has always done great business with media companies and patent holders. But we've never gotten anywhere with the giant consumer brand companies—an injustice that causes our partners many sleepless nights.

"Do you really think we could advance Proctor & Gamble's interests by modifying the copyright laws?" Judy asked, after a long (and rather dramatic) silence.

"Sure. After all, media isn't the only thing that greedy consumers are *stealing*," Josh said, with contempt that most people reserve for otter molesters. "What about anyone with a fake Louis Vuitton handbag? Or a phony Rolex? Or a bogus box of Pampers, for that matter? The people who sell those things aren't the only crooks. The consumers themselves are willfully stealing the brand marrow. That's what you're paying for when you buy the real thing. And that's what people are *pillaging* when they buy a knockoff." It was a clever pitch, and that "brand marrow" term was ingenious. I could see it spreading like swine flu among marketers and management consultants.

"So you're proposing that we amend the laws to criminalize the ownership of fake consumer goods?" Judy asked excitedly. By now, several people around the table were frowning and nodding slowly—aping the way the mighty *Frank* Carter used to show approval back when he was still running the firm. Like many of our founding partner's mannerisms, this one had leached clear through to the firm's lowest echelons.

"Yep. And it would only take a few hundred words to do it." Josh handed her a printout of his proposed text. "Fido could slide it into an omnibus spending bill, and no one would even notice."

"Please," Judy chided. "Let's not call the senator 'Fido.' People might get the feeling that he's our lapdog, or something."

That one was definitely a joke, so we all chuckled merrily.

"But kidding aside," she continued, "you're telling me that if someone walks down Lexington in fake Nikes, your modified legislation could nail him for a hundred and fifty grand?"

"Absolutely."

Now everyone was frowning and nodding, as excitement rippled through the room. If Josh was right, and if the major brands would play ball, entire law practices could be built around this idea.

"But what if someone doesn't know they bought a knockoff?" Randy asked. He has this thing for fairness, which does his career no favors.

"Stupidity's no alibi," Judy snapped. "If it was, Kato Kaelin would be walking the streets today!" Of course, ol' Kato *is* walking the streets, just as he always has. But no one dared to point this out, as bizarre non sequiturs are another Judy trademark. Some whisper that they point to a mild case of Tourette's syndrome. But since they never pop up in client meetings, I'm sure she's just messing with us, Idi Amin–style.

Judy turned to the man of the hour. "Write this up, Josh. I want to present it at the next partners' meeting. It's a brilliant idea." And with that, she spun on a heel and faced me. "But who knows? Maybe Nick Carter is even smarter than you are. We've always wondered."

I felt like my elevator just lost its cable on the hundred and somethingth floor. *Was Randy right?* Had the firm decided to give me a final test, to see if I was worthy of receiving The Omen and sticking around? Or did Judy just want to pummel me one last time before showing me the door?

"Why don't we find out, Nick," she was saying in a steely, even tone. "Top Josh's idea. *Now.*" And with that, Judy achieved the impossible, and drove all thoughts about alien incursions completely from my mind. I was suddenly fully grounded in my ordinary, daily life. And it *sucked*.

I looked at Judy as calmly as I could. "Music and movie piracy . . ."

I slipped into a dramatic pause as I desperately tried to

come up with some idea, any idea. I scanned the room for inspiration, briefly glimpsed Randy and—I had my answer.

". . . are *terrorism.*"

Randy shot me a horrified look. I was about to lay out a notion that he once dreamed up over beers. It was just a sick joke between sophomoric colleagues, and Randy clearly thought I'd get fired immediately if I presented it as a serious proposition. He was right to worry—but this was the only thing I could think of that was more audacious, grasping, and twisted than Josh's idea of suing secretaries and college girls into bankruptcy over their fake Chanel bags. And Judy might just love it.

"I'm all ears," she said levelly.

"As you know, our legal system has traditionally viewed several specific crimes as being acts of terror," I said, as my calming superpower kicked in. "So why not slide a few paragraphs into the Patriot Act to put music piracy and peer-to-peer file sharing right up there with dirty bombs and hijacked planes? We could give Fido some political cover by cooking up a story about al-Qaeda using BitTorrent to transmit their nefarious communiqués."

The room was perfectly silent as everyone waited for Judy to signal whether they should love or loathe this idea.

"A change in the law would oblige Homeland Security to redirect at least part of its budget to the new 'file-sharing front' in the war on terror," I continued. "So the country might end up with a few less police radios and TSA agents. But some portion of the redirected funds would inevitably accrue to this firm, in the form of legal fees." I didn't betray a shred of the yawning horror that I felt. This had to be career hara-kiri. But I was doing it with style.

I went on to cite three relevant rulings, as well as the

sections of the Patriot Act that we'd need to tweak. After I'd laughed so hard at his original joke, Randy had written the whole thing out for me in legalese, complete with this supporting detail. It was so funny and comprehensive that I remembered it all clearly. I now felt cheap and guilty to be presenting his ideas as my own—silly, I guess, given that there was zero chance that he'd *ever* want to use them at work himself. But Judy's scathing performance review said that I did "NO original thinking," and this was clearly a case in point. Still, I could sure do a gorgeous job delivering someone else's ideas, and that was (slightly) better than nothing.

As soon as I fell silent, Judy started circling the table predatorily, like Robert De Niro in *The Untouchables*. "Nick, I . . . don't know what to say."

Step. Step. Step.

"Other than that your idea is demented. It's warped. And it's—well, it's a cry for help." She paused for a good five seconds as she continued to circle. "We're in a state of war." *Pause.* "A global crisis." *Pause.* "One of the few good things to come from this is that Congress occasionally sets aside its greed long enough to do something for the common good." *Pause.* "And you're proposing that we exploit this fact, so as to cynically promote the parochial interests of our paymasters."

"That's an excellent summary," I said. It really was.

Judy halted her pacing, and stood right behind me. "Maybe it's true that our firm . . . *manipulates* the system. Occasionally. Strictly to serve our clients' interests, of course. Cynics might even accuse us of profiteering from it. But you're recommending that we willfully *pervert* it. On an utterly base level."

By now people were gazing intently at various points between their noses and the conference room table. Just as the tension was peaking, Judy cracked an ironic smile. "But the real problem with your idea is that it's so fucking obvious we've already tried it twice, with no luck. So I need you to come up with something more original. And cunning."

Everyone relaxed, and I basked in a warm, giddy surge of relief.

"September 11th was years before you started here, so you're off the hook for not knowing what we tried back then," Judy said, now smiling almost kindly. "We were so close. We'd put together a whole package of measures that would have lumped Napster and Kazaa right in there with truck bombs. And they were actually in *the working draft* of the Patriot Act. But then the press got wind of it. And after that, not even Fido could push it through." The awkward hush morphed seamlessly into a memorial silence for that great, lost opportunity.

The rest of the meeting passed in a blur. I was only half there, my brain fogged over from lack of sleep, cold medicine, the drubbing I'd just taken from Judy, and (oh yeah!) agitation about the incipient alien threat to my planet.

Judy wrapped things up around ten by saying "Okay, everyone but Nick—bug off." Aliens, my monster cold, and sleeplessness fell from my mind again as the room cleared out.

As soon as we were alone, Judy said, "That was brilliant stuff, Nick. Very creative, very topical. And you pulled it out of thin air. But enough about you—here's something cool about me. When I realize that I've been wrong about something, I don't fuss about it. I just embrace the new reality.

Pronto. I'm always triangulating, readjusting. And it looks like I was wrong about you."

I just stood there—less shocked than when Carly atomized my iPhone, sure, but not by much.

"And that frankly changes everything for you," Judy continued. "The rest of the partners like you. But I was a holdout, and we all know I can veto anything. And now you've won me over. So, yay-rah—go you."

I nodded, although Judy wasn't looking at me (uttering some of the most momentous words that a young attorney could hear within these walls, she was meanwhile checking email on her old school BlackBerry).

"So you know the drill from here," she said. "Fido's coming through New York tomorrow, and I have a ten o'clock meeting with him. *Bastard!*"

For a moment I thought she was denouncing our main patron in Washington. But she was just irked by an email. She fell silent, her thumbs thrashing a retort into the keyboard.

"Anyway," she continued, actually looking at me now. "It's my monthly one-on-one with Fido, but you're coming. It's time for you to start meeting the folks who are the firm's bread and butter. So as to establish personal relationships with them to the mutual benefit of yourself and the partnership, blah, blah, blah."

So this was it. The Omen. I was actually getting the call.

"And this'll be a doubleheader," she added. "The Munk's in from L.A. tomorrow, too. We'll be dropping in on him right after Fido."

I nodded again. She was referring to the CEO of a vast music label—one who famously clutches apples and other loose food with both hands when he eats, chipmunk-style.

"You sit closer to the elevators than me, so I'll come by your office at nine-thirty tomorrow, and we'll head out," Judy finished. "Got it? Oh, and since you'll be meeting Fido, why don't you spend the afternoon trying to score him some Milk Bone?"

SEVEN
AVATARD

Like all pets, Fido loves his treats. So every so often, we try to give him one. "Milk Bone" is our internal code for the little goodies that make him feel cherished. And since he has unusual appetites, they're notoriously hard to arrange. Most senators are happy if you rally lots of funding for their campaigns. Others can be wooed with decadent junkets fueled by thousand-dollar single malts. But Fido's a devout Mormon with no funding concerns, so none of that works.

He does, however, have a mad inner craving that we can help satisfy—a primal desire he shares with most red-blooded American men. Which is to say that conservative, God-fearing, and borderline elderly as he is, Fido secretly wishes he was a rock star. To be clear, his rock 'n' roll fantasy is more Osmond than Osbourne. But he takes it incredibly seriously—so much so that he has actually released several albums over the years (mainly on religious and patriotic themes). So, if part of your job is making Fido happy, you occasionally strong-arm someone into putting a snippet of his music into a movie. Or, you get a Nashville D-lister to leave him an admiring voice mail. Or, you blackmail somebody into performing one of his songs in a concert.

Judy had given me a whole list of agents, managers, and label executives to reach out to. But I left that for the afternoon. For now, it was much more urgent that I review the Berne Convention. I scanned through its dozens of articles, and saw no claims of jurisdiction over acts of piracy that occur outside of its signatory nations. Just as I thought. And while a huge number of countries had signed it, all were firmly situated on the Earth's surface. Since this should obviate any licensing concerns that Carly (or any other extraterrestrial) might have, I felt confident that there'd be a solution to whatever quandary our music was causing up there.

Carly had said that the glasses I'd need for our 11:06 rendezvous would arrive three minutes beforehand, along with some instructions. Sure enough, I got an email from "Meeting, Dataspace" at precisely 11:03:

1) Open top right desk drawer
2) Don glasses, connect to computer
3) At 11:06AM click here to enter Earth-based dataspace

I opened my desk drawer as instructed. A pair of pink-lensed Bono glasses were right next to my business cards, attached to a USB cable that had to be twenty-five feet long. All of this had presumably just popped over via a Wrinkle that had just opened up between my planet and Carly's.

Just then, my cellphone rang. The caller's number was blocked, and I picked up, thinking it might be Manda.

"Nick, this is your boss, Judy Sherman."

Boy, was it. It was also a bizarre statement, even for Judy. Her voice is as renowned within my brain's fear and obedience circuits as my mother's was, back when I was a naughty three-year-old. So if she had said "Nick, you are now speaking on your cellphone," the statement would have been no more superfluous.

"Guess where I am," she continued.

"The . . . office?"

"Wrong, Nick. I'm in sickbay—reviewing your medical records. And it appears that *some*body's inoculations aren't up to date."

"You mean my . . . flu shot?" Since when did the firm track our medical histories? And where the hell was "sickbay"?

"It's not a flu *shot*, Nick," Judy snapped. "It's a flu *solution*. But we can't *solve* our flu problems with even one sickly associate spewing flu germs onto everyone else. Don't the words 'herd immunity' mean *any*thing to you?"

They certainly didn't. And I wasn't about to admit this. But before I could come up with a serviceable bluff, I heard some familiar laughter on the line, and it wasn't Judy's.

"Manda?" I asked.

"Well done," she tittered.

"You do . . . impersonations?"

"Not me. The stereopticon. I'm learning its audio mode. And it does perfect impersonations of any voice that it gets a sample of."

"And you . . . sampled Judy?"

"I found a YouTube clip of her guest-lecturing at a law

school about copyright legislation. She's quite the force of nature."

"I'll say," I said.

"Anyway, did the pink glasses show up?"

"They did." As I gave Manda a quick update, I lifted them to my face. Everything took on a rosy tinge. *So this is how the world looks to Bono,* I thought. "T-minus thirty seconds, and I have no idea what's about to happen," I finished, plugging the alien USB cable into my computer.

"Well, be careful. And yank the glasses off if it gets weird."

We said our good-byes, and I hovered my cursor over the mysterious hyperlink. At exactly 11:06, I clicked, and—

The room disappeared.

I found myself in a barren, apocalyptic landscape facing a muscular green hulk with pointy ears and three-inch fangs. Dressed in a red, form-fitting evening gown, he was balder than Mr. Clean. The sky behind him was orange with distant flames, and pierced by ten-foot spears that held up medieval battle standards.

I yelped and jumped backward. This didn't go so well, because I had forgotten that I was sitting on an office chair—which was kind of understandable, given that both the chair and my own body had vanished entirely from my vision. But I sure could *feel* the chair as it tipped backward from the thrust of my legs. I could also hear it crash as I sprawled to the . . . ground? Floor? The surface beneath me looked like packed earth. But it felt more like office carpeting.

I rubbed my fingers across it. Yep, this here was patterned-loop nylon. But I couldn't see my fingers, or any part of myself. I was like a disembodied, floating . . . viewpoint. I looked up and around me. The green giant stood motionless as a statue. The whole landscape was also perfectly still. And silent. This made it all seem a lot less menacing—as did the ogre's ridiculous red evening gown. Reassured, I rose unsteadily. This was surprisingly difficult without my body providing some visual cues. And while I know that sounds pathetic, try standing on one foot with your eyes shut for half a minute, and you'll see how hard it is to balance without seeing your body.*

Once I was back on my feet, I raised my hands to my face and removed the Bono glasses. The office . . . came back. Or rather, it was still there, having never gone anywhere. The glasses had been displaying an animated world to me in flawless 3D—shifting the images in perfect sync with every movement of my head, which made me feel entirely present in that eerie, imaginary landscape.

I cautiously put the Bono glasses on again, and—nothing. The office looked slightly pink. That was it.

My assistant naturally chose that one moment out of an entire half decade to get all concerned and proactive. "I heard a crash," she said, popping open the door without knocking. I stood before her in bug-eyed pink glasses that were cabled to my computer, beside a toppled thousand-dollar Aeron throne that HR had bought in a recent panic over "ergonomic hygiene." "Is everything all right?"

"Everything's fine," I chirped.

"And that sound?"

"Just . . . termites."

---

*But DO NOT DO THIS unless you are wearing full pads and a helmet, and are standing on an OSHA-certified crash mattress with an attending paramedic. And even if you take these precautions, in no event will this book's author or publisher be liable for any direct, special, incidental, indirect, or consequential damages of any kind arising out of, or in connection with, your standing on one foot with your eyes shut.

She nodded slowly, backing out of the door.

"Oh—and Barbara Ann?"

She stopped. "Yeah?"

"A quick request. Could you, uh . . ." I was about to ask her not to disturb me again, but realized that this would make things look even sketchier. "Could you tell me if these glasses make me look fat?"

She looked me over, doing her level best to take the question seriously. I'm one fourth of her boss, after all. "No," she decided. "They don't. They do make you look a little . . . Irish, maybe? And short. Definitely short. But not fat."

"Thanks," I said, and she shut the door.

I looked back at the computer screen. Maybe I had to click the hyperlink again? I righted my chair, sat on it squarely, clicked the link . . . and was back in the tableau.

"Hi Nick!" Apparently the ugly green statue was feeling chatty. I knew its voice from somewhere, but couldn't quite place it.

"Who . . . are you?"

"Oh, the green guy? That's not me. That's *you!*"

I recognized the voice now. It was Frampton. And it wasn't coming from the ogre, it was coming from—nowhere in particular. "Excuse me?" I asked.

"That's you. That's your *char*acter! And I'm sorry about the dress. But I thought it would be cool to make you a Warlock. And, well, that's what level one Warlocks wear, I guess. I tried to make it up to you by making you an Orc, but . . . it all came out a bit silly, didn't it?"

This conveyed precisely zero information to me.

"Anyway, please click the button," Frampton continued. "Carly's kind of impatient, and I don't want her getting p.o.'d."

Button? I looked around and saw it. Hovering at shin

level to the ogre (to *me?*) was a red button that said Enter
World.

"Touch your right thumb to your forefinger, like you're
making an okay sign, and the system will start tracking your
body," Frampton said. I did this, and the green guy started
mirroring my movements precisely.

"How's it doing that?" I asked, amazed by the tiny nuances of gesture that the system was picking up from me
and rendering in my avatar.

"The glasses you're wearing. There's a . . . radar machine in them. Or something."

Feeling like a digital puppeteer, I had my character
reach down to the Enter World button and touch it. With
that, my perspective shifted. It now looked like I was floating above, and slightly behind Greenie. And he (I?) was now
hanging out with two other screwballs. One looked like a
Black Sabbath roadie gussied up for a Halloween roller
derby in the Bronx—massive iron gloves, a steel-tipped ruf-
fled collar, armor held together by a huge skull-shaped
fastener—that sort of thing. The other one looked like a
Moscow whore who'd somehow gotten trapped in a Tolkien
novel. Wearing thigh-high boots and some scant strips of
green cloth that were accessorized with a hunter's bow and
quiver, she had blond hair, pointy ears, luminous green
eyes, and, well—let's just say a nice set of lungs (as I once
heard a squirrelly old bartender put it).

"I'm a Death Knight," Frampton announced, as the
S&M thug did this shuffling sort of dance step. "And Carly's
a Blood Elf." The top-heavy trollop gave me the finger.

"Where are we?" I asked.

"This is World of Warcraft," Frampton said, as his Death
Knight applauded for some reason.

"You're kidding." Two friends of mine play WoW constantly, but I hadn't tried it myself. I just thought it was an online video game with cartoonish graphics. But this was incredible.

"Don't get too excited," Carly said, as if reading my thoughts. "This is actually a highly enhanced version of Warcraft. The virtual reality interface in your glasses, the high visual fidelity, the gesture tracking, and the voice channel that we're using were all created by Refined engineers, and aren't available to human players on Earth."

Boy, that took a lot of fun out of it. "So why are we meeting here?"

"Because the only two-way data connection that exists between Earth and the rest of the universe runs through Warcraft. A group of our hackers built it in order to have some small interactions with humans, since your planet's off-limits to us. It's totally illegal. But inevitable, given the fascination that the rest of the universe has with you. And the Refined beings who use it behave responsibly and don't divulge their origins to the humans they interact with."

"But who do they say they are?"

"Koreans," Frampton said.

Carly's cartoon floozy nodded. "If you ever meet a Korean in WoW, you can bet it's an alien patching in from far, far away. Ask him to name his president, or the main street in Seoul. He'll just stammer."

"The real Koreans are all playing some other game that takes place in an online tree, or something," Frampton added dismissively.*

"Got it. Well, how much time do we have to talk?"

* 메이플스토리

"About fifteen minutes," Carly said.

I had Greenie nod. This was consistent with what the concierge had said about the duration of Wrinkle connections. "And not only can we exchange data, but our bodies can theoretically travel through the Wrinkle during this time, right?"

"Exactly."

"But you'll get trapped on Earth for many hours if you come over, so you won't make the jump."

"We won't," Carly confirmed.

Phew. The last thing I needed was these two stomping around New York in their damned robes, having seizures every time a song came on.

"But you can," she added.

"What?" Somehow I managed to say this calmly.

"But *you* can."

Christ, she said it again! "But . . . I'm afraid of heights."

Okay, that was pathetic (but true—which I guess makes it more pathetic). But no one had mentioned the faintest possibility of me getting yanked through umpteen zillion miles of space, and I didn't like the idea one bit. I mean, I'm a lawyer—not an investment banker! The law is a safe haven for the bright, ambitious, and *cripplingly risk-averse*. I wouldn't even bungie jump—and she wanted me to *what*?

"Something . . . unexpected has happened," Carly was saying. "Something that could be very dangerous. And it calls for more than just a twenty-minute chitchat between us."

"But wait." *Wait!* "Won't I get stuck for a day if I come over there?" Or devoured, or zapped, or probed, or dropped, or crushed in a giant trash compactor, or offed by a mutinous computer, or colonized by an alien fetus, or . . . ?

Carly's avatar shook her trampy little head. "Once we're done on our planet, we plan to take you to a restricted facility that has near-constant Wrinkle access to the entire universe. It's called a Wrinkle Vertex. From there, we can send you straight home, so you won't get stuck."

"Yes, but . . . isn't that dinosaur about to charge us?" This was more than just a cowardly attempt to change the subject (although it did serve that purpose nicely), because a dinosaur really was about to charge us.

"T-Rex, level fifty," Frampton hollered, his avatar turning to Carly's. "Hang back, squishy. I'm on it." He turned to me, pointing at the incoming beast. "That's from a real Warcraft server," he said reverently. "It's exactly how things look to human players on . . . *Earth*." With that, his avatar pulled a monstrous double-headed ax out of thin air, and dashed off to battle the dinosaur. His prey was pretty nicely rendered. But compared to his own avatar's down-to-the-micron fidelity, it looked like a cheap animation.

I turned to Carly's digital harlot. "Look, the Wrinkle won't close for a while yet. So before I put my life in your hands, you need to tell me a lot more about what the hell is going on."

As I said this, Frampton's avatar beheaded the dinosaur with a single blow. "WOOt!" he crowed in a triumphant falsetto as he stomped back toward us. "WOOt, woot, woot!"

"Time is tight, so this will be highly abridged," Carly said.

"Go for it."

She and Frampton proceeded to give me the lowdown on the Refined League's discovery of Earth back in the seventies, and the decades that everyone had since spent ecstatically contemplating our music.

"Which brings us to the reason why we came to you," Carly said several minutes later, having carefully hung on to the punch line.

"Well—yes, I've been wondering." It's hard to tell with an avatar, but I got the sense that she was starting to glower a bit.

"Back when the most ancient societies first became fully Refined, their focus transitioned from science—which they had thoroughly conquered—to the development of culture, which is a never-ending pursuit," she said. "An entirely new social, political, and economic order arose. One based wholly upon the creation, sharing, and savoring of the Noble Arts, which are now the prime focus of our existence. At the core of this order is something that we call the Indigenous Arts Doctrine. It's the basis of our entire economy, moral code, and legal system. It has been the cornerstone of our society for over five billion years. To give you a faint inkling of how ancient and sacred this doctrine is to us, it's about twenty-two *million* times older than your Constitution."

"Which makes it twenty-one point six million times older than the Articles of Confederation," Frampton added professorially, earning a deeply irritated glare from Carly's direction.

"Got it," I said. "So, what does the Doctrine say?"

"Very simply, that every work of creative art must be shared and savored in accordance with the rules and the norms of its society of origin. Those rules are inviolable, whatever they may be. And they must be universally respected."

"That sounds reasonable," I said. If a bit vague. And uptight. "Could you give me an example?"

Carly's manga streetwalker nodded. "Sure. Take live dramatic performances."

"You mean plays?"

"Exactly. Some of the universe's finest plays are created by a society that evolved on a planet with such a nurturing climate that they never had to make buildings, roofs, or cellars. Nothing ever came between their ancestors and their cherished, sheltering sky. And so, by their ancient tradition, their plays must always be performed in open-air amphitheaters, with no roof or other structure coming between the performers and the heavens. This is an inviolable rule throughout the universe—wherever their works are produced, and regardless of who's putting them on."

"That sounds very respectful."

"It is," Carly said. "Which is appropriate. Because they didn't wrap their plays up in some scummy, greedy rule that didn't *merit* respect, did they?"

I said nothing, assuming that this was just a bizarre rhetorical question.

"*Did* they?" she barked.

"Well—no," I allowed.

"Another species creates the universe's most sublime stained-glass patterns. In the dawning days of their civilization, they had an especially feared predator whose skin was the color that your designers call 'harlequin shamrock.' The society's earliest glass masters forbade the use of their predator's hated color in their craft, and that ancient ban remains in effect to this day. So certain frequencies of green light cannot be used in the society's patterns anywhere in the universe, regardless of who's cutting glass for those patterns. Again, the rules and the norms of the society that generates the art apply to that art everywhere."

Right then I had a grim premonition. "And that brings us to the Earth's music, doesn't it?"

"Boy does it. And I must say, the rules connected to your music are quite strange."

"But despite that, they're . . . inviolable, huh?"

"Yes. And they must be universally *respected*." Carly spat out this last word as if it were the name of a barbarous tribe that had conquered her nation, slaughtered her people, and salted their ancestral lands. "And they apply throughout the universe. Wherever, and whenever, your music is shared and savored."

"And according to our eternal rules, when you . . . share and savor our music . . . ?"

"We do so in a manner that your society defines as *piracy*." As Carly said this, her bump-mapped hussy mimed a set of ironic quotation marks so violently that she might have torn gashes in the fabric of reality itself if we weren't in a computer simulation.

"You don't say."

"Ohhh, but I do. And someday, you really have to tell me how the American people arrived at that fine of up to $150,000 for every single copy of every single song that gets pirated. You see, I'm a history buff, Nick. And this turns out to be the single most consequential decision in the history of the *entire fucking universe*."

"Oh. Well, you see, that's an approximation of . . . damages." I actually had no idea how Judy had dreamed up that demented number.

"Damages? *Dam*ages? As in—one solitary person downloading a single copy of a single song causes up to $150,000 worth of *harm* to a multinational media company?"

"Well, maybe they're rounding up slightly, but—"

"Rounding *up*? To what? To the nearest three-twentieths of a million dollars?"

"Wow! Did you just do that in your head? Because if you did—"

"Nick, Can you name one other thing whose price *rounds* to $150,000?"

"Relatively few mass-market goods, I'll grant you, but—"

"Oh, I can tell you, Nick. Lots of four-bedroom houses in Phoenix *round* to $150,000."

"Well, Phoenix is a bit off the beaten track, and—"

"Off the beaten track? It's the *sixth largest city in the most powerful country on Earth*. And McMansions there can cost less than a pirated copy of 'My Sharona'!"

That was tough to rebut, so I shifted topics somewhat. "So how much money does the Refined League owe our music industry at this point?"

"All of it," Carly said flatly.

"All of it? As in . . . ?"

"As in, all of the wealth ever created throughout every cubic inch of the universe since the Big Bang."

"All that, huh?"

"As in, all of the wealth that could conceivably be created by every conscious being that will ever live between now and the heat death of the universe, trillions of years in the future."

"All that, too?"

"As in, an amount that's so much larger than even the *sum* of those first two numbers, that the factor by which it exceeds that sum is itself far too large to even be meaningful in traditional monetary terms."

"*Damn* that's a lot," I said, not following this in the least, but figuring a quick, emphatic response was called for. "And when exactly did you all realize that you had this . . . little debt problem?"

"Nine days ago."

Frampton's animated thug leaned close. "That's less than *one thirty thousandth* of the age of the Magna Carta," he whispered dramatically.

Digital Carly turned and stared at him, eyes narrowed.

Frampton's avatar shrugged defensively, which gave off a thundering clank. "I'm trying to translate this into his terms," he explained, pointing a rusted iron glove my way.

The enraged strumpet kept staring him down.

"Carly. Nick is a *lawyer.* That means he thinks in terms of *laws,* like the Magna—"

As he was saying this, Carly grabbed her own double-headed ax out of thin air and lopped off his head. His body fell almost majestically—like an ancient oak, say—while his head flopped like a suffocating fish. Moments later, his remains vanished.

Carly returned her gaze to me. "As I was saying. We figured this out nine days ago. And I'll tell you, it caught us off guard. Because *trillions* of civilizations have integrated with the Refined League across the ages. *All* of them have contributed art to our shared heritage. *All* of that art came with inviolable, and universally respected, rules. And *nothing* remotely like this has ever happened before. Ev-er."

"Seriously? Across trillions of societies?" I asked.

"Trillions and trillions."

"And over billions of years?"

"Billions and billions."

"And throughout all of that . . . you've seriously, honestly, never encountered anything like the Copyright Damages Improvement Act?"

"Not even close. Our top legal scholars have researched it thoroughly. And they unanimously agree that it's the most cynical, predatory, lopsided, and shamelessly money-grubbing copyright law written by any society, anywhere in the universe since the dawn of time itself."

Wowsers. I was weirdly kind of proud of Judy and the firm for the next four seconds or so. Not even the open-source ayatollahs at the Electronic Frontier Foundation had ever denounced their work quite this definitively. "So that one little law," I marveled, "has turned the entire universe . . . on its head."

"It has," Carly said. "Which is why we think someone's about to destroy the Earth."

"Whoa . . . *WHOA!* To *what?*"

"Destroy the Earth."

"To *WHAT?*"

"Destroy the Earth."

"Destroy the EARTH?"

"Yes. Deee-stroyyy thuhhh Eaaaaaaarrrrrrrrth."

"But *why?*"

"In order to cancel out that ridiculous debt," she said with a bit more relish than I cared for.

"But that's absurd just don't pay the fine it's not like the music labels have telescopes do they I mean not really big ones anyway so seriously they'll never know I mean Christ I'm not gonna tell them am I no siree ma'am!" With that, I all but disbarred myself with a single run-on sentence, since I was proposing that I aid and abet *the entire universe* in reneging on its debts to my own firm's clients.

"It's not that simple," Carly said. "Because the culprits seem to think they can't get around the debt without getting rid of you."

"But . . . that would be un*gentle*manly." I realized how stupid this sounded as I said it. But despite everything that

Carly had told me about the profound logic underpinning the Indigenous Arts Doctrine, it still seemed like the Refined League lived by some deranged chivalric code.

"Exactly how gentlemanly do you think owing someone all the wealth in the universe would make you?" she asked.

Good point. I owed a few hundred bucks on a credit card back in college, and would have gladly destroyed the planet of the collectors they unleashed on me. And it turns out that I live there.

"But there'd be no more Oak Ridge Boys," I argued desperately.*

"People would manage," she answered. "Remember, you've given us quite a legacy to work through."†

Frampton's recapitated avatar rejoined us at this low point of the conversation. "Stupid corpse run," he muttered.

"Okay," I said. "Okay. Okay. Okay. We need to think this through. Okay?"

"We do," Carly said. "But—"

---

*When she was giving me the background on the Kotter Moment and everything else, Carly had mentioned that the band behind the novelty hit "Elvira" has a particularly gargantuan alien following—and then shocked me further by reporting that the boys were still putting out albums, racking up a half dozen releases over the past several years. Surely, a lot of joy would leave the cosmos if this suddenly stopped.

†Carly had also told me that Refined beings can happily spend months digging into the nuances of a single album—and that humanity had therefore already produced far more music than anyone could explore in many lifetimes.

"First thing, you need to tell me about that . . . dangerous unexpected development that just happened."

"No arguments there, Nick. But—"

"And then—I need to tell you about this thing called the
Berne Convention that might just fix all of this!"

"Sounds grand. But—"

"And, oh—I'm meeting with two people tomorrow who
are hugely influential in the music industry. They may be
able to help us!"

"I can't wait to hear more, Nick. But first, you have a
decision to make. The Wrinkle between our planets closes in
forty seconds. If you want to save humanity, you need to
make the crossing. *Now.* I can pull you over here. But I can't
do it without your permission. So—decide."

Forty seconds? I thought. What happened to the two-
minute warning? Isn't there a law about that? And how
could I know who to trust here? That damned parrot hadn't
given me any ultimatums like this—so maybe he's the good
guy. Yeah, maybe he's like a space cop! And Carly's an intergalactic kidnapper! Or maybe she's just completely delu-
sional! And what about the Berne Convention? That would
fix everything, right? So maybe this trip wasn't even necessary! Or maybe it was! Maybe it was incredibly necessary!
But how could I process all of this in *forty seconds*?

But then I realized that she was actually giving me thirty-
nine seconds more than I really needed (well, maybe more
like ten seconds, because this whole thought process clearly
took more time than it should have). My gut told me that
the Earth was in danger. It also told me that the parrot was
the bad guy. And if I was right about this, it meant that
everyone and everything I loved was in jeopardy on this

fragile blue eggshell dot of a flimsy gossamer island planet. That included my family. Puppies. NATO. God. Democracy. Did I mention God? And above all, Manda. And yeah, fine— *that crazy, ne'er-do-well cat of hers, too!*

"All right, I'm in," I said.

"Then this is very important—get *out* of the chair, and crouch down on the floor for safety," Carly said. "And then, Science will do the rest."

"And TAKE OFF THE BONO GLASSES," Frampton shouted. "You'll want to see everything!"

"You have three seconds," Carly warned.

Despite the rush and a sudden surge of abject terror, I managed to carefully remove the Bono glasses as instructed. But I forgot to get out of my chair.

EIGHT
IN THE WHITE ROOM

Imagine you're sitting in a cramped New York office, and the wall in front of you starts receding. It's like some invisible crew has started pulling back part of a movie set. Now imagine that the wall to your right is receding in the same manner. Likewise the wall to your left, and the wall behind you. So we have all four walls pulling back together—and they're picking up speed. You look up, and the ceiling's also in full retreat. You look down, and the floor's in on it, too.

It gets weirder. Although the room is flying *away* from you in six different directions, you now realize that it's not flying *apart*. Walls, ceiling, floor—they're still bound tightly together. And no, they're not stretching or growing. They're all the same size as before, and attached at the same seams—even as they're zipping off on separate vectors.

As you consider this impossibility, you realize that the

room isn't moving—it's *you*. It's like thinking that a neighboring train has started rolling, and then realizing that it has stayed put, and it's your own train that's in motion. In other words, you're moving away from all the boundaries of a stock-still room at once. I guess you might have this sort of experience if you suddenly started shrinking. But that would only pull you a few inches back from each of the walls before you vanished into nothingness. In this case, the walls, ceiling, and floor are moving much farther than that—two feet, then three feet, five, eight, thirteen . . .

In short, you're rapidly moving away, and at right angles to . . . *everything*. Or at least to each of the three simple dimensions that you've known during your life on Earth.

You start drifting in some unnameable direction and the scene shifts. You're now looking into the neighboring conference room. And you see all of it—each of the walls, plus the ceiling and the floor, are fully in your gaze simultaneously. Crazy! But that's nothing compared to the conference table. Somehow you're seeing its . . . *innards*, even as you view its familiar surfaces. You see its wooden fibers, as if you were a termite or something. And this isn't a simple cross-section—you're seeing *all* the insides of the table at once. Somehow it all fits into your field of view, along with the surfaces that you'd normally see if you were standing in the room.

You drift farther, and now all of New York City spreads out before you. And I do mean all of it—the surfaces & innards, the subways & basements—the works. The city's lights then recede into points—points that blur into swirly patterns. And that's when it hits you that you've left New York far behind. Those points of light were stars, those swirls are galaxies, and you're zipping past them at impossible speeds. *This beats IMAX,* you think. Then you're embarrassed to have such a vapid thought as you behold this celestial majesty. *So it beats . . . IMAX 3D?*—and you're mortified that this is the loftiest thought you can muster despite seven years of higher education, until you then decide that "celestial majesty" was adequately clever, and get back to the show.

Now there's one monstrously bright . . . something, and you're blinded by the light, and it must be the surface and interior of a giant star, and whoa, it's approaching fast, and you're zooming up to a planet that's orbiting the star, and toward this vast, wildly modern city—floating buildings, flying cars; *total Jetsons shit!*—but you can't parse it, because it's going by too fast, and you can't really tell surfaces from innards because you've never seen most of this stuff before, but you're coming up to the top floor of this immense building that's *floating* eight miles high above the ground, and then you're looking into this little room, and there are two figures standing there, and you can still see everything—walls & floor, skin & clothes, even blood & organs—and your reptilian brain's trying to view Carly's unclad flesh separately from her clothes & viscera (you pervert) when you're suddenly back in the normal three dimensions, and falling hard on your ass, because the chair you were sitting on when you slid out of the first room is long gone, and on top of that you're popping out at least two feet above the floor.

"That's why you should always crouch when you catch a Wrinkle," Carly said, as I tumbled. "If you start out touching the floor at several distinct points, it will place you on the floor on the other end. If you're not even touching the floor, then who knows?" She said this as if we'd gone over the concept for weeks, and I just refused to get it.

She and Frampton were standing to either side of me. They were wearing their mullah and nun outfits again, only without the sound-blocking headdresses. Carly had a cascade of silky chestnut hair tumbling well below her shoulders, while Frampton had this crazed red mop that sprang out in corkscrews and pleats in all directions (and his jihadi beard—presumably a fake—was gone). The room was totally white, and utterly featureless.

"So where are we?"

"The planet we've been living on for the past six years," Carly said. "It's called Zinkiwu.* And you are now in my home."

"And how far are we from Earth?"

"About eight billion light-years."

Now, that got my attention. Of course, I already knew that I'd traveled a huge distance. But it's one thing to know that in an academic sort of way, and another thing to viscerally grasp the fact that you've just—what, *crossed the universe?* In a faster-than-light manner that upends humanity's entire understanding of physics? As I reveled in the awesome historic weight of my journey, the first words to flash through my mind were *Eat it, Backstreet Bitch!* Now people would taunt *him* for having *my* name. "Who are you—the pissant singer," they'd ask. "Or the man who shattered every law of motion as we'd ever understood them?"

"I just traveled . . . a trillion times faster than light," I murmured, as I processed all of this.

---

*Rhymes with "pinky-boo." And by the way, wimpy planet names like Zinkiwu turn out to be way more common than cool sci-fi names like Alderaan. Yeah, it sucks.

Carly gave me an agonized look. "Please, Nick. That would shatter every law of motion as we've ever understood them."

"Wait—what? Then how far did I go?"

"What did you clock the Wrinkle at, Frampton?"

"Two minutes, forty-one seconds," he answered.

Carly looked at me. "I'd say you came about eighty feet."

"But . . . but I thought you said we were eight billion light-years from Earth!"

"We are."

"Then how did I get here by moving eighty feet?"

"Because we were briefly about eighty feet from the boundary of a nine-dimensional heptagon whose lesser vertex included your office's hypermeridian," she sniffed, like a fallen Nobel laureate reduced to teaching fractions to a dull fifth-grader.

"Whoa, slow it down for the Earth boy. How'd you get me here? In really simple terms."

Carly rolled her eyes impatiently. "For about twenty minutes, the deep geometry of the cosmos allowed us to fold a tiny corner of the universe over on itself in one of the higher dimensions. And that brought your office within eighty feet of here, along a hidden vector. Whereupon we started reeling you in. Quite slowly, as you now know."

"Wait—you *folded* the universe?"

"Yes," Carly said. "The Refined League does that many billions of times per second to move beings and data around. In this case, we put a transitory Wrinkle into a very narrow quadrant of the seventh dimension."

I was starting to see why the ersatz concierge had been unable to explain Wrinkles to Manda and me in formal English. Carly managed to do a decent job of it by way of an analogy, though. She told me to imagine a huge map of the Earth painted onto a gigantic sheet. We can call it Flat Earthland.* Its two-dimensional inhabitants zip around it like cutout dolls on a paper map. Suppose a girl named Flat Stacey moves from Flat Boston to Flat Dubai. That's seven thousand miles, and she's homesick. Now imagine that the vast sheet of Flat Earthland actually exists in a three-dimensional place—and that Flat Stacey has the power to fold it over on itself. If she does this, putting the fault line somewhere in the Atlantic, her childhood home could end up hovering just a few feet above her new pad in Flat Dubai—even as it's also several thousand miles to the west for someone sliding along the sheet.

If Flat Stacey knows how to travel in the third dimension, she can now pop in on her family even faster than she can cross the street. And when she leaves Flat Earthland, she'll experience something like my own short, strange trip through the Wrinkle. First, she'll start moving at right angles to every normal dimension of her daily life. Floating above Flat Dubai, she'll be able to see into closed rooms, and behold the innards of objects that she normally just sees the surfaces of. And much as I had zipped across the universe, she'll be able to travel to the farthest corner of Flat Earthland in moments if it's folded over, and practically touching her starting point.

"I hope that makes sense to you, because we really need

---

*This in honor of the English mathematician Edwin Abbott, who first depicted this sort of scenario in his 1884 novella *Flatland*, as well as Charles Johnson, who led the unrelated Flat Earth Society without a trace of irony until his death in 2001.

to get back to saving humanity," Carly said after describing all of this.

"Oh . . . right." I was so giddy from my journey that this little issue had slipped my mind. "So, you said that someone's trying to destroy Earth. But I thought you'd come to save us from *self*-destruction?"

Carly nodded. "The two are related. To be more precise, we believe that someone intends to *help* you to self-destruct."

"You mean like . . . assisted suicide?"

Frampton shook his head. "More like *involuntary* assisted suicide."

"Which sounds like an antiseptic term for murder," I said.

"What say we go with genocide?" Carly suggested breezily. "There's quite a few of you, after all."

"Well, whatever we call it, who's behind it?" I asked.

"We're not sure," Carly said. "One of several organizations that are dismayed to be losing all their wealth to you."

"But that could be anyone with any money at all, right?"

She shook her head. "Actually, virtually no one in the Refined League harbors any violent intentions toward humanity. We're R*efined,* after all."

"You're also incredibly loved," Frampton added. "We're all way, way happier than we ever were before, and it's because of your music."

Carly nodded. "And most people's lives won't change anytime soon anyway, because individuals will retain full access to their possessions and savings as long as humanity's wealth remains in escrow. Things are different for organizations. Our banking laws have already severely restricted what they can do with their former wealth."

"Got it. And when will everything be . . . transferred to humanity?"

"Not until your civilization is advanced enough to qualify as Refined itself," Carly said.

"*If* that ever happens," Frampton added.

Carly nodded. "An overwhelming majority of species self-destruct long before becoming Refined."

"With or without 'assistance'?" I asked.

"Always without," Carly said. "It's a huge crime to interfere with a primitive society. And like I said—most societies do themselves in anyway. Humanity is actually very lucky so far. You've made great strides against hunger, disease, and extreme poverty. You also did a masterful job of fending off a modern ice age with your CO_2 production. And you've survived for several decades with nuclear weapons. Few get this far. But you're now on the verge of creating a host of highly destructive nano, bio, and olfactory weapons, and you'll have to learn to live with them, too. Only one society in four gets through the final phase of development that you now face."

I considered this. "And the organizations that you mentioned want us to be one of the three out of four that doesn't make it, because that way, they'll get their money back, right?"

"Actually, I'd say that certain brutal factions *within the top leadership* of the organizations want you to self-destruct," Carly said. "I'm sure you're adored among the rank and file."

"So in Warcraft, you said there's been a dangerous new development. What is it?"

She looked at me grimly, clearly preparing to share the most jarring news yet. "Shortly after we returned from

Earth yesterday, we were notified that another alien party had crossed the Townshend Line after us. We don't know who they are, or where they came from. But we fear the worst."

"Oh, you mean Paulie and Özzÿ?" It was weirdly satisfying to have my own bombshell to drop on these two for a change. "Sure—they swung by right after you left."

Now *that* led to an awkward silence.

"Did you . . . happen to notice what they looked like?" Frampton finally asked.

"Paulie looks like a parrot. And Özzÿ looks like a vacuum cleaner. Only with hands." It turns out that I had to say this out loud to appreciate how truly stupid it sounded.

"Are you sure it wasn't swamp gas? Or maybe ball lightning?" Frampton asked, twirling a finger around his temple as he shot Carly a skeptical look. "I'm not saying I don't believe you. But the so-called UFO sightings on your planet always turn out to have simple, natural explanations."

"Oh, I'm sure about this one. I have another witness. Two, if you count the cat."

"Then why did you wait until *now* to tell me this?" Carly demanded.

"Wait until now? I've been here for like five minutes! And when we were in Warcraft, it was *your* turn to do the talking—given that *you* were asking *me* to take an eight-billion-light-year leap of faith!"

Carly didn't even hear this. "Seriously! Why doesn't anybody *ever tell me anything*?"

"I promise, I'll tell you everything, starting now," I said as soothingly as I could. "Paulie showed up first. He met me in a restaurant, about an hour after you left. He's a nasty little hoodlum with a bright yellow plumage. And he tawks like he's from Brooklyn, maybe thirty or forty years ago."

Carly and Frampton swapped an alarmed glance. "You mean he talks like Vinnie Barbarino," Frampton said quietly.

I shot him a blank look.

"John Travolta's character on *Welcome Back, Kotter*?" Carly said, like a teacher chiding me for not having read Chaucer. "*Kotter* was our first exposure to English, obviously. And for a while, everyone spoke it like Vinnie Barbarino. Until we started digging up some of your other shows about six months later."

"That's when I started speaking like Tattoo on *Fantasy Island*," Frampton said. "Zee plane! Zee plane!"

Carly rolled her eyes. "He didn't stop until yesterday. I told him he wasn't coming to Earth talking like that."

"Zee plane! Zee plane!"

"*Stifle*," Carly snapped.

Frampton stifled.

"Anyway, a few groups kept up with the Barbarino thing. Strictly thugs, because we learned that Brooklyn had a rough history. So this isn't good. What else do you know about him?"

"I think his full name is Paulie Stardust. Ring any bells?"

They both shook their heads. "Although that's probably his Exalted name," Frampton said.

Carly nodded. "After the Kotter Moment, everyone took on an Exalted name in the Absolute Universal Language that had just been adopted."

"You mean . . . English?"

Carly nodded again. "American English. As spoken in sitcoms and on AM radio at the time. Anyway, most people usually go by their original names. So if this Paulie guy is famous, we probably know him by the name he grew up with."

"If it helps, he said his organization recently lost something insane like a third of the assets in the universe."

At this, Carly and Frampton exchanged a truly horrified look, and Frampton said something that sounded like "A big ape."

"Huh?"

"It's an acronym," he said. "It stands for the Amalgamated Brotherhood of Intergalactic, Galactic, and Planetary Employees. But we usually just say 'the Guild' for short."

"What is it?"

"The leading union of government employees," Carly said. "And until recently, they were the wealthiest organization in the universe. But now you have all the money. And I suppose they want it back. Tell us more."

I gave them the lowdown on my meetings with Özzÿ and the parrot.

"This is incredibly bad," Frampton said when I finished. He started looking furtively around the empty, featureless room, as if for a hiding place.

"How bad?" I asked.

He turned to Carly.

She folded her arms and shook her head.

"*Dad* bad," he said, looking at her almost sternly.

I was wondering if this was an intergalactic supervillain with a superlame name when Carly sniffed, "He's saying we should run off and beg our daddy to fix all of this for us."

Our *daddy*? I hadn't pegged these two for brother and sister. But it kind of made sense.

"We have to go to Dad," Frampton said, suddenly showing something like a backbone. "He's the only one who can fix this."

Carly folded her arms tighter and stamped her foot.

"But I haven't even *tried* yet. And what can *Dad* do that I can't?"

"He can keep the Secret from being revealed, for one thing," Frampton said. Somehow, I could hear that capital *S* in there.

"Well duh-hickey, the Secret doesn't matter anymore," Carly said. "The Guild has obviously figured it out somehow. They're already on *Earth*."

"But there're a dozen other groups like them that don't know yet," Frampton said. "And if the Secret breaks, we'll have to deal with all of them."

Carly glared at him.

"Look, what's more important to you," he asked. "Proving that you're as good as Dad? Or actually saving the human race?"

Carly just glared some more. Which pretty much answered that question.

"So, uh," I ventured. "We're about to get to the part where you tell me about the Secret, right?"

Frampton nodded. "It's about the Townshend Line."

"What about it?"

"It *sucks*," Carly spat. "It turns out that it's like ninety-nine percent marketing. But no one actually tries to cross it, because nobody knows how crappy it is."

Frampton nodded. "This is probably the best-kept secret in the universe. But it's about to get out."

"And when it does, so many Who fans will show up that the Earth will collapse into a black hole?" I guessed.

Carly shook her head. "That was a heat-of-the moment thing. Everyone's gotten used to living with your music since then. Which I guess is why they never made the Townshend Line really robust. People must have been less interested in bum-rushing the Earth once they all caught their breath. Until this debt thing happened."

"Got it," I said. "And, uh . . . how exactly are you in on the biggest secret in the universe?"

"We're part of a very powerful . . . program that has a rather large research staff," Carly said evasively. "They're good at ferreting out secrets."

"Is it some creepy KGB-like thing?" I asked.

"Oh, it's much creepier than that," Carly said. "And our father runs it."

"And what does your program do?"

"We'll get to that later," Carly snipped.

Oh please. My entire *species* was allegedly on the line, I was risking my life to save it, and she wouldn't even tell me what she did for a living. "Well," I said, "I think it would be appropriate to at least—"

"I said we'll get to that later!"

I had a brief flashback of my iPhone disintegrating in Carly's telekinetic hands, and backed right down.

"For now we're going to Dad," Frampton said, looking at his sister. "Please?"

There was a grumpy silence. Then, finally, "Oh, all right."

Frampton immediately lit up, and turned to me. "Oh— and you should come!" he said.

Carly was already shaking her head. "We can't take him to see Dad without taking him out there," she said, pointing vaguely at the wall.

"You mean I can't leave this room?" I asked.

Carly shook her head. "It would be dangerous."

"Why? Because I'd . . . choke on the air?"

"No. Zinkiwu is identical to Earth in terms of its

atmosphere, size, and gravitational field. By design. The problem is that while humans are hugely advanced in music, you're desperately primitive in every other art. That includes decor, textile design, architecture, cuisine, and scented-candle craft."

"Which means?"

"Which means you could find the sights, smells, and textures of a Refined home as enthralling as the rest of the universe found the *Kotter* song."

"You mean my brain could explode?"

Carly shook her head. "The human aesthetic sense is far too dull to engender such a cultivated response. But you could end up in a useless trance for hours."

"But Nick could help talk Dad into keeping a lid on things," Frampton pleaded. "He's a lawyer—and he's from *Earth*. Dad will have to listen to him!"

Carly considered this. "You may be right. But what happens when he sees my apartment?"

"Oh, he'll be fine. Didn't you see his office? He has no aesthetic sense whatsoever."

"True," she allowed. "But still, I just updated the lighting, and it's simply gorgeous out there. I don't know if he can handle it."

"We can shut it off. It's still daytime, and your apartment gets sunlight."

"But what about my layout? It's so stunning it makes *my* head spin. What'll it do to him?"

"I could go out there first and rearrange the furniture," Frampton offered. "Make it look really crappy?"

Carly considered this, then nodded. "And hide all the art. And open the windows to dissipate the scents. Cover up whatever walls you can. And if there's any food out there, for God's sake, vaporize it. Otherwise he'll be like a panther with a bushel of catnip."

"I'll turn it into a sensory deprivation tank." As Frampton slipped out the door, I shut my eyes so that a stray glimpse of Carly's dangerously brilliant layout wouldn't cripple me. Moments later, we could hear him banging around outside.

"We put these rags back on for you, for the same reason," Carly grumbled, looking at her robes.

"Afraid that your own fashions would overwhelm me?"

"Yes. They're too tasteful for your mind to process comfortably." She was entirely serious.

"Hey, some of *our* clothes are amazing, too—you should see the girls in Rio and St. Tropez.* And why do you dress like a pair of religious kooks anyway? You're not exactly scaling the heights of our fashion—lame as you find it."

"We know how important religion is on Earth. So we thought we might get more respect from people this way. Was it a bad choice?"

"Bad? It was abysmal!" It felt good to be the expert for once. "You look like a couple of nut jobs. A nun and a mullah walking through midtown stand out as much as—I don't know, as much as a Wookiee and a Klingon." That was something of a zinger. By then, I knew that our films were viewed with smug derision everywhere, with our depictions of alien life being particularly mocked.

I was about to follow this up with a truly cutting jab when Frampton opened the door to the living room, changing my life forever.

---

*I should see them, too, by the way, as I've never been to either place.

NINE

FOOL FOR THE CITY

The colors of Carly's living room were lucid in ways I didn't know were possible. It was like I'd spent my life watching some ghastly Nixon-era TV mounted in a huge wooden console, then was suddenly plunked down in front of a hundred-inch plasma screen in James Cameron's house. Nothing was gaudy, it was all just very . . . present. The blues had immense gravity—like they'd been pulled from the depths of an ocean that was distantly illuminated by a thousand suns. The reds actively smoldered—as if a master enamelist had taken the truest red in nature, distilled away its slightest impurities, and then applied a nuclear infusion to give it a deep, plutonium glow. And the dark touches looked like they were carved from black holes—accents of perfect opacity that made the rest of the room look phosphorescent by comparison.

Each color would be a museum-worthy marvel on its

own. But the shades of the textiles, the furniture, and the walls wove together in an immaculately balanced tapestry. It was like a color symphony sustaining the perfect chord—one with both an infinite, fractal complexity and the pure simplicity of a low integer. Lush primary splashes offset fields of bewitchingly deep tones, all bracketed by those impossibly perfect blacks. And everything—textures, reflections, contours—stood in perfect counterpoise. As for the furniture, Carly's humblest footstool could single-handedly transform the lowest Staten Island squat into the swankest bachelor pad in New York. Meanwhile, the carpets were not only gorgeous beyond words, but they caressed and coddled my feet in almost pornographic ways. When I bent down and touched one, I found that it was softer than eiderdown, and deliciously squishy—kind of how a chinchilla blanket might feel if you were on one of those drugs that can make even asphalt feel satiny.

"Oh my God!" Carly murmured as we both took in the room. I assumed its familiar splendor was dazzling even her. Then, "It looks like absolute *crap* without the lights on." She took in the furniture arrangement. "You totally trashed the superasymmetry, too. And who knew this place would look so *dowdy* without the artwork showing. Frampton, you're a genius."

"I've seen a lot of American music videos," he said bashfully, lapping up the rare praise.

"Well, you really *learned* from them. I mean, this is amazing, I'm honestly feeling nauseous. Nick? How are you handling this?"

"It's the most glorious place I've ever seen," I said in a minuscule voice. I was saving every ounce of my energy to revel in the splendor before me.

I soon realized that the room was illuminated by a natural golden glow that was radiating from an immense window. I approached it and beheld the city that I had glimpsed from the Wrinkle's chaos. We were at the pinnacle of a vast building that floated miles above the ground. It was surrounded by thousands of other massive structures— some floating, others freestanding. Each building soared, stretched, inverted, and arched as if it were spun from living gossamer and suspended in zero gravity. And all of the buildings moved in a slow, majestic, ingeniously synchronized dance. As they flowed through their motions, their reflections, lights, and shadows interplayed, causing sublime new patterns to emerge across the face of the city every few seconds. It was as if hyperintelligent counterparts of Frank Gehry, Alex Calder, Dr. Seuss, and Martha Graham had gotten together, dropped a load of acid, and hit the drafting boards.

"What do you call this place?" I asked in my minuscule voice—still preserving energy for ongoing rapture.

"Paradise City," Frampton said.

"Paradise—as in, where The Good go after death?" I asked. This made unimpeachable sense.

"No. Paradise *City*, as in track six of the first Guns N' Roses album."

"This city's an arts center," Carly said. "We built it on rock 'n' roll. What do you think of it?"

"It's . . . it's . . . it's beautiful!" I said. More lyrical, or poetically adequate, words simply eluded me.

I'm not sure what response I expected to this. Softly murmured assent, or some reverential silence would have been nice. Instead I got a gale of guffaws that belonged in a truck stop. Frampton sounded like he was gagging on snot, as Carly leaned on a chair for support, verging on a seizure. "It's . . . it's . . . it's *byooooo-tiful!*" she squeaked in a cartoon falsetto, and she and Frampton lost it all over again.

"Seriously," Frampton said, after struggling for several seconds to regain control. "That's Paradise City. You wouldn't find a tackier place if you . . . if you . . . *looked really, really hard!*" This devastating salvo brought on another round of hysterics.

Once he calmed down, Frampton removed the chunky diver's watch that he always wears. I watched in amazement as it drained of color and reshaped itself into a translucent lump.

"Is that a stereopticon?" I asked.

He nodded. "Have you seen one before?"

"Özzÿ used one when he visited us in my apartment," I said. I didn't mention that we still had the device in our possession. I was annoyed that Carly was stonewalling me about the program they were working for, so I didn't feel like revealing every last card in my own hand just yet.

"Most Refined beings have one on them at all times," Carly said, clasping her bulky, medieval cross. It oozed and melted into the same shape. She pressed it back against her neck, and it re-formed into the crucifix. "They're like a cross between a computer, a phone, a 3D recorder, and a lot more. By the way, put your phone on that table."

I did as she asked. It immediately levitated, then disintegrated into a familiar shower of green sparks. An instant later it reappeared on the table. Carly's crucifix glimmered softly throughout this, and I realized that the telekinetic display that had cowed me in my office was actually an ingenious optical illusion projected by her stereopticon. I thought of Manda, and her idea of using our stereopticon to recruit Judy to our cause—and decided that it was brilliant after all.

Frampton was meanwhile gazing at an information display that his stereopticon was projecting about a foot from his face. "Dad's on the far side of the planet. Should we contact him?"

Carly let off an exasperated sigh. "What did I tell you about the security of the datalinks on this planet?"

Frampton thought hard. "Nonexistent, right?"

Carly nodded wearily. "How are the Wrinkle connections?"

Frampton consulted his data readout. "Totally booked out. Air and space traffic slots are bad, too. The best way to the other side of the planet is a dropway."

"Call an omnicab," Carly commanded. She turned to me. "We're going to travel by a physical route, since the Wrinkles are booked out. Frampton just ordered a vehicle, and it'll be here soon. You mentioned that you were afraid of heights, didn't you?"

I shrugged. "Oh, I wouldn't really say 'afraid.'"*

"Excellent," Carly said, with a puckish grin that I didn't like one bit.

Frampton was meanwhile launching a series of projections from his stereopticon. It was a procession of flawless 3D renderings of common animals and objects, including shoelaces, praying mantises, fire hydrants, cats, KFC-branded "sporks," bedbugs, freeway on-ramps, and hundreds of other things.

"Refined life is so abundant and diverse that many dif-

---

*Nor would I say *abjectly terrified*, because that, too, would be a shameful understatement.

ferent species of it can blend in seamlessly on any given planet," Carly explained. "Frampton's cycling through all the Refined species that resemble things on Earth. They'd be the beings to choose from if someone wanted to infiltrate your society."

"Shoelaces?" I asked no one in particular, looking gravely at my Cole Haan's.

"There's about a thousand Refined look-alike species for Earth," Frampton said, "including some birds." He quickly produced a little feathered police lineup—a 3D tableau that included several species of bird, including a dead ringer for the parrot I had met at Eatiary.

I pointed at it. "That's the species."

Frampton expanded the projection of the parrot and started getting excited. "I—I think I know exactly who visited you."

"Seriously?" Carly turned to me. "He has his weaknesses, but my brother never forgets a face."

Frampton checked something else on his stereopticon. "One of these guys used to be really famous. As in, he was on *Aural Sculptures.*"

I gave him a puzzled look.

"It used to be the universe's most popular entertainment program."

"It featured all of the greatest musicians," Carly added. "The Kotter Moment was the death of it."

"Bingo," Frampton said, looking at another data display. He made a flicking gesture, and a member of the yellow parrot–like species appeared in the middle of the room, standing next to an orange, pus-oozing lizard. The lizard had five bloodshot eyes mounted on stalks that bristled with metallic thorns. Frampton pointed at the parrot. "This guy's Exalted name is Paulie Stardust. So he's the one you saw at the restaurant."

"And who's the heartbreaker?" I asked, pointing at the orange grotesque.

Carly smiled, almost sweetly. "That's Mllsh-mllsh, the show's host."

"This episode ran in the year 2 PK," Frampton added. Seeing my blank look, he added "Pre-Kotter."

"A law passed shortly after the Kotter Moment requires that all dates be expressed in Pre- and Post-Kotter terms," Carly explained.*

Frampton made another flicking gesture, and the static images came to life. Now, I've never heard a rabid hyena

---

*And yes, "Pre-Kotter" and "Post-Kotter" are both abbreviated PK. Being as muddle-headed as everyone else in the months following the Kotter Moment, the Refined lawmakers didn't consider how much confusion this would cause until it was too late. There was a grassroots movement to fix things with a PK/AK dating system (Pre-Kotter/*Anno Kotter*). But it was doomed, because Refined legislative decisions can only be overturned if a subsequent vote passes with a larger proportion of votes than the first one—and the vote that instituted Pre- and Post-Kotter time was unanimous, so it will have to stand forever.

Luckily, the Refined League has done much better by its adoption of our years, days, hours, minutes, and seconds as time units (which the legislature also mandated in those brief, heady days of total obeisance to humanity's awesomeness). All time was previously measured in "Standard Intervals," which are derived from the half-life of iodine-129 (^{129}I). Since ^{129}I has a half-life of 15.7 million years, this was useful in measuring things like the universe's age (876 Standard Intervals). But daily life was larded with clumsy sentences like, "I'm off to mail that letter—I'll be back in 0.000000000000605 Standard Intervals," or "she's way too young for him—she's only 0.0000153!" Everyone was also constantly depressed by the thought that they'd never live to see their first birthdays.

shriek from rectal acid burns. But I'll bet that sounds a lot like Mllsh-mllsh introducing a guest.

Carly and Frampton nudged each other and grinned nostalgically as he spoke. "His lisp was *so cute*," Carly murmured.

Soon the bird was singing. And if this sound could be weaponized, its destructive power would put it somewhere between chemical and biological warheads.* Frampton and Carly shut their eyes and nodded along, adoringly.

"*STOP IT*," I yelped when I couldn't take it anymore. Frampton paused the playback and gave me a hurt look. "Could we, uh—get back to talking about the Earth?"

"Right," Carly said reluctantly. "So, your visitor is an angelic singer."

"Angelic? *Him*?" I must have had a pint of blood gushing through my ear canals thanks to his caterwauling.

"God, yes!" Frampton said. "Didn't you hear his timbre? Or those syncopated glottal stops?"

"Or the polyrhythms?" Carly asked. "His melodic subtlety, or—"

---

*And I mean this literally. The Advanced Societies have hacked every firewall on our Internet in their relentless study of our musical history, and they found that "Malignant Acoustics" was once a key domain of Soviet military research. The program flourished until 1932, when the playback of an especially lethal recording killed everyone within ten miles of the lab that created it. Of course, Stalin would have gladly killed everyone in a *hundred*-mile radius for such a titillating new weapon. But the loss of the entire research team ended its development. As for the local civilian deaths, a cover-up pinned the blame on a lichen famine (lichen being a staple of the Soviet diet back then). The whole episode is memorialized in "Experiment IV," a majestically haunting 1986 hit by Kate Bush, who must be an ex-KGB agent or something.

"All right, all right—I get the point. He's got a golden throat, and makes a living from music."

Frampton shook his head. "You mean *made* a living from music."

"Humanity's emergence made all Refined musicians completely irrelevant," Carly said. "Glorious as it is, their collective output isn't worth a Shaun Cassidy B-side."

"So they must be pissed."

Carly nodded. "They're the only Refined beings that feel anything other than complete adoration for humanity. And even most of them don't mind you, because they love your music as much as anyone. But there are some bitter ex-singers out there."

"And this guy's one of them," Frampton said, consulting another data readout. "His career was just taking off around the time of the Kotter Moment. He was so mad at the universe that he ran off and joined the Guild's Enforcement Brigade."

Carly gave a low whistle. "Refined beings tend to be . . . rather docile," she explained. "Only the most powerful organizations dare to bend the rules even slightly. The Guild is one of them—and their Enforcement Brigade is the closest thing we have to the Hells Angels. I wonder if his partner has a similar history. What does he look like again?"

"A vacuum cleaner with hands," I said.

Frampton found Özzÿ's race on his stereopticon. "Whoa," he said, "this species is made of metallicam! And it's the only metallicam species that can blend in on Earth."

"So this is a very carefully chosen pair," Carly said. "We have a human-hating ex-singer, and a metallicam being. Both of whom can fit in somewhat on Earth. And let me guess—Paulie's the boss, and Özzÿ's an ass-kissing pushover."

I nodded. "Definitely. But how'd you know?"

"With no personal grudge against your race, Özzÿ is probably as gaga about humans as anyone else," Carly explained. "So the Guild needed to send someone Paulie could manipulate and brainwash."

"Makes sense. So what're they going to do?" I asked.

"Something with metallicam," Carly said. "That's why you hire metallicam beings—because they can handle it safely. They're too thick to do much of anything else."

"And metallicam's both an energy source and a weapon, right?"

Carly nodded. "In its raw form, yes—it's kind of like uranium, or plutonium, only far more powerful. When it's integrated into a living being in its organic form, as with Özzÿ, it's no more dangerous than carbon or oxygen."

"So do you think they'll hit us with . . . a metallicam missile?"

Carly shook her head. "They need to do something much more subtle. Remember, it's illegal to harm a primitive society. So they have to make it look like you've done yourselves in."

"Right, but how would metallicam play into that?"

"It would completely destabilize your geopolitical system if anyone gained access to it," she explained. "Energy supplies, balance of power—all of that would change, which could easily trigger wars. So maybe they'll give it to Pakistan, or something. The program that we work for has . . . considered this scenario on a broad level. But we haven't fully fleshed it out yet. So I'm not entirely sure how it might unfold."

Ah, the mysterious program again. I forced myself to sound less snippy in discussing it this time. "I assume you can't tell me about your program because it's top secret."

"Oh, it isn't *secret*," Frampton tittered.

Carly glared at her brother. "Yes, it's . . . very much out in the open. But the public doesn't know about the internal work that's done by our researchers."

"You mean your spies?" I asked.

She shrugged. "Yeah, sure. Our spies. Frampton and I are privy to their research. They recently uncovered the truth about the Townshend Line. And then another team with the program . . . *predicted* that one of several powerful organizations might try to engineer your self-destruction. That's why we came to New York—to try to settle the debt, so that nobody would have any reason to harm you."

"Then why are you so shocked that the Guild is already on Earth?" I asked. "It seems like you should've expected them to be here."

"We did. Only not this soon. The secret about the Townshend Line hasn't broken yet."

"Well, who knows the secret besides you?"

"Only a very, very high-ranking group of beings," Carly said. "Have you ever heard of the Guardians?"

I nodded. "I have. In fact, for some reason, Özzÿ and Paulie think that *I* might be a Guardian."

Carly gave me a stunned look. "But Guardians are wise, and dignified, and cosmopolitan. Haven't these creatures met you?"

"Yes. They've met me. As I told you. And they think I might be a Guardian because they know that *some*body crossed the universe last night, just to pop into my office and pretend to disintegrate my iPhone."

Frampton caught his breath. "Seriously? *Who*?"

Carly glared at him. "Well, keep them fooled, because they won't do anything as long as they think a Guardian is watching them. That's your planet's sole defense for now, because the Townshend Line obviously can't protect it."

"Well, luckily, I might have come up with something else that can," I said, eager to share my other big news.

"I doubt it," Carly said. "But let's hear it anyway."

"Okay. Let me start with a couple of questions. Have you ever heard of a treaty called the Berne Convention?"

Carly gave an oddly noncommittal shrug.

"It's an international accord governing copyright enforcement on Earth," I continued. "So in light of that, is there any possibility—even a remote one—that the Refined League might have signed it?"

"Of course not," she snorted.

"Excellent. Next question. According to the Refined League, what legal system has precedence on the Earth itself? Our own laws and agreements, like the Berne Convention? Or Refined laws?"

"Your own laws," Carly said. "The autonomy of primitive societies is sacrosanct in all matters, particularly legal ones."

"Great," I said. "So everyone agrees that the Berne Convention is the law of the land here on Earth. And meanwhile, the Indigenous Arts Doctrine requires the Refined League to honor humanity's laws, rules, and norms as they pertain to humanity's own artistic output. Correct?"

Carly rolled her eyes. "Of course. That's what the Indigenous Arts Doctrine *is*."

"So then what if our laws actually say . . . that our rules *don't apply* to you? Wouldn't your doctrine require you to respect our right to hold our own laws null and void in relation to you?"

"Of course," Carly said. "But the Copyright Damages

Improvement Act doesn't seem to provide an exemption for alien civilizations, now, does it?"

I shook my head. "No. But it doesn't have to. Because my society doesn't claim any restitution for acts of piracy that occur outside of the nations that have signed the Berne Convention. Seriously. So as far as our laws, rules, and norms are concerned, you can copy as many of our songs as you want to on your own planets, and never incur a fine."

"I see," Carly said. "So the fine only applies if we make allegedly pirated songs on the territory of a signatory nation?"

I nodded smugly. "You got it."

"Which means countries like the United States?"

"Yep."

"Which means cities like New York?"

"Well, yes. New York being located in the United States and all."

"Which means places like the train stations and tunnels beneath New York?"

"Sure. Don't, uh . . . go pirating any music down there."

"Well, oops," Carly said. "It turns out that every copy of every human song that the universe is listening to right now was made right under Track Sixty-one of Grand Central Station."

I was briefly mute as the absurdity of this sunk in. Finally, "You . . . seriously make your copies—on Earth?"

"You got it," Carly said.

"Under Grand Central Station?"

"Yep."

"In *New York*?"

"Well, yes. Grand Central being located in New York and all."

This couldn't be. "Seriously," I said. "Of all of the billions of planets in the universe—"

"Sextillions," Frampton clarified.

"Fine. Of all the *sextillions* of planets in the universe, why do you have to copy all of your damn music on *Earth*?"

"First of all, it's *your* damn music," Carly snipped.

"Well—yes, that's kind of the problem, isn't it?"

"And secondly, the original plan was just to set up a listening post."

"A listening post?"

Carly nodded. "No one wanted to lose access to your music after the Townshend Line went up, so our engineers had to build a monitoring station to pick up the new songs in your radio broadcasts. And it had to be somewhere on Earth itself, since the force field prevented them from putting a probe anywhere within a hundred and forty-four light-years of your solar system."

"But why pick Grand Central?"

"They wanted to install just one outpost, so as to minimize the risk of discovery," Carly said. "And New York was the right city, because of the quality and density of its radio stations. The only place they identified that was likely to lie undisturbed indefinitely was an abandoned underground spur connected to Grand Central's rail network. So they built the listening post there—and then popular demand forced them to put the copying facility in there, too."

"Popular demand?"

"Sure, everyone thought it would be really cool to have copies of your music that were made right in the NY of C," Frampton explained. "I mean, why not?"

"Well, there's up to 150,000 reasons why not per copy," I said. "But that aside, isn't it just insane to make a billion copies of a song on Earth, and then send all of them to Planet X? I mean, it's a lot more efficient to just send one copy to Planet X, and make the rest of them there, right?"

Carly shrugged. "In theory, sure. But in reality, our networks are so fast that efficiency concerns are irrelevant."

"Well, great then," I snapped. "So because you have fast networks and a crazed appetite for digital souvenirs, you set up shop in New York and started making trillions of illegal copies of our songs."

"Thousands of octillions," Frampton clarified.

"Okay, sure. That many. And in doing that, you completely screwed up the Berne Convention angle. Fine. Bravo. But still, there *has* to be some other loophole we can exploit."

"Such as?" Carly sneered, clearly convinced that no simple solution could possibly exist, given that she hadn't come up with one.

"Well . . . I don't know, what about exchange rates? Our multinationals are always pushing income and debt into different currencies to minimize taxes and whatnot. And you guys are multi*galactic*. So don't you suppose there's a way to get rid of the debt using exchange rates?"

"No," Carly answered, without a moment's thought.

"Seriously, though. The American dollar can't be widely used in the rest of the universe. So why not make the exchange rate really favorable to yourselves? Decree that a million bucks is worth just one of your transmeteorite dinars, or whatever."

"Nick," Carly said, "you don't know a thing about astrophysics, do you?"

"It wasn't a huge subject of mine at law school, no."

"Well, if it was, you'd know that the common heavy elements are all created in supernovas, which are distributed fairly evenly from galaxy to galaxy. That makes the noble metals similarly rare—and similarly precious—everywhere."

As if that explained a thing. "What are noble metals? And why do I care?"

"Silver, gold, iridium, platinum, and so on. Since they're similarly rare and precious everywhere, they're the natural basis for exchange rates throughout the cosmos—just as they have been throughout much of your own history. And since the various hard currencies of Earth already buy certain amounts of these metals on your global spot markets, we can't set exchange rates for your money arbitrarily. They're set by your metal prices and by ours."[*]

I sighed heavily and gazed at the bewitching landscape of Paradise City, hoping it would cheer me up. "Okay, then

---

[*]While it sucks that this system plugged a loophole that could have saved humanity from imminent destruction and all, it does have some cool practical advantages. For instance, should you ever pop over to the nearby Andromeda galaxy, you'll be able to tip the bellman, load up on souvenirs, and pay your hotel bill by converting dollars into the local currency based on the spot rates for certain metals. You'll also be able to tell any passing Andromedan roughly what he owes on that pirated copy of "Da Ya Think I'm Sexy?" that he's been rocking out to all morning. It could be as much as six pounds of platinum. Which will be unwelcome news, given that your average Andromedan earns maybe three ounces of platinum per month. He'll probably curse you a blue streak, just like Carly tends to when the subject of our fines comes up. But while the novelty value of watching a hot young nun swear like a sailor is immense, hearing that from an eight-ton cockroach covered in genitalia-like tendrils would be another matter. And creatures fitting this description are actually on the cuddly end of the spectrum in Andromeda.

it sounds like the only way out of this situation is to get a massive legislative change through the U.S. Congress somehow. Or to get a deal done with some key players in the music industry. So my first question is, do we really need to cut deals with . . . *each* of the major music labels?" The answer was probably yes, given that we had supposedly bankrupted the entire universe. But maybe Carly was exaggerating for effect when she told me that.

"No," she answered.

I immediately relaxed. *Thank God.* Dangle a bunch of cash out there, and you can often talk one, or even two of the major labels into doing an experimental licensing deal— particularly if they think they can somehow screw everyone else over by doing this.

"There's no way that the settlement can just be limited to each of the major music labels," Carly continued, to my horror. "It has to be with absolutely everyone in the music industry. Literally. Every music label, big and small. Every music publisher. Every performing rights society, licensing collective, singer/songwriter. In short, it has to be with absolutely every music rights–holder on your planet. In every single nation and territory on Earth. Except North Korea."

When you face something extraordinary that your entire history has prepared you to appreciate, time can all but stand still for you. They say this happened to Salieri when he first encountered Mozart's music. To Edwin Hubble when he realized that the universe was expanding. And it happened to me as I considered the vast, utter, and yawning impossibility of Carly's proposal:

The settlement has to be with absolutely everyone in the music industry. Literally.

My, but where to begin? The industry has tens, even hundreds of thousands of bickering, autonomous players. A few major labels, hundreds of midlevel players, and countless ankle-biters. It would be impossible to get that many people and entities to agree on *anything*, even if they were all levelheaded, smart, and decisive. And the captains of the music industry are none of the above. Levelheaded? They still think they can wish (or sue) the Internet away despite a decade and a half of overwhelming evidence to the contrary. Smart? They pay my firm millions a year to fight that doomed battle, when no number of lawsuits or Judiciary Committee perversions could really delay the arrival of The Future by one nanosecond.

And as for decisive, these people are clinically paralyzed by ignorance, arrogance, politics, bureaucracy, and, above all else, *fear*—fear of doing the wrong thing. And it's not fear of hurting themselves that has them hamstrung. No—what brings on the night sweats is their fear of doing something that might inadvertently *benefit* someone they hate. And this is a real risk, because the giant music execs seem to hate everyone their businesses touch. They hate each other, for one thing. And boy, do they hate the musicians (spoiled druggie narcissists!). They certainly hate the radio stations that basically advertise their music for free (too much power, the bastards!). And they loathe the online music industry (thieving geek bastards!). They hated the music retailers, back when they still existed (the bastards took too much margin!). They hate the Walmart folks, who account for most of what's left of physical CD sales (red state Nazi cheapskates!). They've always hated the concert industry (*we* should be getting that money!). And they all but despise the music-buying public (thieves! they're all a bunch of down-loading geek bastard thieving-ass thieves!).*

"What if we just get all of the major labels on board?" I asked desperately. "They represent about eighty percent of the market. What if we cut deals with them, and only pay the fines to the rest of the industry?" Scary as the majors were, I was even more worried about the hordes of people who

---

*And ironically, the music label brass reserve their harshest bile for any-one who manages to rescue them from looming oblivion. For instance, you could power a city on the hatred that any decent label exec feels toward MTV. This loathing began the moment MTV put the decrepit record business back in the forefront of youth culture in the eighties, ushering in an era of unprecedented prosperity. *Bastards!* the label guys still snarl if you ask them about this today. "They were makin' money *offa our stuff*!" A more recent case is Apple. Back in the late nine-ties, the labels sued many of the early online music pioneers out of ex-istence. Then, for years after that, they refused to let the survivors sell their catalogs. This amounted to embargoing their music from the le-gions of young folks who wanted it in a digital form, and insisting that these would-be customers either steal it, or do without it. Thus they managed to drive an entire generation of music lovers to discover and master the tools of digital piracy, and—surprise!—music sales collapsed. Eventually the major labels released limited chunks of their catalogs online. But they did this with so many restrictions, exceptions, asterisks, and raised middle fingers that the pirating hordes they had midwifed barely noticed. Then a miraculous lifeline appeared when Apple launched the dead-simple iPod music player, and then later connected it up to an online store. Suddenly, people were buying downloadable music in droves. For a decade after that, Apple was the main bright spot in the labels' business, growing when almost all other channels were shrinking, and gradually becoming the world's number one music re-tailer. And of course, this earned them gales of rage from the labels. *The cheapskate geek bastards!* they'll snarl if you catch them after a cou-ple of drinks on the right night. "They have too much power! They take too much margin! AND they're makin' money *offa our stuff*!"

held the rights to just one or two published songs. I shuddered at the thought of merely tracking all of those people down. Forget about cutting deals with every last one of them—it simply couldn't be done.

"You really don't have the faintest idea of how much money we're talking about, do you?" Carly asked.

I shook my head.

She turned to Frampton. "I think we need to spell it out for him."

He nodded, fired up his stereopticon, then reached into his pocket and pulled out a handful of Carter, Geller & Marks pens that he must have swiped from my desk. "These'll come in handy," he said, hanging on to one and setting the others down on a nearby table.

"The main issue," Carly said, "is that every Refined being in the universe is carrying around personal copies of about twenty-five million of your songs."

Frampton traced the number *25,000,000* in the air using the pen. The stereopticon tracked his movements, and beamed the digits into the space between us in his achingly gorgeous cursive.[*]

"Oh, come on," I said. "That's an insane number of songs." I have 25 *thousand* songs on my computer, and it's way more than I need.

"It's actually *all* of the songs," Carly said. "At least, it's all the songs with any faintly meaningful commercial distribution on Earth."

"But why do each of you need to have copies of every single one of them?"

---

[*]Penmanship being one of the many Noble Arts for which pretty much any nonhuman could win international awards on Earth.

"Let me answer that with a question: How many contacts do you store on your iPhone?"

"I don't know—thousands." Every name that has ever entered my Outlook software has made its way to my phone.

"And I'll bet you really only call a few of them. But it's trivially easy for you to store all that data, so why not? You never know when you might need a certain number. And who has time to organize them anyway? So you might as well keep all of them with you."

I nodded. That was my thinking precisely.

"It's the same way for us with music," Carly continued. "We can store all of your songs in a microscopic space. So why not always have our own copies of all of your music with us? That way, if we ever think about, hear about, or read about any particular song, we've already got it. Even if the local network blinks—or even if we're in a Wrinkle, and can't access a network. So everybody has a copy of every single song on them at all times. Then, as you know, the maximum fine is $150,000 per song." Frampton jotted this second number in the air. The stereopticon did the multiplication, and beamed out the number $3,750,000,000,000.00 in a perfect mimicry of his glorious handwriting.

"And that's uh . . . thirty-seven . . . ?" I was straining to parse all the zeros.

"Just under four trillion dollars *per being*," Carly said. This vastly exceeded America's all-time record budget deficit. "Which wipes out every individual in the universe. And as for the organizations, they typically copy backup data on behalf of the beings that work for them, or are affiliated with them. So they're wiped out, too. Your idea of paying off twenty percent of the liabilities to get rid of the tiny plaintiffs would require each and every Refined citizen to write a check for up to $750 billion. That's way over 10,000 tons of gold, and almost nobody has that kind of money. And then we'd still have to deal with the major labels, obviously. You see, the maximum debt is simply ruinous. And I don't think you really fathom its magnitude."

"Okay, fine. Then what *is* the maximum debt? Across everyone?"

"Well, with about four hundred billion galaxies in our bubble of the universe," Carly said, as Frampton scribbled madly, "and an average of about twenty-five Refined species per galaxy, and about eighty billion beings per species, we get to—that."

The number $3,000,000,000,000,000,000,000,000,000, 000,000,000 appeared at the bottom of all the calculations.

"$3,000,000,000,000,000,000,000,000,000,000,000,000." Frampton said solemnly. "Do you have any idea how much money that is?"

"How do you even *say* $3,000,000,000,000,000,000,000, 000,000,000,000?" I asked.

"Three trillion yottadollars," he answered. "And I know it's hard to even conceive of that much money. But if you can imagine that this pen represents a trillion yottadollars," Frampton held up the pen that he'd just been using. "Then three trillion yottadollars would look . . . like *this*." He grabbed two more pens from the table, and gestured grandly at the trio.

"And a yottadollar is . . . ?" I asked.

"One septillion dollars,"* Carly said. "That's the net

---

*Carly later explained that she derived the term *yottadollar* from the language of data storage, which is pretty expressive when it comes to big numbers. If you're over twenty-five, you may remember that we

worth of maybe twenty trillion Bill Gateses. And to repeat—
we're talking about that, times three *trillion.*"

"I guess the musicians of Earth are all . . . pretty rich
then."

"The *people* of Earth are all *sickeningly* rich," Carly corrected me. "You included."

"But I don't own any music rights."

"You don't have to. You just have to live in a country with
at least one remotely successful songwriter, or music label. If
you do, then a certain percentage of their gargantuan wealth
will go to your government, in taxes. That then becomes sov-
ereign wealth—which is jointly owned by each of a nation's
citizens. And the Refined League's citizens are listening to
music from every nation on Earth. Except North Korea. So
all non–North Korean humans are revoltingly rich."*

"But a hundred and fifty thousand dollars per track is

---

used to measure hard drives in megabytes—which are units of a million bytes. By the midnineties we started counting in gigabytes—or
billion-byte units. These days, most new hard drives are measured in
terabytes. Meanwhile, big boys like Google work mainly in petabytes—
the next thousand-X move up the food chain. To measure all of humanity's data, you have to go up at least another notch to exabytes (it's
said that everything ever uttered by every person in human history
could fit into a five-exabytes text file). And if that's not enough, a
thousand exabytes make up a zettabyte (a word I hadn't heard before
Carly introduced me to it, but Wikipedia tells me it's real). Finally,
there are a thousand zettabytes in a yottabyte—not that any human
has ever seen one. And just as a yottabyte is one septillion bytes, a yottadollar is one septillion dollars.

*To give you a sense of how much money is involved here, consider
Greenland, which has the planet's second-least popular music catalog.
Exactly one of their songs made it to the Refined League (by way of a
world music album that sold briefly in a few Starbucks stores, and

just the maximum fine," I said, frantically. "Jammie Thomas herself was never fined much more than half of that."*

Frampton crossed out the three and the first zero from his grand total, and replaced them with a "15" followed by thirty-six zeros. This number was still a bit on the large side. But then I thought of something that should help a whole lot more. "And wait a second—since you guys didn't actually *know* that you were infringing, I think there's a provision in the law that could knock the fine *way* down . . . to something tiny, like two hundred dollars a song!"

"Gee, that would add up to a mere five billion dollars per being," Carly said, "which would only bankrupt most people a few thousand times over."

"Oh . . . right," I said.

"And besides, we'd need to have '*no reason to believe*' that we were infringing in order to benefit from the loophole you're talking about," Carly added, quoting directly from the law in question. "And we've had access to every law on your books since you first started posting them to your Internet—which surely qualifies as 'having a reason to be-

---

ended up on Napster). The cut that each Greenlander is hypothetically due from that one song vastly exceeds the Earth's entire GDP.

*Ms. Thomas is a legendary figure in my line of work—akin, say, to the first enemy soldier captured during a world war. The first file swapper to actually go to trial, she was sued for sharing an odd mix of twenty-four songs (ranging from Vanessa Williams's unspeakably schmaltzy "Save the Best for Last" to Def Leppard's porn-tastic metal anthem "Pour Some Sugar on Me"). After the first jury found against her (in all of five minutes), her fine was amended so many times via appeals, judicial motions, and a retrial that I've lost track of what she's owed over the years—but it's been as low as a couple thousand dollars per track, and as high as $80,000 each.

lieve' that we were infringing. So I'm afraid we can't fix the ridiculous cosmic mess that your demented laws have created quite that easily."

That did it. "That *our laws* created? I've got news for you, Carly. We created *our* laws for *us*. We never asked *you* or anybody else to follow them. *You're* the ones with the deranged honor code that says it's better to exterminate a species than to violate the letter of one of its idiotic laws!"

"*Nothing* in our code says *any*thing about exterminating *any* species," Carly snarled. "Particularly not humanity—which the Refined League adores, respects, and reveres in ways that human minds are too puny, backward, and pathetically underpowered to comprehend!"

"Well, if we're so revered and backward, why didn't you try looking out for us a bit? By—oh, I don't know, maybe glancing at our legal code before making jizillions of yotta-copies of our music? And by the way, the Copyright Damages Improvement Act was written decades *after* you set up shop in Manhattan. If just one of you had stopped having songasms long enough to look it over, we never would have gotten into this mess!"

"But we had waited for *most of the universe's history* to discover your music. Compared to that, the time since the Kotter Moment has been the batting of an eyelash! We were just indulging in a fleeting appreciation of your ingenious art before exposing ourselves to the rest of your barbaric society!"

"And you couldn't even have a *cheap intern* glance over our legal code?"

"It's not that easy, Nick. Interns are unionized in our society, and—"

The entire apartment suddenly vibrated gently, kind of

like a cellphone receiving a text message (a really huge cell-phone that you and two other people are standing inside of).

"The omnicab's here," Frampton announced, clearly re-lieved to change the subject. He walked over to a door just to the left of the giant window looking onto the city, popped it open and—stepped right out of the building. Carly fol-lowed him. And there they stood, suspended in midair, im-patiently waving for me to join them. I tiptoed to the edge of the abyss. Using both arms to brace myself firmly on the inner doorjamb, I peered down. There was . . . nothing. Just miles of empty space between us and the ground.

Carly heaved a sigh, and somehow walked across the air toward me and slid an arm around my waist. Then in one fluid motion, she tipped me backward, spun me ninety de-grees, and popped me right through the doorway toward her. This happened so fast that I didn't even move my arms from their raised, bracing position until I was already beside her on the far side.

My pores instantly doused me with ice-cold sweat as adrenaline flooded my system. And—nothing happened. It took my body several seconds to accept that it wasn't falling. "How are we . . . doing this?" I finally managed to half gasp.

"Doing what?" Carly asked, as if we were just sitting around the kitchen table on a sunny afternoon.

"Floating, in . . . midair," I managed.

"Nick, we're standing on solid concrete!"

But as she said this, Frampton suddenly fixed us both with a look of bug-eyed horror. He caught Carly's eye and slowly shook his head, pointing downward. They both looked at their feet. And then—just as Wile E. Coyote stops defying gravity the moment he realizes there's no ground beneath him—we started to drop.

TEN

FREE FALLING

We all screamed. A yawning, plunging void replaced my guts, and the bucket brigade cranked it up in my pores again. After what seemed like eons of shrieking chaos, a tiny, isolated sector of my brain noticed that I wasn't feeling, or even hearing, a trace of wind. Instead, there was just a voice saying something about . . . living in Reseda? I stopped screaming and saw that Carly and Frampton were doing a sort of zero-gravity boogie to the song "Free Fallin'" by Tom Petty, while mouthing its lyrics with these daft, blissed-out looks on their faces.

Right about then a sense of solidity returned to the soles of my feet. It increased until I was standing firmly on an invisible, but perfectly solid, floor as our descent slowed. At this, the soundtrack switched to "It's a Miracle" by Barry Manilow. The pressure on my feet kept growing as the song built, until we had not only stopped falling, but had begun to hurtle across the landscape, chasing the setting sun. Soon we were traveling many times faster than any jet I've ever been on. Looking carefully, I could faintly make out the outlines of an ovular pod around us. It was maybe twenty feet long, and all of its features were invisible. As we picked up speed, the music transitioned to "All Right Now" by Free.

I wanted to ask Carly and Frampton about what we were riding (and to curse them out for that evil Wile E. Coyote prank). But nothing could reach them in their wigged-out musical state. This was the first time I'd seen it for more than a few moments, and it wasn't pretty. Their faces were twisted into Manson-like grins. Their eyes were unfocused and adrift. And the worst part was this shuffling stomp that they were doing. An anthropologist would probably get all politically correct, and call it "dancing." But it lacked any kind of rhythm or connection to the music, and looked like the gait of an undead duo stumbling back to the crypt after slurping down some cerebellum stew.

Since they were clearly useless, I turned my attention to the landscape zipping below us. It was undulating in a regular, but dramatic pattern. First, we'd soar over a long, jagged series of towering peaks. These had to be stupidly tall, since we'd barely clear their summits, despite flying high enough to plainly see the planet's curvature. We'd then cross over the rim of an immense, half-bowl-shaped valley. The ground would then drop away steadily for miles as we flew over the bowl part, until a towering wall of cliffs topped with more airless peaks reared straight up to cap off the valley's far end. Beyond that, there'd be a short stretch of peaks before the ground sloped into another, almost identical half-bowl valley. The valleys seemed to be empty, apart from some scaffoldlike structures that I could barely pick out at the lowest part of each valley floor, right up against the cliff line.

"All Right Now" faded to silence after a single chorus, and Carly and Frampton started calming down. Meanwhile, a vast, black pit appeared on the horizon. As we approached it, we started buckling under a strong wave of apparent gravity as the pod decelerated. Carly managed to rasp out "Don't worry," just as we slowed to a stop above the darkened maw.

"Why not?" I asked, amazed that my voice still functioned after all that screaming.

She pointed at the pit. "It's bottomless." And with that, we started to drop.

Since the last few minutes had given me boundless faith in our omnicab (while essentially shocking the fear of heights right out of me), I watched with more fascination than dread as we plunged toward the abyss. The pit's mouth was about a mile wide, and many other vehicles were hurtling toward it as well. As we approached the rim, I saw that its walls were smooth and machined, rather than jagged and natural. That was all I had time to make out, because everything went dark the moment we crossed the threshold. It was perfectly silent in there, and we were completely weightless. I instinctively looked up at our only light source, which was the rapidly contracting circle of light way up at the pit's mouth. This shrank to a point, then vanished. Now it was utterly dark.

"So, uh—where'd you say we were off to?" I asked after a few seconds of complete sensory deprivation.

"The far side of the planet," Carly said. "This hole goes clear through. A perfect vacuum is maintained within it, so we'll be in a state of constant acceleration and weightlessness until we reach the planet's center. Then gravity will start slowing us down, until we pop out on the far side at the same speed we entered at."

"But that's completely gratuitous," I said, feeling a fresh wave of panic at the very thought of this preposterous route. Why couldn't people with this kind of technology get around without being so *gimmicky* about it?

Suddenly the interior of our pod was bathed in a faint violet light. Frampton was floating a few feet away from me, already dead asleep. Carly was just beyond him, illuminating everything with her stereopticon. "Does that help?" she asked.

"Yes—a lot." It actually made the plummeting pod feel almost womblike. I stretched out cautiously, and discovered how relaxing weightlessness can be. "So," 1 continued, catching my breath. "How long 'til we . . . pop out?"

"A bit over forty minutes. Then it'll be another five minutes to the performance canyon."

"To the what?"

"Performance canyon. We flew over several of them between Paradise City and the mouth of the tunnel. The planet's covered with them."

"Wait. So those valleys are like . . . stadiums?"

"Stadia. Yes. Planets like this one exist so that people like us can do our shows."

"Your . . . ?"

"Shows. Frampton and I are performers."

"But I thought you were *spies*."

"What a stupid notion. Why?"

"Because of that . . . program of yours. The one that digs up all the secrets?"

"Mmm—more on that in a bit."

"So what kind of shows do you guys do?"

"Lip sync, duh."

And so I learned about Carly and Frampton's day jobs. Of the trillions of Refined species in the universe, theirs resembles humans most closely. They're called Perfuffinites, after the wimpy-ass name of their home planet. Most music lovers crave live experiences—and by looking so human, the Perfuffinites give Refined beings the closest thing they can get to rockin' out at a hot gig on Earth.

Of course, they can't sing for shit, and they're even worse if they get their hands on a musical instrument. But they just have to get up there and mime it to a famous recording, and the crowds go nuts (catch a Britney Spears show to see something similar here at home). Perfuffinites perform throughout the universe. But their top elites play on one of about a dozen artificial planets like Zinkiwu that are purpose-built to host as many gigantic concerts as possible. So Zinkiwu is like Branson, Missouri, on a boundless scale. And the Perfuffinites are an entire race of Milli Vanillis—except the fans know they're faking it, and love them anyway.

"So, then," I said when Carly finished telling me all of this. "I guess you guys are out to save humanity for economic reasons, huh?" The destruction of the planet that cranks out the hits couldn't be good for the Perfuffinite business model.

"Not at all," Frampton said in a sleepy voice, having woken up toward the end of our chat. "We already have enough material to last until the stars burn out. For instance, Carly hasn't added a new song to her show in three years, and she's sold out for decades."

Carly nodded. "Remember what I told you about the

Oak Ridge Boys? There's already enough human music out there to last everybody forever. That's an objective fact. But we Perfuffinites can't think about these things pragmatically. We're a race of Artists, after all."*

"We're also your cousins," Frampton added. "We'd do anything for you."

I nodded politely. That was probably all there was to it, for Frampton. But Carly seemed to have deeper motivations. And based on the squabble they'd had about taking our troubles to Daddy, I figured it had to do with him. "We sure do look a lot alike," I said neutrally.

"It's not just looks," Carly said. "We're almost identical to you on a genetic level."

"Apart from having eight toes on each foot, double-jointed shoulders, and no tonsils," Frampton clarified.

"But there must be something special about the two of you, compared to other Perfuffinites," I said. "Because there's only a handful of these giant concert planets, right?"

Carly nodded. "Normal Perfuffinites have to schlep it from star to star, doing shows for twenty or thirty million

---

*Actually, I later learned that they're more like a race of busboys. Although they showed some early promise after joining the Refined League two billion years back, the Perfuffinites eventually settled for being a migrant labor force scattered across a half-dozen backwater galaxies. They tended toward simple, dirty jobs that were too boring or undignified for more eminent races. Then the fallout from the Kotter Moment hit them with the most implausible windfall since the Big Bang. This was nothing but the dumbest of luck, as most Perfuffinites will bashfully acknowledge. But a few of them confuse their outrageous fortune with Destiny, and write interminable ballads pushing this idea. They drive their audiences crazy whenever they insist on weaving these songs in with their lip sync shows, because the premise is so arrogant, and of course nobody wants to hear their crap music.

beings who'd barely even cross a galaxy to see them." She said this in a tone that Sting might use to describe someone who'd gladly sing for two peasants and a pig in a Mongolian yurt.

"So why are you guys different?"

"Because we're physically almost indistinguishable from two massively beloved human celebrities." Frampton asserted this shyly and quietly, but with enormous pride.

I smiled and nodded cluelessly.

"Massive," he repeated, a bit less confidently.

I kept smiling and nodding like a Burmese bellhop hoping for a hard-currency tip. The silence grew awkward.

"Really, *really* massive . . . Right?" This with a growing edge of desperation.

Carly was now glaring at me expectantly.

"Oh—oh, of course," I nattered. "Massive. Really, really massive! But I'm . . . so awful with names. Could you just remind me? Which ones? Which—celebrities? You . . . look like?"

Frampton took on a morbidly dejected air. He tried to respond, but nothing came out.

"I tried to warn you," Carly said, putting a sisterly hand on his shoulder.

He made another failed attempt to speak.

"And why does it matter who's famous on Earth anyway?" she continued. "To the rest of the universe, to the entire universe, *you're* a giant star. And through you . . . *so is he.*"

Frampton gave me an accusing look, then blurted out something that sounded like "HUGNLL."

I couldn't tell if this was a garbled word or a gagging sob. "There there," I said, going with the latter.

"H-H-...HUGNLL!"

"There there."

Frampton collected himself, then finally managed "Mmmmick."

"There there."

Now he caught his breath, gathered himself, then slowly enunciated, "Mick. Hucknall."

I turned to Carly for help.

She mouthed something silently, but I don't read lips.

"Mick Hucknall," Frampton said, almost steadily. "M-I-C-K. *Huck*nall."

I went back to smiling and nodding, but was obviously hearing this name for the first time.

"I'll bet our mothers couldn't tell us apart," Frampton cried, suddenly almost delirious. "Our *mothers*!"

Carly faded back a few feet and jabbed at her stereopticon, which was back around her neck in its crucifix form. The words "'Holding Back the Years,' dumbshit," beamed out just behind her brother's head, where he couldn't see them. This rang a faint bell, but I was still lost.

"Our grandmothers," Frampton was railing. "Our *sisters*! Our third, fourth, and ninth cousins! Nobody! *No* one! Nobody could tell us apart—I'm *sure of it*." He drifted across the pod, turned his back to us, and started hyperventilating.

Since he seemed to be safely delirious, Carly chanced an explanation. "Lead singer from Simply Red," she whispered in a barely audible voice. "One-hit wonders from the eighties."

Frampton snapped his head around like a hungry cobra hearing a dinner bell. He glared, and defiantly thrust a peace sign into her face. "Two," he whispered. Carly gave me a withering look and stuffed her fingers into her ears, an

instant before he shrieked *"TWO! TWO-HIT WONDERS!"*
Then, in a soft, broken voice, "Five hits in New Zealand . . ."

"But Fram," Carly cooed. "You *know* New Zealand
doesn't count. It's like Canada. But to *Australia.*" They'd
clearly been over this point many times.

"So . . . who do you look like?" I asked Carly, as her
brother slunk off to get back to his hyperventilating.

"I don't suppose you remember Chrissy Amphlett.
Huge for eleven weeks in 1991. I'm basically her at twenty.
Only thinner, and with blue eyes. And a much nicer ass, I'm
told."

"Two," Frampton was murmuring on the far side of the
pod. "Two hits. *Mini*mum!"

"You're twenty years old?" I asked.

Carly shook her head. "My body is biologically twenty,
thanks to Refined medical technology. But I've been
around . . . a bit longer than that."

We all fell silent, and soon Frampton was snoring. I shut
my eyes, figuring that I'd either fall asleep, or find out what
weightless meditation was like. I took a deep breath. For
some reason this felt incredibly good, so I took another. I
was inhaling for the fourth or fifth time when it hit me. *My
cold was gone.* It had been dogging me for weeks. But now
there wasn't a trace of it. In fact, I felt healthier and more
energized than I had in ages.

I caught Carly's eye, then drifted over and mentioned
this to her.

"I thought that might happen," she said. "Since you're
so close to the Perfuffinite genome, the planet's Health
Vigilance system probably gave you an ambient wetware upgrade."

"You know, I figured it was something like that. Only . . ."

"You have no idea what I just said."

"Exactly."

Carly explained that just like humans, the Refined species are in a constant arms race with the diseases that prey on them. Only while our cures and treatments are like clubs and slingshots, Refined doctors are packing the medical equivalents of kinetic lepton implosion rays.* Their arsenal includes surveillance systems that constantly monitor the disease base of every Refined planet. When new threats emerge, they develop countermeasures in the form of small changes that can be written right into the genetic code of the local Refined species. Nano delivery systems can distribute these changes throughout an Earth-sized planet in just hours. Once an upgrade enters the body, tiny molecular robots replicate trillions of times, and bring the new instructions into the nucleus of each and every cell, where the changes are entered into the DNA.†

"Once they're done, it's like every part of your body is suddenly operating from a new script," Carly said. "Even certain physical, structural changes can take place in your body, as trillions of cells shift around to take up new positions."

"Wow. So then . . . where did my cold go?"

"The planet's Health Vigilance system probably identi-

---

*I have no idea what these are, but I totally want one.

†And yes, strange as it may sound, DNA-like molecular structures are wildly abundant throughout the universe—because it turns out that the ickily-named "panspermia hypothesis" is largely accurate. This posits that the core building blocks of life spread throughout the cosmos by piggybacking on asteroids and comets. Add a high propensity for proto-life-bearing rocks to find their way into Wrinkles (a complex phenomenon that I don't pretend to understand), and you have a formula for incredibly widespread, distantly related life-forms.

fied you as a Perfuffinite, checked your DNA, found a bizarrely broken version of the species genome, and updated it. If I'm right, your cold is gone because you're now genetically immune to it—thanks to a long-ago update to the Perfuffinite genome that you now have."

"So you think your doctors came up with a cure for this year's *North American cold virus* back in the day?"

"Actually, I'm sure they came up with cures for all cold viruses back in the day. Along with all flus, infections, cancers, and autoimmune disorders. In fact, I doubt if there's a remotely common disease that you're vulnerable to now."

"Seriously? That's . . . an incredibly valuable gift." I'd definitely downgrade to a cheap HMO the next time we signed up for insurance plans. *And that was just the start . . .*

"Well, let me verify this before you get too excited." Carly pulled up her stereopticon and peered at me through it. "I have an app in here that detects genetic version numbers. And you are . . . up to date with the current Perfuffinite genome. But don't take my word for it. See if you can do this." She arched her shoulders back far enough to give a yoga master the creeps.

I tried the same impossible move, and . . . found that it was easy. "What happened?" I asked, thoroughly freaked out.

"Frampton told you that Perfuffinites are double-jointed in the shoulders. So the system identified your lack of double-jointedness as a genetic flaw, and . . . repaired it."

"Christ, that's eerie," I said, arching my shoulders again.

"Oh, I wouldn't give it much thought. It would change your life if you were a pitcher. But otherwise, it's just an oddity that I'm sure you'll forget about."

"You know, you're right," I said, feeling a bit better. "And it's not like it's a visible change that other people can see."

"Yeah, well—about that."

"What."

"I'm sure the system also . . . fixed the mutation that was depriving you of your six missing toes."

"My *what?*" I ripped off my shoes and socks, and saw that she was right. I now had eight digits at the tip of each foot. They were all proportionately smaller, so my shoes fit fine. But anyone spotting these . . . *tines* would run screaming. Now, if I ever actually won Manda's heart, I'd need an excuse to keep my socks on. For like sixty years.

All of this seemed to put Carly into a giggling fit, which struck me as awfully insensitive. I was about to chew her out when I realized she was gazing at me through her stereopticon again, and laughing at something that she saw in it.

"What's so funny?" I asked.

"Just a junk joke," she snickered.

"What's a junk joke?"

"Well, every time the bioengineers push out a genetic update, they write a bunch of jokes into the junk DNA. Then the rest of us can read them whenever we scan someone's genome."

"Wait—*junk* DNA?"

"Yes. Your body only pays attention to about two percent of your genome. The rest of the DNA's just along for the ride, which is why it's called junk. But every base pair can carry two bits of information. That adds up to over a half gigabyte of space for jokes, rumors, graffiti—that sort of thing."

"I don't think I like that."

"Well, get used to it. Millions of junk jokes are now written into your cells. Mine, too, and Frampton's, along with every other Perfuffinite. But don't worry—it doesn't affect your health one bit." She turned to her brother. "Hey, you're gonna love this new one."

"Oh, let's hear it!"

"Why did the Octarian Weevil upload its ganglions to both instantiations of the OverNet, instead of just one?"

"I don't know, why?"

"Because it wanted to have . . . *second thoughts!*"

This turned out to be even funnier than my fondness for the Paradise City skyline.

"Can you *please* delete that?" I asked after what seemed like ages of cackling.

"Sure . . . sure," Carly said, still giggling. "Junk DNA can be personalized. I'll log a request with Health Vigilance." She started manipulating her stereopticon furiously. "There. Within an hour, all the jokes in your cells will be wiped out. And instead, we'll upload . . . this!" The chorus of "Never Gonna Give You Up" filled the omnicab. She paused it before she or her brother could slide into that musical delirium of theirs—although by now, the two of them were laughing so hard they could hardly get any giddier.

"You're putting a *song* into my genome?"

"Sure, there's a half gigabyte in there," Carly tittered. "That's enough room for entire albums. How 'bout some . . . *Simply Red?*"

That put Frampton into hysterics.

"That's a really respectful use of the Code of Life," I grumbled to no one in particular. I not only had sixteen toes to live with, but was now lugging trillions of Rickrolls around in my cells. As Carly and Frampton cackled madly, I went back to my deep breathing. Within seconds, I was sound asleep.

ELEVEN
BŌNŌ

I woke up flat on my back in normal gravity. Stretching and blinking, I saw Carly and Frampton doing the same on either side of me, and noticed that the omnicab had popped out of the pit. Darkened mountaintops were now zipping beneath us, as a brilliant night sky spangled above. Moments later we crossed a ridge line, and the floor of a mammoth performance canyon plunged below us. It was an awesome sight. There had to be tens of millions of beings down there, gathered before a stage that was many times larger than a football field, and so brightly lit that it could surely be seen from space. It was surrounded by acres of video screens, and packed with amplifier stacks the size of office towers.

Carly pointed at a live feed of an energetic singer on the main video screen above the stage. "That's Dad."

He looked like a fifty-something Sonny Bono, only with

the shaggy hair, drooping mustache, and groovy threads of the young Sonny of the seventies. As he mouthed lyrics and sashayed across the stage, he made melodramatic crooning gestures that were so exaggerated I thought he might dislocate his neck. After a few seconds, the live feed toggled to a canned scene of Dad running while a sexy blonde chased him in a red Mustang. The background shifted from freeway, to desert, to lunar wasteland as he repeatedly looked back at his hot pursuer in mock terror. Then the scene cut back to a few more seconds of Dad on stage—and then to a slutty Pocahontas stalking our hero through a forest, bow taut and arrow drawn. Then to a bit more live Dad; then to a mob of ecstatic, sobbing teenyboppers; and then finally to a leggy redhead in a trench coat and a fedora chasing Dad through an Egyptian temple at night.

"I'm kind of dying to hear the audio," I admitted.

"Only for a moment," Frampton said. "Me and Carly can't afford to freak out right now." He made a flicking gesture, and the music streamed in briefly. Dad was faking it to "It's Not Unusual" by Tom Jones. *Perfect.*

"So your dad can stop the secret about the Townshend Line from spreading any further?"

"I suppose he can if he wants to," Carly said cagily.

"Great. But how?"

"Dad's a very influential journalist," Frampton gushed.

I thought journalists were more in the business of spilling secrets than containing them. But I knew better than to press when Carly had made up her mind to be evasive. "I see," I said. "And can he help us with the Guild, given that they already know the situation?"

"Maybe," Carly said. "And no matter what, he should have insights into how they found out. Which could help us figure out how to get them to back down. Anyway, the show's ending, and we need to get backstage."

We dropped violently and leveled off about twenty feet above the ground, where we drifted above a towering rank of creatures who looked like praying mantises in executioners' hoods. They held tiny flames in their appendages and waved them in humble supplication for an encore, as their fangs dripped acid that made the ground sizzle and burn. We slid forward, passing over acres of vile antlike creatures the size of boxcars. Next were some glowing red cubes whose surfaces were covered with alien text that changed at blinding speeds. Then there were these puppylike critters who danced on their hind legs and backflipped with joy (they were outlandishly cute, but like everyone else down there, they had zero sense of rhythm). Overhead, the sky was dense with soaring raptors that made Mothra look like Tweety Bird.

Soon we were closing in on the stage, and I could plainly see the great man himself, preening for the folks in the fancy seats. There were at least fifteen guitarists up there, positioned every few dozen yards to give everyone toward the front someone to look at. They windmilled their arms over phony Stratocasters without a trace of synchronization among them. Meanwhile, the dozen-ish drummers made valiant but doomed efforts to fake a beat.* Inept as they all were, it was charming to see everyone trying so hard to mimic our forms. And this turns out to be the whole point of

---

*It turns out that only the singers are actual Perfuffinites in Zinkiwu performances. The bands consist of several near-miss species that can pass for humans from a distance but not close-up. Everyone on stage wears sound-blocking gear, which is hidden beneath a hat or an outsized hairstyle.

Zinkiwu—authenticity. No matter how primitive the technology, how awful the design, or how revolting the cuisine (for those who can digest it), if they have it at Lollapalooza, they ape it on Zinkiwu. Thus the set's patently un-Refined design, and the atrociously Earthly clothes that everyone was wearing onstage.* The audience members were also in on the game, doing their best to scream like humans, clap their appendages, and sing along.

As Dad flounced off the stage and the crowd went wild, our omnicab zipped through a gap in the wall of lights, amplifiers, and video screens. Right behind the stage was a small warehouse-like building with an opening in its roof that we dropped through. It was empty inside, apart from a spread of sofas, easy chairs, and lamps that looked to be straight out of Pottery Barn.

"Welcome to the backstage lounge," Carly said as we landed next to it.

"It looks very . . . Earth-like." As I said this, Frampton walked right up to a sofa and flopped onto it. Given that he didn't smash his nose on an invisible wall, I figured that our pod must have soundlessly unfurled a cargo door.

Carly nodded. "People like to see Earth-like furniture in our shows, because it helps them imagine that we're always acting human."

"So you use this stuff as props onstage?"

"No, this is where we shoot backstage scenes for our broadcast show. It's the most popular reality program in the universe."

---

*This is really taking authenticity seriously, given how our fashion sense revolts the Refined. It would be like pumping sewage odors into a movie theater to heighten the realism of a film set in a Calcutta slum.

"Wait—the Refined League does *reality* shows?"

Carly gave an embarrassed nod.

"But I thought you were all highbrow. Theater and sculpture, and découpage, right? Are you telling me reality programming is one of your—what do you call them? Noble Arts?"

"No, it's a Vulgar Art, clearly," Carly sniffed.

"We discovered it when *The Osbournes* came out," Frampton said.

"And the entire universe found the very concept to be perfectly revolting," Carly added righteously. "But quintillions of metal fans held their noses and watched."

"And then—let me guess," I guessed. "They decided they liked it."

"No. *Loved* it," Frampton said.

I nodded. "So now you have your own show. What's it called?"

"Sonny & His Sirelings," Frampton said proudly.

"It's named after Dad," Carly explained. "And it's about our immediate family, which is about as famous as it gets. Dad's been famous since the Kotter Moment, because Sonny Bono was already a celebrity back then, and Dad's obviously a dead ringer for him. Several years went by, and then a couple of singers emerged who looked a lot like me and Frampton.* And this suddenly turned us into a family with three human celebrity look-alikes."

---

*But unlike their father, Carly and Frampton never adopted the names of their human doppelgängers. The reason was that they were already established as performers before Simply Red and the Divinyls (Chrissy Amphlett's band) swept the universe—because like every other Perfuffinite, they had taken on the names of random human pop stars, and launched lip sync careers shortly after the Kotter Mo-

"The only one in the universe," Frampton said.

"So when they decided to do an *Osbournes* knockoff, we were the obvious stars," Carly added. "Anyway, I'm not exactly proud of *Sonny & His Sirelings*. But we learned about the Townshend Line situation through our work with it, so it could just save humanity."

"Wait—*this* is the program you guys work for?" I asked.

"Well, duh."

"But I thought it was a government program. Espionage, or something?"

"That was your own odd conclusion," Carly reminded me. "I just referred to it as a *program*."

"Well, gee, thanks for not letting me get confused about things."

She shot me an icy look. "No problem."

I felt like chewing her out, but decided against it. The brief, giggly mood of our trip through the planet's core was long gone, and Carly was back to her crabby, sarcastic self. *What's with her?* I wondered. She was gorgeous and smart—and apparently spectacularly rich and intergalactically famous. So why was she always such a . . . brat? "So now that I know more about your program," I said carefully, "could you please tell how it helped you discover the truth about the Townshend Line?"

Carly shrugged awkwardly. "Sure. Our show has a research staff that rivals the major intelligence services in terms of

_____

ment. Incidentally, since all of the Perfuffinites rebranded themselves at once, the celebrity names of the *Kotter* era still dominate their society. Manilow is almost as common among Perfuffinite men as Mohammad is among Muslims—followed by KC, Cat, Donny, Orlando, Mangione, Mercury, Frampton, Sly, and Boz. Meanwhile, Dolly, Carly, and Agnetha top the charts among Perfuffinite women.

resources. They've cracked into every email server and phone exchange on Earth, and they're always making huge discoveries. We found out about Schwarzenegger's love child five years before humanity did. About Lohan's arrest as it was happening. And we have stuff on Ryan Seacrest that would shock even a Fark reader. Anyway—I don't know how, because nobody ever tells me *anything*—but somehow, our team got the facts about the Townshend Line out of the Guardian Council."

"Even though it's the best-kept secret in the *universe*?"

She nodded. "They're that good." She didn't sound remotely proud of this.

"But it won't be a secret for long, because the truth's about to get out, right?" I asked.

Another nod.

"How so?"

"We're uh . . . going to tell them."

"We? As in . . ."

"Our program," Carly finally confessed. "The whole purpose of our research team is to dig up juicy facts about humanity and human celebrities for our writers to weave into our story line. And nothing makes Dad happier than getting a huge scoop."

"Remember, he's a very influential journalist," Frampton burbled.

Carly rolled her eyes. "Please. Before the Kotter Moment, he used to serve snacks to a small-time editor in a backwater globular cluster, and he never got over it. He's about as much of a journalist as a—"

"*Whoa*," I said. "Wait! Let's not change the subject here. You're telling me that the entire universe is about to find out about humanity's complete defenselessness because of *your* reality show?"

"Our bad," Frampton confessed, holding his hands above his shoulders like a surrendering soldier.

"But it wasn't our idea!" Carly blurted. "They just handed us these scripts a couple days ago, and had us perform these horrified reactions to learning the truth about the Townshend Line. That was honestly the first that Frampton and I heard about *any* of this! And even when we were acting out the scene, I figured they were just going to use it for a dream sequence."

"Wait—you have dream sequences in your *reality* shows?" I'd heard that scripts and writers were routinely used in producing that crap. But dream sequences should strain the gullibility of even reality show fans. I mean, right?

Carly shrugged and nodded.

I didn't know what to say. After all the high-handedness that I'd put up with because she was trying to save my species, it turned out that her own boneheaded family business was directly imperiling us! Offended and infuriated, I felt a sudden urge to call her an arrogant, duplicitous dolt.

"You arrogant, duplicitous dolt," I said.

Carly looked like she was about to cry. "You . . . you're right. I am arrogant. And I'm a dolt. And I didn't used to be either! I swear, I used to be really, really *humble*. So humble. And smart! And then this . . . *fame* thing happened to me. All this wealth and fame was thrust on me, and I became a tool to these managers, producers, and agents! And this show is the worst part of it. Before it came out, we at least had our privacy when we weren't onstage. But now we're *always* onstage! And we're just tools to these—these *scriptwriters*. It's like no word that comes out of my mouth is really my own!"

Deeply touched that Carly could let herself be this vulnerable with me, I was overwhelmed by affection and pity. I was about to reach out to hug her, when a voice erupted right behind me. "Aaaaaaaaaaand *SCENE!*"

I turned around and saw a truly terrifying creature. I can handle orange pus-oozing lizards with stalk-mounted eyes, like Mllsh-mllsh. I can handle acid-drooling praying mantises. And I can handle junkies, muggers, meter maids, and any other human flotsam. But this . . . *thing* was an almost-human. And something about that was viscerally horrifying. He was about my height and size, had a full head of blond hair, and looked to be about thirty. Only instead of eyes he had—whites. No pupils, no irises. Just the whites of the eyes. He also had perfectly smooth flesh where his mouth should have been, and a vertically oriented mouth embedded in his right cheek.

Other than that, he was your basic dude in Dockers. He was holding a perfectly normal finger up to his perfectly normal left ear, and seemed to be listening to some small device. After a few moments, he bellowed again. "Ya know, gosh darn the luck, Carly, but it sounds like there was a teeeeeny little audio boo-boo right toward the end. Could you take it from . . . I dunno, maybe from 'now we're always onstage'?"

Carly sighed irritably, composed herself, then took on a forlorn air and said, "But now we're *always* onstage! And we're just tools to these—these *scriptwriters*. It's like no word that comes out of my mouth is really my own!"

"Thaaaaat's perfect," Sidemouth said. "Great work, Carly. Okay, all of you—take five."

I looked around, and saw that we were suddenly surrounded by a dozen other near-human freaks. They were toting around lights and microphones, fussing over a table full of snacks, and manhandling three gigantic TV cameras that slid around soundlessly on these squat, rolling platforms. All of them could pass for human from a middling distance (including Sidemouth, if you saw him from the right angle). But a second look showed that this one's feet were oriented backward. Or that one had three elbows, which gave him a series of . . . *links* for arms. Or that one had four nostrils on an upturned nose.

Before I could process any of this, I heard a commotion coming from behind one of the false walls. Moments later, Sonny himself zipped around it, surrounded by three near-human lackeys. One was carrying a tiny platter of caviar, another held out a dish filled with blue M&M's, while the third bore a black ashtray that held a smoldering stogie. They maneuvered with ingenious dexterity, always keeping their little offerings within reach of Sonny's hallowed hands as he strode forward. The production crew meanwhile surged into action. Within moments they had a boom mike hovering over our little group, with lights and cameras positioned to capture our every movement and expression.

Sonny strode up to his son.

"Frampton, Frampton, Frampton," he scolded, waving a finger foppishly. "I left you in charge of your baby sister for half a day. And now Asteroid Command tells me you spent the entire time zooming around . . . in *outer space!*"

Frampton leapt to his feet. "You'll never guess where we went, Father."

Sonny grimaced and waved a hand in front of his nose. "To the monkey house, by the smell of it," he said. Gales of laughter came from every direction at once. It sounded like a besotted audience of hundreds of people. At this, Carly buried her face in an open palm and started shaking her head. A camera zoomed in for a close-up of this.

"No jive, Dad—try to guess where we went!" Frampton was hopping from one foot to the other.

Sonny suddenly took on a stern air. "I hope you weren't running around with those Peterson boys again." He grabbed the cigar from his lackey's ashtray and gave a concerned puff.

Carly looked up. "Dad, we need to stop production and clear the set for a minute," she said flatly.

Sonny gave one of the cameras a puzzled look. "These kids have the *strangest* expressions these days." His lips weren't moving, but his voice was booming in from somewhere overhead. "Just last week she said some boy was taking her to the 'submarine races.'" He shrugged, and gave the camera a look of zany confusion, to adoring laughter.

Now he stroked his chin and gazed at the ceiling. "But, hmm—I don't want to look like a *square* to my kids," his disembodied voice mused. "So I'll just pretend that I know what she's talking about, and figure it all out later." He smiled, nodded smugly, and winked at the camera.

Carly leapt to her feet. "Dad, we honestly need to cut the slapstick crap for like five minutes."

"*Oooooooo,*" the invisible audience goaded.

Carly waved her hands like a ref declaring an incomplete pass. "No, I'm dead serious. Cut. Stop. Shut down the set. We seriously need to talk in private."

Sonny gave her a pensive look. "Something's . . . really wrong, isn't it?"

Carly sighed. "Yes. I have an omnicab here—it can give us some privacy." With that, the outlines of our pod appeared, glowing faintly with a violet light. After we had exited it and walked over to the set, it had apparently parked itself about thirty feet away.

Sonny turned to Sidemouth. "Okay, shut it down for a few minutes. And put the writing team on standby. It looks like we're gonna have to come up with a new final scene for today's episode." Sidemouth nodded, gave a hand signal, and the crew shut off the lights and climbed down from the cameras.

Carly gave her father a grateful look. "Thanks, Dad. This . . . this really means a lot to me."

"Oh, Carly," he said gently, then started talking like a retarded child. "Daddies need to be dere for deir wittle girls, don't dey?" I followed the three of them to the omnicab. Right at the threshold, Sonny jerked a thumb at me. "By the way—who's this palooka?"

"This is Nick," Carly said. "I'll explain what—"

"No, no, no," Sidemouth hollered from the set area. "Sorry boss, but 'palooka' is way too sitcommy. Remember, you're supposedly off-camera now."

"Oh. Then how about 'dude'?"

Sidemouth shook his head. "Sorry boss, that's a bit . . . well, don't take this the wrong way, but 'dude' is a bit young for you. I'd go with 'guy.' "

Sonny shrugged, nodded, carefully repositioned himself at the pod's threshold, and jerked a thumb at me again. "By the way—who's this guy?"

Now I was completely baffled. Hadn't they stopped recording the show?

"This is Nick," Carly said. "I'll explain what he's doing here as soon as we're in the omnicab. It's all good. Trust me."

I looked around for a live camera with a zoom lens, but the gear was all shut down, and the crew was clearly on break.

Once we were in the pod, its faintly violet door shut and we shot up about a hundred feet. As soon as our altitude stabilized, the walls turned opaque, resembling brushed steel.

Carly looked like she'd just stepped into a sauna after a long, stressful day. "Thank God. The omnicab can't be bugged. And with the walls blotted out, no one can peek in and read our lips." She pointed at me. "This is Nick Carter, Dad. He's a human. From Earth."

Sonny gave her the exact look that my own dad would give me if I introduced a new friend as Xzjerthåan from the planet Mwrgørrr. "Carly, you've just suspended production on the most profitable show in the universe. Every minute we spend up here is costing us tons of moolah, and we don't have time for one of your harebrained schemes."

"Dad, I'm totally serious. Nick is from New York City."

Sonny squinted at me suspiciously. "Oh, really? Then tell me, City Boy. Which Yankee plays for the World Series?" He grinned triumphantly at my baffled look. "All right. Open wide." Before I could ask what he meant by this, he grasped both of my inner shoulder blades with his left hand, which somehow activated a painless but powerful muscle spasm that completely immobilized me. His right hand then brushed my cheek while making an odd squiggly gesture, and my mouth flopped open. He gazed down my windpipe. "Nope, nope." He squinted and pulled in for a closer look. "Noooooo. Uh-uh. I'm not seeing any icky red blobs back there." He touched my cheek again and my mouth snapped shut.[*]

---

[*]Sonny turns out to be a passable practitioner of a Noble Art called "Combat Dance." In its gentlest form, this involves the ingenious ma-

I wanted to say something, but I was like a marionette in the hands of a master puppeteer, and had no control over my own larynx. So I just stood there and puzzled over all of this. Then it hit me—Frampton had said that one of the three differences between Perfuffinites and humans was a lack of tonsils. So Sonny had just established that I . . . *wasn't human.*

"Dad, he had a wetware upgrade," Carly said. "So don't bother pulling his shoes off. You just have to take my word for it."

"Oh, sure. Suuuuure. Daddies need to twust their wittle pwincesses, don't dey? So I'm sure he's as human as rayon slacks. Where'd you pick him up?"

"On Earth. Seriously. Please just pretend to believe me for two minutes."

Sonny suddenly got very stern. "Okay. In that case, remind me what we promised our daddy? Something about *never* leaving the galaxy without having our big brother along to look after us?"

"Frampton was with me," Carly said through gritted teeth.

"Great—then what did you have to go zipping off to Earth for? Big sale at Claire's Boutique? Recipe swap at the nail salon? Pony day at the knitting store?" Sonny finally released my shoulder blades to give his son a laddish nudge.

"Dad, I'm sick of being typecast like that. I'm an *adult*. And it's time for my role to reflect that!"

Suddenly not at all playful, Sonny gave her an indignant

---

nipulation of pressure points—something that I first experienced when Carly twirled me into the omnicab while it was perched above the abyss beside her apartment.

look. "Oh d'you think? So what did you do, then? Stomp off to Earth to get some footage of yourself acting all *adult* and heroic, so you could sabotage the character we've been carefully developing for years?"

Carly looked awkwardly at her feet.

Sonny glared at her. "Carly, we've been over this. Our show already has a bright young hero. His name is *Frampton*. And if we were making some fantasy garbage like *Super Friends,* I guess we'd all get to be heroes. But we're not. We're making a *reality* show. And in *reality,* what does every hero *actually* have?"

Carly said nothing.

Sonny grabbed her shoulders, forcing her to look him in the eye. "A dizzy little sidekick who's always causing problems. And you're the most famous one *in the universe.* So why are you suddenly going rogue on me?"

Carly shook her head. "I . . . I'm not. Not at all. I decided to go to Earth *strictly* because of the episode that reveals that the Townshend Line is just a rickety piece of garbage."

"Oh, *that*? Well, what about it?"

"It was obvious that once it aired, the Guild—or somebody—would start scheming to destroy humanity. And I just couldn't sit by and let that happen. So I went to Earth to negotiate an end to the debt before it was too late."

"But the Earth is perfectly *safe*," Sonny said. "The Townshend Line is the most masterful piece of engineering crafted by any civilization since the dawning moment of the Big Bang. Bar none!"

Carly gave him an incredulous look.

"And by the way, that's how I know City Boy here is just another Perfuffinite, no matter what you say about hooking up with him in the Big Apple," Sonny continued, jerking a contemptuous thumb my way. "I'll bet the Guardian Council's Inner Republican Guards couldn't even get past the Townshend Line. So how could *you* pull it off?"

"Because it *doesn't work*," Carly said. "Just like our research team discovered by spying on the Guardians!"

"That wasn't a discovery," Sonny snapped. "That was a subplot."

Carly looked completely aghast. "A *what*?"

"A subplot, duh." Sonny took a couple deep breaths, then softened his tone. "Carly, you know our ratings have stunk since the news of the debt broke. And it makes no sense. I mean, I dig that people want to talk about the universe's complete financial collapse. But after *ten days* . . ." He shrugged, shaking his head theatrically. "Anyway, the show needs a debt angle to stay relevant. So me and the writers cooked up the idea that the Townshend Line is caca, and we're afraid that some unspecified bad guys will find out. Over the next few episodes we're gonna have Frampton fix everything, using Science. And then you'll almost mess it all up by seducing a rugby team. You know—the usual stuff. Only with a *debt* angle. See?"

Carly looked like she was on the verge of tears. "But . . . I didn't have any idea."

"Of course you didn't," Sonny said gently. "Nobody tells you anything. We told your big brother, though. Didn't we, Frampton?"

Frampton furrowed his brow. "I think so."

Sonny turned back to Carly, and pinched her cheek fondly. "You're so precious. Always believing everything you see on reality shows—even your own. It's a good thing you're surrounded by smart, brave men who protect you."

He gazed proudly at his son and clapped an arm around his shoulder.

"Well, with all due respect, sir, I think your subplot might have inadvertently gotten things right, because the Townshend Line has been awfully porous this week," I finally said. "And I really am from Earth. I know you have cached copies of our Internet handy. So if you don't believe me, just Google the entertainment law firm Carter, Geller & Marks, click the 'Our Team' link, and then click on 'Associates.' You'll see me listed under 'C.'"

Within moments, the relevant webpage had replaced one of the omnicab's metallic interior walls. Sonny stared hard at my head shot, then looked at me with something verging on reverence. "Hold the phone . . . It's *you!*"

It took five minutes and several Google searches to convince him that I had nothing to do with the Backstreet Boys. Once he was over his crushing disappointment (almost a half hour), I gave him all the details about Paulie and Özzÿ. As I told the story, he got increasingly excited and agitated. By the time I finished, he was pacing the length and breadth of the pod—a giddy, kinetic bundle.

"So, Dad," Frampton said in a relieved tone. "It looks like you've figured this one out."

"Right on. Land the flying saucer."

I felt us descend and settle gently on the ground.

I turned to Sonny. "So what do we do?"

"First, we plug the leak on our team."

"Meaning?"

"Meaning that *some*body told the Guild all about the Townshend Line episode that we just shot. Only whoever it was didn't realize that it was all phony baloney."

I nodded. "Which is how the Guild got the idea that they could cross the Townshend Line."

"Exactly," Sonny said. "Why any of you actually *could* cross the Townshend Line is beyond me. But the Guild clearly got the *idea* that they could cross it from someone who spied on the taping of our episode. Along with a bunch of other cockamamie ideas, I'm sure. So the culprit was on our set when we shot it, but doesn't know doodly squat about what's really going down."

Carly's eyes widened. "Catering?" she guessed.

Sonny nodded. "Obviously. They're unionized, so they have ties to the Guild. *And* they're the most clueless people with the show." He patted his daughter gently on the shoulder. "Present company excepted."

Carly gave her father a murderous look. "So then what do we do now?" she managed.

Sonny smiled ecstatically. "We'll push the broadcast of our Townshend Line episode up. Way up. In fact, we'll broadcast it *tomorrow*. Only we'll add some footage of Earth Boy here walking onto our set, because that proves that the Line is really down."

"But . . . why do that?" Carly asked.

He smiled even more rapturously. "Because the Earth is *doomed*. However impossible it is, you got through the Townshend Line. And now the Guild's Enforcement Brigade is down there! For some reason they think Palooka Face here is a Guardian. But as soon as our episode tells them that he isn't . . ." He paused, then flung his arms back triumphantly and bellowed, "KA-*BOOOOOOM*!"

"Right, right," I said. "And that makes us happy because?"

"Because? Be*cause*? Because it turns out I was *right* about the Townshend Line, meathead. And it's the biggest scoop in the history of the universe—ever! So tomorrow's episode won't be reality programming, will it? No. It'll be *journalism*, dig? And people will finally know how seriously they should take me."

"Daddy, don't you dare," Carly whispered.

"Don't I dare what? Finally prove that I'm more than just another gorgeous face?"

She nodded, stepping between me and her father like a mama bear shielding her cub from a pushy time-share salesman. "It would be the end of humanity."

Sonny shook his head. "Carly, even if I wanted to hide the truth—and as a *journ*alist, *I don't*—but even if I wanted to, Gotham here walked onto our set today. He's all over our footage, and our production people have all seen it by now. One way or another, they're gonna figure out that he came from Earth. And when they do, they're not gonna keep their yaps shut. Sure, I can keep a lid on this for a day or two. And I'll definitely keep Catering in the dark so the Guild doesn't go and blow up the Earth before we can get our episode out there. But if I don't run the story, the truth will come out anyway. And that would put humanity up the exact same creek they'll be up tomorrow. Only *we* wouldn't get the credit. Or the ratings."

Carly gave him an imploring look. "But . . . but the episode will at least say that the bad guys are Guild people, right? Because then they can't destroy humanity. Because everyone'll know it's them, right? *Right?*"

Sonny shook his head. "Carly, are you nuts? We don't actually have *proof* that it's the Guild down there. They'd sue us for eons! And even if we did have proof, do you think I want their Enforcement Brigade on my ass?" He shook his head again. "No. The episode just depicts us worrying about some unknown bad guys. That's how we shot it, and I'd be *bonkers* to change it."

He started toward the pod door, which was still closed.

"Well dammit, Daddy," his daughter hissed. "There's more to life than ratings."

Sonny stopped and turned, cocking an eyebrow. "Like what?"

"Like justice." Carly suddenly sounded very tired.

Sonny paused and considered this for a moment. "You know, I really *liked* that," he said. "But I think we both need to sell it a bit more."

Carly nodded obediently. Then Sonny started toward the door again and she shrieked, "Well *dammit,* Daddy. There's more! To life! Than *RATINGS!*"

He wheeled around and stared at her for a long, tense moment, then whispered, "Like what?"

"Like . . . *justice.*" She crammed this through bitterly gritted teeth. With that, Sonny turned on a heel. The pod door flew open, and he stomped off. An instant later the door shut, and we rocketed skyward. The walls became transparent as soon as we were a couple thousand feet up. By now the sun had risen over the performance canyon, and the audience had gone.

I really wanted to let Carly have it at that point. And it would have been a great release to vent about her dad for an hour or three. Oh—and to unleash a primal scream to mourn my species' awful fate. But our team needed to stay united if humanity was to have even a tiny chance of surviving, and Carly needed to remain calm. This made her toxic family dynamics a great subject to avoid. There was meanwhile a much safer topic that was baffling me, which also seemed important.

"So," I ventured, "I couldn't help but notice that you guys kind of . . . re-shot a couple of scenes—even though the cameras weren't on you."

"Cameras?" Frampton giggled.

"Nick, the great big things with the lenses down there are called 'props,' " Carly explained, in the voice of a mommy who had brought her special-needs preschooler to work for the day. "And the people operating them are 'actors,' who play 'production crew members' in our 'reality show.' "

Apparently. One dumb question from me was all it took to bring Carly right back to normal. "They're actors?" I confirmed.

"Well, more like extras," Frampton said. "That's why they all look kind of half human."

"We want the show to look like it's completely staffed with Perfuffinites, because that makes it more glamorous," Carly added.

Frampton nodded. "But real Perfuffinites are expensive. So we hire our extras from these near-miss species."

"And as for our actual cameras, stereopticons can record everything that happens in their presence from every conceivable angle simultaneously. And they do it in such a rich format that when you play a segment back, you can zoom in on anything, or move your de facto camera position to almost any point in the room. It's all in the self-organizing light." Carly touched her chunky medieval crucifix. It oozed into its compact, translucent form, and she held it up to me. "These are the real cameras. By wearing mine around my neck, I can record in three hundred and sixty degrees."

"And does your audience really believe you're making the show with that big crew, and all that old-school equipment?"

Carly shrugged. "I'm sure some folks do. And others have fun suspending their disbelief, and playing along. Pretending to use the same sort of gear that was used to create *The Osbournes* is one of our gimmicks. Since reality shows are a human art form, it's seen as virtuous to create them using only human technology. But part of the art form is deceiving viewers into believing that fake things are real. So Dad decided that it's fine to use Refined equipment when we pretend not to."

"He's . . . very committed to the show," I said.

"You mean because he's willing to *humiliate his only daughter* just to boost his ratings?"

"Yeah. And to—you know, destroy humanity. Assuming he's actually serious about that."

"Oh, he's serious," Carly said. "You can bet he plans to air that episode tomorrow morning at nine fifty-eight. But there's really nothing to worry about."

"Why not?"

Carly clutched my right hand with both of hers, went down on one knee, and fixed me with a freakishly intense gaze. "Because . . . I have a vow to make, Nick. Right now. In front of you, and in front of my brother."

And in front of your stereopticon, I thought. But I just nodded and let her continue.

"No matter how great the risks. No matter how terrible the odds." She paused dramatically. "I am *not* going to let Dad embarrass me."

"Yeah, I . . . wouldn't let him get away with that." There were nobler vows that she could have made at that point. But humanity needed all the allies it could get—and if this was the credo that would keep her fighting, I was all for it. "So now what?"

"We go to see pluhhhs," Frampton said. He'd been off on the far side of the pod for the past little bit, working on something with his stereopticon. "I sent them an emergency signal, and they're bringing us straight out to their planet."

Carly gave her brother an amazed look. "That's actually kind of smart, Frampton."

He beamed.

"We're going to see who?" I asked.

"pluhhhs," Carly said. "They control the Townshend Line. They're the ones who let us through it yesterday. And they're the ones who notified us that someone else crossed it right after we returned—although at that point, they didn't know who the trespassers were. By now, I'm sure they know it was Guild guys, and have probably figured out how they got through. And if anyone can bounce those bastards out, and never let them anywhere near Earth again, it's pluhhhs."

"Sounds fantastic," I said, wishing we had gone straight to these badasses instead of wasting our time with Daddy.

"And because of the needs of the Townshend Line operation, their planet lies right on a Wrinkle Vertex," Carly added. "Which means it can usually connect to most points in the universe almost immediately."

"Great, so we don't have to wait half a day to see them. When does our Wrinkle leave, then?" I asked.

"Now," Frampton said.

This time I remembered to crouch down to the floor before everything got weird.

TWELVE
pluhhhs

My second Wrinkle started out like the first one. But it ended in an eerie ultraviolet haze that seemed to go on infinitely, in all directions. I felt paralyzed and half mad, and I lost all sense of time—unable to tell if seconds or centuries were ticking by. Then it was over, and we were in our pod, high above a topaz landscape that was covered with an intricate network of serpentine rivers and tiny lakes.

"What was that?" I asked, relieved to be out of there.

"We passed through the penumbra of a gamma ray burst," Carly said. "It happens every so often. Gamma ray bursts are the most violent events in the universe, and they severely warp the fabric of space and time." She looked at Frampton. "How long were we in there?"

He consulted a display from his stereopticon. "About five hours."

"*Wow,*" I whispered, unsure if I was surprised at how long or how brief this was.

"We got lucky," Carly said. "Sometimes it's days. And we don't have days."

"Right," I said, alarmed. "The episode airs around ten tomorrow morning, doesn't it? What time is it now?"

"Not quite seven at night on the East Coast," Frampton said. "And we're five minutes from the Townshend Line's headquarters."

"Got it," I said, shaking my head to clear it out. "Well, while we're heading over there, why don't you tell me more about the Pluhhhs. They sound like total badasses."

This put both Frampton and Carly into stitches.

"What? What's so funny?"

"First of all, it's not *the* pluhhhs, it's just pluhhhs," Carly managed through her giggles. "And second, pluhhhs are anything but badasses. In fact, they're the most tedious, irrelevant, and forgettable species in the entire cosmos."

"Which is why they took on the job of quarantining your planet," Frampton said.

Carly nodded. "Back when every Refined being in the universe wanted to storm the Earth to catch some live music, the team responsible for keeping them all out was guaranteed to become the least popular group of beings in existence. So only the folks who *already were* the least popular beings in existence would take the job. Enter pluhhhs."

They're called pluhhhs, she explained, and not Pluhhhs, pluhhh's, nor (certainly) *the* pluhhhs because they're too boring and inconsequential to merit any capitalization, punctuation mark, or definite article.* They hail from a planet that spawned ten different intelligent species deep in its evolutionary past. The other nine were all hulking, violent, venomous carnivores. In the local schools (which everyone attended together, due to a well-meaning but ultimately disastrous court ruling), gang activity and interspecies strife pushed annual homicide rates into the double digits—and any faintly interesting or charismatic pluhhh was taunted, wedgied, and devoured long before it could reach reproductive age. Under this evolutionary pressure, pluhhhs gradually became a stunningly monotonous and unassertive species. Eventually they were so bland, passive, and inoffensive that their population was able to explode and dominate the planet. This caused its other intelligent inhabitants to become so lethally bored and disengaged from the world that they lost all interest in life, and gradually died out.

"But pathetic, drab, and trivial as they are, pluhhhs should be able to shed some light on what's happening with the Townshend Line," Carly said.

"They also have access to the Wrinkle Queue," Frampton added.

Carly nodded. "It displays all the Wrinkles that are booked throughout the universe at any given time. It'll let us see if Paulie's arranging to bring anything to Earth."

---

*The capitalization rule is a particularly hard one. While pluhhhs are absent from virtually every article, reference text, story, and song ever written about the universe's inhabitants, they're mentioned in countless punctuation guides, all of which are unyielding on the point that "pluhhhs" should absolutely never be capitalized, even if it's the opening word in a sentence, or is in a chapter or book title. Most of these guides go on to castigate the hypothetical author who would even mention pluhhhs in passing anyway—much less feature them in any sort of title.

"Like metallicam?" I asked.

"Exactly."

I shuddered. "Well, it sounds like it's a good thing we came. Is there anything else that we should get from the Pluhhhs while we're here?"

"*pluhhhs!*" they corrected me.*

"And yes, there is one other thing," Carly said. "Özzÿ told you that he and Paulie are staying at 'the local base.' I'm sure this is the music collection and copying facility under Grand Central, because it's a Guild operation, and there's no other Refined outpost anywhere near Earth. pluhhhs know all about this facility, because it uses the Townshend Line's infrastructure to transmit music out of New York. So they can probably tell us how to access the base from the city's surface."

"Interesting," I said. "But what would we do there?"

"The species that runs the New York operation is gentle and friendly. So I doubt they know a thing about what their uppermost bosses are planning for Earth. If you tell them what's happening, you may be able to drive a wedge between them and Paulie."

As she said this, my jacket pocket started to hum with a familiar buzzing.

"What the hell," I said, pulling out my phone.

"Text messages?" Carly guessed.

I nodded. About a dozen had queued up since I'd left Earth, and they were all coming in now.

"While it's relaying all that music out of New York, the Townshend Line infrastructure picks up other electromagnetic signals, too," she explained. "I guess your SMS fre-

---

*Making a major grammatical blunder of their own. No sentence containing the word pluhhhs should ever be exclaimed!

quencies are among them.* But don't even think about replying—it's a one-way thing."

I looked back at my screen. There were five increasingly shrill texts from Judy demanding to know where the hell I was, and how far I'd gotten in procuring some Milk Bone for Fido. She'd sent the last one about an hour before. It simply said GUESS I WAS WRONG WHEN I DECIDED I WAS WRONG ABOUT YOU.

Dammit! Judy's outrage was understandable, as it's unheard of for an associate to go AWOL on a senior partner right before a key meeting. Of course, the terminal career ramifications of this would be entirely moot if I didn't derail the metallicam plot. But on that far more important front, I *needed* to recruit Judy as an ally. She might then help me recruit Fido, or the CEO of the giant music label that we were also supposed to meet with tomorrow. If anyone could arrange the sweeping licenses that we needed, it would be the three of them, working together. But that wasn't going to happen if Judy cut me off.

There was also a series of texts from Manda. It began with some updates on her exploration of the stereopticon's feature set. Once she mastered the voice mode, she tried her hand at rendering objects in ways that made them seem physically present. Around 2:00, she'd sent me an image of herself posing with a cartoonish baby elephant in front of my couch. By the way, where bf are you she added in text. An hour later, she sent a shot of an entirely real-looking baby elephant winding up to smash its trunk through my plasma screen. DUmbo's getting really worried about you, CALL DAMMIT or the tv gets it. A couple hours later, she sent a photorealistic ren-

---

*Somehow this resulted in a seven-figure roaming charge, and it took me days to persuade Customer Service that it had to be a billing boo-boo.

dering of Judy popping out of a giant layered birthday cake in my kitchen. Judy promises a raise and a piece of cake if youd call. OK fine the cake is a lie but seriously WHERE R YOU am really starting to panic.

As I was processing all of this, the omnicab started dropping rapidly toward the ground. Seeing two messages from Pugwash in the queue, I decided that whatever he was pestering me about would have to wait.

The omnicab touched down beside a structure that looked like a small adobe hut. Its sole feature was an ornate door etched with arabesque patterns that were so beautiful they made my eyes ache. "One more thing before we go in," Carly said. "While it's easy enough to grasp the concept of pluhhhs, you'll find that it's very difficult to maintain awareness of an actual pluhhh individual. They're just too tiresome to merit the slightest bit of attention. So you'll have to concentrate very hard whenever you interact with one."

We exited the omnicab and the glorious door slid up. It opened directly onto a platform that was perched at the pinnacle of a soaring chamber of cathedral height. As soon as we all stepped onto it, the platform swooshed us soundlessly downward.

The chamber's floor was staffed by a teeny receptionist. Heeding Carly's instructions, I locked my eyes on her and focused intently. She looked like a gray, bedraggled lemur, with hunched shoulders and patchy fur. As we approached, she glanced up and froze in place. With that, her body lifted off her chair, twisting violently at the torso. It completed a full circle, then dropped to the floor where it sprawled, arms and legs pointing upward at obtuse angles. With that, her retinas ignited.

Eccentric as this greeting was, it almost put me to sleep. "What was that all about?" I yawned.

"Fame differential," Frampton whispered. "It affects almost everybody we meet—but no one as badly as pluhhhs."

I looked to Carly for help. "Fame is a by-product of Conscious Attention," she explained, "which itself is one of the six fundamental forces of nature as organized under String Reality.* As such, it creates measurable fields that can impact the physical world."

Frampton nodded. "Kind of like a magnet."

"Fame stores up in a sort of battery that's attached to your body in the fifth dimension," Carly continued.† "Whenever you, or something you've created, draws attention, a charge builds up in that battery. Then when you encounter another conscious being who recognizes you and knows of your works, your fame fields interact. If there's a very large difference between them, the being with the weaker field is impacted in some way."‡

---

*String Reality is the deep physics of the universe. Our physicists only understand it faintly, and for now they're cautiously calling it String Theory.

†If it's hard to imagine your body stretching into an invisible dimension, picture something analogous on Flat Earthland. Suppose its otherwise flat inhabitants have these crazy retractable arms that can stretch for thousands of miles into the third dimension. They're not aware of these strange limbs—but if one of them is mad at someone, his invisible arm might reach out and bop his rival, even from far away. Neither party will be consciously aware of this. But the person who gets hit will start thinking hostile thoughts about the jerk who just bopped him, and at some point his own invisible arm will strike back. As for us humans, it turns out that all kinds of crap sticks out of our bodies into the fourth, fifth, and eleventh dimensions—including fame batteries (and, yes, retractable arms for unconsciously bopping our enemies).

‡The way this works mechanically with humans is that as soon as you recognize someone famous (which feels like it happens from a dis-

"Usually they just act really, really stupid, and do whatever we tell them to," Frampton said.

"But pluhhhs are so thoroughly irrelevant that they have this sort of antifame charged up in their batteries," Carly said, "and when they recognize someone hugely famous like me or Frampton . . . well, you've just seen the effects. Come on, the control room is this way."

We walked down a short hallway and entered a towering gallery that was dominated by a wall of massive 3D monitors displaying renderings of Earth from every conceivable angle. There were aerial views of cities, topographical maps with minute resolution, heat maps, real-time population maps, and brilliant Earth crescents rising above the lunar surface. In front of this was an enormous bank of switches and buttons, and a sea of brightly colored lights that winked on and off in frenetic patterns.[*] Five gray pluhhhs were milling about in the foreground.

Frampton strode in like the giant celebrity he is, making little pistol shapes with his fingers that he waved at the team. "Love your work, boys. Love your work!" he said.

---

tance, but actually involves some icky physical contact in the eleventh dimension), the difference in charges between your attention batteries forms a current of sorts (fifth dimension), which gets a series of mechanical gears whirring in hyperspace (fourth dimension). These wind up and thwack your amygdala (third dimension—if you dissected a sheep's brain in biology class, you've cut through one of these). Your thwacked amygdala then pumps out a cocktail of hormones and other goo, and now you're stammering, dropping things, and generally making an ass of yourself.

[*]Carly later told me that none of this stuff actually does anything—it's just there to impress the churlish bands of schoolkids that troop through on field trips every few days.

Four of them made garbled sounds and contorted right into variations on the receptionist's akimbo position. Frampton turned to the one who was still standing. "Hey there, mlah.* So great to see you again."

mlah quavered, but stood his ground.

"mlah has a remarkably celebrity-resistant constitution," Carly told me. "He's the one who helped us get to Earth yesterday."

"How'd he do that?"

Carly blinked. "I have no idea, actually. Because of the fame field, Frampton and I usually just sort of . . . ask for things, and they happen."

"So, mlah," I said, trying my best to focus on the monotonous gray blur in front of me. He locked eyes with me instantly—no doubt relieved to be talking to a fellow nobody for a moment. "How'd you, uh . . . enable these two to go to Earth yesterday?"

"I suspended the force-field generator temporarily," mlah said in this impossibly flat, bland voice that was hard to heed even slightly.

"Hey, speaking of Earth, we have a little question for you," Frampton said.

mlah braced himself and looked at his incandescently famous visitor.

"Remember how you told us that someone else crossed the Townshend Line right after we got back from Earth?" Frampton said, then paused and checked his diver's watch, his concentration clearly going to hell. Then, "Oh yeah.

---

*Short for mlahh. This is what passes for a jaunty nickname among pluhhhs.

Any, uh, guesses as to how they might have gotten through that . . . incredibly awesome force-field thing of yours?"

"We were wondering if you'd ever ask," mlah managed. "When you and Carly crossed the Townshend Line's boundary after I suspended the field generator, it had the effect of destroying the force field. Completely and permanently."

"Huh. That's incredibly interesting," Frampton said, clearly not the slightest bit interested in any of this boring-ass crap. "Why'd it, uh, have to go and do that?"

"Because it was what's known as an autoliquidating force field," mlah droned. "This is an immensely powerful, but very fragile construct that collapses irrevocably if it's penetrated, even by an authorized visitor."

This faintly got Carly's attention. "You should have warned us," she chided absently, wagging a finger at no one in particular.

"We did. Several times. But you paid no attention."

I struggled to tune in to this wearying blather. As mlah's voice drifted in and out of focus, I started to entertain myself with mental lists of the errands I wanted to get to next Saturday. ". . . we simply couldn't resist the will of celebrities of your stature," he droned. ". . . impossible to reconstruct the force field . . . anyone can now Wrinkle through . . ." And so on, and so on, and on, and on, and on . . .

A distraction finally rescued me when my iPhone vibrated. I checked it and saw that I'd just received a third text from Pugwash. I pulled it up along with the two unread messages that I had from him, and started by reading the first one. He'd sent it only twenty-five minutes before:

M I losing my mind there's a parrot here talks in complete sentences says he knows you hPs hPs hPs

A few minutes later he had written:

Locked self in bathroom at my place get here now I blame you

And this most recent one said:

HPs he's singing make him stop can't take it

I was processing all of this when Carly tugged violently on my sleeve, hauling me over to something that looked like a well.

"What's this?" I asked.

"The only full-access view of the Wrinkle Queue in the entire universe, apart from the one at Guardian Head-quarters itself. This is part of the reason why we came to see pluhhhs." With that, she shoved my head into it.

"*Good God,*" I whispered. It was the most . . . intricate sight I'd ever seen. I was surrounded on more sides than I knew I had, by millions of little twisty segments, all different. They came in an insanely wide range of lengths, and about a hundred distinct colors. Each was also spinning in one of about a dozen different ways, and they were all scintillating in one of maybe thirty distinguishable patterns. The segments were all in rapid motion. And as they scooted around, their front ends would often vanish, and then reappear in distant parts of the display. The image seemed to have an infinite resolution and depth to it, and I found I could zoom my perspective in and out at will, and also look at it from countless different directions simultaneously.

"Ghetto-ass 5D display," Carly muttered from some-where nearby. "You'd think they'd have a higher budget around here."

"It's . . . beautiful," I said.

She let off an irked sigh. "You *would* think that. But I'll grant you that it's hugely interesting. Now, look at that tiny empty region. Over by the midsized thicket of slow-pulsing ultraviolet segments."

Somehow I was able to locate this easily.

"That's the one-hundred-forty-four-light-year sphere surrounding Earth," Carly explained. "Nothing's Wrinkling in and out of there, because so far nobody but we and the Guild know that the force field's gone. Now I'll have the display show us something that's scheduled to happen in a few hours. Watch."

With that, a midsized muddled-orange segment with a slow-twitching counterclockwise spin and a foggy blink to it started shooting straight into the empty region's heart. "What's that?" I asked.

"It's a transfer that's scheduled to happen around ten-fifteen tonight. The point of origin is unknown for now, but it's slated to arrive at the transmission facility beneath Grand Central Station. What's-his-face says it was booked about a minute ago. That's why I dragged you over here to look."

"Who booked it? And what is it?"

"pluhhhs are still looking into that. But I'm sure Paulie booked it. Worst case, it's the metallicam shipment we've been worrying about. Although it seems a bit early for that since he still thinks you're a Guardian. Okay, out of the pool." Carly yanked my head from the well-like display, and we were back in the control room. And that's when Pug-wash's most chilling message arrived:

hmfs this guy is so cool he and I am going to
make a fortune no need to come in fact PLEASE
DON'T all under control

I looked at Carly, holding up my phone. "It's from my cousin. Paulie's had him cornered in his apartment for the past half hour."

She shot me a concerned look. "Is it a hostage situation?"

"No," I said, fighting a wave of panic. "They're . . . making friends." I looked back at the text. Pugwash must have written it while Paulie was booking that shipment. The two things had to be related.

I was about to mention this when Frampton waved frantically for my attention. "What . . . *is* that?" he asked when he caught my eye.

"What's what?"

Then I noticed it, too. There was a slight disturbance in the room. It was . . . a flicker of light? A whisper of sound? Microscopic sparks?

Carly joined the guessing game, but was also stumped. So we held our breath, listened intently, and carefully scanned the room. Then it hit all of us at once—it was that lemur critter. Remember him? He was doing . . . something incredibly inconspicuous that we could barely catch out of the far corners of our eyes. In fact, he was . . . ah yes, he was standing in a blinding spotlight about a foot away from us, screaming into a deafening megaphone, and waving a magnesium signal flare.

"Come again?" I asked, straining to keep my attention on that piddling, vacuous, lethally boring speck of irrelevance that we know vaguely as mlah.

"I *said*," mlah bellowed, "detailed instructions for getting to the transmission facility beneath Grand Central are written on the back of *this*." He pressed a New York subway map into my hand.

"Gee, thanks," I yawned, then struggled mightily to remember who I was thanking, and for what. Then I was fighting a looming narcosis, and Carly was bundling us out of the control room with the help of . . . someone, and we were back in our omnicab and rocketing skyward.

We had to replay the key points of our conversation with mlah several times from Frampton's stereopticon before the details really stuck with us. And as the facts settled into my mind, a righteous fury gradually built in my chest. It was bad enough when I thought that Carly's show was just going to *tell* the universe that the Earth was vulnerable to attack. But now we knew that she had *directly destroyed our defenses* when she insisted on getting passage through the Townshend Line!

After we watched the playback for the last time, I turned to Carly. "One could almost argue," I said through gritted teeth, "that by coming to Earth to allegedly rescue us, you made something that . . . verged on being a misstep."

"Yeah, I suppose," she spat. "Technically, maybe. If you want to get all technically *tech*nical about it. But seriously— who the hell's ever heard of anything as weird and obscure as a . . . what did he call it? An *autoliquidating* force field?"

"I would guess . . ." I struggled to maintain a tone of dignified understatement. "Pretty much anyone who knows . . . *the first fucking thing about force fields.*" Oops.

Carly suddenly looked like she was going to cry.

"So what do we do now?" I asked, much more gently. And I wasn't going soft just to make her feel better. I really did need her advice on what to do next. She was the savviest person in our group, and she had really good instincts.[*]

Carly seemed to flirt briefly with an emotional collapse. Then I saw the old flintiness return to her eyes. "Well, I guess I got you into this mess. So dammit, I'm gonna get

---

[*]Well, usually.[†]

[†]Or at times, anyway.

you out of it. And it's pretty clear that this is a job for the Guardians themselves." She turned to her brother. "Frampton, can we Wrinkle to Fiffywhumpy anytime soon?" She turned back to me. "That's the planet where the Guardians are headquartered. It has even better Wrinkle access than this planet, so we should be able to get there quickly."

Frampton consulted his stereopticon. "The Wrinkles are wide open, of course. But Fiffywhumpy has incredible defenses, and access to it is completely restricted."

"I'm sure pluhhhs can cram us through somehow. The Townshend Line gives them all kinds of administrative superpowers in the Wrinklesphere. Contact . . . that creature. Insist that he put us through straightaway. And tell him to drop us into the office of humanity's Intake Guardian, if he can."

"Humanity's what?" I asked, as Frampton contacted mlah through his stereopticon.

"Intake Guardian," Carly said. "It's a long story, but he's the guy who will one day decide if and when your species is ready to get promoted, and become Refined. Every primitive species with any shot at becoming Refined is assigned to one. And who knows, maybe your Intake Guardian can accelerate you through the process. That could solve everything, because not even the Guild would dare to harm a Refined species."

My eyes widened with hope, and Carly struck a noble pose. "I told you, there's nothing to fear. Because my word is my bond. And I am *not* going to let Dad embarrass me!"

Frampton looked up from his stereopticon. "mlah is putting us though."

"Brace yourself," Carly warned me as we hunched down for the Wrinkle. "You're about to visit the most secure planet in the universe."

THIRTEEN
THIS IS THIRTEEN

The end of this Wrinkle was even creepier than the last one. This time, everything went blank as we approached our endpoint. Not *black*—that would have been claustrophobic, but familiar. Here, it truly went blank. It was an absence of input so complete that it was chilling. It was beyond a black-out, beyond blindfolding—maybe even beyond blindness, because not only were my senses shuttered, but I briefly had no ability to imagine, or even recall, any sights or sounds. Then it was over, and we were crouching on the floor of a dark, egg-shaped chamber.

"What *happened*?" I asked. "Toward the end, it was like a . . . like a . . ."

"Sensory embargo?" Frampton said.

"Yeah, that's—a great way of putting it." Bizarrely so, coming from him.

"He's not being poetic," Carly said. "SensoryEmbargo™

is a trademarked term. It's a security product that prevents beings on inbound Wrinkles from peeking at sensitive installations."

"Oh. So we're in a top-secret building?"

"A top-secret planet. Fiffywhumpy is the Guardian Council's headquarters. Everything about it is secret."

"Wow. Have you ever been here before?"

"That's classified," she snapped.

Frampton was consulting his stereopticon. "We're surrounded by thirty feet of lead on all sides. It's as if we're in some kind of a . . . solitary, removed, and forsaken corpuscle."

"Solitary, Removed & Forsaken Corpuscles™ make the universe's most secure prison cells," Carly explained. "Our Wrinkle appears to have been hijacked at the last instant, and funneled into an isolation chamber in one of the Guardian Council's dungeons."

"Wait. We're in *jail*? For what?"

"For violating one of the sternest laws in the universe."

"What . . . did we do?"

"We trespassed on the Guardians' planet." She took in my horrified expression and shrugged. "Yeah, it was a totally criminal move. Sorry." As she said this, a manhole-sized indentation formed in the wall, and then sank away from us, leaving a tunnel in its wake. "Oh my," Carly yawned. "It looks like an extruded pathway to a summary courtroom." She crawled a few feet into the dark, leaden tunnel. "Helllooooo? Mr. Jailer? Can we step on it?"

Frampton turned to me while she was briefly out of sight. "Don't worry," he whispered. "She's just messing with you. Like when we stepped into the omnicab, and pretended we were falling."

"More *pranks*? Seriously? Wasn't it enough to scare the crap out of me once?"

"Dad made her feel stupid, and then you almost made her cry," Frampton whispered. "This is her way of . . . moving on. And it's a lot better than the way she dealt with things when we were kids. So trust me—it's all under control. Just play along, and pretend you're really scared. It's the best thing for all of us."

"C'mon, Jailmeister," Carly was shouting, as she crawled back into our cell. "Let's get this trial going; we don't have all day."

"Actually, I have to arraign you before I can try you," boomed a deep, rumbling voice from the tunnel. "But luckily, I'm a full-service guy. Incarceration, arraignment, trial, sentencing, *and* punishment. We can get through the whole shebang in twenty minutes or less—guaranteed."

There was a sludgy, gurgling noise, and a mountainous snail-like creature hove into view. Its mucus-drenched head protruded from a spiky metallic shell. It had something of a face, which was dominated by a solitary, unblinking eye. Beneath this was a gaping maw that seemed to contain a pilot light. As the creature oozed out of the tunnel, its body and shell expanded—kind of like a balloon coming out of a narrow tube. Once it fully entered our Solitary, Removed & Forsaken Corpuscle™, there was hardly any room for the rest of us.

I had no trouble acting scared like Frampton requested, because it turns out to be remarkably easy to feign terror in the presence of alien beasts that horrify you on a deep visceral level. This one left a fetid brown slick wherever it slid. Its breath smelled like the entrails of kittens and bunny rabbits who had been given hours to dread their fate before being slowly devoured and digested. It had four gigantic, lobsterlike pincers that seemed to be made from corrugated steel and barbed wire. And the worst thing was that giant eye. When it turned toward me, I felt like I was naked— naked under a floodlight attached to a huge magnifying glass operated by my entire eighth-grade science class, including the impossibly hot Heather Logan, and that Forlenzo guy who always took my lunch money.

After staring me down, the grim peeper turned to Carly and Frampton. There was a moment of recognition as it faced two of the most dazzling stars in all of creation. This was followed by several quite uneventful moments, during which Carly shifted from a completely blasé posture to one of morbid horror. *Damn, she's good,* I thought. Her faked vertigo in the omnicab had been slapstick, in retrospect. But this was Oscar material.

Our jailer pointed a pincer toward the tunnel. "After you, Fame Girl," he rumbled.

Frampton gave me a wild-eyed look as his sister crawled into the leaden passage. I grinned and winked. He shook his head and started trembling. I winked again, and faked some trembling of my own. He trembled more violently, and I stole a glance at Bugeye to see if he was buying the act. But he wasn't even looking at Frampton—he was peering down the tunnel after Carly. Which meant that Frampton wasn't acting at all. Which meant that he was genuinely freaking out. Which couldn't be good. I thought back to his whispered words from moments before. "Trust me," he'd said. "It's all under control." Based on that, I had assumed that Frampton—*Frampton*—had everything under control. Shit.

"Now you two, go," the rumbling voice commanded. Frampton and I started crawling down the tunnel. Bugeye brought up the rear. All was pitch-dark after he plugged the entrance with his shell and his massive gut. His slimy underparts made gruesome slobbering noises against the tunnel floor as he crawled behind us.

"What's wrong?" I whispered to Frampton.

"The fame field. I don't know what happened, but it didn't work."

"You were counting on your fame to get us out of *this*? Please—it's not like this place is staffed by the Pluhhhs!"

"pluhhhs," he corrected me. "And no, we knew it was protected by some tough guards. But *everyone's* vulnerable to our level of fame. Nobody but pluhhhs twist into knots with burning eyeballs. But one way or another, everyone always completely loses it in front of us. Until now."

As he said this, I saw a faint gray patch ahead of us as we approached the end of the short tunnel. It led into a darkened room with maybe five watts of ambient light illuminating it. As my eyes adjusted, I saw a stone podium in front of us, and a single stone bench facing it. It was hard to be sure in the darkness, but I could have sworn there was a framed portrait of Saddam Hussein hanging on the far wall.

The creature gestured for us to sit on the bench, and took his own position beside the podium. He rummaged behind it, and hauled up something that looked like a sheep's carcass. When he hoisted it onto his head, I realized it was a powdered wig.

"The Wholly Autonomous Boundary Court of Fiffywhumpy is now in session," he rumbled. "You are all hereby accused of violating the planet's sovereignty by entering its gravitational well without permission. If you feel that you are not guilty, one of you may now address the court. Otherwise we'll move straight to sentencing."

I gave Carly a desperate look. But she was already giving me a far more desperate look. "Say something," she hissed. "You're the lawyer."

She had me there. So I turned to the jailer, my eensy superpower's calming energy kicking in. "Your Honor. Before I begin my statement, may I ask if you know exactly who your defendants are?"

"Yes," the beast rumbled. "I read the metadata attached to your Wrinkle. From this, I know your names, and the identities of your home planets. And of course, I recognize your two colleagues."

I know your names, and the identities of your home planets. As the words were leaving his lips, I knew what I had to do—but I hated it fiercely. Cynical as the legal profession can be (and cynical as I can be about it), I had long ago promised myself that I would never lie in a courtroom. However flawed, humble, or alien a court might be, it's a sacred space of justice. Yet I was now preparing to tell the most personally debasing lie that I could imagine—and I would be doing this as an active counsel before a magistrate.

"You may begin your statement now," the jailer said impatiently.

I stepped toward the podium; begged Moses, Themis, and every other law-giving prophet and goddess for mercy; and began. "When I first joined the Backstreet Boys, I was a young idealist, fresh out of law school. And I've since learned that . . . Sadness is beautiful. Loneliness is tragical. So check out the shape of my heart." With that, a little bit of my soul died. I prayed that this would do the trick, so that I wouldn't have to lie again.

The mighty eye gazed at me. "You're *that* Nick Carter?"

I smiled bashfully and nodded once, figuring that a simple flick of the neck shouldn't count as a second lie.

"*Millennium* is one of my favorite albums," the voice rumbled. "Proceed." There was a brief silence, then, "I believe you left off with 'check out the shape of my heart.' So . . . proceed."

"Right. Well. Even with all of my youth and idealism, I didn't realize that I was embarking on a path that would soon make me one of the most famous beings in the entire universe."

"I see," the jailer rumbled. "But it's not going to work, you know."

"What's not going to work?"

"Oh, don't pretend you're some naive, uneducated nitwit—it's beneath the dignity of a Backstreet Boy. I'm talking about the fame thing. It's not going to work. You see, I'm famous, too. Famous enough that nobody else's fame charge can even affect me."

"Wait a second," Frampton said. "I know you. You were on *Aural Sculptures!*"

"Over a hundred times, across a period of thousands of years," Bugeye said. "You must remember this one."

He took a deep breath, but before he could make a sound I gave a panicked yelp. Everyone looked at me. "Please," I said. "No singing while court is in session. We . . . take an oath about this on Earth. And I'd hate to break it."

The jailer held his fire. Meanwhile, the interruption had given me an idea.

"Your Honor," I asked. "If you were a regular guest on *Aural Sculptures,* it would imply that you were a renowned singer until my planet's discovery ended your musical career."

"That is correct."

"In light of that, shouldn't you recuse yourself from these proceedings, given that you have personal reasons to deeply resent at least one of the defendants?"

"That will not be necessary, because I have nothing but gratitude for you and the other songsmiths of Earth," the jailer rumbled. "For one thing, I adore your work even more than most Refined beings. For another, my personal circumstances actually improved significantly the day I stopped singing professionally." He turned his eye to Carly. "I'm from a collective patrimony species, you see."

Carly turned to me like a court interpreter. "It means his species has always made its artistic output the shared property of its entire civilization. In societies like his, artists earn no income, and live in collectives that are supported by philanthropy. Kind of like monks—only with lots of parties, drugs, and groupies."

"When we became Refined, the Indigenous Arts Doctrine mandated that we continue to follow our ancestral customs pertaining to art," the jailer added. "So our artistic output became the shared property of our new community, which is now the Refined League as a whole. And we maintained the ancient rules preventing our artists from making personal incomes from their work."

"So being a singer didn't pay so well?" I asked.

"It didn't pay at all," he groused. "We had to take vows of eternal poverty in order to get into Noble Arts school."

"That's *nuts*," I said indignantly. It never hurts to bond with your jailer.

"Tell me about it! I mean, it was fine when I was two thousand years old and only wanted to party and nail hotties. Particularly because music is absolutely my first love. But as I got a bit older, I started wanting a place of my own."

"Sure. And maybe a little nest egg," I goaded.

"Exactly—a little nest egg! Then the Kotter Moment came. And suddenly our services were no longer desired by anyone, and we singers were released from our vows. So now I get to live the second half of my life just for me."

"So being a jailer is actually closer to your heart?"

"Closer to my colon," he corrected me. "We don't have hearts, because our veins pump our blood. So we associate love and passion with our colons. Anyway, in answer to your question, jailing sucks. But in a few years I'll earn my pension, and then I can devote my last four millennia to macramé, which has always been my second love."

"Wait . . . you get four thousand years of pension for working—how long?"

"Forty-three point three years. I've been at it since the Kotter Moment, and I still have a few years to go. Shocking, huh?"

"Well, it may be a little . . . imbalanced."

"A *little*? It's completely imbalanced!" the jailer said bitterly. "I have friends who started working right after their larval stage, and they got pensions for the *full* eight thousand years of their adulthood, for the same forty-three point three years on the job. So you'd think they'd cut the work requirement in half for someone like me, right?"

Carly turned to me. "Rules governing Art aren't the only things that are frozen in place when new civilizations join the Refined League. Laws connected to state pensions are also immutable. And since gaining access to Refined technology often results in huge jumps in life expectancy, many societies get locked into contracts that give their present civil servants, as well as all of their future civil servants, lifelong pensions in exchange for working less than one percent of their productive years."

"But how can they afford that?"

She shrugged. "They can't. In cases like that, the society ends up owing its government retirees its entire economic output for all of eternity. Something like this happens in roughly one society out of three. Which is how the Guild came to control a third of the assets in the universe."

"But that's insane! Why are state pensions so sacred?"

"Because government workers want them to be. And government workers run our government, odd as that may sound."

"*Wait* a second." I turned from Carly to the jailer. "You must be a member of a government union, right?"

"Of course I am."

"Which makes you a member of the Guild."

"Naturally."

"Then there's no way you can preside over this trial—you have a huge vested interest in getting rid of us!"

"Do not," the jailer said.

"Do so!" Frampton snapped, clearly no stranger to courtroom polemics.

"*Do not.*" The jailer thundered this so loudly that a thick curtain of dust fell from the ceiling. The rest of us fell into a stunned silence. "So with that settled, why don't we get back to our little trial?"

"Okayyy," I said. "Shall I make an opening statement?"

"You've already made it, Backstreet. You have also been arraigned, and have entered your plea. And I hereby find all of you guilty of aggravated trespassing on the Guardian world of Fiffywhumpy, thereby violating one of the universe's sternest laws. And I sentence you to death by incineration."

"To *what?*"

"Incineration. What do you think this thing's for?" The jailer made the pilot light in his mouth glow several times more brightly for a moment. Then he turned away and blew hard against the wall behind him, coating it briefly in a deep blue flame.

"Wait a second—we want to appeal," I demanded. "To an actual Guardian."

"Your request is hereby solemnly received, carefully considered, and curtly denied."

"But . . . shouldn't it at least be considered by a higher authority?"

"Normally, yes. But this is a *Wholly Autonomous* Boundary Court. That means there is no higher authority than me."

"Are you saying your authority exceeds that of the Guardians? On their own *planet?*"

"Of course not," the jailer said. "But the legal boundary of the Guardians' planet is about twenty feet thataway." He pointed at the floor with one of his pincers. "We're right under the roof of a building that's over a hundred miles tall. That puts us just barely into low orbital altitude—which means we're beyond the jurisdiction of any planet. That's why it's called a Boundary Court."

"But that makes a complete mockery of any notion of justice! How can you even call this a legal system?"

"Hmm, you raise a good point," the jailer allowed. "But if we were in the star-spangled banana republic that you call home, do you really think a case like this would have Guantánamo fair judge than me? Oops—I mean, *gone to a more* fair judge than me?"

I turned to Carly and Frampton. They both had their

eyes shut and were moving their lips furiously, as if atoning with some deity.

"Guys," I said. "Do something . . . famous!"

Carly popped open an eye and shook her head. "It's hopeless, Nick. This guy's a superstar himself. And there's also no way we can Wrinkle out of here. The SensoryEmbargo™ system would prevent it, even if we had prebooked an outbound Wrinkle. And we didn't."

"Carly's right," the jailer said. "There's no way out. And even though I've personally attended three of her shows on Zinkiwu, and am a huge fan of hers—I'm a huge fan of *all* of you, really—I have to do what I have to do. But I do have one small piece of good news."

"What's that?" I asked.

"The oath that you made to never listen to singing during a trial is now moot, because court is adjourned. So before your incineration, I can honor you all with my own race's equivalent of the song 'Taps.' It's somber. It's moving. It has a great dance beat. And because of the collectivized ownership of art in my native society, it's now the patrimony of all of the Refined League. So in a sense, it's *your* song, too." He took a deep breath.

I wouldn't have thought it was possible for any sound to be more brutal than Paulie Stardust's singing on *Aural Sculptures.* But this guy was the Slipknot to the bird's Hannah Montana. I almost begged for an immediate incineration. But even as my will to live collapsed under the sonic assault, my mind instinctively scrambled to find a way out. Certain phrases that the jailer had said kept running through it. *I'm a huge fan of all of you . . . Music is my first love . . . I adore the music of Earth more than most Refined beings.* By the time his song ended, I had a desperate, long-shot getaway plan.

"So," the jailer rumbled. "Do you have any last requests?" He looked at Carly and Frampton, but their eyes were still shut tight, their lips moving a mile a minute. He turned to me. "How about you?"

"Just one," I said.

"What is it?"

"*Please take me thaaaaat way,*" I crooned, pointing at the floor. Carly and Frampton's eyes immediately popped open.

"*Tell you what—we're only here by mistake,*" I ad-libbed to the tune of the Backstreet Boys' cloying, insipid hit, "I Want It That Way."

"*Tell you what—please do this just for my sake . . .*" I started snapping my fingers in time with the song. The jailer's eye widened, and his pilot light went out.

"*Tell you what—I never really meant to stay . . .*" Now the jailer's eye was rolling up, up, up, revealing a bloodshot mass of tissues and green goo lying beneath it. Carly's and Frampton's legs started to spasm violently.

I pointed at the floor, swaying my hips like Shakira. "*So please take me thaaaaat way.*" With that, Carly and Frampton busted out their shambolic dance moves, and the jailer joined in with a sort of epileptic two-step. As I launched into a second chorus, it struck me that this was the first time that a human had sung a note in the actual presence of any of these music-addled aliens. Sure, it was an a cappella version of a crap song performed by a nonsinger. But I can more or less carry a tune. And the scale of the Perfuffinite concerts on Zinkiwu had demonstrated how much these loons love even the least authentic live performances. As for the jailer, however immune he was to fame, *no* Refined being is inured to our music—and my song was rapidly enslaving him.

As I hit the third refrain of the chorus, I started clapping in time with the beat, and strutting around the courtroom. My groupies followed me, doing this creepy-ass zombie march. I started pointing theatrically at the floor every time I said "please take me that way." Soon enough the jailer caved in, and rotated his eye in a peculiar way while facing the podium. This caused half of the floor to drop like a trapdoor.

As the floor fell away from us, it transformed into a sort of carpet that flopped down and covered the top several steps of an otherwise transparent staircase that descended below us as far as I could see—maybe the full hundred miles to the planet's surface. It was your typical stairwell, with about twenty steps separating each landing, and the staircases switching back and forth as they went down. But the steps and landings were clearer than museum glass and were surrounded by these unreflective, jet-black walls. The effect was one of an endless tunnel, tapering downward to a point beyond seeing. I pointed at the top step, commanding my disciples to lead the way. Comfortable as I'd become about heights, there was no way I was blazing a trail into that seemingly infinite pit.

So the jailer went first. And this was a very lucky thing.

FOURTEEN
STAIRWAY TO HEAVEN

The jailer had just started descending the staircase when his gooey underside suddenly released its grip on the steps. As he started to slip, his head whipped backward, its gruesome eye suddenly lifeless and unfocused. Moments later, he started to roll. Anyone standing below him would have been carried along and crushed when he hit the wall at the base of the first landing—a violent collision that flung him backward and down the next set of steps. It took maybe three bounces for him to reach the second landing down. He bashed its wall even harder, then cleared the next set of steps with a single bounce. After that, he just ricocheted from wall to wall on his way down, slamming harder and harder, and flying faster and faster—like some kind of repulsive, sludgy pinball. We watched him career down dozens of flights of steps until we could no longer pick him out.

"Lucky fellow," Frampton murmured as he vanished from sight.

"*Lucky?* Didn't I just . . . kill him?" This thought sickened me. Our jailer hadn't been human, but he'd been intelligent and conscious. Did that make me a murderer?

"Actually, it's more like you sent him to paradise."

"Almost literally," Carly agreed. "His body went limp when his brain hemorrhaged on a massive overproduction of endorphins. This not only creates a sense of supreme bliss, but it causes subjective time to halt. So you basically drove him into a state of eternal ecstasy." Misinterpreting the horrified look that hadn't yet left my face, she added, "Don't worry—it's a nonsexual sort of feeling. For the most part." With that, she started us down the steps again.

"Humanity's music did this to entire societies early on," Frampton reminded me as we followed her.

"That's right," I said. "But I thought that everyone who was vulnerable to it kind of . . . died out."

"Apparently, live music is more lethal than recorded music to some beings," Carly said. "We always suspected this, and now we know." She stopped abruptly in front of the wall at the end of the third staircase down and gazed at it closely. "I think we're here."

"Where?"

"Guardian territory. We're below orbital altitude." With that, the wall before us snapped up like an old-school roller blind. Behind it lay an empty, octagonal room with transparent walls and a matte black floor. It was nighttime outside, and a dazzling galactic core sparkled in the sky overhead. I looked down, and saw that we were in the tallest building of a unending city that glittered below and around us. The planet's curve was plainly visible at the horizon.

"Come in, come in, whoever you are," a grumpy voice urged from the octagon's far corner. "And make it snappy. You're not on my calendar, so when my next appointment arrives, you're out. But since you're here, you may as well state your name, species, and planet of origin—and tell me why you're barging in on me."

Carly and Frampton both looked at me. Apparently I was now our spokesman. And I realized with a start that I was okay with this. More than okay, in fact. I'd been following everyone's lead but my own since Carly and Frampton first showed up. And until I took over with the jailer, things had gone steadily from extremely bad to unspeakably awful. Of course, the situation was still within the tiniest rounding error of unspeakably awful. But at least it was finally improving.

I strode confidently into the spacious room, which seemed to be empty. "My name is Nick Carter," I said in my courtroom voice, wondering if this was, in fact, the "Intake Guardian" who would one day determine if humanity was ready to become Refined. "Individuals in my species are referred to as humans. And my planet of origin is Earth."

The voice considered this. "You know, I actually fell for that once. It was in the year 9PK. Joking about the Planet of Song was still beneath even the lowest beings back then, so I was caught off guard. The perpetrator—I had him defenestrated, by the way—did a reasonably convincing human voice. But I must say, yours is much better. The attack in your consonants has every nuance that's associated with the human palate. The resonant frequency structure is impeccable, and the inharmonicity levels are precisely as they should be. I am therefore impressed. But you will be defenestrated anyway. Lying to a Guardian is a serious crime.

So is barging in on one without an appointment, come to think of it. As is stepping on a Guardian's testicles. So will you kindly move your left foot?"

I yanked my foot off the floor, but had no sense that I had been stepping on anything. Then I saw a ghostly hint of motion down there. It was like a tiny splash of light, or a flicker of shadow.

"Thank you," the Guardian said.

"I—I'm sorry about that."

"Oh, don't worry about it. It actually felt kind of good. Not that I swing that way."

Gazing closely at the floor, I could faintly make out an exotic geometric form drifting right in front of us. It was perfectly flat, and had an irregular, kidneylike shape. Its interior was filled with a complex set of interlocking segments and patterns. Bending closer, I could see that countless tiny points of light were swarming along a network of intricate pathways that connected its internal regions.

"He thinks you're beautiful, Your Illustriousness," Carly predicted in a bored tone. "And please forgive our intrusion and my colleague's confusion. He is in fact human, and he's never seen a two-dimensional being before. And we just escaped from detention in low orbital altitude, having been abducted by a Guild-affiliated jailer who intended to execute us."

"You mean they're back to doing *that*?" the Guardian huffed, as if she'd said that someone had just left the lights on in the garage again. "We'd ask them to stop, but they'd only go on strike. Clerks and peasants unite, blah, blah, blah. The government allegedly works for us. But you try telling a public sector union what to do. Anyway, what brings you here?"

"We were hoping that Your Illustriousness might be the Intake Guardian responsible for Earth," Carly said.

"Yes, I'm with Intake, and humanity is among the many, many candidate races that I'm responsible for tracking and eventually promoting or rejecting."

My pulse quickened and I felt almost giddy. Carly had said that not even the Guild would dare to harm a Refined species. So maybe this guy was our salvation! "Your Illustriousness," I said. "Please pardon my ignorance, but what are the criteria for graduating to Refined status?"

"They involve attaining minimal thresholds of competence in thirteen technical disciplines. A civilization that reaches them without self-destructing is deemed to have survived its adolescence. It can then be entrusted with the Refined League's truly sophisticated technologies without any fear that it will destroy the universe, reverse the flow of time, or otherwise cause a nuisance. Our criteria are very strict. But they are also entirely objective, and extremely fair."

"And how is humanity doing against them, Your Illustriousness?" I asked.

"Oddly. When we first discovered you in 1977, you seemed to be on the threshold of what we call the Great Acceleration—a period when compounding improvements in a diversity of scientific areas push a society forward with stunning momentum. A Great Acceleration would normally take you from your hopelessly backward state to a full mastery of the Thirteen Disciplines in less than a quarter century. And once a civilization gets to that point, it's just a standardized test and a few simple essay questions away from joining the club."

"So what happened?" By that schedule, we should have made the cut ten years ago.

"Your development almost stopped in its tracks. Which probably isn't evident to you, since you are in fact modestly more advanced than you were in 1977. But you should have started experiencing drastic advances in computing technology about thirty years back. And that simply didn't happen. It's quite baffling to the entire Intake team."

"Seriously?" It seemed to me that digital technology had been moving along at blinding speeds my whole life.

"Absolutely," the Guardian said. "You suddenly started having terrible problems with software. And your crap software has hobbled everything else. Biotech, caliology, nanotechnology, materials sciences, oikology—you'd be flying along in all of these areas if you had just one or two decent programmers between you. Not to mention that your dismal ECAD tools have crippled your integrated circuit design—so your software problem has also become a hardware problem."

"And have we always been this bad at software?"

"That's the odd thing. You were actually pretty good early on. I mean, the PDP-11 was an elegantly balanced package of hardware and software, for its day. But then it was like someone lobotomized your entire population of digital engineers. It's strange. But I'm an Intake Guardian—not an anthropologist. So I can't begin to guess at what went wrong. What I can tell you is that humanity falls drastically short of our promotion standards. And we can't relax them for any species—not even yours."

With that, the Guardian fell silent, and the lights circulating in his innards briefly sped up. "Oh crap," he said.

"What is it?" Carly asked, suddenly anxious.

"The hospitality union just filed a grievance against you. They say you killed one of their best greeters right after you Wrinkled in. Line of duty, distraught widow and orphans, blah, blah, blah . . ."

"One of their *greeters*?" I said. "But he wasn't trying to greet us—he was trying to kill us!"

"Well, duh. Don't you have euphemisms where you come from?"

"Trespassers are commonly executed at Guardian facilities," Carly confirmed. "I knew that before we came. My miscalculation was in not realizing they'd have a celebrity greeter that Frampton and I couldn't incapacitate."

With that, there was a thunderous knock at the door. It sounded more like a battering ram than a friendly request for access.

"That would be security," the Guardian said. "Our facilities are run by strict and precise rules. I'm not required to open the door for them. But if I don't, they can let themselves in after a short interval. So . . . I'm afraid you have just under three minutes to live."

"But you have to stop them, Your Illustriousness," I blurted. "This is all part of a Guild plot to destroy humanity!"

"Oh please—don't tell me you're one of those conspiracy nuts," His Illustriousness snorted. "I'll admit, I'm no fan of the Guild. But I can't imagine they're hatching some diabolical *plot* against your species."

"But—" Carly said.

"And no, the Guild wasn't behind nine/eleven, or the weird murals at the Denver airport."

"But—" she tried again.

"And whatever the tinfoil-hat crowd says about alien involvement, I can assure you that NASA faked the lunar landings entirely on its own," the Guardian added smugly. "We've looked into that one carefully."

"But Nick is right, Your Illustriousness," Carly finally managed. "The Guild has definitely positioned two operatives in Manhattan. And they clearly intend to destroy Earth."

There was another surly thud at the door.

"That's an interesting claim," the Guardian said in a more thoughtful tone. He was silent for a moment. "I don't actually believe it, because harming a primitive species is strictly forbidden—and I also don't think the Guild is quite *that* awful. But I've just filed an urgent request to Wrinkle your tetrahedral asses out of here. Wrinkle connections are wide open to everywhere, so I can send you right to your respective home planets. But it takes a few minutes to formerly process a Wrinkle request."

Now the pounding was coming in persistent, frenetic waves.

"So you will have to fight them off, at least briefly," the Guardian continued, after apparently consulting some data source. "They'll be entering in just over ninety seconds. And it looks like I can't Wrinkle you away for three and a half minutes."

"So we'll have to survive for two minutes after they get in here," I said grimly.

Frampton turned to me. "Did you *seri*ously just figure that out in your head?"

The pounding got louder and more insistent. It sounded like a vengeful tribe smelling enemy blood.

"Are they from the same race as the greeter that we already fought off?" Carly asked.

"I'm afraid not. They're photophobes." As the Guardian said this, the exterior windows that made up seven sides of the room started turning opaque, one by one. It was suddenly getting very dark in there.

"What's going on?" I asked.

"Photophobes are highly allergic to light," Carly said. "They navigate by sonar, like bats. And they only enter pitch-dark places." The third window went dark.

"It was clever of the Guild to send them," the Guardian said. "My office is designed to darken whenever a photophobe arrives, since I can't see into your dimension anyway. So when they enter, you'll be blinded, and they won't be." The fourth window blackened.

"But what about the fame field?" I asked. "Are they all celebrities out there or something?"

"That's why they're sending photophobes," Carly explained as the fifth window darkened. "I'm sure they don't know who they're arresting. And since they'll have no way of recognizing us, our fame fields won't act on them."

"Then I'll sing to them!" I said, starting to panic as the sixth window blotted out.

"I'm afraid these beings can only hear ultrasonic sounds," the Guardian said. "Give us 'I Am Woman' at six octaves over High C, and you'll have them. Otherwise, you'll be wasting your breath." With that, the last window went dark. This left only a faint ambient glow coming from the floor, which itself started to dim. Moments before it faded into darkness, a brilliant light ignited to my left, and the whole room was suddenly brighter than daylight. I looked over and saw that Frampton was using his stereopticon to beam white light in all directions.

"Great thinking," I said. I had just enough time to get this out before the light cut out and we were plunged into utter blackness.

"Exahertz disruption field," the Guardian explained. "The guards are using one to shut off all Refined technology in here. No device running on molecular valves will work within these walls as long as it's on."

"But that's *every*thing," Frampton said.

"Not quite," said the Guardian. "Human technology is premolecular valve. Got a cellphone, Nick?"

"Yes!" I yanked my iPhone from my pocket and clicked at it desperately, but nothing happened. "It's—not working."

"Hmm," the Guardian said. "I guess they have terahertz, gigahertz, and megahertz disruption fields as well. That knocks out modern human technology. Very thorough of them. You don't have a couple of sticks to rub together, do you?"

I just let off a panicked whimper.

"All right, then go fetal," the Guardian said. "Tuck your face into your chest, roll yourself into a ball, and be still."

"Why?" I asked, as we all collapsed to the floor and followed his instructions.

"They don't know that you're about to Wrinkle out. That's your only advantage. If you're boring and unthreatening, they might be in less of a rush to kill you. You only need to last for two minutes."

I squeezed myself into the tightest and most boring ball I could manage. Figuring my hands would be my most captivating feature in the dark, I tucked them deep into my suit jacket's inner pockets.

"They'll be entering in five seconds," the Guardian said. "Four, three, two, one."

After all the pounding, I expected our pursuers to enter the room with an explosion of noise. But the door slid open soundlessly, and I heard only the faintest drumming of tiny feet as they fanned out into the octagon. Whatever they were, there were dozens, even hundreds of them.

"I can hear their vocal range clearly," the Guardian said. "But they can't hear mine, so I can give you a running commentary. Thus far, they find you terribly boring. Keep up the good work."

Several of them were running over my body by then. One trotted across the exposed part of my neck. It was furry and weighed about a half pound. I pictured a putrid ratlike creature with venomous fangs and a black licorice tail, and almost vomited from revulsion.*

"They don't know who or what you are, but they're very upset about having to kill you. They're following orders reluctantly, because their pensions are on the line. A minute thirty to go. This might just work."

I heard more pitter-patters. Then the tip of something that felt like a hypodermic needle was positioned against my neck. I recoiled, plunging my hands ever deeper into my innermost jacket pocket and—*what the hell was that?* My fingers had just brushed a mysterious plastic lump.

"They're going to have a Parcheesi tournament to console themselves when this is over. They'll eat food that's not unlike popcorn and gingerbread cookies. Somebody just converted the new Melinda Doolittle album into an octave they can hear, and they're eager to listen to it. And—wait a second." The Guardian fell silent for a moment. "They . . . they're gossiping about one of the Guild operatives who was sent to New York. He hates to be called . . . Dyson?"

I ran my hand over the base of the unidentified foreign object in my pocket as the needle's tip pressed harder into my neck, almost breaking my skin.

"They—they think this New York team has been dis-

---

*I can't even tell you how much licorice disgusts me.

patched to do something awful to humanity. I'm very sorry that I doubted you. It seems that your story is true."

I racked my brains to recall what I'd put in my pocket.

"Terrible news. They've agreed that they should just get this over with. Lethal injection. And we still have almost forty-five seconds to kill, if you'll kindly forgive the pun. And now the photophobes are weeping. They feel terrible about what fate has forced them to do. I'm . . . afraid we're out of time."

Then it hit me. I'd been so exhausted that morning that I'd blearily put on the same suit for the second day in a row. Which meant that this was the jacket I'd worn last night, at Eatiary. I yanked the device from my pocket, flicking desperately with my thumb. A faint glimmer filled the room as the bulbous Paraguayan cigarette lighter cast indigenous, carbon-sequestering photons in all directions. I remained in my fetal position, with my eyes shut tight, as a sickening splattering sound came from all directions. Then I detected a faint gleam through my scrunched eyelids as the floor's ambient light returned, and the windows cleared.

"Well done," the Guardian said. "I'm not sure what you did. But there are no more living photophobes in the room."

I could hear Carly and Frampton getting slowly to their feet, but I stayed on the floor with my eyes shut tight. This was worse than killing the jailer. Once again, it had been a life-or-death situation, and someone had to die. But this time I had massacred a small army of beings. Ones who were into Parcheesi, gingerbread cookies, and *Melinda Doo-little*! Who no doubt loved their families, and who truly wished us no harm. Can anyone really commit mass murder in self-defense?

"Get up. Stand up, Nick," Carly said. "You're safe. And

we're Wrinkling out of here any second now, so we need to make plans."

I climbed unsteadily to my feet with my eyes still shut, praying that I'd find myself surrounded by the universe's most vile and noxious-looking corpses. It wouldn't change anything, but it might make me feel just a little bit better.

Carly snapped her fingers in front of my eyes. "Jesus, Nick. Rise and shine."

I opened them slowly and saw that we were surrounded by . . . *slaughtered teddy bears*. The cutest, fuzziest, and most gentle-looking critters that I could imagine existing anywhere, they made Ewoks look like giant maggots. Some were clutching tiny blankets in their lifeless paws. Others were wearing clip-on bow ties. Several had eensy helium balloons tied around their little arms. From their expressions and contorted postures, they had clearly died agonizing deaths. Major arteries had ruptured on all of them, dousing the entire scene in gallons of crimson blood. The only faintly good thing in all of this was that the nearest pool of gore had narrowly missed my clothes and shoes.

"Get over it already," Carly said, seeing how upset I was. "Live and let die—it was us or them." She turned toward the Guardian's flickering form. "How many seconds 'til we're out of here, Your Illustriousness?"

"Actually, since there's no longer any reason to rush, I've put your Wrinkles on a temporary hold. I'd like to discuss the Guild situation some more."

"By all means," I said unsteadily, as I tried to decide if I had just become a war criminal.

The little lights inside the Guardian were now pulsing at a furious pace. "The Guild is cunning, and cautious," he said. "And since they know how illegal it is to destroy a primitive species, I just don't see them doing it. So what are they up to?"

"Actually, their plot has to do with humanity *self-destructing*," I said.

"But that doesn't explain anything, nor would it break any rules. Self-destruction is what primitive societies *do*, after all. Fewer than one in a thousand survive long enough to master the Thirteen Disciplines. Hell, half of them don't even get past longbows. If humanity self-destructs and the Guild applauds from the sidelines, it would be horribly crass of them—but not illegal."

"The Guild is actually planning to *expedite* humanity's self-destruction," Carly broke in.

The Guardian considered this. "I suppose that makes slightly more sense. But how do you know this?"

"It's a bit embarrassing, Your Illustriousness," Carly said. "But it seems that they plagiarized their plans from the scripts of a show that I'm featured in. And the expedited self-destruction was . . . kind of our scriptwriters' idea."

"You've *got* to be kidding," I groaned. Could Carly and her fameball family have *possibly* screwed us over any more?

"Then tell me how the story line in question ends," the Guardian said, ignoring me.

"We never wrote a sequel to the episode in which the broad idea was introduced. So they're on their own to figure out the details."

The Guardian considered this. "Well, it won't be easy for them. You see, they'll have to manipulate human society into heading down an obviously self-destructive path. And they'll want the rest of the universe to witness this, via its ongoing monitoring of Earth's media."

"Why?" I asked. "Because if we just . . . explode out of the blue, it won't look like self-destruction or something?"

"Exactly," the Guardian said. "Whereas if CNN presents breathless coverage of your final hours, it will look quite authentic."

"Well, whatever their plans are, they almost certainly involve metallicam," Carly said.

The Guardian considered this for moment. "Now *that's* clever. Metallicam is extremely destabilizing when it's first synthesized by a civilization. The first nation to do this is often tempted to take over the rest of its world—which leads to planetary annihilation so frequently that it's practically a cliché."

"But we don't have metallicam yet," I said. "So how can they use it in their scheme? If it shows up on Earth, it'll be obvious that some outsider's trying to destroy us, and you'll . . ." what was that word he'd just used? "defenestrate them, or something. Right?"

"Not necessarily, I'm afraid," the Guardian said. "With the Townshend Line down, it's entirely imaginable that a random, well-intentioned ninny will ship some metallicam to humanity in a misguided attempt to be helpful. Remember, metallicam can also be an unlimited source of clean, free energy. Things like this have in fact happened occasionally over the eons, and the Guild is no doubt aware of that. And in every prior case, the Guardian Council ended up voting not to intervene, on the logic that the society was facing just another test of its ability to handle technology responsibly— even if the circumstances were unusual."

"But how is that . . . fair?" I asked.

"Fairness is irrelevant when the universe's survival is in jeopardy. Which would be the case if we ever let an exces-

sively violent species become Refined. The package of technologies that are granted to newly Refined species are
simply too dangerous. I mean, we have *dental* treatments
that could destroy entire galaxies if they fell into the wrong
hands."

"So what's your job, then?" I asked. "Is it making sure
that worthy species become Refined? Or making sure that
unworthy species don't?"

"It's both," the Guardian said gently. "And when the two
goals conflict, we're morally obliged to err on the side of
keeping unworthy societies out of the club."

"Okay," Carly said. "I can see why you can't make humanity Refined prematurely. But you can at least stop the
Guild from endangering them, right?"

"Not yet, I'm afraid," the Guardian said. "For now this is
all guesswork and hearsay. You have no evidence that the
Guild is up to anything. And while I do personally believe
you, I'm just one Guardian out of five thousand. I couldn't
even call the Council to session without having some fairly
damning proof. And even if I could, you can bet that the
Guild would have the best lobbyists and lawyers in the universe on hand to deflect the blame, and promote the idea
that the Earth should be left to its own devices with the metallicam, for the safety of all."

Carly looked at me glumly. "He's right. If they make it
look like the metallicam's coming in via an anonymous care
package, they'll have a really good chance of getting away
with it."

"So I guess I have to come up with some clear evidence
of the Guild's involvement," I said.

Carly nodded. "And the place to start is the transmission
facility under Grand Central. You have instructions for get-

ting there. Meanwhile, Frampton and I can work on a way to sabotage the broadcast of tomorrow's episode of our show. If we can just knock it off the air for a day or two, it'll give us a lot more time to make something happen with the Council."

"Sounds great, but how will you do that?"

"I don't know. I have a couple of vague plans for now. But I need to hammer them out a bit more."

"Sounds like a good approach," I said, although I was half lying. We did need more time, and it clearly made sense to fight on multiple fronts. But the last time Carly hammered out one of her vague plans, she ended up destroying the force field that had protected humanity for decades.

"Meanwhile, these might help you, Mr. Carter," the Guardian said. I heard a tiny clinking, as if a vending machine had just spat out a couple of quarters.

"My *God*." Carly was pointing at two cheap-looking ZZ Top key chains that were now in the center of the floor. "Are those . . . Foilers?"

"They are," the Guardian said. "Only Guardians have access to these devices, Mr. Carter. Carry one, and you cannot be Dislocated. That's the legal term for Wrinkling somebody against his will. Keep the blue one on your person, so that I can track you. You can give the red one to any collaborator you might have on Earth."

"Do people get Dislocated a lot?" I asked, pocketing the chintzy-ass things.

"Hardly ever, since only the highest government bodies have the power to Dislocate. But since the Guild largely runs the government, I won't be surprised if they illicitly issue this power to their operatives on your planet, in hopes of disrupting your actions. That's why I'm giving you my

Foilers. Only the Guardian Council itself can Dislocate someone who's carrying one. And even then, only with a formal subpoena. Anyway, the Wrinkle connections back to your planets remain wide open. Mr. Carter, where shall I place you?"

"Can you put me in front of my apartment building if I give you my address?"

"I can put you in your bedroom if you give me your unit number."

"Perfect," I said, and told him where to send me.

"Meanwhile, we should get Your Illustriousness's identity, so that we know where to send any evidence that we might gather against the Guild," Carly said.

"Guardian 1138 is my formal title."

"Got it." Carly turned to me. "Nick, a data connection will open between our planets at eleven thirty-two tonight, your time. Meet us in Warcraft then. That will hopefully give you time to scout out the transmission facility, and for Frampton and me to start working out our plans."

"Sounds good," I said, suddenly exhausted.

"Your Wrinkle will proceed in three seconds," the Guardian announced.

Moments later, everything started sliding away from me as I began my journey home.

FIFTEEN
THUD!

Soon I was crouching on the floor of my bedroom, just as the Guardian had promised. I got up and stretched. The city was dark, and my wall clock read 8:03. For a moment I just stood there, arching my many toes, twisting my neck, and making other fidgety moves. The evening racket of Manhattan that sometimes drives me nuts was as soothing as a spring rain drumming on a rooftop.

Then I remembered the text messages. Pugwash's demanded the most urgent reply from me:

Stay put and DO NOT BELIEVE A WORD the parrot says he's dangerous am on my way!

Judy was next on the list. We needed to recruit her to our team—and she had all but disowned me because I'd been AWOL when I was supposed to be finding Milk Bone for our pet senator. So I tapped out a groveling apology, claiming that I had been off organizing some spectacular treats that Fido would never forget. That done, I walked on down the hall.

Manda threw the door open moments after I knocked, and Meowhaus leapt right up to nuzzle my leg. "Thank God!" Manda said. "I've been calling you for hours—where've you been?"

"The far side of the universe. Literally. I just got back." This earned me a pleasingly awestruck look. "I'll tell you the story in the cab. For now we've got to get to my cousin's place, pronto." I pulled up his messages and handed her my phone.

"You were getting texts? On the far side of the *universe*?"

I nodded, grabbing a coat for her.

"You obviously don't have AT&T," she murmured, glancing through the messages.

Meowhaus wasn't happy to be left behind. But we had nothing to carry him in, and Manda said it had been raining off and on all night. So we left him in her apartment and walked on down the hall. As we waited for the elevator, I saw that she was wearing a chunky, floral necklace that was glittering with gems that even I could tell were fake—an odd choice for a fashionably understated hipster. "New look?" I asked.

Baffled, she followed my gaze, then laughed and said, "I have a lot to tell you about, too." She grabbed at the necklace. It melted into her hand, then quickly cohered into the familiar form of Özzÿ's stereopticon. "I've been working with this thing all day, and it's amazing. It can take the form of about a dozen different necklaces. They're all tacky as hell. But it records everything that happens in any direction when I wear it around my neck."

"You've really figured that thing out," I said, as we entered the elevator. "Carly wears hers like that, too."

"Cool, then I must be doing something right. Now, check this out." She beamed an image of her kitchen against the elevator's back wall, home-movie style. "This was recorded while I was walking around my apartment this afternoon. Check out how we can zoom in on anything we want during the playback, with an insane level of detail." She focused on her kitchen table, zeroing in on a transparent saltshaker. The image zoomed in so close that the individual salt grains soon looked like glassy boulders covering the elevator's wall. "I can also make a 3D projection out of anything that I have an image of." She tapped at the stereopticon, and a perfectly rendered saltshaker appeared in midair. "I couldn't get the projection mode to work outside, because I guess it needs walls to bounce the light off of, or something. But indoors, it's amazing."

Soon we were standing across from a new Baby Vuitton store at Second Avenue and Thirty-second Street, getting drenched. The temperature was right around freezing, and I was afraid of the roads getting icy. I gave Manda my rundown on the day as cab after occupied cab zipped by. I was wrapping it up and handing her the extra Foiler that the Guardian had given me when we heard a familiar *gggggggggh!* sound coming from under a rickety, oversized van that kind of looked haunted.

Manda ran up and peered under the van. "Meowhaus?"

I joined her, soaking my pant leg on the curb. And there he was—regally perched on an elevated patch of pavement that was surrounded on all sides by water flowing toward the gutter. It was hard to be sure, but he looked perfectly dry. He gave us two of his impeccable *meow*'s, threw in a *gggggggggh!*, then started calmly grooming his left arm.

"How'd he get down *here*?" I asked.

"Fire escape?"

Normally I'd laugh that off. But if Meowhaus had in fact popped open the window, shot down the fire escape, and dodged every raindrop en route to that isolated dry patch beneath the van, it would have been one of the less weird things to happen that day.

"We need to get him out of the rain," Manda said worriedly.

"I actually think he could teach us some profound lessons about staying out of the rain ourselves."

"Maybe. But—hey, look!" She had spotted a taxi coming toward us on Thirty-second. The car number on its roof was lit up, marking it as available.

"I'm on it." I splashed out to the street. The cab was still a half block away, and I trotted toward it, waving madly. Our stretch of Thirty-second was deserted, so there was no competition. But the driver flashed his Off Duty light the moment he saw me. He knew I'd bring buckets of water in with me, and wanted to keep his cab dry for people waiting under awnings (where the real tips would be, assuming a correlation between common sense and earning power). Just as I was about to flip him off and curse impotently, he slammed his brakes, and skidded to a stop just short of me. Through the windshield I could see him looking up in pop-eyed horror, his face awash in a pale white glow. Screaming like a doomed B-movie extra, he pointed a trembling finger upward. I looked over my shoulder. A ghostly, three-story saltshaker was blockading the street.

"Get in the cab before he takes off," I said, flinging open the door. Manda slid right in, followed by a flying wad of mottled fur that made a faint *gggggggggh!* sound as it soared by. I slid in right behind Meowhaus, and slammed the door.

The stereopticon continued to project a faint, flickering salt-shaker into the street until Manda shut it off.

"Raindrops," she whispered. "It didn't work outside at all earlier. But I had a feeling the raindrops might help. Like when nightclubs use fog machines to make light beams stand out."

"That is what?" the terrified driver asked her, staring at the alien device.

"You mean this . . . flash? Light?" Although talented in many ways, Manda's a dismal liar.

"America good!" the driver said obsequiously, apparently confusing us for government operatives, and the stereopticon for a potent cloak-and-dagger tool.

Manda pressed it to her neck and it formed right into that necklace—which didn't help the driver's state of mind one bit. I gave him Pugwash's address, hoping he'd get us there without flying into a panic.

As we started to roll, the driver muttered into his cellphone in a language that had a spectacular density of consonants. After listening intently for a few seconds, he turned to me. "North Vietnam?" He shook his head derisively. "Very, very bad." He listened some more, then denounced Brezhnev. Apparently someone on the other end was now mining an old history book for statements that he could use to prove his loyalty to the secret agents in his cab.

After sitting through heated condemnations of Kaiser Wilhelm, the Mexican troops at the Alamo, and King George III, I pulled up a picture of Pugwash on my phone and showed it to Manda. "This is my cousin, by the way."

"Ohhhhh. He's the guy I kind of hate, right?"

I nodded. Several weeks back, Pugwash had used the Phluttr service to ambush me while she and I were out having drinks. I was lucky to get Manda to myself once a month, and was savoring the occasion—when suddenly Pugwash was slithering onto a stool that had miraculously opened up right next to her after I'd stood there for an hour, wondering how I'd ever casually touch my shin to Manda's while she was seated and I was not. It turns out that Pugwash has Phluttr tweet him whenever FourSquare flags one of his Facebook friends within eight blocks of him at a Zagat-rated bar that has at least three stars on Yelp, and has not been tagged as "long line at door" in the past hour by other Phluttr'rs*—and I'd hit the tripwire.

After some awkward introductions, the conversation turned to Phluttr itself, which Manda described as diseased and (worse) derivative, since "it's just a wad of used chewing gum sticking some other services together." Pugwash retorted that this made it a *mashup*—a far higher form of creativity than any of the simpleminded services that "sit beneath it." He followed this up with some muddled thoughts about the work of mashup DJ's like Girl Talk and Danger Mouse. Manda had some insights on this, being a critically acclaimed musician and all. Pugwash rejected her points categorically, then declared that social media and the "Semantic Web" were "resuscitating" modern music by "reimagining" and "repurposing" it.

Manda said that social media was becoming a cancer, with Exhibit A being GawkStalker.com—a site where hordes of wannabe paparazzi publish cellphone photos that they sneak of even the most obscure stars, including hundreds of pictures of her. Pugwash mentioned that he was an investor

---

*As the service insists on calling its users, in its inimitable fingernails-on-blackboard style.

in GawkStalker. Manda said he should consider marketing it to the thought police in Pyongyang. Pugwash critiqued her pronunciation of Pyongyang, and then enunciated it slowly, sounding like a white guy impersonating an Egyptian trying to speak Korean. And so on. I'd kept the two of them from crossing paths since then. But there was no avoiding that tonight.

Or was there? As I opened the taxi door, a loud, shattering sound came from the top floor of the neighboring building. I leapt from the cab, gazed upward, and saw something large and Pugwash-shaped accelerating toward the ground. It landed with a sickening thud about eight feet away. It was my cousin's battered and bloodied corpse.

SIXTEEN
PAUUUUULIE

Manda was just getting out on her side of the cab when Pugwash splatted, and saw nothing. The driver was denouncing the Algonquian tribe to me (they apparently fought against us in the French and Indian War), so he was facing my way, and saw everything. Already plenty rattled, that was it for him, and he took off—saving us a hefty $13.40 fare (plus tip!).

As the cab lurched forward, Meowhaus made a frantic leap through Manda's door to the sopping street. From there, neither rain, nor sleet, nor cadaver was going to deflect him from the shortest possible path to the nearest awning. This meant a soggy, furry cannonball shot right through Pugwash's remains. Yes—*through*. Afraid that he'd blasted a little canyon through my dead cousin (or perhaps left a wake), I edged toward the corpse. But there was no sign of Meowhaus's passage. Nor was there any trace of moisture on Pugwash, other than blood. His hair was oddly unaffected by the torrential rain, and his clothes looked bone dry.

Suddenly Manda was clutching my arm like a tourniquet. "Oh my *God*," she whispered. It really was a gruesome sight. And it didn't help that hundreds of tiny worms were already crawling out of Pugwash's mouth. Worse, he was starting to decompose. His flesh rotted before our eyes, revealing a seething mass of maggots feasting on his internal organs. They all died after just a few chomps, and turned right into dust—along with his remaining innards. This left only his skeleton, which looked like it had spent years bleaching under the Kalahari sun. Within moments, it collapsed and joined the dust pile, which then spun into a tornado pattern that rocketed up six stories, and right into Pugwash's open window.

Somewhere between the worms and the dust storm, we both realized that it had to be some kind of trick. Having seen countless low-tech versions of this sort of thing as a kid, I transitioned smoothly from shocked grief to a clinical appreciation for the creativity and attention to detail that had gone into it. But Manda's from a civilized family that doesn't rank faked deaths alongside whoopee cushions in the pantheon of harmless childhood larks. Badly upset by the gory scene, she flew into a righteous fury when she realized that someone—let's call him "Pugwash"—was just messing with us. "Son of a *bitch*," she whispered, staring hard at something. I followed her gaze and saw that a trio of mirrors had been arrayed a few feet from the building's front door— fragile antiques that were unlikely to survive the rainstorm. "Self-organizing light," she hissed, jabbing a finger at them.

"Huh?"

She pointed up at the window that the dust devil had vanished into. "I'm sure he pointed a stereopticon at those mirrors. They must have helped him bounce that sickening scene down here."

"Ah. That would explain a lot, wouldn't it?"

"The *jackass!*"

Pugwash lives on the top floor of a six-story building in a decadently spacious loft. Entering it is like walking into a scrapbook. His every phase, voyage, and achievement is commemorated—by furniture,* carpets,† framed certificates under museum-quality glass, poster-sized photo prints,‡ and bulky conversation pieces. This last category of *objet* includes a four-man Harvard racing shell that hangs from a living room wall and dominates the space. From this, the casual visitor might suppose that he rowed at . . . well, at Harvard. Rather than at the small Schenectady college where he splashed and whined his way through one semester of intramural crew (and where the boats must be in hot demand from collectors, given that he had to settle for the Harvard one).

Pugwash curates items for his little museum on the basis of their potential to up the odds—however slightly—of a female visitor dropping her panties. And I respect this ob-

---

*Rajasthan is heavily represented, which makes the place feel a bit like an Indian restaurant.

†From the looks of things, you'd think he spent a Fulbright year in Iran, although it was actually a morning in a Tunisian rug market.

‡Pictures of Pugwash with decent-looking women and minor celebrities dominate, along with shots of him standing on top of tall things with merry groups of fellow travelers. At least a hundred different people are depicted on his walls, and I'll bet he hasn't talked to more than ten of them in the past year.

jective. But he'd have more luck if he'd just cut the propaganda campaign, and give his apartment some breathing room to work its own inherent charm. His living room ceiling arches dramatically, soaring from about ten feet at the front door to well over twenty at the far wall, which is all glass. And while he doesn't have an unobstructed panoramic view, I think he looks out on something much better—a sawtooth jumble of buildings, rooftops, and water towers that's as distinctively New York as the Statue of Liberty, and as varied and unpredictable as the city itself. It really is dazzling. But walk in there, and all you see is that damned Harvard boat.

Unless you're Manda. She missed the boat. She missed the view. She missed the sixteenth-century maps, the vintage Sinatra records, the first-edition Vonnegut novels, the signed Picasso print, and even the huge yellow parrot who snarled "who's da dame?" when she burst in. She ignored everything but my cousin, whose idea of an appropriate use of alien technology was faking his death for two people who had just raced across town out of concern *for him,* for Pugwash; who repaid their concern with that gory simulated homicide or was it a suicide well whatever it was he followed it up with special effects that would sicken a horror movie fanatic and did he even consider what they would have done to the psyche of a small child if one happened to be there?

Pugwash was about to respond when a panicked flurry of yellow feathers landed on his head. "Hey, don't mess with my bodyguard," Paulie hollered, sinking his talons into my cousin's skull. "He knows kung fu!" At that, Pugwash jumped sideways, trying to dodge Meowhaus, who was rocketing straight for his groin. But he jumped too late. Already off balance at the moment of impact, Pugwash was toppled by the collision. Badly spooked, he leapt right back to his feet. This was good news for Paulie, whose aerie on Pugwash's scalp ended up safely beyond Meowhaus's reach. But it enraged Meowhaus, who reared up on his hind legs and sank his front claws deep into Pugwash's thighs, fixating on his prey like a dog treeing a squirrel.

"Aright, enough adat, jeez," Paulie said, flapping off to the top of a bookcase made from rare Burmese hardwoods. "Someone tell Simba to back th' hell down."

"Come here, Meowhaus," Manda called. He instantly ceased hostilities and trotted right to her side, more like a border collie with marine training than a feral cat who'd had a day to learn his name.

Paulie quickly composed himself and turned to Manda. "What's your name, little girl?" he asked smarmily.

"I'm Manda. And you?"

"You can cawl me Paulie."

"Well, it's good to meet you, Polly. I'd offer a cracker, but I'm fresh out."

"*No,* not that. It's *Pauuu*lie." He sounded like he was spoofing the Brooklyn word for "cawfee."

"Like I said. Polly."

"*Pauuuuulie!*"

"Paulie's a trade envoy from a distant galaxy," Pugwash announced. His nasal voice told me that he'd caught my cold, just as expected.

"We've met," I said.

"Oh—I know."

Paulie drew closer by fluttering to a rosewood side table which (as my cousin loves to trumpet) was briefly owned by the vice president of Belize. "Good to see you again, Your Illustriousness," he said to me, sarcastically overenunciating the title that Carly had used to address the Guardian. He started into a deep bow, then stopped abruptly. "Oh, wait— that ain't really yer title, is it?"

I was suddenly as dizzy as I'd been in that plummeting omnicab on Zinkiwu. Paulie had already figured out that I wasn't a Guardian. The Earth was doomed.

"Anyways," he continued, "I'd love to stay and yap. But my Wrinkle outta here's finally about to open. So, see ya."

"Hey, when can we get something signed?" Pugwash gurgled urgently through his congested nose. "We need to get that business incorporated, pronto."

"I'll, uh, have my people draw somethin' up," Paulie muttered.

"Meanwhile I can keep the prototype, right?" Pugwash asked, holding up a stereopticon.

"'Fraid not," Paulie said. "That'd be against interplanetary, uh, trade rules. So why doncha set it down here. Yer gonna have millions a them things soon."

Pugwash reluctantly put the stereopticon on the end table next to Paulie. It turned into a translucent puddle that flowed up his feathers and formed into a nautical-themed pashmina afghan (his answer to Manda's chunky necklace and Carly's crucifix, apparently). Moments later, both Paulie and the transformed stereopticon vanished.

Pugwash turned to me. "You're quite the con artist." He didn't say this judgmentally, but with professional respect.

"Me?"

"No, I'm talking to the cat."

"*Gggggggggh!*"

Pugwash turned to Manda. "Nick convinced Paulie that he was our Trade Regent to Asia. As if there's any such thing."

"I *what?*"

He kept addressing Manda. "Paulie's looking for a business partner, so he was here doing a reference check." He turned to me. "Quite the childhood you invented for yourself."

"You told him about my childhood." I now understood why Paulie had dropped in on Pugwash. At Eatiary, he must have guessed that we were related somehow. And he knew that any humanoid Guardian coming to Earth with the so-called trespassers right before the Townshend Line went up in the seventies would have been an adult. So he just needed to hear a couple of stories about me running around as a tot in the eighties to verify that I was nothing but a harmless Earthling—and he figured Pugwash would cough that up readily if we were in fact related. Particularly if he was bought off with the prospects of earning a quick fortune in intergalactic import-export.

"Nick told Paulie that he was raised from infancy in a Swiss boarding school for future Trade Regents," Pugwash chuckled to Manda. "As if." He turned back to me. "Paulie didn't know whether to believe this. So he asked me to show him some old family photo albums, and I'm afraid I did. I would have backed you up if you'd brought me in on the deal. But you wanted to keep it all to yourself, didn't you?"

"*What* deal?"

Pugwash turned back to Manda. "Paulie's gonna export these projectors to Earth. You saw what they can do. And I'm sorry that the test pissed you off. But I wanted to see how well they could work outside, and Paulie said I'd need some mirrors relaying the light down there. Then we decided to have some fun with it when Nick texted that he was coming over. I'll bet my mirrors are ruined, huh?"

"Yeah, they're kind of shot," she said. *Along with humanity's future.*

"Too bad. Anyway, the projector's the first product Paulie's bringing to Earth. But he has exclusive rights for *all* trade to the planet for the next fifteen years, and he needs to work with someone here. And, well," Pugwash turned to me. "Sorry, but he was pretty upset about you faking your résumé."

"So let me guess—he'll be working with you instead?" As I had figured, it was no coincidence that Paulie had booked his shipment to Earth right after Pugwash texted me that the two of them had become buddies. And given that he knew the truth about me when he did this, it was no doubt a payload of metallicam, a half day before we expected it.

"He's gonna do more than just work with me. He's making me his *part*ner." Pugwash turned back to Manda. "An alien Peace Armada is planning a big White House landing in just a few weeks. They'll mainly be opening diplomatic channels. But Paulie's sponsoring it, so he has a few minutes in the program to demo the projector. Talk about product placement! It'll be the biggest event in human history. And, uh," he edged a bit closer to her. "I can get you great seats."

I sighed. On top of everything else, Pugwash was now waging a ham-fisted campaign to get into Manda's pants. He wouldn't act this way if he knew I was crazy about her— because while I've probably made it hard to believe, he's kind of a decent guy. Of course, my feelings for Manda should have been clear to him. But Pugwash tends to view other people as being charismatic androids who exist primarily to shuffle opportunities and obstacles in and out of his life. So he tends to miss obvious signals, and is prone to being a major jerk by accident.

It took about fifteen minutes to get the truth about the aliens across to him. This should have gone faster, given that he's way too bright to be gulled by something as improbable as that nonsense about me pretending to be a "Trade Regent." But when sinister parrots materialize in our apartments bearing mind-blowing alien technologies, it's not unreasonable to accept whatever they say after they've laid out their initial bona fides. The fact that Pugwash was highly disposed to embrace everything that Paulie told him made him all the readier to drink the Kool-Aid. And when Manda and I finally laid out the truth, it was emotionally wrenching for him to let go of the trade monopoly that he briefly thought he held with the rest of the universe, and the journey from denial to acceptance took some time.

"So now what?" he finally asked dejectedly. "Is he gonna blow us all up with a photon torpedo?"

I shook my head. "He can't harm us directly. So he needs to get us to destroy ourselves somehow. And it's a safe bet he'll be using the shipment that he booked right after he figured out that I'm not a Guardian."

"You mean right after I *told* him that," Pugwash said, perhaps feeling something verging faintly on guilt.

"Well, he was going to learn it from that reality show tomorrow morning anyway," I said.

"Maybe," Manda snipped, still irked about the faux suicide. "But we'd be a *lot* better off having until tomorrow morning instead of—what time did you say that damned shipment's coming in tonight? Ten-fifteen? That's barely more than an hour from now!"

Pugwash nodded miserably. "You're right, we need—" he said nasally, then gasped. "Need to—" he paused, and held his hands out to either side of his torso, like a kid edging onto a balance beam.

Here it comes, I thought.

Pugwash suddenly reared back his head, then snapped it forward like a rattlesnake, while emitting an explosive, sodden bark. Manda jumped back three feet. The normally unflappable Meowhaus leapt up to an impressively high point on a bookshelf. And I looked around for a tissue. Pugwash's sneezes had been a source of wonder throughout my childhood. I almost wouldn't mind being sick myself, since it meant that my brothers and cousins would also be sick, and we'd be entertained for days by these nasal M-80s.

"We need to talk to him," Pugwash finally said. "Convince him you're a Guardian after all. I can tell him I made everything up, and say the pictures in the photo album were of some other kid."

"That sounds like a long shot," Manda said. "And besides, it's not like we can just drop in on him."

"Actually, we can," I said, pulling the subway map with the directions to the alien base from my pocket.

SEVENTEEN
DECAPALOOZA

The directions on the subway map were very precise. Step one was going to the lobby of the Waldorf-Astoria hotel, a half dozen blocks north of Grand Central Station. The rain had stopped, and we found a cab quickly. But traffic slowed to a crawl for several blocks around Union Square, and we really should have taken the subway. Once at the Waldorf, we found our way to an unmarked door along a hallway off the lobby. This opened onto a long staircase that led to an industrial maze of bare concrete floors, exposed lightbulbs, and noisy pipes. We followed our directions through about a dozen left and right turns, before getting to a squat metal door that opened onto a pitch-dark staircase.

"*Gggggggggggh!*" Meowhaus darted down it fearlessly, then turned around to peer at us. His flashing eyes showed that we only had about twenty steps to descend. Pugwash bombarded them with his "light cannon," a monster flashlight that he picked up in Paraguay, right before trekking out to visit some primitive tribe that he hoped to wow with modern technology.*

"Some people have to do the damnedest things to get laid," Manda said, setting off down the steps.

"My research in Pahra*khwai* had nothing to do with that," Pugwash retorted. "It was a sociological experiment."

"Proving once again that dumbshits with flashlights can look like gods to geniuses, if the geniuses are from the technological past," Manda said, fingering the tacky necklace that was Özzÿ's stereopticon in disguise.

Downstairs we found a network of steam tunnels, where our instructions called for several more lefts and rights. At one point we passed a huge black circle that was painted onto the wall, along with three menacing orange triangles. A peeling sign read: F LOUT SH LT R. Right after that, we got a big scare when a leviathan roar began somewhere deep in the tunnels, then approached us at a terrifying speed. It was a subway, of course. As it thundered by on the far side of an ancient wall, Pugwash insisted that he could tell it was the uptown 5 train from its distinctive rattling.

After a few more turns, we got to a final metal door that was coated in rust. I forced it open. On the far side, a vintage locomotive loomed. It rested beside an abandoned platform, on a set of tracks that led up around the bend into darkness. A single car was attached to it—an aging behemoth that looked like it was heavily armored. I went to the passenger car's last door, as directed. It was stubborn but

*His flashlight, hand-cranked radio, and Mardi Gras beads failed to impress, however, since the chief's son had recently brought in three crates of Pop Rocks and an iPod Touch.

unlocked, and opened into a sort of rolling conference room. A long, sturdy table sat in the middle of it, surrounded by a dozen heavy, formal chairs. Everything looked decades old—in terms of both style and state of decay. Above it all loomed the Seal of the President of the United States. "Odd place for a cabinet meeting," I muttered, making my way to the table's far diagonal corner, where I flipped over a chair as instructed. On its underside I found a small, glowing panel with seven colored buttons. Referring to my directions, I pressed in a quick combination.

A soft ambient light immediately bathed the car in the golden tones of sunset. Moments later, a closet door on the far side of the conference table popped open. "So, it finally happened," came a friendly voice. "Everyone said there'd never be a human visitor. Never, ever! But I'd always say— sure, there will be. You just have to be patient. And, optimistic!" We all craned our necks, but saw nothing. "Hey, I'm down here."

Just then, an energetic critter rounded the corner of the table, which loomed several inches over its head. It was a Decapus—a species whose anglicized name is inspired by its ten limbs.* When a Decapus walks, its limbs cluster below it and weave slightly, like a group of mingling drunks. All locomotion comes from its digits, which wriggle frenetically and propel it forward. Their muscular torsos are covered in

---

*You can't really call them "arms" or "legs," because each of them doubles as both of those things—as well as a trunk of sorts (they breathe through them, like elephants), reproductive gear in two cases (there's no telling which ones), and an off-ramp for liquid waste in another (but if you ever meet one of these guys, don't worry—Decapus etiquette will protect you from shaking hands with the limbs that you'd rather not touch).

silky, chestnut-colored fur, and they have the faces and attitudes of relentlessly upbeat squirrels (except when they're on the clock).

"Bruce is the name," the Decapus said, raising three limbs to shake hands with each of us at once. "But everyone just calls me The Boss."

"Big Springsteen fan?" I guessed.

"Who isn't?" The Boss finished shaking our hands and gave us three thumbs-up signs. "Especially with Jersey being just a couple miles that a way." A fourth limb pointed directly behind him. "But mainly, they call me The Boss because I'm the foreman here." A fifth limb pointed toward the closet that he'd just popped out of. "Anyways—my instructions are to give access to anyone who knows the access code, no questions asked." Limb number six saluted. "So, this way to our little outpost." He started toward the closet and I smiled. Carly had said that the folks staffing the transmission center were friendly and gentle, and so far, she seemed to be right.

"You know, we've waited so long to see a person in person that I can't help but wonder what you're doing here," The Boss continued, as we followed him. "Even though I'm sure it's none of my business."

"I don't mind telling you," I said. "We were sent to meet with Paulie and Özzÿ."

It was as if I'd just sucked half the oxygen out of the room. "Oh," The Boss said, without a trace of enthusiasm. "Them. I guess I should have guessed, I guess. What with you showing up so soon after them, and all."

So Paulie had already alienated the local team. Bravo. "Between you and me, Boss," I said, dropping my voice conspiratorially. "We're, uh . . . not such big fans of Paulie's. We just need to have a quick chat with him."

The Boss's sunny mood snapped right back into place. "You know something? Don't tell anybody, but I'm not the biggest fan myself. I mean, anyone coming in from Central is important. Obviously! But we're all workers and peasants, right? Class unity and all? So you'd think he'd treat his equals as equals. All things being equal." He opened the door to the closet, which turned out to be a mechanical capsule of some sort.

"So how do you feel about his . . . project?" I fished.

"Fine, I guess." The Boss waved us into the capsule, which barely fit us all. "Bringing unlimited energy to the Earth is a good thing. Especially if it frees people up to write more music, like Paulie keeps saying."

"You're talking about his plans for the metallicam, right?" The reference to "unlimited energy" almost had to mean this—but I wanted verification. Manda was recording everything on the stereopticon, and we needed all the hard evidence that we could get for Guardian 1138.

"Exactly." The Boss swung the capsule door shut. "Hold on tight." We dropped as fast as a sack of lead for a couple of seconds, then slowed to a gentle stop. "Anyways, I'll take you to see Paulie now. And hey! We're gonna cut right through the main shop floor. It's where we've been ripping, uploading, and distributing the music since day one. Want a quick tour?"

"If it's right on the way, why not? But we're in a hurry."

The wall in front of us slid open, revealing a long, low-slung room that housed hundreds of vintage turntables and cassette decks sitting on little cabinets. Everything had the boxy lines and fake wood veneer of the Carter era. At least eight Decapuses were clustered around each component, and maybe half were sound asleep.

"When we got here right after the Kotter Moment, the Guardian Council approved a single surface run, so we could grab a bunch of music," The Boss explained as we took this all in. "There was this Disc-O-Mat store in the main concourse of Grand Central back then. So we triggered a little blackout up there around three in the morning, and swiped all the merchandise. But when we got it down here, we realized we needed something to play all the records and tapes on. And our blackout was almost over! So we ran back up, and grabbed a whole stereo store belonging to this crazy guy called Crazy Eddie.* Remember him? Anyways. The gear's been here ever since."

"And it all still works?" Pugwash marveled. I'm sure he was wondering how much vintage hi-fi's could fetch on eBay.

"Probably. But who cares? Your music's all digital these days," The Boss said.

"But you still seem to have lots of folks . . . doing things with the stereos," Manda pointed out.

The Boss gave her an incredulous look. "*Doing* things? They're not doing shit—they're working!"

At the mention of work, the nearby Decapuses opened their mouths and made a noise that sounded like steel claws savaging a chalkboard. After a few jaw-grinding seconds, I started picking out some words. There was "live long," "pension spiking," "card check," and countless hi-ho's. It

---

*I later learned that the rushed schedule forced them to "grab the whole store" quite literally—leaving nothing behind but a smoking shell laced with exotic compounds that are unknown on Earth. Our federal government did a brilliant job of covering all of this up, and to this day, several top-ranking agents are completely freaked out over it.

was a work song. The most gloomy, crotchety, lazy-ass work song ever heard this side of Athens.

"So how long has it been since you actually had a new album to encode?" Pugwash asked after the workers shut up.

"Late seventy-eight. We grabbed the Disc-O-Mat that summer, and ran everything through by December.* Then we pulled stuff off the radio for maybe twenty years. After that, we switched to the Internet."

"And these guys still show up and get paid, even though they don't have anything to do here?" Pugwash was almost indignant about their good fortune (perhaps forgetting that this had been his own de facto arrangement at Google for all those years).

The Boss nodded vehemently. "I'll bet some of them would show up even if they *did* have stuff to do. Remember, we're government. Do you have any idea of what our benefits are like?"

Recalling that he was a multimeta-intercultural relativist, Pugwash managed to nod politely. "Yes, I see. It's quite enriching to learn about this . . . alien style of hard work."

"*Alien?*" The Boss said. "It's as human as farting! Haven't you ever been to the DMV?" By now, we were heading along the main aisle toward a door in the back of the shop.

"And how are the wages?" I asked.

---

*When this happened, sophisticates throughout the universe delighted in the newly unleashed archives of jazz and classical. But to this day, most folks remain loyal to the pop, disco, and (above all) blistering hard rock that dominated the airwaves during that first magical year of discovery. For this reason, hip-hop, which didn't emerge commercially until late 1979, never caught on in the Refined League to the degree that it did here on Earth.

"They're fine," The Boss said. "Not that they make up for the isolation of living and working on Earth, right boys?"

The three Decapuses who happened to be awake at the nearest workstation shook their heads lethargically. "The Man is screwing us," one of them mumbled.

"And not that it makes up for the backbreaking *nature* of the work—right boys?"

Two of the Decapuses shook their heads again (the third had since nodded off).

"And not that it makes up for the dangerous, deadly *dangers!*" The Boss practically yodeled, hitting a revival hall crescendo.

His audience ignored him. One of them had just opened a cassette door, and the other was busy closing it.

"What *dangers* are you talking about?" Manda asked.

"Well . . ." The Boss was stumped. Then, "Okay. Suppose we stacked up all of these turntables over there." He waved seven of his limbs as if he was shooing the gear into a corner. "And then the whole pile fell. Right . . . on your *head!*" He pounded his limbs onto his head, which flattened dramatically for a moment. I tried to picture this, but just couldn't get past the part where the workers found the gumption to stack up the turntables in the first place.

By then we had reached the far side of the shop floor, and an automatic door slid open onto a bustling warren of tunnels. The main ones were wide enough to allow a dozen Decapuses (or the three of us) to walk shoulder to shoulder, and were lined with eateries, dance halls, and other public spots. All of these places were open to the street (let's call it that), and were gently lit by a soft, golden gleam that reminded me of candlelight. Tributary tunnels branched off the main ones at every conceivable angle. These were too narrow for any of us to enter (except Meowhaus), and looked like they led into quieter residential areas, where pools of golden light cascaded from snug little windows.

The whole setup was as cozy as a Scandinavian mountain town on Christmas Eve. And everywhere—the major tunnels, the tributaries, and all of the public spaces—was thronging with energized, gibbering Decapuses. Our group got some curious looks as we passed through. But most of the Decapuses were too engaged in each other to give us much attention. I couldn't imagine any one of them drooping lifelessly over a Kenwood tape deck. But I guess we all have a work persona.

After a few minutes we entered a spacious cavern. It was about fifty feet tall, and broad as a small city square. The Boss pointed at a box-shaped building about the size of a suburban garage right in the center of it. "They're in there," he said.

As we approached the building's front door, a passerby pointed at Manda with seven limbs, and made an excited gibbering sound. Its companion pulled a stereopticon out of a sort of marsupial pouch, consulted it, and gibbered something back. At that, they started jumping up and down, making high five–like moves with their limbs. Then they took off at a dead run.

The Boss looked at Manda. "So. You're a singer?" he asked.

"Yes, actually," she said. "Did those guys . . . recognize me or something? I'm not exactly famous."

"Well, from what they said, you've got an album out on Merge."

Manda nodded. Merge is in fact her label. They don't

put a ton of money behind their artists, but have enough indie cred to affect the tides.

"We distribute everything on Merge," The Boss said. "That puts your music into over four hundred billion galaxies. And while you're no Arcade Fire, some of the kids around here listen to everything that's local."

"There's a lot of local music in New York," Manda said, clearly astonished by all of this.

"No, I mean locally local." He pointed up toward the city's surface with several limbs. "As in midtown-ish. You live in Murray Hill, right? These kids are loyal to their neighborhood. Anyways. Let's go in and see those two." He led us up to the main door, which snapped open to admit us.

Özzÿ was stationed right inside, next to a small table that stood at about hand height to him. He was shifting several coasterlike pads around its surface very carefully. Paulie was hovering like a hummingbird about five feet above him, peering intently at a long series of thumbnail images that were beaming out of a small stereopticon that was draped around his neck. Each image seemed to depict a tiny document. An enlargement of one was floating above the rest— a page that looked like it was written in Russian.

"Paulie, you got visitors," The Boss announced. When Paulie saw us, he dropped halfway to the ground from shock, then fluttered to a safe landing. Özzÿ continued shuffling his coasters, ignoring us.

"Paulie, so good to see you again," I boomed. "How goes the, uh—unlimited energy project?"

"Who're you to ask?" Paulie turned to The Boss. "And whaddaya doing, bringing humans in here?"

"They knew the access code, so I let 'em in," The Boss said hotly. "Rules are rules. And that's the rule!"

"The energy project, Paulie?" I repeated. "Details, details."

Paulie glared at Pugwash. "Tell your cousin to quit buggin' me. Or my deal with you is off."

"He's not actually my cousin," my cousin said, following our script. "I just know him through work. I made that cousin stuff up because I wanted you to think he was a liar, so you might make me your partner instead of him."

"Yeah, right," Paulie chuckled. "I don't have time for none a you." He made a quick gesture with his wing, and Pugwash vanished.

"Where'd you put him?" I asked in a shocked tone.

"Wh-what're you still doin' here?" Paulie asked in an even more shocked tone. He looked around wildly, and saw that Manda was also still with us. "And *you?*"

"Dammit, tell me where you sent my c—colleague," I demanded (almost blowing everything by calling Pugwash my cousin).

"I dunno—somewhere in midtown. Wherever the shortest Wrinkle connection would put him," Paulie said. "But why are *you* still *here?*"

His growing panic made me realize that things were going even better than I'd hoped. It seemed that the Guild had, in fact, given Paulie the power to Dislocate, or Wrinkle beings without their permission. And he'd apparently just tried to Dislocate all of us up to the city's surface. But since Manda and I were carrying the Guardian's "Foilers," we couldn't be sent anywhere against our will. And Paulie surely knew that only Guardians have Foilers.

Time to spook him even more. I bent down and ran my hand across the floor. "Hey, Boss. This floor feels really nice.

What's it made out of?" As I said this, Manda started strolling around the transit bay, turning her head to and fro with every step. She was still capturing everything she could on the stereopticon.

"Some nanosubfiber, I think," The Boss said, utterly confused by all of this.

"Well, it feels so silky soft, I just have to see what it's like to walk on it." I removed my shoes. As I pulled off my socks, Manda averted her gaze per my request—but Paulie fluttered up a few feet to get a better view. As soon as he saw my sixteen toes, he dropped halfway to the floor from shock again.

I took a few steps. "Wow, this nanonanofiber is fabulous, Boss—I should get some for my apartment." With that, I put my shoes and socks back on, and Paulie started fluttering around in anxious little circles. He had plenty of reasons to be nervous. My toes had just identified me as a Perfuffinite—so I couldn't be the ordinary human that Pugwash had portrayed me as earlier in the evening. And since I'd definitely been living on Earth since long before Carly and Frampton knocked out the Townshend Line, I pretty much had to be one of the mysterious "trespasser" aliens who arrived in 1977. That, and the bizarre immunity that Manda and I had to Dislocation, would have made it seem virtually certain that I was a Guardian after all.

"So, Paulie," I pressed. "The energy project. Tell me more. And please—use my title. I'd hate to have to incinerate you for disrespecting me."

Paulie landed and stared hard at the ground. "Right to silence, Your Illustriousness. I ain't sayin nothin' without no lawyer from the Guild."

"Then why not *sing* something?" I jeered, angling to enrage him into saying something stupid. "Oh, that's right—no one wants to hear your singing anymore. Do they?"

The physiological differences between Paulie's species and our own parrots must be significant. Because over the next several seconds, his feathers went from canary yellow, to bitter orange, to kamikaze red. As he spun through the color wheel, Paulie started vibrating with rage—much as Özzÿ had when Manda taunted him. But he held his peace.

I turned to his sidekick. "How about you, Özzÿ? Why don't you tell me about your little table?"

Özzÿ pushed the coasterlike things around it more frenetically. "I've never seen you, never ever, not even once in my life, Your Illustriousness," he wheezed.

Ah yes—I'd talked him into keeping Paulie in the dark about our first meeting. Well done, Özzÿ. Glancing at my watch, I decided to quit while I was ahead. I was supposed to meet Carly and Frampton in Warcraft in less than an hour. And my work here was done, since Paulie clearly wouldn't be trying anything rash until after tomorrow's episode of *Sonny & His Sirelings* proved that I wasn't a Guardian after all. I turned to The Boss. "These two aren't talking, so please take us back to the surface."

He nervously consulted his stereopticon. "That might be tricky. It turns out that it's . . . a little crowded outside."

"A little crowded?"

"Maybe a lot crowded." The Boss walked over to one of the walls. "Now, don't panic. This'll be like a one-way mirror. No one outside can see us."

He waved three of his limbs in a complex pattern. With that, the walls and the ceiling all vanished, and we beheld . . . *every Decapus on Earth*. They filled the entire cavern, and every tunnel feeding into it. The floor was completely invisible beneath their tightly packed bodies.

"Whoa," Manda said.

This being my first spontaneous subterranean alien mob, I was briefly terrified. But then I realized it was a *peaceful* spontaneous subterranean alien mob. No one out there was pushing or shoving. A few were chattering, but most were silent. And everyone was holding limbs with three or four neighbors in a way that was almost reverential. Then I noticed the first placard. It looked like a slapdash sign made by one of those Meadowlands drunks who paints his face green, and sobs when the Jets lose. It featured three hand-drawn glyphs—an eyeball, a Valentine-like heart, and a ravenous fish. Scanning the crowd, I saw a few similar signs, as well as a banner that was covered with a vertical cascade of words: Musical, Angellic [*sic*], Nice, Debutantey, and again, Angellic (and again, [*sic*]).

I turned to Manda. "Hey, it looks like you've got some . . . fans." The eyeball, heart, and toothy fish had to mean "I Love Shark." And the first letters in the cascade of words spelled out M-A-N-D-A.

"Holy shhhhhhh . . ." She didn't finish the thought, but I got the gist.

Paulie had put two and two together as well, and turned to The Boss. "You coulda warned me that you'd brung your colony's favorite singer down here." He was testy, but had more or less reined in his temper (and his feathers were almost back to their normal yellow color).

"I didn't," The Boss said defensively. "She just became their favorite singer a couple minutes ago." He went on to tell Paulie about the sighting that occurred as we were approaching his work space. "My team says that after that, the news that an actual singer had actually come to the actual cavern spread like lightning," he concluded, consulting his stereopticon. "Even though most folks hadn't heard of her, the whole colony naturally started listening to one of her songs. And it's already the biggest hit down here since 'Macarena.'"

Paulie instantly relaxed and got a blissed-out look on his face. "God, I love that song," he whispered huskily.

"Don't get me started!" They both sighed and gazed absently into the distance—The Boss mouthing the words to the Macarena song, and Paulie miming the steps of the Macarena dance.

"*Gggggggggh!*" Something about this fascinated Meowhaus.

"Maybe next time, we can get Los del Río down here," Paulie said wistfully.

"Are they the ones who sing 'The Macarena'?" I guessed.

They both looked at me like I'd crashed the State of the Union and asked who the loudmouth at the podium was. "*The* Macarena?" Paulie asked. "*The* Macarena? It's *Macarena*! No goddamn definite article, you troglodyte! And yes—Los del Río is the band behind the greatest dance song since the Big Bang."

"Pardon my ignorance, but I was raised by wild dogs. Now, tell me how you're getting us out of here? And don't forget to call me Your Illustriousness this time."

Since there'd be no getting through Manda's adoring public, we quickly agreed that the only way out was a Wrinkle. Paulie figured out that he could place us within a block of where he'd put Pugwash. And this time, we let him send us.

EIGHTEEN
AVATARDIER

"Seriously? He *canceled* it?" I leapt to my feet and did a little jig that looked even stupider on my Warcraft avatar's brawny green body than I expected. Carly celebrated by having her Blood Elf avatar flash me with that pornographic chest. Then Frampton's Death Knight leapt toward me with his right hand overhead. I bounded toward him and met the high five, briefly forgetting that my actual body was surrounded by the fragile flotsam of Pugwash's live-in scrapbook of an apartment. Out there in reality, my hand connected with something that felt indigenous and expensive—silky fibers arrayed on some sort of twig skeleton that I smashed to atoms.

"Dammit," Pugwash's disembodied voice whined from outside our Warcraft scene. "That merkin stand was from *Borneo!*"

"Sorry, dude," I said. "But saving the world calls for a bit of celebrating." I'd just learned that Paulie had canceled the inbound Wrinkle that Carly and I had seen in the queue at pluhhhs base. Since he'd surely rebook it once *Sonny & His Sirelings* made it clear that I wasn't a Guardian the following morning, I'd only saved the world for ten or eleven hours. But it was a start.

"So tell me more," I asked Carly's virtual tart.

"Well, from the timing records that pluhhhs gave me, I can confirm that Paulie booked the Wrinkle right after your idiot cousin told him about your childhood."

"Why are you calling my cousin an idiot?" I asked. The answer to this was self-evident. But Pugwash could only hear my end of the conversation, and I thought he'd enjoy knowing what the most famous babe in the universe had just called him.

Carly ignored the question. "pluhhhs also told me that the Wrinkle was just ninety-eight seconds from activating when you suckered Paulie into shutting it down. So that was truly brilliant work." Her smutty little avatar flashed me again.

"And was it metallicam?"

"Apparently. The Wrinkle was to originate in a metallicam depot."

"And how long will it take them to rebook it after the episode airs?" I asked.

"The episode broadcasts tomorrow morning at nine fifty-eight, New York time. And Paulie will be able to establish a connection between the depot and Grand Central just an hour and a quarter after that."

"So we're looking at eleven-fifteen or so."

Carly's ray-traced jezebel nodded. "And one other thing. Paulie apparently intended to relay the metallicam out to five different points on Earth shortly after it arrived under Grand Central. pluhhhs haven't figured out exactly where the target destinations were, but they're working on it."

"I might actually have some evidence on that front." I finally told her that Manda and I had ended up with Özzÿ's stereopticon. I then described the thumbnail documents that Paulie was looking at when we entered the transit bay. Given the stereopticon's panoramic lensing and unlimited resolution, Manda should have picked up detailed images of all of them.

Carly told me to have Manda jab a USB cable into the stereopticon (assuring me that a perfect socket would form to accommodate the plug as she did this), and to connect the other end of it to the computer that my Bono glasses were attached to. "So why didn't you tell me that you guys had a stereopticon?" Carly asked grumpily, as Manda followed her instructions. The answer was that I'd been annoyed by all of her stonewalling right after I arrived on her planet, and had decided to keep that fact to myself for a while. Then we got all distracted by fighting for our lives and whatnot, and I'd simply forgotten to mention it.

"Because nobody tells you anything, duh," I said, shrugging.

Once we had access to the stereopticon's recorded footage, Carly summoned a virtual plasma TV (not a standard Warcraft feature, I'm sure), and we gathered our avatars around it as she fast-forwarded through the evening. At one point, she slowed it down for a scene of Manda, Pugwash, and me walking through the city streets. "Bear with me, this is actually really useful," she said, shifting to a playback angle that set me off against the city's skyline. She tweaked at this for a few seconds, then jumped to the part where we all joined Paulie and Özzÿ in the transit bay. Here, the first thing she zoomed in on was Özzÿ sliding the coasterlike pads around his small table.

"Do you know what he's doing?" I asked.

"Practicing," Carly said. "When the metallicam Wrinkles in, it will arrive on that table. He'll then need to array the containers in just the right way for the outbound five-way Wrinkle to work. A burger-flipper could probably do it. But given that it's metallicam, he's wise to practice his moves." She paused the playback and stared at Özzÿ.

"What do you see?" I asked.

"I see . . ." She gave me a worried look, and pointed at the TV screen. "I see an incredibly useful recording. One that you're telling me was made with Özzÿ's own stereopticon. Which is bizarre, because Paulie should have deactivated that thing the instant he knew it was missing. It's a huge security hole for them."

"I've been wondering why it hasn't been shut down myself. But why would *Paulie* be the one to do it?"

"Because Özzÿ's stereopticon is a sensitive part of the Guild's data infrastructure. So I'm sure he was supposed to report it the moment he lost it. And Paulie or someone else in his chain of command should have investigated, and crippled the thing by now."

"Aha. In that case, I think I know what's going on." I reminded her about how I had persuaded Özzÿ to not let on that I'd caught him in my apartment. "So the poor dumbshit's so scared for his job that he can't tell anyone that he lost his stereopticon," I chuckled.

Carly's anime ho nodded slowly. "That, or it's all a setup, you're the dumbshit, and they're using the stereopticon to spy on you."

"Oh, well, I've . . . carefully considered that possibility, and believe that it's quite remote."

"Yeah, right. I'd say it's a fifty percent chance, and you're considering it for the first time right now. But since we're already sunk if you're the sucker, let's assume that Özzÿ's the dumber-shit of the two of you for now, and play it that way."

"Got it. Great . . . plan."

"And if Özzÿ really is that stupid, we can bet he'll get caught soon enough. And when he does, they'll definitely start spying on you through his stereopticon. Unless Paulie throws a tantrum and cripples the thing before it occurs to him to do that."

I thought of how Paulie couldn't stop himself from brawling at Eatiary when he should have focused on interrogating me. "I'd give the tantrum high odds."

"Let's hope so. Anyway, let's look at those images."

Carly had no trouble enlarging Paulie's thumbnails until they were easily legible. They turned out to be letters in several human languages, which she converted into documents that we could hold in our virtual Warcraft hands.

"God*damn,*" I said flipping through the English material. It included a letter addressed to the president, as well as ones to the heads of the CIA, the Joint Chiefs of Staff, the NSA, and so forth. The letters identified several unstable regimes and violent insurgencies that had just gotten their hands on an immensely destructive substance. They assured our leaders that the recipients had been fully apprised of the substance's inherent dangers, and that they would therefore *surely* use it responsibly. However, the letters said:

I still thought you might want to know about this anyway, just in case you feel funny about these guys controlling something that makes your entire Nuclear Arsenal look like a flaccid spitball. Oh, and PS! I should mention that this stuff could also be used as an inexhaustible source of CLEAN ENERGY. Cool, huh?! Of course, that doesn't do you much good, because it's sitting at the coordinates that I've listed below, none of which lie in territory that you control (at least not yet, huh??? ;-)

Oh, and PPS! I've also forwarded all of this Information to the leaders of Russia, China, India, Israel—and even Estonia (why not?!). I figured they might want to know, too. In fact, I kind of hit "send" on my note to the Chinese an hour early by mistake (oops!). For all I know, they may already be on their way to try and seize the stuff (sorry 'bout that!).

The letters ended with latitude and longitude numbers that pinpointed the locations of the five metallicam caches down to the millimeter, followed by a flurry of X's and O's. Attached to each was a page of elaborate mathematics.

"What's all this?" I asked, looking at the equations.

"Scientific proof of the letter's claims," Carly said. "Any skilled physicist who examines it will know this is all for real." She turned to her brother's avatar. "How's the foreign stuff looking?" As she and I read through the English material, Frampton had been applying translation tools to the rest of it.

"Very reassuring," he said.

"Why? What did you find?" Carly asked suspiciously.

"The letters are mostly instructions for using metallicam as an energy supply. Which is good, right?"

"Sure," I said. "Assuming we want all of the world's energy to come from—" I glanced at the list of metallicam recipients. "Al-Qaeda, Myanmar, a band of Hutu rebels, the Serbian Maoist party, and some guy named Mahmoud in Karachi."

"But I'm sure those guys will do the right thing if they finally feel *needed*," Frampton insisted. "And on top of that, Paulie's sending them all tons of safety instructions."

"Seriously? What do they say?"

"Well, let's see . . . this letter to al-Qaeda warns them to absolutely never follow a certain eight-step process with their metallicam, because if they do, Israel will be destroyed by a monstrous wave of radiation. It's very detailed, so Paulie obviously takes safety seriously. He even underlined the words *absolutely never* twice!"

A quick inspection showed more of the same in the other documents. Paulie was basically giving some raving lunatics the tools and instructions they needed to wipe the Earth clean of the nations that most annoyed them. He was meanwhile divulging the details of this to some lesser lunatics with massive militaries at their disposal. Once the latter group had Paulie's letters authenticated by scientists, five nuclear-armed nations (and Estonia!) would plunge into a mad, violent race to snatch the metallicam out of five global flash points before somebody else did. Humanity's self-destruction was the only plausible result of this—either with or without the eventual detonation of the metallicam itself. And one way or another, the crazed scramble would surely trigger unlimited news coverage during the days (or hours) before everything blew up.

"Is this enough evidence for Guardian 1138 to get the Council to shut Paulie down?" I asked.

"Maybe," Carly said slowly. "But remember what he said about the Guild having the best lobbyists and lawyers in the universe. They may be able to obfuscate things if we manage to raise the issue to the Council."

"Seriously? But how?"

"Guardians are famously logical and literal-minded. So they might completely miss the irony in these letters. And even if they don't, they might be persuaded to let things take their course and see if humanity survives. Remember—their highest duty is always to make sure that self-destructive species actually self-destruct before they become dangerously sophisticated."

"So then what do we do?"

"I've been giving this a lot of thought, and I think I know someone who could turn the tide for us. After our show became such a huge success, Dad decided to build an amazing legal team for our family's media company—and he found a real superstar to become our lead attorney. This guy's actually argued three cases in front of the Guardian Council in the past, and he's hugely respected."

"He sounds incredible. But how will you get him on our side? Doesn't he take his orders from your father?"

"He does. So step one is getting Dad on our side."

"And how do we do that?" She was the one who had persuaded me that this was hopeless in the first place.

"By carrying out the plan that Frampton and I have already developed to sabotage the airing of tomorrow's show. All of this actually fits perfectly with it."

"Great. What is it?"

"In a few hours, I'm holding a press conference in which I'll tell the universe that I'm in a romantic relationship with an Earth-based Guardian," Carly said. "It'll be a colossal news story. When Dad sees how huge it is, he'll definitely want to run with it. Which means he'll have to play along with the idea that there's a Guardian living on Earth. Once he's on board, I'll show him our proof that the Guild is on the cusp of destroying humanity. And then he'll definitely let me take our lawyer to the Guardian Council."

"But he doesn't seem to care about protecting humanity."

"He doesn't. But he'll definitely want to protect his new story line."

"That sounds . . . kind of nuts. But it could work."

"It only has to work for a couple of days—maybe a week, tops. Because once our lawyer gets a chance to address the Council, humanity should be safe, and we can call the whole thing off. But you need to try to buy us some time on your side, too, because this is no shoo-in, and we need a Plan B."

"I agree—and I think I might have one," I said. About twenty minutes earlier I'd gotten a text from Judy that grudgingly accepted my apology for being MIA all afternoon, and confirmed the next day's meetings with Fido and the big CEO. And I had some ideas for those meetings that could just set off some fireworks.

"Two minutes until our connection breaks off," Frampton warned. Earth and Zinkiwu wouldn't be able to reconnect again until the next morning.

"We'll need to schedule things very carefully during the coming days," Carly said. "Because along with everything else, you and I need to generate some more footage together."

"We . . . what?"

"Nick, I'm about to tell the universe that I'm in a relationship with an Earth-based Guardian. I can't just make a wild claim like that without some evidence."

"Which means?"

"Which means that *you* have to play the Guardian that I'm involved with. My own stereopticon has captured lots of footage of you and me together, and of you with my family. And now we have Manda's recordings of you running around New York, which is a huge windfall for us."

"Why?"

"Because it shows that you're really from Earth. Nothing that's shot with a stereopticon can be modified without the changes being logged in a metafile that viewers can access. So everyone will know that the New York footage is authentic. That, combined with the footage of you and me together, will be enough to electrify the entire universe at the press conference. But we'll need more than that to keep the story rolling for the next few days. Remember, *Sonny & His Sirelings* is high-budget reality programming. Everything needs to be scripted very carefully, or it'll seem fake."

"O-kay. Got it. Well . . . what do we need?"

"Scenes of the two of us eating in two or three different restaurants. A quarrel about my career. Me lost in thought in a taxi. You bringing me a box of chocolates to apologize. Us building a sand castle that towering waves fail to destroy. A motorboat chase involving guns and a grenade launcher through the canals of Venice."

"Sounds . . . fine."

"That, and about twelve hours of sex tapes should get us through a week of episodes."

"Wait—*what?*"

"Nick, the viewers would see right through a relationship that isn't completely saturated in sex. In Refined society, the reproductive arts are second only to music."

"*Seriously?*"

"Absolutely."

I desperately needed time to process Carly's bizarre suggestion. It pointed to dimensions of Refined society that I didn't know existed, and raised hundreds of profound questions about cultural relativism on galactic scales.

Well—one, anyway. "And are you guys as . . . adept at the reproductive arts as you are at, say, interior design?"

"Oh, we're way, way adepter."

With that, my id seized uncontested control of my mind. I let it have its way for a moment before launching a clumsy bid to reclaim my moral center. "But . . . well, it's complicated," I nattered pathetically. "I mean, she's not my *girl*friend. Not yet, and—probably not ever. But . . ."

Carly's rasterized nympho nodded understandingly. "Manda, right?"

"Exactly."

"I think she's perfect to play your neighbor. It fits great with the footage that we already have, obviously. We'll just keep her as a minor figure for the first two episodes. Then the third one will start with you coming home from buying me flowers, and finding a refrigerated package addressed to Manda down in your lobby. She won't answer when you buzz up. So you'll use a spare key that she's given you to put the package into her freezer before it thaws. And when you walk into her kitchen, you'll find the two of us having sex on a counter."

I just looked at her.

"Trust me on this one. Nothing works better in a story line than infidelity and female bisexuality. It's an iron law of physics."

"Five seconds until the connection breaks," Frampton said.

"Now try to get those music licenses," Carly said. "My idea might not work." And with that, the connection broke.

NINETEEN
PLAN B

Manda, Meowhaus, and I were still in Pugwash's apartment at eight o'clock the next morning. We were running on exactly two hours of sleep, having spent most of the night creating our "recruiting pitch" for Judy. Pugwash had learned how to access a stereopticon's library of pre-rendered objects and effects when he and Paulie assembled that scene of him falling from the window. Between that and Manda's recording and projecting skills, we were able to concoct a 3D show that could shock & awe anyone into believing that aliens are entirely real. The plan was for Manda to hide behind my office desk when Judy came by to take me to the meeting with Fido later that morning. I'd get Judy to shut the door on some pretext, and then Manda would crank things up on the stereopticon. This should get Judy on board. Then we'd basically repeat or modify the process as appropriate in our meetings with Fido, and with the music label CEO that we call The Munk.

I was feeling good about our prospects. We didn't actually need to change the law or get impossibly sweeping music licenses to achieve our goals. We just needed enough cooperation from either Fido or The Munk to buy us some time. A rough outline of a law to erase the universe's debts signed by the senator might convince Paulie that we were on the cusp of getting him what he wanted. Or maybe a nonbinding memo of understanding to the same effect from The Munk. Something impressive but meaningless (and therefore painless for Fido or The Munk to write) should do the trick. And we only needed to buy a few days. By now, Carly would have routed our evidence to Guardian 1138. And if her campaign to recruit her show's lawyer went as planned, they should have their audience with the Council soon.

"Holy crap," Pugwash bellowed. "Are you sure there's no way we can license this?" He was standing in the middle of his living room with my Bono glasses on, snapping his head around as he took in the sights of the enhanced alien version of Warcraft. He'd be hanging out in there until Carly or Frampton showed up with an update on their progress—presumably when the next Wrinkle connection opened, in a bit under an hour. After that, he'd go wait in the Waldorf's lobby, in case we needed him to rush down to the cavern beneath Grand Central to talk to Paulie or the Decapuses.

As he checked out the Warcraft vistas, Pugwash started wriggling and rubbing his hands over his body in a creepy, but oddly familiar way. "I haven't had this much fun since puberty," he said. "And I'm just moving an avatar around!" He wriggled some more.

"Are you doing . . . ?" I asked.

He caressed his hips with both of his hands.

"Is that the Macarena?"

"Makha-*reeeeee*-nyu," he corrected me, sounding like a Pakistani samurai hailing a cab. "And yes, I can't get that damn song out of my head."

"Speaking of music, see if you can get a digital copy of the awful song that our jailer sang right after sentencing us all to death," I asked, vaguely wondering if that precise sentence had ever been uttered in the English language before. "Both Carly and Frampton should have captured it on their stereopticons." Of course, there was probably no way to get their audio into a format that our computers could read, but it wouldn't hurt to ask.

"Sure—what do you need it for?" Pugwash asked, transitioning to a Texas two-step.

"An insane backup plan that I thought up while I was falling asleep. The jailer said that his song is the jointly owned property of everyone in the Refined League. So maybe we can get Google or someone to make a zillion illegal copies of it, to offset the copies that everyone in the Refined League has of our music?"

"What a stupid idea," Pugwash said, easing into the cha-cha.

"Probably. But I want to get every iron into the fire that I can. Anyway, don't hurt yourself in there. And remember to contact me the *instant* you hear from our alien friends." The last thing we needed was for him and Frampton to break into an impromptu dance party and lose all track of time.

"Don't worry, I'll call," Pugwash said, switching to a groovy sixties-looking boogie. A couple steps into it, he started making those kiddie-on-a-balance-beam moves that I know so well.

"Incoming!" I shouted instinctively. But neither Manda nor Meowhaus know my family's argot—so the warning was lost on them, and they both jumped halfway across the apartment when Pugwash unleashed another twenty-megaton sneeze.

Once everyone had recovered from that, Manda, Meowhaus, and I headed downstairs and hailed a cab. I was going straight to the office, while Manda would be swinging by her apartment to change into her paralegal garb, and to drop off Meowhaus.

"Your idea for copying the jailer's song is interesting," she said as our cab headed north.

"There's actually a ton of problems with it. But our other plans could all fall through, so we may as well have an extra backup."

"Then why don't I set up a C-Corporation to own the song's copyright?" she suggested. "A lawyer that I work with specializes in start-ups, and I incorporate things all the time. We can figure out how to distribute the stock to the Refined League later, if we actually need to."

"Sounds good, but how long will it take? Remember, we have Judy at nine-thirty."

"Seconds. My firm has this template that makes it go incredibly fast. And if I file the documents with Delaware, they can incorporate it in less than an hour for a thousand-dollar fee."

"Seriously?"

"Absolutely. And if Pugwash manages to get me a copy of the song, I can also hit the Library of Congress website and register the copyright in the C-Corp's name."

By 8:45 I was in my office and struggling to keep my eyes open. Right around 9:00, my assistant Barbara Ann rang through. "I have Joseph Stalin on the line for you. Says he's calling from . . . Prussia?"

"Ah, Stally. Please put him through." This would be Pugwash. He resents Barbara Ann for being both attractive and completely indifferent toward him (common as this is), and retaliates by identifying himself as renowned figures that she's too dim to know about whenever he calls. I have amassed quite a collection of Post-it notes saying things like "Kissinger can't make lunch on Tuesday," or "that Steven Hawking guy called again," or "Oogo Shavez has an extra Mets ticket for tonight."

"Dude, turn on your Skype," Pugwash said as soon as he was patched through. "I've got Carly networked in through Warcraft via my computer, and she has news. And keep me on the phone so I can listen in—I can only connect her to one Skype account, and that'll be yours."

I fired up Skype and answered an inbound call from SpaceVixen4Uxxx. Up popped a window displaying Carly's cybertramp.

"Bad news," she said as soon as our connection was live. "There's a wildcat strike under way on Zinkiwu. Everything connected to media and communications is completely shut down. It started five minutes after I announced my press conference. So there's no way I can hold it now."

"Let me guess—the Guild's behind it."

"Obviously."

"Do you think they know what you were planning to say?"

Carly's saucy little proxy shook her head. "Not a chance.

Only you and Frampton know that. But they do know that I'm working with you."

"How so?"

"Apparently, the jailer reported that we were traveling together right before he . . . stumbled down the steps."

"So they shut down the press conference as a precautionary step to keep you quiet."

"Exactly," Carly said. "Meanwhile, the episode that spills the beans about there not being a Guardian on Earth goes live throughout the universe in an hour and a quarter."

"Of course. So now what?"

"You *definitely* need to buy us a few days by getting something promising for Paulie from your senator, or that CEO. Meanwhile, pluhhhs are going to pull me and Frampton over to their planet as soon as you and I are done talking. Then they'll try to push us through to the Guardians' planet again. I don't know if we'll make it, though—the Guild will be watching for us there, and we know what happened last time."

"Well, for God's sake, be careful."

"We will be. pluhhhs will keep a tracking beam on us, and they'll yank us back if someone tries to hijack our Wrinkle at the very end of the trip again. And whether we make it through to the Guardians or come back to pluhhhs, we'll be on a planet that's at a Wrinkle Vertex. So we'll be able to come straight to Earth at any time, if circumstances warrant."

"Got it. Then let me tell you my schedule, so you'll know where to find me." I gave her the details on my meetings with Judy, Fido, and The Munk.

"Got it," Carly said. "Don't be surprised to see me or Frampton at some point."

"I won't be. Do me a favor though, and skip the religious garb, okay?"

The Blood Elf said nothing.

"I mean, there's lots of hats and things that you can wear to hide your sound-blocking gear, right?"

She was motionless as well as speechless.

I jiggled my mouse, and the cursor was motionless, too. *Naturally.* My PC was having one of its thrice-daily seizures. "Goddamn Windows!" I snarled under my breath.

"Crashed again, huh?" I'd forgotten that Pugwash was still listening in on the phone.

"How'd you guess?"

"You know, you really should have made the switch years ago." Pugwash is a committed Mac snob, and not even the apparent advent of doomsday on Earth could diminish the smug warmth that this fresh sign of the PC's inferiority was giving him. "Anyway, I should go see if I can reconnect with Carly in Warcraft. I lost her when I put her through to talk to you on Skype. But before that, I did manage to get a copy of that god-awful song for Manda."

"You *did*? How did you translate the audio from their format to ours?" I can barely send a spreadsheet from one computer to another without encountering some boneheaded compatibility issue.

"It was easy. Your Bono glasses are connected to my laptop through that USB cable. So I just recorded the audio that flowed through the computer while Carly played the song. Things like that are really easy on a Mac."

"Great. Anyway—"

"Also, my computer never crashes, and it's practically immune to viruses."

"Well, that's great, too. Listen, Manda's about to get here and—"

"And best of all, wireless networking's a breeze. Unlike on a PC. And the retail stores are a great resource. I can walk to *three* of them from my loft. Have you heard about their training classes?"

I eventually got him off the phone. A few minutes later, Barbara Ann rang to tell me that Manda had arrived. "Send her in," I said.

Despite everything, my heart gave a little flutter when the door opened. Manda is simply stunning in her professional garb—no surprise, I guess, coming from someone who's stunning in a Radiolab sweatshirt. She was wearing a gray pencil skirt, along with a blue satin blouse and a navy blazer that was nipped in at the waist. It all made for a fine display of her curves, while still being appropriately modest for a modern American office. The only thing that didn't fit the look was that garish necklace, but it was the least tacky form that Manda had found in the stereopticon's repertoire.

We had fifteen minutes before Judy was supposed to drop by to take me to Fido. Given how late she always runs, I figured this would give us at least a half hour to ourselves. "So you got the song?" I asked.

Manda nodded. "Your cousin emailed it to me while I was in the cab coming over. And here on Earth, it's already the copyrighted property of Intergalactic Music—a bouncing baby corporation that entered the world just a few minutes ago."

Before I could high-five her, Barbara Ann rang through again. "Judy's here," she announced.

Of course she was. The innate sense that tells Judy exactly how much lateness will make a media baron think she's maximally awesome must also alert her whenever an early arrival will be cripplingly troublesome for the person she's about to meet with.

"Dammit, Judy's here," I told Manda. She didn't have time to take a single step toward her hiding spot behind the desk before the door blasted open.

TWENTY
SHOCK & AWE

Judy made a beeline for Manda, who must have looked like a professional homunculus of herself, being similarly gorgeous, elegantly dressed, accessorized with a lawyerly attaché—and infuriatingly young. "I'm Judy Sherman," she said, extending a hand, and oozing warmth. "Who are you, and why the fuck are you here?"

Manda tried to launch our "recruiting pitch" as she shook Judy's hand. But she hadn't mastered the stereopticon's controls in its necklace form, and she did something wrong. It gave a promising glimmer as self-organizing light poured from it. But all it generated was a golf ball–sized version of Özzÿ's heavy metal orb, which rose from the floor about a foot from Judy's left shoe.

"Nasty—what *is* that?" Judy asked, stomping on it with a Louboutin heel. The stereopticon processed this development, decided that the orb had been killed, and rendered it clinging lifelessly to the leather-clad spike that had impaled it, its orange blood and viscera dripping into a revolting little pool on the carpet.

With Judy distracted, Manda clutched at her neck to make the stereopticon ooze into its more familiar form, then jabbed at its controls while kicking the door shut. An instant later, my office turned into a completely enveloping star field. I swayed briefly as an infinite, glittering abyss seemed to replace the floor beneath us—but Judy didn't flinch. "Your constellations are all screwed up," she groused, like a jaded teen irked by a sloppy special effect. "Cassiopeia's way too far from Perseus." Then a brilliant rendering of Earth appeared overhead, and she fell silent.

Our message was short and to the point—and delivered by none other than Richard Nixon (courtesy of the impersonating mode that Manda discovered in the stereopticon).[*] Nixon declared that greedy intellectual property laws were imperiling our planet. As he spoke, wads of money[†] flew in like asteroids, gradually blotting out the entire scene, until

---

[*]When we were choosing a voice to narrate our piece, Manda asked me if Judy had any heroes that I knew of. I said no, but that Eric Cartman from *South Park* and Nixon were probably good candidates. Manda sampled Nixon's voice via an online clip from his resignation speech, and it just kind of stuck.

[†]Specifically, Vietnamese dong, because this was the only human cash in the stereopticon's library, for whatever reason. Pugwash naturally insisted on calling them *dawooong*, even after Google revealed that the Vietnamese themselves say something similar to our own pronunciation of the letters d-o-n-g. I retaliated by referring to the 100,000 dong bill (which we used because it's the only green Vietnamese note) as "50,000 double dongs," which aggravated Pugwash even more than I had hoped.

we were surrounded by nothing but drifting piles of space cash. Then the money started to burn. And as the scene dissolved into an image of the Earth ablaze, Nixon said that *only you* can save our race from destruction, whereupon the flames vanished and a heart-shaped rainbow encompassed our world. Nixon then urged Judy to believe everything that I was about to tell her about the alien threat to our planet, regardless of how fantastic it sounded.

Judy remained silent for several seconds afterward, then turned to me. "Aliens, huh? Well, I'm convinced, because that was incredible. How'd you do it?"

I glanced at Manda. She held up the stereopticon. "Self-organizing light," she said. "Extraterrestrial technology."

"Oh, I could have done the graphics in PowerPoint," Judy quipped. "It was Nixon's voice that amazed me." She leaned toward Manda. "Richard Nixon is *dead*," she said slowly, as if explaining meiosis to a Playboy bunny. She then turned back to me, and unleashed a barrage of smart, probing questions.

Judy always says that when she realizes she's wrong about something, she embraces the new reality, and immediately casts her old, invalid beliefs aside. And true to form, she adjusted to the alien situation with impressive speed. She inhaled the facts as fast as I could utter them. We covered almost everything within twenty minutes—and then *I* was the one who turned to *her* and said, "So now what?"

"Now what? Nick, please. We do what we've been doing for our entire careers." She glared at Manda. "Yes, really— all eighteen minutes of it." She turned back to me. "We have a client. It's called humanity. We have an adversary. It's some goddamn union. We even have a hot little paralegal who I'm sure you're trying to bang. Most important, we have a legal system of some sort, and we have a high court."

I'd been so focused on getting Judy to help out with Fido and The Munk that it took me a moment to realize what she was getting at. "Are you saying that we should . . . go and plead our case to the Guardian Council?"

"As opposed to leaving it to some lip-syncing martian slut whose bumbling got us into this mess in the first place? Of *course* I'm saying that we should plead our case to the Guardian Council. More precisely, I'm saying that *I* should plead it to the Guardian Council. *You* can be my supporting counsel. And Mindy here can be our Vanna White, and hit the buttons on her little projector when I tell her to." She glared at Manda and raised her left heel. "And you can start by getting this noxious thing off my shoe." The punctured orb was still rendering there, and had started to shrivel and dry in disgusting ways. Manda's fingers flew across the stereopticon's surface and it disappeared. "Okay," Judy said, "any questions?"

"Just one," Manda said in a hostile tone. She paused, waited for the silence to get really awkward, then said, "Nobody told you that Carly's a slut. So how did you know that?"

Christ, Manda knows about the kitchen-counter scene! I thought wildly.

Before I could launch into some stammering explanation, Judy grinned. "She's funny," she said to me, pointing at Manda.

"I am," Manda smiled—and I realized that she was just putting Judy in her place a bit, and making it clear that she wasn't some kind of bimbo.

"But Carly really is a slut," I said, idiotically trying to

play along. "You should hear what she did with these Vulcans last week."

The temperature in the room instantly dropped about thirty degrees. "Nick," Judy said. "Just like blacks can use the N-word with impunity, and queers can use the F-word, and orientals can use the A-word, Mitzi and I are within the bounds of decorum when we joke about other women being sluts. But as a man in a phallocentric society, you cross a bright, red line when you do that—particularly in a professional setting. Is that clear?"

My hands turned to ice as my adrenaline surged and my reptilian brain flipped a coin between fight and flight. I was about to take off for the elevators at a dead run when Manda looked at Judy and said, "You're funny, too."

"I am," Judy said, and they both fell apart laughing. As I calmed down, it struck me that these two were going to work beautifully together, and that they'd probably love Carly, too. However effective I'd been with the jailer and the Guardian, I should probably just hang back at this point, take their drink orders from time to time, and otherwise let the three of them save the world.

"Anyway," Judy finally said to me. "It sounds like there's no way to get in touch with the Guardians until astroslut turns up again. So when do you expect her?"

"I'm not sure. A bit over a half hour ago she and Frampton went to see the Pluhhhs."

"pluhhhs," Judy corrected me irritably. Damn, she learns fast.

"Right—pluhhhs. They're going to try to put her on the Guardians' planet. She might get blocked out, but wherever she ends up, both of those planets have this special Wrinkle geometry that makes them accessible to most of the universe around the clock. So she could turn up on Earth at pretty much any time."

"How'll she find us?"

"She has our schedule, and the addresses of our meetings today," I said. "As well as my phone number, email address, and whatnot."

"Great. And we're definitely going to those meetings. I'm sure I can get something out of them that will buy us some time with Paulie and the Guild—and we don't know how long it's gonna take us to get in front of the Guardians. Now, is there anything else I should know before we shove off?"

I nodded. "It's kind of a long shot, but Manda and I have set up a C-Corp that already owns the copyright to an alien song here on Earth. I was thinking we might try to register the corporation's ownership to the Refined League as a whole."

"Why would we do something as demented and useless as that?"

"Well, I was thinking that if we copyright the aliens' music for them here on Earth, then our fines should apply to any pirated copies that are made of their songs down here."

Judy nodded slowly. "I don't see why not. But what does that get us?"

"Maybe we could put together a huge server farm to make zillions of illegal copies of their songs. Then the fines that we owe them on their music could offset the fines that they owe us on our music."

"Gee, great thinking there, Nick. One little problem. It sounds like each and every human is personally owed a massive fortune, since half of the alien debt to the music companies will flow to national governments in taxes, and from there it will be the property of all the citizens. So we'd have to talk each and every person on this planet into personally making zillions of copies of that crap alien music, so as to voluntarily eradicate their own personal intergalactic fortune. Somehow, I don't see that happening."

"Then . . . we should have all the governments make the copies?"

Judy gave Manda an aggrieved look. "Your man writes a great brief, but he sucks at math. He always drops or adds a zero—sometimes two." She turned to me. "And in this case, maybe nine. Because from what you've told me, the entire human race can't possibly have enough disc space to offset even a sliver of the debt in the way you're suggesting."

"Oh, right. There's that."

Judy looked at her watch. "Okay, let's move it. We'll be about nine minutes late for Fido, which is perfect. Then between me telling him what to think, and Mimi here hitting the buttons on her Hot Topic necklace, we'll get him on board. My car's waiting downstairs."

Judy trolls Manhattan in a nonstretch limo with the driver's compartment sealed off behind an opaque barrier. This let us flip through our selection of visual effects in private as we rode to the meeting (and a midtown traffic jam gave us ample time for this, despite the fact that it wasn't even a mile away). When we showed Judy the full rendering of Özzÿ's orb with the thunder and lightning effects and that booming, supernatural voice, she seized on it. "That's the one for Fido. Only we won't say it's an alien. We'll say it's the spirit of Brigham Young, or Joseph Smith or something." She turned to Manda. "Fido's a psycho Mormon, and he'll totally buy it. The stereopticon turns anything you say into that crazy voice, right?"

"It does if I'm holding it right," Manda said.

"Good. Just turn your back to Fido when the orb pops out of the floor. He won't pay any attention to you once Brigham shows up."

"But I don't know a thing about Mormons—what do I say?"

Judy shrugged. "You've got a phone—ask Wikipedia. We're five blocks away, that's plenty of time. Just come up with something that's close enough. It's not like he's gonna start a theological debate with Brigham Young." She thought for a moment. Then, "No, screw Brigham. Make it Ronald Reagan's ghost!" She turned to me. "This wingnut'll do anything Reagan says, guaranteed."

Just then, I had an alarming thought. "Wait a second. Carly and Frampton's episode is airing in just a few minutes—which means that Paulie's about to learn the truth."

"Right, we know this," Judy said impatiently.

"I was just thinking that his immediate reaction might be to go ballistic on Özzÿ, since he was supposed to go through my apartment and figure out if I was a Guardian in the first place."

"Sure. Poor Özzÿ. But why do we care?"

"Because if he grills him hard enough, Paulie might end up learning that we have Özzÿ's stereopticon."

"And that matters because?"

"Well, for one thing, he could start using it to spy on us."

Judy considered this for a split second. "Let him. He'll see us negotiating with Fido. Which is exactly what he should want us to do. If we're lucky, he might even put everything on hold, and sit down to cheer us on."

"Good point," I said. "But—well, the other possibility is that they'll throw a kill switch, and disable the stereopticon before we can use it to win over Fido or The Munk."

"If that happens I'll just improvise, and get what I want from those two anyway. Trust me. This is what I *do*."

I immediately relaxed. I'd never known Judy's confidence to be misplaced. And ultimately, she was a more powerful secret weapon than any alien gizmo. Still, something was bugging me as we arrived at the Four Seasons. Something connected to . . . Judy herself? But with all of the adrenaline and sleep deprivation, I couldn't quite put my finger on it.

Fido was staying on the hotel's fifty-first floor. His fabulous suite had its own small library, where an assistant stuck us while his earlier meeting wrapped up.

"Is it hot in here?" Manda asked, shifting uncomfortably moments after we were seated.

"I'm actually kind of cold," I said.

Manda shifted some more, only her shifting was more like writhing, then her hands flew up to her throat, and she yanked like mad, and hurled her necklace to the floor. "*Oh my God*. It's like it was on fire." With that, the disguised stereopticon started glowing—white hot, then blue hot—then it burst into flames, and vanished.

We all stared at the scorched little patch of carpet that it left behind. "Kill switch," we said in unison.

An instant later the library door opened and the assistant stuck her head in. "The senator will see you now."

As we all rose, I figured out what had been nagging at me, and immediately started frisking myself for the ZZ Top key chain that the Guardian had given me. I found it in my right front pocket, and jammed it into Judy's hand, saying

"You *need* to take this." Now that Paulie was on to me, it was only a matter of time before he started picking off my allies. If he'd surveyed the stereopticon's immediate surroundings before hitting the kill switch, he might have marked Judy as a potential enemy. And I couldn't take the risk of him snatching her.

"Nick, get serious," Manda said when she figured out what I was doing. "You can't be without a Foiler—we need you on Earth."

"So long as Judy has one of them, I'm happy," I said.

"Judy Sherman, greetings," Fido boomed from the suite. Judy pocketed my Foiler with a confused look and walked in. As we followed her, Manda shoved her own Foiler into my outer jacket pocket.

Fido's suite was much bigger than it needed to be for a bunch of small meetings with lobbyists and donors. But it was just the right size to project the power of his office, and the wealth of his campaign (which had financed this fancy trip). The folks from his prior meeting lingered to say hi to us, and they were a familiar bunch—executives from one of the major global music labels.

The guy that I knew best was Del McCann, who'd joined the label's public policy group a bit more than a year before. Prior to that, he'd been a Judiciary Committee staffer for ages. Back then, he was the music industry's go-to guy on the committee—always tweaking bills in ways that favored us, pushing for hearings that promoted our viewpoint, or sounding the alarm when something was brewing that we'd want to fight. Committee staffers are extravagantly powerful, in that they have de facto final say on the text of most of the country's laws. But they're also anonymous, overworked, and underpaid. This makes them incredibly vulnerable to manipulation by way of cosseting, flattery, and the prospects of future payback during the staffer's post-government career. And nobody is better at working this system than Judy.

"So how's life as a gazillionaire?" I asked Del, only half-jokingly.

He gave me a wry smile. When he'd had enough of committee life, Judy had personally arranged this new job for him at two and a half times his old salary.*

Once the music executives gathered up their briefcases and left, Judy introduced me to the senator as a rising superstar in the firm (which made me briefly giddy, despite everything that was going on), and Manda as her Hungarian niece Mysti, who couldn't speak a word of English, but still made a remarkably good living in Manhattan as a performer.

The senator fixed me with a serious and appraising look as he shook my hand. This made for a regal moment, as he's the Hollywood ideal of the silver-haired statesman. At six-two, he towers, but doesn't loom over most of his supplicants. He's lean but not scrawny, wears impeccably tailored suits, and tops them off with colorful ties that are creative

---

*This kind of patronage amounts to a sort of asynchronous bribery. Since the music industry wouldn't dare to secretly pay off a guy like Del while he's writing the rules that govern it, it instead pays him off *openly* as soon as his reign is over, by hiring him into one of its leading companies at nakedly inflated wages. This amounts to paying him in arrears for obediently serving the industry's interests during his term on the committee staff. All of this is based on tacit, unspoken understandings rather than a formal quid pro quo—so no laws are broken, the industry gets monumental influence for a bargain price, and everyone (mostly) stays out of jail.

but not excessively so. The only odd touch is these straitjacket-like shirts that he wears. They're starched enough to retain their shape in a trash compactor, and have extralong collars that must put his neck into traction whenever he buttons one up. It's whispered that he wears them because he got sick of media consultants and handlers always telling him to hold his head high (a constant refrain in Washington, where jowl minimization is a citywide obsession). And it works—but at the cost of giving him the air of a remarkably career-oriented turtle.

After the introductions, Judy got right down to business. "Believe it or not, Senator, I'm bringing you a matter today that's more connected to your work on the Intelligence Committee than your role on Judiciary."

"In that case, I'm all ears," Fido said. And he wasn't alone, as I had no idea what Judy was going to say now that our stereopticon was gone. But the Intelligence Committee reference made me worry that she was about to ad-lib some kind of tie between our licensing needs and an imaginary Third World terrorist threat. This wouldn't be a bad idea in theory—except that Judy has this strange dyslexia when it comes to geography. She's also militantly disinterested in (and therefore uninformed about) developing countries, what with their paltry markets for legal services.

"Sir," Judy began, "are you familiar with Abdulistan? I'm talking about the breakaway province of Pashtun. Not the . . . emcee."

I was quite certain that neither existed, but Fido nodded gravely.

"There's a criminal gang out there that's very well known to my firm. Ex-apparatchiks from the local Soviet party. We once sued them in Dubai for pirating CDs, and won a huge judgment. But they slipped across the border into Pakistan before it could be enforced."

Pakistan and Dubai don't share a border any more than Brazil and Alabama do. And Fido knows the region well from his work with the Subcommittee on Terrorism and Homeland Security. But he just nodded again—and I started to relax. Judy speaks with such charisma and authority that when she says something that everyone knows is factually wrong, her listeners just feel embarrassed for not understanding the world properly.

"Anyway," Judy continued, "it seems that these guys have graduated from penny-ante music piracy to weapons of mass destruction. Happens all the time. In this case, an informant in the file-sharing world tells us that the Abdulistanis have snagged some dirty bionukes from Mongolia."

"That's alarming." Fido's obvious concern made it clear that Judy's superpower was working its usual magic.

"Luckily, they're crooks and not ideologues," she continued. "So they're willing to trade their weapons away. Cuba's offered them a fortune in barter. But you have something that they want more than venison and cheap gin."

Manda shot me a desperate look. As the daughter of an international relations professor, she knew Judy was claiming that an imaginary nuclear weapon had leaked from a nonnuclear nation into a breakaway region of Pashtun— which itself is a language, and not a country. She might have tried to nudge the conversation toward sanity, but having been cast as a Hungarian monoglot, she was in no position to do so.

I caught her eye and gave her a reassuring smile. I was no longer concerned in the least.

"So what do the terrorists want?" Fido asked.

"Freedom fighters, Senator. It turns my stomach, too, but we have to call them that to have any shot at a deal with them. What they want is the unilateral, retroactive, and unconditional suspension of the fines in the Copyright Damages Improvement Act. All fines ever accrued under the law revoked. In Abdulistan, and all points beyond. Infinitely beyond, in fact. That part's important."

"They want to suspend the Copyright Damages Improvement Act? But . . . why?"

"It's their *generalissimo*," Judy said, lowering her voice as if to foil Abdulistani bugs. "Macaca something. He's some kind of techno anarchist. Lessig must have gotten to him."[*]

Fido looked at Judy with a combination of alarm and desperate confusion. "But we can't negotiate with terrorists!"

"Freedom fighters, Senator. And it's not a negotiation. It's more like haggling. There's a difference. And we've only got a few hours to show them that we're serious about striking a deal."

"But . . . how do you think our *friends* will react to this?" Fido was getting frantic. The media magnates who drip out the trickle of feigned artistic validation that he so craves would rabidly oppose any change to the Copyright Damages Improvement Act—even if it meant that a few cities

---

[*] Lawrence Lessig is a legal scholar whose writings challenge many aspects of today's copyright regime. The media companies view his work with the sort of horror that the last czarist court must have had for *Das Kapital*.

had to take it in the teeth from a "dirty bionuke." Forced to choose, he'd probably do the right thing. But he'd desperately hate to enrage his patrons if he could possibly avoid it. It had been almost a year since two seconds of one of his songs had accompanied a scene transition in an Adam Sandler movie, and Fido was craving more Milk Bone.

"That's the beauty, Senator—the labels will support this one hundred percent." Judy looked slyly back and forth, as if verifying that we were alone. "It's Bono. He's the linchpin to the whole thing. He met Macaca at the TED Conference last year, and is negotiating with him right now. And he's figured out a way to get the label people on board. The plan is to act like we're giving the Abdulistanis exactly what they want. But then we'll pull the deal at the eleventh hour—and placate them by putting on a huge festival to benefit their rain forest. It'll be like Live Earth—only without Al Gore." That last bit was a cunning jab at a raw nerve. Fido had been teed up to make a fleeting, but ego-stroking walk-on appearance at 2007's Live Earth Festival. But Al Gore was Live Earth's coproducer, and put the kibosh on this.

The whole performance was vintage Judy. And within twenty minutes, we walked out of there with the skeletal outline of a mock bill to eradicate the fines that were enacted by the Copyright Damages Improvement Act. It was even printed on Judiciary Committee stationery, because Fido's assistant had set up a little office in one of the suite's rooms. The odds of our draft actually becoming law were drastically lower than my odds of becoming the Shah of Peru. But it only needed to wow Paulie into giving us a couple of extra days.

Once we were back in the town car and heading toward our meeting with The Munk, Judy pulled the Guardian's

Foiler key chain out of her suit pocket. "So what's this?" she asked, pinching the tacky thing between a thumb and a forefinger and holding it far from her body, as if it were a rat carcass.

"A Refined device in disguise," I said. "It'll prevent Paulie's people from Wrinkling you against your will."

"Not that you don't deserve it," Manda said. "I mean, were you trying to make the senator think that I'm a Hungarian stripper, or something?"

"I figured Romanian would be a bit far-fetched," Judy said absently, as she pulled the key chain up to her eyes and gazed at it in fascination. "So this little thing can seriously stop me from disappearing into a—"

Puff of smoke.

No, she didn't say those words—she disappeared into one. Strictly speaking, it was more of a puff of fog, I guess, because it didn't smell like anything, and it left a moist residue on her seat. But whatever it was, Judy was gone, daddy, gone. And so was the draft outline of that law, which she had carefully stored in the attaché case that disappeared along with her.

TWENTY-ONE
STREET FIGHTING MAN

Manda and I just stared at the empty spot that Judy had occupied as the town car inched toward our meeting with The Munk. "So much for Guardian technology not sucking ass," I finally said.

"Do you think she's . . . okay?" Manda asked.

"I think so. Paulie could have sent my cousin to the ocean floor when he Dislocated him out of the cavern last night. Or to Pluto. But he sent him to a street corner. So he probably just put Judy someplace where she'll be fine, but out of the way." For the next few hours. Whereupon he'd basically sentence her and every other living person to death.

"That's my sense, too." Manda was silent for a moment. Then, "So now what?"

"We could . . . tell Fido that Judy's been abducted? By an Abdulistani splinter cell? And that we need another copy of that document to spring her?"

Manda shook her head. "I'm sure Judy already stretched his gullibility to the breaking point. I can't imagine he'd buy that."

I nodded. "And I'm sure he's in another meeting by now, and we'd never get access to him without Judy anyway."

Manda considered this. "So what else?"

I thought hard. "I guess we could try to get something compelling from The Munk. He runs one of the world's biggest music labels—so that could be almost as impressive as the document that we got out of Fido. The trouble is that he doesn't know me. And we don't have Judy with us. And we don't have the stereopticon. And even if we could win the guy over, his label is just one of many, big as it is."

"That doesn't sound very promising," Manda said. "Although if there's any lever to pull in the entire music industry, he'll know about it, right? So he might come up with a way to fix this mess that we haven't thought of ourselves."

"True. So should we go and tell him exactly what's going on, and hope for the best?"

Manda shrugged. "Why not? If he doesn't believe us, we'll bail after five minutes, and try something else."

I nodded slowly. This was better than nothing. Just. "Meanwhile, we should try to do something to derail Paulie down in Grand Central."

"Like what?"

I thought for a moment, then it hit me. "Start a mutiny."

Manda looked at me blankly.

"I'm serious. Everybody down there loves you. They also love humanity, and our music—and they don't seem to like Paulie any more than we do. If you tell them what's happening, I'll bet they'll rally to you." I grabbed at my suit jacket pocket and found it empty. "Dammit—where's the map to the transmission facility?"

"Pugwash has it," Manda reminded me. "You wanted him in position at the Waldorf, in case we need him to go down there."

"Right. Let's get him on the line."

I called Pugwash and put him on speaker, and we quickly formed a multipronged plan. I would meet with The Munk, and try to come up with something as compelling as the memo that we briefly had from Fido. Manda would meanwhile head straight to the Waldorf, and connect with Pugwash. The two of them would then go down to the Decapus settlement, start a mutiny, and corner Paulie. If that didn't work, Pugwash would try to persuade Paulie to give us a bit more time. This was a perfect role for my cousin, because he's actually a decent negotiator—and he and Paulie are cut from a similar cloth.

"How much time do we need?" Pugwash asked.

"Whatever you can get from him," I said. "A week, a day, a few hours. Hell—twenty minutes, if that's all you can manage. Everything we're doing right now is strictly meant to buy us more time. So do whatever it takes to get some."

"Whatever it takes?"

"Absolutely. Whatever it takes."

The car pulled up in front of the Peninsula Hotel just as we were finalizing all of this (the three-and-a-half-block drive having taken over ten minutes in midtown traffic). We were there because The Munk famously does business out of hotel penthouses when he's in town from L.A. There's no practical reason for this, because unlike Fido, he has extensive offices available to him in New York. In fact, the *headquarters* of the label he runs are in New York. He just never shows up there, because slumming it under the same roof as his minions would subtract too much from the theater of being the boss. So instead, he has them navigate snarled traffic, oozing slush, or hellish humidity to reach his realm.

As Manda took off on foot for the eight-block journey to the Waldorf, I entered the Peninsula's sumptuous lobby, and found my way to the elevators. Up on the nineteenth floor, the hallway outside of The Munk's suite was practically blockaded by the torso of a guy who could single-handedly manage security in Detroit's roughest nightclub. Essentially a building with feet, he stared at me for about fifteen seconds after I gave him my name, and then wordlessly opened the door. Inside, the bouncer's twin took over as my minder. The place made the setup at the Four Seasons look slummy. It featured a grand piano in the living room, a dining room table set for ten, and a library that made the antechamber in Fido's suite look like a small magazine rack. I also spotted a full-sized Jacuzzi through an open bathroom door.

The inside bodyguard showed me to a seat at one end of the living room. On the far end, The Munk was talking to someone on a landline. He'd throw in a threat or a creative expletive every so often, but his end of the conversation was mainly gruff monosyllables.*

"Ey. C'meee-y'h," he said. His inside guard lumbered

---

*The Munk speaks a gutter dialect of English that makes Tony Soprano sound cuddly. Its roots were in a neighborhood that was known as Italian Harlem almost a century ago, until the roughest Italians moved over to the Bronx. It's mainly heard in witness protection safe houses these days—but there must be pockets of speakers at Swarthmore, Yale Law, or maybe the Hebrew school that The Munk attended as a tot, because he clearly picked it up somewhere.

over to him. I was about thirty feet away, but clearly saw The Munk stuff a thick wad of cash into a Peninsula Hotel envelope. He spat out a slurry of vowels that indicated that the envelope was meant for a certain notorious rapper, and handed it off. The bodyguard pocketed it and lumbered out of the suite. A minute later, The Munk hung up and joined me on my end of the living room.

"So who're you, and where's Judy?"

I gathered up my nerve. "I'm an associate at her firm. As for Judy herself, I'm not sure where she is. She disappeared before my eyes about fifteen minutes ago—probably snatched by members of an advanced alien society who don't want her meddling in a music rights issue that's unfolding between Earth and the rest of the universe."

The Munk stared at me silently. Taking this for encouragement, I dove into the rest of the story. Over the next several minutes he nodded or grunted after every few sentences, and muttered something like "the *fuck*as!" whenever I talked about Paulie or the Guild doing something egregious.

"Look, kid," he said when I got to the end. "I know all about this stuff."

"*Seriously?*" My heart raced. If the labels had their own histories with the aliens, it opened up all kinds of possibilities.

"Yeah, sure. You think there's a market for our music anywheres that I'm not on to?" *(dat ine nadawwwn ta?)*

"I'm not sure I . . . understand."

"Ah, Christ. I been talkin' to these jokers fuh years. And yer space parrots aren't the only ones pushin' for this deal. I mean, take Mars." *(Mahhhz.)* "Those guys want in on this thing in the worst way. And then there's those guys up in—

whassit called? Orion. Yeah, Orion. They been all over me, tryin' ta get a piece a this. But I'm tellin' 'em all—no deal. No deal, not even a meetin'." He paused for effect, then pointed at me. "Until I get wit Judy's people."

So, the good news was that he was either accepting my story, or tacitly agreeing to play along with it. He'd done very well over the years believing practically everything that anyone from my firm ever told him in private (or at least pretending to).* The bad news was that having bought into my pitch, he was doing what he always does when presented with a deal: he had invented two imaginary bidders, and was now trying to start an auction.

"Anyways," he said, as if breaking some bad news, "the fact that these guys're workin' wit you. Hey, it helps. But I got shareholders to think of. So the deal's gotta go to the top bidder. Just like always."

So he was assuming that the aliens were our clients. And the whole thing about them annihilating Earth was of no concern to him, because, in his world, even the chummiest negotiations open with blood-chilling threats. For instance, I represent his people in talks with a Web start-up that operates entirely within the law. This is a company that the labels respect, and are dying to do business with. Despite

---

*It's entirely possible that he thought I was speaking in some bizarre code so as to foil a government bugging device, and was cautiously following my lead. Organized crime permeated the fringes of rock 'n' roll in the early days, and old-timers like The Munk get a kick out of imagining that they still menace society enough to merit the feds' attention. One aging bigwig is sure to ask if I'm "calling from a secure line" whenever I get him on the phone. Others use needlessly confusing ciphers when discussing business in public. It's kind of pathetic, but also charming in a way.

that, the first meeting between the two sides consisted solely of the label folks railing at the start-up team about copyright laws, threatening them with lawsuits and prison, and *discussing the high incidence of homosexual rape* in the prison in question.

"So anyways—let me tell you about me," The Munk continued. "It might help you understand my position."

Here it comes, I thought.

"We didn't have no astronomy teacher at my school. And I don't know much about aliens, physiatry, or space travel." He started wagging a finger. "But what I can tell you is this." *A long pause.* "I'm—a street fighter." *A shorter pause.* "So is every guy in my organization. And most of the guys at the other labels, too. We're all just a bunch of street fighters." *A feckless shrug.* "That's all we know." This was maybe the thousandth time I'd heard the street fighter confession since becoming a lawyer to the music labels. You'd think that every executive in the industry had come up from some remote section of the Bronx that was filled with crumbling tenements, angry teens, and switchblade emporia. Every year, the neighborhood would stage a street-fighting Olympiad. And only the victors were granted internships at Arista Records.

Things continued in this vein for a few more minutes. Having established his credentials as a street tough, The Munk informed me that he did business by gut, always by the gut, not by no spreadsheet or Jap management technique, and looking me in the eye, he knew he could trust me, and that this was worth more than a stack of contracts in the world of tattooed, heat-packing reprobates that spat him forth. All of that said, in the starch-collared world that he'd joined, he had to do business by the numbas, and so while he'd sign right now and worry about the numbas later if it was up to him, he'd have to take this back to his numbas guys, and he'd be in touch soon, and by the way, he'd always wondered, is that Judy a dyke or what?

It took about twenty minutes, but I did manage to get a meaningless, but highly impressive document to bring back to Paulie. It was a memo expressing The Munk's earnest desire to reach an agreement granting the Refined League unlimited retroactive rights to his entire catalog for all points one hundred forty-four light-years beyond the Earth's stratosphere. It also said that he intended to use his considerable influence to rally the entire music industry into striking similar deals. His outside bodyguard turned out to be an outstanding typist, and once the document was done, he printed it up on stationery that must have cost five bucks a sheet.

As The Munk walked me to the door, he asked me if there was anything—and he really meant anything at all—that he could do for me personally, or for the industry at large, because while it was a vicious, crooked, two-faced business, at the end of the day he loved it, because he *loved the music,* and he'd do anything he could to help the bigger cause, particularly—and he said this last bit while fixing me with a meaningful gaze—in Washington.

I gave a knowing nod. D.C. is Judy's beat, and she expects everyone to help with the care & feeding of the politicians. "Actually, I have a small request for you from Senator Orrin Hatch.* I just met with him."

The Munk sighed. "From Fido?† What's he want this time?"

---

*(R.Utah)
†Ibid.

"He wants to play cowbell for U2 on their next tour."

"That's a big ask. What'll he cave to?"

"How about a chummy voice mail from Steven Tyler?"

"Done. But he *can't fuckin' tweet about it* this time."

The moment I reached the street, I heard someone calling my name. I turned and saw a familiar mullah waving a series of crazed hand signals at a passerby.

"Nick—it's us," the voice repeated. I turned a bit farther and saw Carly standing about eight feet off. She was hiding behind a pair of cheap sunglasses, pretending she didn't know her strangely clad brother (she, after all, was respectably dressed as a young actress off to shoot a fetish scene with some monks).

I ran up to her. "Carly—how'd it go with the Guardians?"

"Nick, it's us!" This was very loud.

"I can hear you. And I thought you were going to ditch those ridiculous outfits."

"It's me, *Carly*."

"Yes, it is. Look, I'm glad you're here. We need to go to the Waldorf immediately."

"*Carly*," she practically screamed. "And *Frampton*." She pointed at her brother, who was wrapping up a small transaction with a businessman.

Ah yes. They were wearing their deafening apparatus—a good thing, as a Camaro packed with chubby Jersey girls had just started blaring "La Vida Loca." I pointed at my eyes, then pointed at Carly, and gave her a big grin and a thumbs-up sign.

She flashed a relieved smile. "You *recognize me*."

By now, Frampton was miming something spasmodically to a new pedestrian. I caught Carly's eye, pointed at her brother, and gave an exaggerated shrug.

"He's selling *pencils*," she bellowed. "That way, everyone will think he's *really deaf.*"

And that was when the whole of midtown ground to a sudden halt. Taxis, stoplights, buses, iPads, ATMs, LEDs, neon signs, the IRT—anything using a microprocessor, electricity, or even any sort of mechanical engine simply ceased. It was a Y2K nightmare times ten. Like practically everyone, my immediate reaction was to look from side to side, then up and down in wonder. The arrest of all mechanical motion wasn't the most jarring part, because things didn't *look* much different from your basic gridlocked rush hour. No—it was the near-total silence that was beyond surreal. There were no idling engines, cellphone ditties, car radios, jackhammers, honking, sirens—absolutely no sound except for a few scattered human voices, which all promptly fell silent.*

Carly saw everyone go all slack-jawed and gave me a confused shrug. I mimed the removal of a headpiece, then pointed at her ears. She looked at me suspiciously, but did as I asked.

"You don't have to worry about hearing any music," I said, as her hair fell down. "Everything's just . . . *stopped.* But what's happening?"

"Metallicam," she said immediately. "It must have just arrived. In its raw, inorganic state it has so much stored energy that it temporarily disrupts every electromechanical

---

*With the inevitable exception of some joker who bellowed *"D'oh!"* at the exact right moment.

process within a couple-mile radius after it Wrinkles into an area."

"So we're out of time."

"Almost." She waved a hand in front of Frampton's nose to distract him from counting the cash from his latest sale. He saw me and gave me a joyous hug, then removed his headpiece when he saw that Carly had done the same.

"So what happened with the Guardian Council?" I asked.

"We were shut out," Carly said. "The Guild was on to us, and they booted us right off the planet."

I gave Carly and Frampton my own update while we headed toward the Waldorf. As we covered the short distance to the hotel, the area started to throng with people. Drivers were cautiously stepping out of their cars. Workers and residents—mindful of the lessons of September 11—were pouring from their buildings. And everyone was tense. There was no way to access outside information, so people were left to their imaginations in interpreting the situation.

At first we hustled down the middle of Fifth Avenue, jigging around stalled cars. But soon even the streets were getting tight, as every building in midtown flushed its occupants onto sidewalks that just couldn't contain them all. By the time we got to the Waldorf, hotel security was aggressively turning away nonguests. Rumors of terrorist involvement were by then rampant. So if there's ever been a good time to try talking your way past New York security with a carrot-topped mullah in tow, this wasn't it.

"I'm sorry," a huge guy with a very small head repeated

to me. "There's entirely no way you're getting into the hotel without a key proving that you're a guest."

I tried to argue, but this only brought his thug of a boss over. "We got a problem here?" the boss asked Pinhead. I cringed inwardly, because I knew the boss's type all too well. Pushing three hundred pounds and sweating in the February chill, he'd no doubt failed the psych exam to work for the city cops three times.

"Yeah," Pinhead said. "These people are insisting on accessorizing our lobby without a key."

The boss made a gesture and two more guards came over. "Look," the boss said to me. "It's within our discretion to incarcerate, if necessary, in times of emergency. And I don't want to have to do that to you and your little friends."

Things were starting to get heated when a forty-something guy in a suit strode out of the lobby, eyeing Frampton carefully. The guards quieted down as the suit walked up. Clearly he was management. He came closer, looking at Frampton more and more intently. He was practically nose to nose with him when he broke into a huge, deferential grin. "Mick?" he asked.

Frampton straightened his back and beamed.

"Mick *Huck*nall?"

You could power a city with that grin.

"But you haven't aged a *day*," the manager gushed. "I mean—throw on that beret, and pinch me, but I'm watching the 'Money's Too Tight (to Mention)' video!"

I guess everyone has a little superpower—and Frampton's had just saved the day, as this guy was apparently America's solitary Simply Red fan. "Crikey!" was all he could manage (in the fakest accent since *Chitty Chitty Bang Bang*).

The manager swept us past security and into the lobby. As he raced off to get some paper for an autograph, we spotted Manda. "Where the hell's your cousin?" she demanded. "He was supposed to meet me here." She turned to Carly and Frampton. "And hi, I'm Manda."

I was stumped about Pugwash, and shrugged.

"Then Paulie must have Dislocated him," Manda said grimly. She turned to Carly. "Can you get us to the Decapus facility?"

Carly nodded. "I've got it mapped, and our devices still work. They don't use electricity or silicon-based microprocessors."

"It's all molecular valves," I added dashingly, feeling like Mr. Science.

Carly removed her crucifix, which flowed into a compact stereopticon form with an enlarged display surface. She navigated us down a long hallway that took us to a service staircase. It got pitch dark as soon as we left the lobby and the murky natural light filtering through its glass doors. From that point on, we had the place to ourselves, since not even flashlights were working in the metallicam's disruption field. Frampton had his stereopticon generate a dim glow that we could see by without attracting too much attention. Once we entered the service stairway, he turned it into a floodlight.

We were back at the presidential train within minutes. "What's the deal with this place, anyway?" I asked as Carly headed toward the chair with the access panel.

"FDR used to enter the city by way of a secret underground track, so the press wouldn't see him getting lifted in and out of trains on a wheelchair. This is where it would pull in, and then he'd magically emerge in the Waldorf."

She keyed in the color combination, and that soothing, golden light enveloped the room again. Moments later, the closet door opened and a familiar voice rang out. "Always with the visitors this week. Thirty-something years without even a Jehovah's Witness, and now all of a sudden, it's like Grand Central Sta—" The Boss rounded the conference table's corner and almost rammed Carly and Frampton. "Whoa, superstars!" He extended two limbs to each of them to double-shake their famous hands.

Then he spotted me. "And, a *criminal!*"

TWENTY-TWO
WELCOME BACK, SHERMAN

The Boss thrust four limbs in front of Manda to protect her from me. Four other limbs were already shaking hands with Carly and Frampton. And since Decapuses need at least three limbs to stand on, this sent him sprawling. Ancient reflexes cause Decapuses to clench their digits and violently retract their limbs whenever they fall. This yanked Carly and Frampton right off their feet, bringing their heads together with an impressive *crack*. The Boss's torso bounced on the floor like a soggy tennis ball, then he slowly released their hands. As his limbs reextended, Manda tried to grab one to help him to his feet.

"No, no—I piss out of that one," he warned. She backed right off. "Anyways, I'm sorry, but I have strict orders to deny entry to wanted persons." He gazed at me sternly as he regained his footing. "Or, to unwanted persons who are traveling with wanted persons," he added, giving everyone else a desperately flustered look. The fame field was clearly wreaking some havoc—but The Boss was no pluhhh, and he more or less kept his cool.

"Who says I'm a criminal?" I asked.

"The Guardian Council itself. A communiqué came in from them right after that Pugwash guy showed up."

"And let me guess—it came to you via Paulie, didn't it?"

"Who told you?"

"Criminal masterminds have ways of knowing these things," I said. "Although I don't know what I'm accused of."

"Arson in a state prison," The Boss said in a scandalized tone. "Armed robbery of citizens, banks, and post offices." He started ticking off allegations on the digits of various limbs. "The theft of sacred objects. Perjury. Bigamy. Passing counterfeit money. Kidnapping, extortion. Receiving stolen goods, selling stolen goods. Inciting prostitution. And, contrary to the laws of this state . . ." He paused, struggling to remember the final charge.

"Using marked cards?" I offered.

"Exactly!"

I nodded. These accusations had dogged me throughout my childhood. They come from *The Good, The Bad, and the Ugly*—a film my cousin would quote from endlessly whenever we'd play Cowpersons & Native Americans.* So Pugwash clearly had a hand in writing the bogus Guardian communiqué that had ordered The Boss to keep us out of the Decapus colony. But why?

---

*His mom, my aunt—who was a student radical for several weekends in the early seventies—insisted on this nomenclature. She also spent half of Pugwash's childhood trying to say "Nicaragua" with a Sandinista accent. So yes, that's where he gets it from.

"Boss, that's bullshit," Manda said hotly. "Paulie made it all up because he wants to keep us away from his metallicam. Don't you know what he's planning to do with that stuff?"

"Sure—he's gonna solve your energy problems and give you all a lot more time to write music."

"Not even close," Manda said. "He's planning to destroy the Earth with it."

"Come on—that's illegal!"

"Only if he does it *to* us," I said. "But he's figured out a way to make us destroy ourselves."

"I don't buy it. All of us Decapuses would get killed, too. And we're union!"

We went back and forth like this for a while. Much as he disliked Paulie, The Boss couldn't believe that the top echelons of the Guild would order this sort of destruction. And he wasn't about to take a one-man crime wave's word for it.

Carly figured out a way to break the deadlock before too many precious minutes ticked by. "Listen, Boss," she said. "Believe what you want to about Paulie and the metallicam. But the other reason we're here is to capture that Pugwash guy."

"What for?"

"For trying to kill Manda. He set up a booby trap in her apartment."

"He *what*?" The rest of our conversation was instantly forgotten. As its most adored (and internally famous) singer, Manda had become the Decapus colony's emotional Achilles' heel.

"He tried to kill her," Carly repeated. "She clobbered him playing Settlers of Catan, and he couldn't take it. He came down here to flee the police."

"So that's why he had Paulie set up that force field," The

Boss growled, balling up the digits of several limbs into fists. They took on a metallic color, and puffed up like balloons.

"He had Paulie do *what?*" I asked.

"Right after he got here, he told Paulie and Özzÿ to lock everyone else out of the transit bay," The Boss snarled. "So Paulie used some metallicam to power up a force field. The three of them are behind it now."

"Oooh—that's really bad," Carly murmured.

"I asked Paulie how he could block out his brothers in the Guild like that," The Boss said as he herded us into the elevator. "It's unheard of! He said it was that Pugwash guy's idea."

"Metallicam force fields are completely impenetrable by any means," Carly warned me as the elevator plunged.

"Really? You know, we're so lucky to have a force-field expert on the team."

She glared at me. "I'm just saying that Paulie and your cousin are incredibly serious about keeping us out if they're using up some of their metallicam to power a force field."

Their metallicam. The phrase chilled me. What the hell was Pugwash up to?

We left the elevator and The Boss activated a small panel on the wall just outside of it. "It's me, calling everybody," he bellowed into it, and I heard his voice echo throughout the surrounding tunnels. "Manda's here. Manda! And that Pugwash guy is trying to kill her! Meet us at the transit bay."

The tunnels were roiling within seconds. All of the Decapuses had balled their digits into those huge metallic fists, and a pissed-off phalanx of them formed around us to keep us from getting trampled underfoot as we raced through the tunnels. It was as if a giant clan of pint-sized linebackers had just heard that their kid sister was at the junior high school dance with R. Kelly. A seething mob had already surrounded the transit bay by the time we got there. It parted like the Red Sea for Moses the instant Manda's beloved form was spotted. Within moments, we were standing at the force field's perimeter. The gibbering mob fell silent as my cousin strode out of the transit bay door with Paulie perched on his shoulder.

"Damn, you were right," Paulie said to Pugwash, flicking a wing at the furious crowd. "Mutiny. Led by that broad. You sure called it."

"So are we on?" Pugwash demanded.

Paulie nodded. "A deal's a deal. And you delivered."

"Delivered *what*?" I demanded.

"Information," Paulie said. "Your cousin showed up here about a half hour back. Said things was goin' sideways. But he wouldn't give me no details. So I say, tell me what's brewin'. If your warning pans out, you get two percent."

"Two percent of *what*?"

"The assets the Guild recovers."

I felt a familiar overwhelming urge to belt my cousin. And for the first time since eighth grade, I made no attempt to resist it. "*Owwwwwwwwww!*" I hollered as my hand connected with a solid, invisible wall.

"Eighty thousand times stronger than steel, right?" Pugwash asked.

"More like eighty-one," Paulie answered, then turned to me. "Metallicam force fields're tough on the dukes. I wouldn't knock it again."

"And calm down already," Pugwash added. "It's not like I did anything wrong."

"Apart from getting the world destroyed?"

"Actually, I *saved* the world." He turned to Paulie. "Tell him about the rest of our deal. You're making me look bad."

Paulie shrugged. "I said if his warning pans out, I give humanity an extra twelve hours to get us our money back."

"I asked for a full week," Pugwash said righteously.

"And I started at a fifth of one percent," Paulie said. "A bit of back and forth, and we settled at twelve hours and two percent. Everybody wins."

I turned to Pugwash. "How . . . could you?"

He glared at me. "How *could* I? Please. What would have happened if I'd waited for Manda like you told me to—and then Paulie saw us coming before your little mutiny could take him prisoner? He would've nuked us, or something— and then we'd all be doomed. I figured our odds of pulling it off were one in ten, max. And if we failed, it was all over."

"Well . . . *may*be," I said. "But—"

"And meanwhile, what was my prime directive? Let's see, wasn't it something like, 'Everything we're doing now is *strictly* meant to buy us more time. So do *whatever* it takes to get us more time. *Absolutely* whatever it takes.' Did I get that right, Nick?"

I just clammed up and fumed. I felt like I was nine years old again, and losing a semantic debate about the rules of Monopoly to my older, smarter cousin. And hadn't I since *gone to law school* specifically so that I could win a few of these arguments? I silently vowed that if I survived this, my professors would receive the most withering demand for a refund that had ever been written.

"So you sent me down to *negotiate* for more time with Paulie," Pugwash continued, moving in for the kill. "And let's see—what did I have to bargain with? Oh, that's right— *nothing*. Except for this one piece of information that I knew he'd find valuable. The details of your pathetic little plan for throwing him off of his perch. *That* was the one thing I had to bargain with. And while I was at it, I also needed to come off as being believable somehow."

"So in order to be believable, you sold out humanity's future in exchange *for a commission?*" I asked.

"Of course!"

Paulie nodded. "Smart," he said to me. "I mean, you gotta admit. No way he'd'a been believable as a do-gooder."

"Exactly," Pugwash said, beaming smugly.

"And this way, he saves the world *and* gets that two percent if things work out," Paulie added.

"Ex*act*ly," Pugwash said, beaming even more.

"And safe passage outta here and a Guild pension for life if everything blows up instead."

"That was the, uh . . . other provision," Pugwash stammered.

I glared at him.

"Oh come on, Nick—it would be over already if I hadn't gotten us that extra time. Admit it."

I considered this, then nodded grudgingly. He hadn't done it with a shred of class or dignity. But if you really wanted to get all hair-splitting about it, my cousin had, in theory, saved the stupid, goddamn, motherfucking, worldwide world. Technically. For a few hours. Maybe.

"Okay, fine," I said, turning to Paulie. "So let's get this in gear. I already have the ball rolling with the biggest music company on the planet." I pulled The Munk's note from my pocket and held it up to the force-field boundary for him to see. "And I'll get a lot closer with the rest of the rights-holders over the next twelve hours. But I'll probably fall a little short. So what do you say we check in ten hours from now? I'll make enough progress by then that I'll be close to clinching the deal. So hopefully you'll be willing to give me a small extension at that point." Of course, it would probably take decades of global martial law with me as Maximum Leader to get all of the sign-offs and approvals necessary to fully reverse the debt. But I was just playing for time. And every hour I could scrape up would give us that much more leeway to somehow get an audience with the Guardian Council.

Paulie's eyes narrowed. "Not a chance. This is startin' to feel like a goddamn setup. So no way do you get even an extra minute to pull somethin' on me. I want the Guild's money in twelve hours. Or the Earth gets it."

"O-kayyy. Well, in order to get anything done, I need to get Judy back."

"You need to get *what?*"

"Judy. My boss. The woman you Dislocated an hour ago. She's the one who knows everyone at the labels and in the government. I can't get anything done without her. So where'd you put her?"

"Put *who?*" Paulie sputtered. "I don't even know the broad." He didn't seem to be faking this. He gave Pugwash a deadly look. "This is smellin' more and more like a setup. Get me my money, now. Without no help from no imaginary friend. Or this whole planet's goin' up in a—"

Puff of smoke.

No, he didn't say those words. Judy suddenly appeared in one. She was on our side of the force field, but practically eyeball to eyeball with Paulie.

"Goddamn disco effect," she said, waving a hand at the haze in front of her face. "With all this technology, you'd think they'd come up with something clever."

"Who the hell're you?" Paulie demanded.

"I'm Judy Sherman, bitch. And you're in infinitely deep shit." She turned and scanned our side of the force field, zeroing in on the saucy nun. "And you must be Carly. Manda here tells me you're a hopeless slut."

Carly turned to Manda and gave her a shocked look. "How did *you* know?" she demanded.

Judy turned back to Paulie. "And where do you suppose I just came from, seed muncher?"

"I do *not* eat no goddamn seeds. I'm from the dark planet of Doopipoopibippyfoo. A cold, brutal, heartless world . . . of *carnivores!*"

"To answer my own question—I just came from the Guardian Council," Judy continued. "Where I talked the members through a barrage of evidence that astroslut here sent to them in hopes of scoring a meeting."

"How'd you end up at the Guardian Council?" I asked.

"I was subpoenaed," Judy answered. She held up my ZZ Top key chain. "Or strictly speaking—*you* were subpoenaed. But you gave me *your* Foiler. So when the Guardian Council tried to haul your ass in, they got my ass instead. A lucky break for humankind, wouldn't you say?"

"But . . . I thought Foilers are supposed to *stop* people from hauling you in," I said.

"Right. They'll stop anyone. *Except* for the Guardian Council operating under a formal subpoena."

"Oh right," I said, recalling that Guardian 1138 had said something along these lines. "So it wasn't Paulie who snatched you, after all."

"That's what I been tryin'a tell ya," Paulie said reproachfully. "I don't even know this broad."

"But I know *you,* cracker whore," Judy sneered.

"I don't eat no goddamn crackers. I eat meat—*raw meat*!"

"Oh, I'm sure. Well, eat this—the Guardian Council has reviewed Carly's evidence. They've heard my testimony. And they're now officially serving you with an Entreaty to Please Kindly Back Down." She held up a seal-encrusted document that was utterly gorgeous.* "A *Most Heartfelt Entreaty*—bitch."

I shot her an incredulous look. A "Most Heartfelt Entreaty" sounded like something that a brainy ninth grader would issue to a mousy girl in hopes of getting a homecoming date.

Judy caught my eye and flashed a gesture that I'd seen her make many times at work. It roughly translates to "this is the best I could get out of these hopeless pansies."

"Fuggedaboutit," Paulie snapped. "I'm on *this* side of the force field. And you? You're on *that* side. And the Council can entreat my feathered ass. Gimme the Guild's goddamn money. Or it's curtains for your planet."

Judy looked at him in astonishment. "You know something? That's . . . exactly what *I'd* say in your position."

Paulie beamed at the unexpected praise. "And that's—that's exactly what I *did* say!"

"Boy, did you," Judy said, dropping the Most Heartfelt Entreaty onto the cavern's floor and fixing him with an admiring gaze. "You're something. I've never seen so much backbone in someone. You're like a . . . Viking bird."

"I—I think Vikings are great," Paulie said. "Norwegian pirates! Pining for the fjords or somethin', right?"

Parchmentry is one of the Hundred Lesser Arts, and of course, Refined Leaguers kick ass at it.

Judy nodded. "And they tell me you can sing," she purred, pivoting straight to the Milk Bone strategy. "You know, Willow Smith needs a talented parrot for her next video. And her manager owes his job to me."

Go, Judy! I thought.

But her spell was broken when Pugwash let off one of his monstrous sneezes. I instinctively reached out to the force-field boundary, hoping it had been shattered. No dice.

"Aright, dammit," Paulie said, coming to his senses. "I'm about to push this metallicam out. Only one thing can stop me. Our *money.*"

And that's when it hit me. Pugwash and his cold. And me and my lack of a cold. I had the answer. I turned to Judy. "Take me up to the Guardian Council. I can fix it." I turned to Paulie. "I can get you your money. All of it." Then I caught myself, and recalled the lessons that my life among lawyers had drilled into me. "Minus . . . ten percent. Deal?"

"But I'm already giving your damn cousin two percent!" he snapped.

"And I'm sure he'll relinquish that in order to get the deal done and save the human race," I said, glowering at Pugwash. "Right?"

"Yeah, fine," he muttered through clenched teeth.

I turned to Paulie. "So—ten percent, total. You get the rest. Deal?"

"Deal," he barked. "But get it done."

I looked at Judy. "I've seriously figured it out," I said. "Take us up."

She nodded, mystified, but approving. "Stand by me, my apprentice," she said. And we were gone.

TWENTY-THREE
TO THE CORE

The Guardian Council meets in an immense spherical chamber called The Core. It floats over a perfectly conical volcano that towers fifty miles above the magnetic north pole of their world. The planet's interior is rigged up with a sort of pulmonary system that spews massive jets of plasma and flaming gas out of the volcano around the clock. The force of this suspends The Core about a mile above the volcano's spigot, while spinning it in a brain-meltingly complex, hyperdimensional manner. The spin creates a local gravitational field that pulls The Core's occupants outward—away from its center. This makes walking around The Core's interior as natural as walking on the surface of a planet. The only difference is that you're on the inside of a sphere, rather than the outside of one (kind of like an ant exploring the interior of a beach ball).

Despite the steady tug of gravity, the place is hopelessly

disorienting—and humbling. The reason is that wherever you are in The Core, gravity tells you that the point beneath your feet is *down*. This makes it feel like you're always right at the base of a vast, spherical room—one whose floor slopes uphill in every direction, until it all arches above you and meets at a point high overhead. As a result, everyone else in The Core always seems to be peering down on you from on high (particularly the folks on the far side of the chamber, who seem to be stuck to the ceiling). Being largely transparent, The Core is also illuminated by the hellish volcanic flames that bathe its exterior.*

"I'm back, Your Illustriousness," Judy announced right after we materialized in this strange place. I noticed that she was gazing at her feet, so I looked down. Our two-dimensional patron, Guardian 1138, was flitting about the floor.

---

*The Council used to meet in a suitably dignified space whose every contour, measurement, and ratio combined to create a physical embodiment of the elegant equation that mathematically proves the eternal correctness of the Indigenous Arts Doctrine. Then came the Kotter Moment—and some months after it, a wild rumor that the band Black Sabbath was coming to the Guardian Council to issue some odious demand. The Guardians immediately redesigned their digs in hopes of making the band feel more at home, on the slim chance that the rumor was actually true. They have yet to revert to their old quarters because, well, you just never know . . .

For the same reason, the Earth's atmosphere and gravity are perfectly replicated within The Core—as well as at every other Guardian facility (including the entire planet where pluhhhs managed the Townshend Line. This required major engineering, as it used to have twice our gravity, and an atmosphere that, by eerie coincidence, almost perfectly mirrored the chemical composition of Drakkar Noir).

"I sense that you have company, Judy," he said.

"Yes, Your Illustriousness," I said. "It's me, Nick Carter. Thank you for bringing us here."

"Bringing you was the easy part. Moving the Council to action is . . . well, it doesn't happen often. But this Judy of yours is quite the force of nature."

As he said this, it started getting very bright in our immediate area. I looked left, right, and upward at the dizzying ranks of exotic faces, and saw that the lights were dimming on everyone else. We were on.

"The human has returned with a compatriot," boomed an amplified voice that sounded like the British guy who narrates all those nature documentaries. "And as Speaker of the Council, I hereby call this session to order. Ms. Sherman— were you able to deliver our Entreaty to the Guild member?"

"Yes, Your Illustriousness," Judy said.

"And did it have its intended effect?"

"No, Your Illustriousness. He is determined to proceed with his plans."

A low murmur arose throughout The Core in countless alien tongues.

"I see," the Speaker said after some contemplation. "You didn't happen to tell him that it was a . . . *Most Heartfelt* Entreaty, did you?"

"Yes, Your Illustriousness. I pointed that out quite firmly. But he's now holed up inside a metallicam-powered force field. And he intends to proceed with his villainous plot, unless the Guild recovers its assets within twelve hours."

A somewhat louder murmur arose.

"To be candid, Your Illustriousness," Judy continued, "I believe that your Entreaty lacks something in the . . . teeth department."

A still-louder murmur followed this, but was quickly overwhelmed by an impossibly deep and gravelly voice that thundered down from somewhere high above us. *"That's what I've been saying all along!"*

Everyone else fell silent, and I struggled to catch my breath. This terrifying roar was like a physical presence that had slapped me bodily, knocking the wind from my gut.

"We must respond to the Guild in the most *ruthless* way available to us!" the new voice demanded. "We must set an example that will chill the hearts of the wicked—until the *very stars go cold*! Fellow Guardians. I move that we enact . . ." It paused dramatically. Then, in a tone so deep that it skirted the bottom range of human hearing, "the *Dark Contingency*."

At that, a rumbling enveloped us from all directions. I squinted into the bright lights and saw that many of the Guardians had started pounding the floor in apparent agreement.

"I like the way you're thinking," Judy said after the pounding subsided. "Tell me more."

"A great regional athletic festival is scheduled to be held on the rogue parrot's home planet, scarcely three centuries hence," Deep Throat growled in a muted, conspiratorial tone. "The Dark Contingency is a callous, and *cunning* plan . . ." Another dramatic pause. Then finally, at an agonizing volume, *"TO BOYCOTT THE OPENING CEREMONIES!"*

The entire Council maintained an eager, agitated silence as Judy considered this. Milking the moment, she let the seconds tick by, then finally looked up and said, "You've *got* to be fucking kidding me."

"Why—why, no," Deep Throat stammered. "Isn't that how Carter got the Russians out of Afghanistan?"

Judy shook her head in disgust, and made like she was packing up her papers to call it a day. The rumbling resumed, the Guardians now pounding the floor in apparent dismay.

"Enough, enough," the Speaker of the Council's cultivated, Bond-like voice demanded. "Stop that pounding this instant—or I'll have you all incinerated!"

The Core immediately fell into total silence.

"Now *that's* more like it," Judy said brightly. "And you know what, Mr. Speaker? Incineration would be a great topic to raise in a revised version of that Entreaty of yours. You know—something to get that damned bird's attention. And maybe we can drop some of that 'please kindly back down' crap while we're at it. I mean, what's *up* with that?"

"It's . . . a bit embarrassing," the Speaker said. "But we don't actually—have the means to *enforce* our will anywhere outside of our own planet. So when things go badly out there, we tend to . . . entreat."

"*And* express dismay," a high-pitched, foppish voice added. "That has been highly effective on several occasions."

"And that seriously keeps the whole universe in line?" Judy asked.

"Oh, absolutely," the Speaker said. "Any faintly aggressive species is sure to self-destruct long before it can even escape its own solar system. This means that the surviving races that we preside over are basically a bunch of sissies. Just look at how they name their planets."

"But if you can't enforce your will anywhere, why is the entire universe convinced that there are horrible consequences for harming a Guardian? Or for destroying a primitive society? Or for disobeying you in general?"

"Well, those are very useful rumors from our perspective, aren't they?" the Speaker said. "They make our Entreaties work. And from the general population's standpoint, they're rather *fun* rumors. They take our monotonously safe, just, and peaceful universe, and give it just a tiny bit of edge. Rumors that are useful to the powerful and fun for the rabble always spread quickly, and are widely believed. It's an iron law of physics."

"But has anyone ever called your bluff?" Judy asked.

"Until now, no," the Speaker said. "So I'm afraid you're finding us in a new, and rather awkward, situation."

Judy nodded slowly, then abruptly turned to me. "Well, luckily, Nick here has come up with an awesome little fix for you guys—haven't you, Nick? Take it away, kid."

The light on Judy dimmed, and the space around me brightened like the sun. I felt an unfamiliar stab of stage fright as I realized that I was about to pair my long-standing superpower with some of that "original thinking" stuff that Judy deemed me incapable of. Then I calmed right down, and focused on *giving good meeting*.

"Your Illustriousnesses," I began. "Let me start out by confirming a few facts. First, the Indigenous Arts Doctrine forms the absolute legal, moral, and economic foundation of your entire confederation of societies, correct?"

"It does," the Speaker said. "It's so deeply ingrained in everything that our entire civilization would unravel if it were ignored, or even suspended briefly."

"And this Doctrine defines a 'Collective Patrimony' species as being one that has always treated its artistic output as the jointly owned property of every member of its society."

"That is correct," the Speaker said. "And when such a species becomes Refined and joins us, its artworks become jointly owned by every individual citizen of the Refined League. Legally, it's as if we all become coequal shareholders in that work."

"I see. And what about independent, primitive civilizations? If the artwork of a society like mine ends up in one of your societies, does the Indigenous Arts Doctrine apply to it?"

"Of course it does. That's precisely why we find ourselves in the current situation, duh."

"Of course. And what about *within* my society? Does the Indigenous Arts Doctrine also apply inside of primitive societies like mine?"

"Certainly *not*," the Speaker said indignantly. "Primitive societies live by their own laws and traditions. For us to impose our beliefs upon them would be imperialistic, specist, and ethnocentric."

"I see. In light of that, if a work of art that originated in a Refined society were somehow published in a primitive society—what copyright rules would apply to that artwork *within* the primitive society itself? Those of the Refined League? Or those of the primitive society?"

"Why, those of the primitive society. Vital as the Indigenous Arts Doctrine is to us, it would be immoral for us to impose it on outsiders."

"And they'd probably just ignore our Entreaties anyway," the deep, gravelly voice added sulkily.

"So to be more specific, Mr. Speaker," I said. "If I were to take one of your Collective Patrimony songs and copyright it in Washington, American laws would apply to that song within the boundaries of the United States. And then those copyrights would be protected elsewhere on Earth by way of the Berne Convention."

"I'm not entirely familiar with your laws, but that sounds correct."

"He's got it right, Your Illustriousness," Judy said, giving me a baffled look. "He definitely knows his way around the Berne Convention."

"So if that Collective Patrimony song were then copied illegally on Earth," I continued, "American penalties would apply to any human violators, and those penalties would be due to the registered owners on Earth."

"That is correct," the Speaker confirmed.

"Okay. Now let's suppose that I create an American-based company that is jointly owned by each and every Refined League citizen. And then let's say I register the copyright of a Collective Patrimony song to that company in the U.S." I paused briefly to let this notion sink in. "Then, let's say some guy living in New York pirates a copy of that song. The financial penalty for his copyright violation will theoretically be due to the citizens of the Refined League—each and every one of whom would be entitled to a tiny, coequal sliver of it, right?"

"Why yes, that's true," the Speaker said.

"So in theory, if I registered a bunch of *your* songs to *you* on Earth . . . and if the people of Earth then made as many pirated copies of *your* songs as you've made of *our* songs—our respective debts should cancel out, yes?"

"That is theoretically true," the Speaker said slowly. "But by your own laws, only the person who uploads, or makes an illegal copy is liable for any fines on it. This of course is fair, and logical. But from the standpoint of canceling our debt, it's problematic—because *each and every* non–North

Korean on Earth is technically owed vast sums of money, by way of the wealth that's due to record labels, musicians, and other music rights-holders being redistributed by taxes."

"Oh, I see," I said. "So in order to reverse the universe's debt, it isn't enough to simply make lots of illicit copies on Earth. Instead, each and every non–North Korean has to *personally* make lots of illicit copies."

"Exactly."

"Thank you for clarifying all of that, Mr. Speaker." I paused briefly to indicate that I was shifting gears. Then, "Mr. Speaker, are you familiar with something called a 'junk joke'?"

The Speaker chortled. "Why of course, and I'm most fond of them. They're the jokes that medical technicians insert into their work when they update the genetic code of a species. Have you heard the one about the Octarian Weevil who uploaded its ganglions to both instantiations of the OverNet?"

Boy had I. Frampton had practically asphyxiated when Carly told him this doozy. And I already had this crowd eating out of my hand. Was I about to save the world . . . *and* launch an intergalactic stand-up career? "Do you mean the Octarian Weevil who wanted to have—*second thoughts*?" I asked.

Utter silence.

"You need to work rather hard on your delivery," the Speaker said gently. "But yes, that's the junk joke I was referring to. Anyway, how is all of this related to our debt?"

"Well, as you may know, we humans store complete copies of our genomes in each and every cell of our bodies."

"I didn't actually know that, but that's a very common evolutionary strategy, so I'm not surprised."

"And the human body has up to a hundred trillion cells in it, each of which divides many times in its lifetime. And *each* division of *every* cell creates an entirely new copy of the person's entire genetic code."

"Why . . . yes, that's not surprising," the Speaker said, with a hint of comprehension starting to creep into his voice.

"And there's approximately half a gigabyte's worth of junk DNA in each and every one of those cells. That's enough data to carry over eight hours of music at high fidelity, and up to fifty hours at low fidelity. And that's just using human technology—I'm sure you guys can do much better."

"So—so what are you proposing?" the Speaker asked excitedly.

"I'm proposing that your technicians push out an update to the human genome. One that's loaded up with lots and lots of songs that are part of the Refined League's Collective Patrimony. I will copyright those songs in the name of a Delaware-based company that is already set up, which we'll register in the name of the Refined League. As soon as the genetic update goes out, each and every person on Earth will start making trillions and trillions of unauthorized copies of your intellectual property, around the clock. You can then carefully track the number of copies that each person has made against the wealth that they are personally owed by the Refined League, and strip the songs out of their DNA once that wealth is almost entirely depleted. Is that possible?"

"Well, this is a bit more complicated than a normal genome update, since we'd have to track and manage individuals rather than a planetary system as a whole," the

Speaker said. "But to our technicians—it would be child's play."

The pounding started again, this time at a positively deafening level. The Speaker allowed it to continue for quite a while before silencing it. "This sounds extremely promising," he continued, once it was quiet again. "But let's explore the details. You said 'once that wealth is *almost* entirely depleted.' Do you intend for the Refined League to still owe the people of Earth some fraction of the existing debt?"

"Yes. I would propose that the people of Earth retain roughly ten percent of the universe's wealth. That seems fair, because we're giving so much back unilaterally, and because our creative works do in fact bring incalculable joy to every citizen of the Refined League. This means that every Refined individual and organization will retain ninety percent of their current wealth. The ten percent that goes to us will buy each of you an eternity of access to our entire music catalog. Which is an excellent entertainment value."

This was welcomed with more explosive pounding.

"Speaker," Judy said after it tapered off, "I must say, my hireling's solution is quite brilliant." She then turned and gave me a meaningful look, adding, "It's also . . . *extremely original.*" The thundering resumed, and I flushed with the pride of a young Jedi getting a public attaboy from Yoda himself. "He and I will need to do some tweaking to make it completely bulletproof," Judy continued, once the chamber quieted down. "But none of that should take long. How long will the genetic work take on your side?"

"It's already done," the Speaker said. "I told you it would be child's play. And we can push out the update to all sectors of your planet quite quickly by taking advantage of the favorable Wrinkle geometry that we have on our world. So once you've done your legal work, massive copyright infringements can start taking place in every non–North Korean human body forthwith."

"Fantastic," Judy said. "So we have everything figured out. Provided Paulie keeps his word. Which is a concern. He's still protected by a metallicam force field, so we won't have many options if he breaks his promise."

"Oh, that won't be a problem," the Speaker said. "We've been monitoring the situation in the Decapus cavern closely. Apparently a black cat was hiding in the building on Paulie's side of the force field. Moments after you left, it jumped him, and now has him pinned. The cat seems to be taking orders from the woman you call Manda. And the vacuum cleaner is laughing too hard to do anything about the situation. So, I'm sure that Paulie will keep his word."

EPILOGUE
THE GREAT DECELERATOR

Things stayed pretty crazy for several weeks. As soon as Meow-haus and Manda got Paulie to drop the force field, he and Özzÿ were Dislocated to the Guardians' planet, where they were locked up to await trial. The prosecutor demanded a penalty of "continuously repeated incineration," which sounded bad (and familiar to Manda, who was raised nominally Catholic). But neither Paulie nor Özzÿ had prior criminal records, which bolstered their pleas for leniency. The prosecutor was also as happy as anyone to get ninety percent of his money back, which wouldn't have happened if the perps hadn't tried their very best to destroy the Earth. So after a respectable amount of haggling, the two sides settled on thirty days* of "Enhanced Domestic Exile" in a plea bargain.

---

*When Judy howled about the lenience of this, it was decided that the term would be served without any possibility of parole.

This particular penalty hadn't been handed down since the earliest days of Refined history (there's hardly any crime out there, since Refined beings truly are a bunch of wimpy little Do-Bee's). It requires that convicts be exiled "beyond the Refined League's outer boundaries," and also that they be placed under house arrest. This sounded fine until it was time to send them off, when everyone realized that the Refined League doesn't actually have outer boundaries anymore, and even if it did, Paulie and Özzÿ didn't have second homes out there.

By then, a new force field had been constructed around our planet (under the name of The Bieber Line, I hate to say). So someone suggested that they be exiled to a place that fell within it, since that would put them beyond the Refined League's boundaries in a manner of speaking, anyway. Of course, the only habitable planet within the Bieber Line was Earth itself, and the convicts didn't have homes here either. So after lots of debate and costly legal motions, Paulie was exiled to Pugwash's apartment, and Özzÿ was exiled to mine.

Özzÿ actually turned out to be a great roommate. Although a nincompoop by Refined standards, he's a technical genius by ours, and within a week, he had created an amazing home recording studio for Manda's place, and a spectacular media system for mine. And he can say what he wants about not being a goddamn vacuum cleaner—but for the entire month that he stayed with me, there was never a speck of dirt on the floor.* For their part, Paulie and Pug-

---

*Pugwash, meanwhile, ended up buying an awful lot of multigrain Wheat Thins for someone who was hosting a cracker-loathing carnivore.

wash were at each other's throats constantly. But it's now been three months since the term of the exile ended, and Paulie has yet to move out.* Manda thinks they're scheming to literally take over the universe. She's probably right.

There has meanwhile been lots of work to do. The basic outlines of my proposed solution to the debt crisis held up remarkably well, but there have been tons of loose ends for Judy and me to nail down. For instance—Angola (among others) never signed the Berne Convention. But somehow the country got a few songs onto Refined playlists everywhere. This makes it really complicated to work down the debt that's owed to its citizens, for a bunch of arcane reasons. Meanwhile, Paul McCartney doesn't have quite enough cells in his body to discharge the debt that's owed to him, unless he lives to be 164 or so. And what about the record labels, and the many other companies that own music rights? Much of their windfall goes to their governments via taxes—but how do you offset the vast wealth that remains with them, given that companies don't have DNA, or cells?

There are solutions to these, and several other technical legal problems that have cropped up (for instance, Judy easily bullied Angola into playing ball, Refined biotech can see to it that Sir Paul lives to 164 and beyond, and companies are owned by shareholders, so we've traced the wealth that's in corporate hands up through brokerage accounts, mutual funds, and private stock ledgers, in order to take it out of the cells of the people who ultimately own equity in

---

*At first I figured he was just sticking around to get into the Willow Smith video that Judy had mentioned. But they taped his part weeks ago, and he's still here.

them). But it's a lot of work for two lawyers* and a paralegal.†
And much as I've lobbied to at least bring Randy onto the
case, for now Judy insists that we keep it entirely under
wraps.

Another challenge arose when Earth's force field collapsed again. This time the Guardians themselves knocked
it down when they sent Paulie and Özzÿ through it to serve
out their Enhanced Exiles on Earth (duh). Rather than
rebuild the damned thing a third time, they just pushed out
a Consummately Heartfelt Entreaty to every citizen of the
Refined League demanding that they stay the fuck away
from Earth—or else. Judy wrote it personally, so you don't
have to worry about flying saucers turning up at the next
Bonnaroo.

With Earth safely sealed off behind a wall of fiery rhetoric, the big challenge now is to find—and to do something
about—the beings who already snuck in. All we know is
that nine "trespassers" came to Earth back before the
Townshend Line was fully activated in the late seventies. But
who (and what) are they? We naturally suspect Perfuffinites,
because they can fit in so well among humans. But there are
also eleven hundred other Refined species that could blend
in to our environment to some degree. Since her Consum-

---

*It would indeed be a lot of work for two *million* lawyers if we didn't
have access to Refined analytics tools that can handle labyrinthine instructions like, "figure out the precise sums owed to all of the ultimate
beneficial shareholders of the Warner Music Group based on its entire
catalog of music and territorial rights, and add those amounts to the
individual accounts that the shareholders' respective Cellular Infringements are being charged against."

†Judy's first action back on Earth was to poach Manda from her law
firm.

mately Heartfelt Entreaty went over so well, the Guardians asked Judy if she'd head up the effort to find them—and she agreed. I think it's brave, and even kind of noble, of her to take this on (some of those guys might be armed, after all). But it embarrasses her when I say this, and she insists that she's only doing it because she's power-hungry and greedy.

There's of course some truth to that—and there actually *is* a huge monetary dimension to Judy's mission. The issue is that while every non–North Korean on Earth is now staggeringly rich (ten percent of the universe's wealth carved up between us is a buttload of terra, exa, or zettadollars per head—I forget which), none of us can touch our loot until humanity becomes Refined. And we can't become Refined until our technology starts advancing at a reasonable rate again. So for now, virtually no one on Earth knows a thing about what's happening between us and the rest of the cosmos. And meanwhile, your money and mine (and, yes, Judy's, too) is sitting out there in escrow someplace. Judy agreed to hunt down the trespassers in part because she suspected them of causing our technology slowdown. And it turns out that in the case of at least one of them, her instincts were spot-on.

I learned this not long ago, when I received an urgent email from Judy. It was early in the evening, and her message ordered me to grab Bootsy (her current name for Manda) and go home to await a visitor. I've found my first trespasser, her email said. It's a Perfuffinite—and THIS IS THE BASTARD who's behind all of our tech problems! The message went on to say that the Guardian Council had issued the guy a Most Heartfelt Entreaty to come to The Core and explain himself. But he had refused, and Judy expected at least a month of bureaucratic handwringing before they got around to Dislocating him. He also wasn't willing to meet with Judy for now (maybe he was already terrified of her). So after some negotiating, she had persuaded him to sit down for an initial deposition with me.

Right at seven, he knocked. "Let me get it," Manda said. "You should be at our desk, looking magisterial." As Manda headed to the door, I tried to look as magisterial as a guy can, sitting at a plywood desk covered with cheap rosewood veneer.*

There was silence for at least three seconds after Manda opened the door. Then finally she said, "It's . . . *you?*"

"In the flesh," answered a nerdy voice that I didn't recognize.

As my visitor entered, I twirled on our squeaky desk chair in a way that I hoped would come off as imperious. A trim, fifty-something guy with brown hair and glasses was standing just inside the doorway. "Bill . . . Gates?" I asked.

"In a manner of speaking," he said.

"You're—an alien?"

"Please don't tell me you're surprised. Hey, nice cat!"

"*Gggggggggh!*"

"Have a seat," Manda suggested, gesturing grandly at our couch. Bill Gates made himself at home.

"So," I said, feigning nonchalance reasonably well. "You said that you're only Bill Gates 'in a manner of speaking.'"

Our desk used to be her desk. Although made from a cheap kit, it's much bigger than my old one, so we kept it when we consolidated our furniture into one apartment.

"I did. When I came to Earth back in seventy-eight, I tracked down a guy who looked just like me, and kind of replaced him. He was the original Bill Gates. He'd already started Microsoft a few years before that, and it wasn't going anywhere."

"And what did you . . . do to him?"

"Several cruel experiments. Then I drained all the fluids from his body, put his brain in a jar, and buried the rest of him under this giant crop circle that I made about forty miles north of London."

I gave him a horrified look.

"Ha—gotcha! Actually, I made friends with him, told him what was going on, and talked him into swapping places with me."

"How'd you do that?"

"Oh, it was easy. He was a college dropout living in Albuquerque with a crap software company, no girlfriend, and a huge science fiction collection. And I was touring dozens of galaxies, doing this John Denver show that was packin' 'em in. Hey, didja know that Johnny-D was born in Roswell? Anyway, I clinched the deal by telling him about the chicks."

"What chicks?" Manda asked.

"You wouldn't believe how easy Perfuffinite girls are," Bill Gates said.

"Oh—I know," I murmured, realizing an instant later what a truly idiotic thing this was to say in front of my girlfriend.

Manda shot me a withering look. "Wow," she said to Bill Gates. "Fame, floozies, and money? Any man would love that. Why'd you give it all up?"

"I didn't give anything up. I'm rich and famous here. And American girls are complete tramps. You should know—you are one."

Manda wound up to hit him.

"Ha—gotcha! Actually, American girls are total prudes compared to Perfuffinites. But it was worth coming to Earth because I love your music more than anything else. And I knew your musical output would be in terrible jeopardy if I didn't do something to slow your technical progress to a dead crawl."

"Because of the Great Acceleration?" I asked.

"Exactly. Great Accelerations are lethal three out of four times. All this technical, biological, and nano know-how is suddenly available to almost anyone. So tiny groups of crazies can take out entire cities, instead of just buildings. Or border skirmishes between fifth-rate powers can kill off whole planets. Or a few hundred individuals behaving recklessly and selfishly can destroy an entire biosphere. And it's hard to avoid a Great Acceleration—because a fundamental force of nature drives successful societies to ever-increasing levels of technical sophistication once they pass a certain threshold."

"So how do you prevent one?" I asked.

"The messy way is to lobotomize a society, by killing off every educated person within it."

"Sounds . . . unfriendly."

Bill Gates nodded. "It is, but it works. Just ask anyone who lived under the Khmer Rouge. The gentler approach is to gum up the works, by causing billions of little time-sapping, schedule-wrecking, and train-of-thought derailing problems every year. Target them at the productive ranks of society, and you'll stomp the brakes on its progress without really hurting anyone."

As I was considering this odd notion, Manda suddenly said *"Whoa."*

We both looked at her.

"You're talking about . . . *Windows,* aren't you?"

"Exactly. And DOS before that."

"Wow," I whispered as I processed this. "That . . . kind of makes sense."

"It makes perfect sense," Bill Gates said. "I mean, seriously. Now that you think about it, could Windows really be anything *but* an alien conspiracy?"

"No!" I said, chilled to the bone. "So how does it work?"

"This year I'll knock about a hundred and eighty billion productive hours out of human society. That's up from maybe a hundred and sixty-three last year. I like to keep the number somewhere between a hundred and twenty to a hundred and fifty hours per machine, per year."

"You mean through . . . crashes or something?" That sounded like three or four full working weeks (for a sane nonlawyer), which seemed like a lot of crashes to me.

"Among lots of other things. I hit maybe one percent of you with catastrophic disc failures every several months. Get zapped, and you might be out hundreds of hours. But most people won't get zapped this year. Other things are more evenly distributed, though. Like needless version compatibility issues. They eat up a couple hours per year, for most of you. Then I get everyone with those momentary screen freezes. They can total up to over twenty hours a year, for heavy users. I also snatch a couple hours from most of you by messing with your printers. Booting and rebooting grumpy systems varies a ton with the OS, but call it ten hours a year, on average. But the real bonanza is in my ingeniously designed user interfaces. Gratuitous complexity and obtuseness can derail almost any creative or productive process, and that sucks up dozens and dozens of hours a year from every one of you. And people are so used to it, they don't even notice."

"But how does that stop society from advancing?" Manda asked. "Even a hundred fifty hours is just a fraction of the working year."

Bill Gates chuckled. "True. But that's just the raw hours that the software confiscates. I get most of my leverage from timing."

"Meaning what?" I asked.

"My systems are thirty-eight times more likely to crash when you're at the tail end of a major project. Haven't you noticed? They're also twenty-two times more likely to have a screen freeze *juuuuust* when you've finally come up with the exact right word to put into a document. And they're almost sixty times more likely to drop off the network when you have a hugely urgent email to send, as opposed to when you're just browsing porn on the off-hours."

"That's . . . fascinating," Manda said.

"It is. I can't really explain how I do it, because it involves higher dimensions, and some concepts that don't even have words in English. But I call it 'irony detection' for short. I'm a big Alanis Morisette fan, see."

"But how's a hard drive crashing at the end of a big project *ironic*?" I asked. "That's just . . . bad timing, isn't it?"

"Like I said, I'm a big Alanis fan. Anyway—my irony detector also takes account of who's doing the work. And a true genius can crash one of my systems just by looking at it."

"So that keeps the best and brightest on abacuses," Manda marveled.

Bill Gates nodded. "And much more important, it keeps you guys from Greatly Accelerating. Which keeps the great music coming for the rest of the universe. Of course, I haven't ground your progress to a dead halt. I let a few technical goodies trickle into your society every so often, so you'll think you're still advancing."

"Thanks for 4G," Manda said respectfully.

"No problem."

"And you had all of this figured out before you took over Microsoft?" I asked.

Bill Gates shook his head. "I had no plan whatsoever at first. I just needed to get to Earth before the Townshend Line went up. My next move was coming up with someone to swap places with, and the original Bill looked more like me than anyone else that I found. It was only then that I started developing a plan to use Microsoft to save the world. Step one was turning it into a juggernaut—which definitely wouldn't have happened without me running the show."

"I guess being Refined made it easy for you to outwit all your competitors," I said.

"I didn't outwit anybody," Bill Gates joshed. "I *killed all* of them."

"Another joke, right?"

"More of a pun," he said with an impish smirk.

"Anyway," I continued, "once Microsoft became a monopoly, I guess you used it . . . to hijack and pervert our entire tech industry?"

Bill Gates nodded. "I prefer to say 'embrace and extend,' but you've got the gist."

"But there are other computers," Manda said. "There's Macintoshes, and Linux. You may dominate the tech world, but you don't completely control it. So someone can still build a great machine independently of you, right?"

"You mean someone like Steve Jobs? Sure. And he was brilliant. But like every great talent, he needed great competitors to push him to his full potential. So early on I set the bar so low that it took less than ten percent of his creative capacity to make my stuff look like crap. You're too young to remember DOS, but trust me on this. I upped the game a bit with Windows. But I was careful to never make him break a sweat."

"But isn't your own software starting to . . . suck less?" I asked. I'd heard a rumor to this effect.

"You mean Windows seven and eight?" Bill Gates chuckled. "I'm just going easy for a few years, because I got a bit carried away with Vista. That one was so bad that the real-life X-Files guys in the government started getting suspicious about me. But I'm gonna pour it on again with the next version of Windows. That one'll set everything back by at least twenty years."

"But the PC's over, and it's all about the Internet and mobile now, right?" Manda pressed. "Can't companies like Google push things forward without you?"

He chuckled again, a little diabolically this time. "Like I said—wait for the next version of Windows. Anyway, I gotta hop. I told Melinda I'd meet her for supper at eight."

"Hey, don't let us stop you," I said, standing up deferentially. Judy was going to kill me for being such a pushover with this guy. But while I seriously needed to think things over, everything he said really seemed to add up.

"And thanks for saving humanity," Manda added politely.

"Hey, let's not get carried away. You had a one-in-four

shot at making it through the Great Acceleration. So there's a decent chance that I'm just screwing you over. But in case I am, I'm trying to make it up to you by putting all my money into saving lives these days."

"That's right—and thanks for that, too," I said, opening the door for him. I'd heard many times that Gates's wealth will save untold millions of lives eventually, given how meticulously and brilliantly he's investing it to fight poverty and disease.

"Did I really just thank Bill Gates for using Windows to save humankind?" Manda asked, right after he left.

"You did. And it sounds like he actually did just that."

"Or at least, there's a seventy-five percent chance that he did."

"Did you seriously just do that in your head?"

Manda smiled at our running joke. "And you know there's no way Judy'll put up with this," she added. "Not with all her space dollars tied up in escrow."

I considered this. "So you think she's going to try to make him back down?"

"As opposed to living out her years stuck on Earth, kissing congressional asses, and suing file sharers? Of course she will."

I nuzzled Meowhaus's cheek with my index finger, and nodded. Manda's right, of course. There are enough loose ends out there that this whole mess is probably just beginning.

MANDA'S PLAYLIST

1	Intelligentactile 101 (Acoustic)	*Jesca Hoop*
2	Daddy's Car	*Cardigans*
3	Nightlight	*Little Dragon*
4	Voice Yr Choice	*The Go! Team*
5	Dance Anthem of the 80's	*Regina Spektor*
6	Hit	*Sugarcubes*
7	Silly Fathers	*Rubblebucket*
8	Combat Baby	*Metric*
9	One Divine Hammer	*Breeders*
10	Rill Rill	*Sleigh Bells*
11	Same Rain	*Sam Phillips*
12	The Real End	*Rickie Lee Jones*
13	Elijah	*Alela Diane*
14	Stoney End	*Laura Nyro*
15	Hurricane Drunk	*Florence & The Machine*
16	The Apocalypse Song	*St. Vincent*
17	Speak for Me	*Cat Power*
18	Holy Holy	*Wye Oak*
19	Mushrooms & Roses	*Janelle Monáe*
20	Written on the Forehead	*PJ Harvey*
21	Don't Talk to Me About Love	*Altered Images*
22	Duel	*Propaganda*
23	The Mummers Dance	*Loreena McKinnit*
24	Central Reservation (The Then Again Version)	*Beth Orton*
25	Undress Me Now	*Morcheeba*
26	Evening	*Vanessa Daou*
27	Ronco Symphony	*Stereolab*
28	5:55	*Charlotte Gainsbourg*
29	Occident	*Joanna Newsom*
30	Teardrop	*Massive Attack*

ÖZZŸ'S PLAYLIST

1	You Shook Me All Night Long	*AC/DC*
2	Living After Midnight	*Judas Priest*
3	Pour Some Sugar on Me	*Def Leppard*
4	Dude Looks Like a Lady	*Aerosmith*
5	Too Daze Gone	*Billy Squier*
6	Beautiful Girls	*Van Halen*
7	Round and Round	*Ratt*
8	Rock You Like a Hurricane	*Scorpions*
9	Like Never Before	*Steelheart*
10	Crazy Train	*Ozzy Osbourne*
11	Wild Flower	*The Cult*
12	Paradise City	*Guns N' Roses*
13	Not Gonna Take It	*Twisted Sister*
14	Cum on Feel the Noize	*Quiet Riot*
15	Tonight I'm Gonna Rock You Tonight	*Spinal Tap*
16	Rock and Roll All Nite	*Kiss*
17	There's Only One Way to Rock	*Sammy Hagar*
18	School's Out	*Alice Cooper*
19	Godzilla	*Blue Öyster Cult*
20	Turn Up the Radio	*Autograph*
21	Looks That Kill	*Mötley Crüe*
22	Unskinny Bop	*Poison*
23	One Way Ticket	*The Darkness*
24	Blue Collar Man (Long Nights)	*STYX*
25	Mother	*Danzig*
26	Paranoid	*Black Sabbath*
27	Run to the Hills	*Iron Maiden*
28	Metal on Metal	*Anvil*
29	Enter Sandman	*Metallica*
30	When the Levee Breaks	*Led Zeppelin*

PUGWASH'S PLAYLIST

1	Le Rai C'est Chic	*Cheb Mami*
2	Nefertiti's Fjord	*Nefertiti's Fjord*
3	Africa	*Amadou & Mariam*
4	Panis Et Circenses	*Os Mutantes*
5	Twiggy Twiggy [Twiggy Vs. James Bond]	*Pizzicato Five*
6	Chocolate	*Pacifika*
7	Tunak Tunak Tun	*Daler Mehndi*
8	Rabba Remixed	*Falu*
9	Bananeria	*Bebel Gilberto*
10	Eple	*Royksopp*
11	Ana (Hisboyelroy Smooth Dub)	*Vieux Farka Touré*
12	Narayana/For Your Love	*Krishna Das*
13	Azul	*Natalia Lafourcade*
14	Tinindo Trincando	*Novosbaianos*
15	Aquas de Marco	*Rosa Passos*
16	Sodade	*Césaria Évora & Bonga*
17	Makambo	*Geoffrey Oryema*
18	Lam Tooro	*Baaba Maal & Mansour Seck*
19	Svefn-g-englar	*Sigur Rós*
20	Money	*Sharon Jones & The Dap-Kings*
21	Money, Money	*Grateful Dead*
22	Money	*Pink Floyd*
23	Taxman	*The Beatles*
24	Money	*Flying Lizards*
25	Gimme Some Money	*Spinal Tap*

MEOWHAUS'S PLAYLIST

1	Cat People (Putting Out Fire)	*David Bowie*
2	Up on the Catwalk	*Simple Minds*
3	The Lovecats	*The Cure*
4	Make a Circuit With Me	*The Polecats*
5	He War	*Chan Marshall*
6	Lucifer Sam	*Pink Floyd*
7	An Cat Dubh + Into the Heart	*U2*
8	Panthers	*Wilco*
9	Superficial Cat	*Edwyn Collins*
10	Tiger Lily	*Luna*
11	Year of the Cat	*Al Stewart*
12	Honky Cat	*Elton John*
13	Another Saturday Night	*Yusuf Islam*
14	Stray Cat Blues	*The Rolling Stones*
15	Rumble in Brighton	*Stray Cats*
16	Panther Dash	*The Go! Team*
17	Photograph	*Def Leppard*
18	Cat Scratch Fever	*Ted Nugent*
19	Back in Black	*AC/DC*
20	Teenage Pussy from Outer Space	*Buck Naked & the Bare Bottom Boys*

CARLY'S PLAYLIST

1	Lost In Space	*Fountains of Wayne*
2	Bitch	*The Rolling Stones*
3	Rock Music	*Jefferson Starship*
4	Take It Off	*The Donnas*
5	Walkin' on the Sun	*Smash Mouth*
6	Killer Queen	*Queen*
7	Venus	*Bananarama*
8	Planet Earth	*Duran Duran*
9	Bike Ride to the Moon	*The Dukes Of Stratosphear*
10	Stars	*Hum*
11	Drops of Jupiter	*Train*
12	Saturn 5	*Inspiral Carpets*
13	Back Door Man	*Doors*
14	Sing to Neptune	*Tribe*
15	Hallucinating Pluto	*The B-52's*
16	Star 69	*R.E.M.*
17	Star Shaped	*Blur*
18	It Don't Come Easy	*Ringo Starr*
19	I Touch Myself	*Divinyls*
20	Trick or Treat	*Peaches*
21	Sex (I'm A . . .)	*Berlin*
22	Space Age Love Song	*A Flock of Seagulls*
23	Surfing on a Rocket	*Air*
24	We Are All Made of Stars	*Moby*
25	Sudden Stars (EP Version)	*Stereolab*
26	Universal Speech	*The Go! Team*
27	Astronaut	*Blitzen Trapper*
28	Ladies and Gentlemen We Are Floating In Space	*Spiritualized*
29	Under the Milky Way	*The Church*
30	Have You Seen the Stars Tonight	*Jefferson Airplane*

FRAMPTON'S PLAYLIST

1	Money's Too Tight (To Mention)	*Simply Red*
2	I'm Not the Man I Used To Be	*Fine Young Cannibals*
3	Love of the Common People	*Paul Young*
4	Skin Deep	*The Stranglers*
5	Stars	*Simply Red*
6	Be Near Me	*ABC*
7	Silver	*Echo & the Bunnymen*
8	Communication	*Spandau Ballet*
9	What Have I Done to Deserve This?	*Pet Shop Boys*
10	Fascination	*The Human League*
11	Vienna Calling	*Falco*
12	Wonderland	*Big Country*
13	The Last of the Famous International Playboys	*Morrissey*
14	Temptation (Original Version)	*Heaven 17*
15	Never Gonna Give You Up	*Rick Astley*
16	Hymn	*Ultravox*
17	Things Could Be Beautiful	*The Colourfield*
18	King for a Day	*Thompson Twins*
19	Europa and the Pirate Twins	*Thomas Dolby*
20	A New Flame	*Simply Red*
21	New Gold Dream (81-82-83-84)	*Simple Minds*
22	Arizona Sky	*China Crisis*
23	Do You Really Want to Hurt Me	*Culture Club*
24	Head over Heels	*Tears for Fears*
25	Father Figure	*George Michael*
26	This Is the Day	*The The*
27	Careless Whisper	*Wham!*
28	If You Don't Know Me By Now	*Simply Red*
29	Heaven	*Bryan Adams*
30	Holding Back the Years	*Simply Red*

PHOTO: © JEFF LORCH

ROB REID founded Listen.com, which built the pioneering online music service Rhapsody and created the unlimited-subscription model since adopted by Apple, Spotify, and many others. He is the author of the *New York Times* bestseller *Year Zero,* a work of fiction; *Year One,* a memoir about student life at Harvard Business School; and *Architects of the Web,* the first true business history of the Internet. He lives in New York City with his wife, Morgan, and Ashby the Dog.

Twitter: @Rob_Reid
Medium.com/@RobReid

EXPLORE THE WORLDS OF DEL REY AND SPECTRA.

Get the news about your favorite authors.
Read excerpts from hot new titles.
Follow our author and editor blogs.
Connect and chat with other readers.

Visit us on the Web:
www.Suvudu.com

Like us on Facebook:
Facebook.com/delreyspectra

Follow us on Twitter:
@delreyspectra

DEL REY SPECTRA